CLINTON SMITH lives advertising guru, film short story writer. His television commercials have won him thirty local and international awards, his short stories seven more. He has shot commercials in many countries, surviving aerobatics with Air Force instructors, helicopter journeys with the Navy and tank rides over obstacle courses with the Army.

He's stalked big-game at Sabi Sabi and chased storms in a wooden ketch around the Barrier Islands. He's filmed cars towing autogyros, women dangling out of truck doors over cliffs, and hang-gliders flying off New Zealand mountains. His shoots have commandeered the Trevi Fountain, Colosseum and Arc de Triomphe, stopped traffic in Times Square and disrupted the Monte Carlo Rally. People as diverse as Edward DeBono and Ronnie Barker have fronted his campaigns.

He uses his contacts to authenticate miltary details in his thrillers and is personally familiar with the settings in this book. His writing reflects his love for a country he seems to be rapidly adopting.

Also by Clinton Smith
The Fourth Eye

THE
GOD
GAME

CLINTON SMITH

HAZARD PRESS
publishers

Acknowledgements

I am grateful for the assistance of numerous members of the Royal Australian Armoured Corps. Also to members of the Royal Australian Infantry and Artillery Corps and the Australian Intelligence Corps. I thank the Defence Library, Holsworthy, the NSW Fire Department and the NSW Department of Agriculture.

I was aided by professionals in many fields: Dr Warwick Harper (medical, surgery). Dick Frew and Brett Drinan (rural). George Lewis (aeronautical). Siobhan McCammon (broadcast, cinematic). Betty Goldsmith (chiropractic, catalytic). Clare Lewis (equestrian). Rex Stapleton (viniculture). I am particularly indebted to Sergeant Dallas Gavan (and Sergeant Norman Davis) for applying such military erudition to sections of the typescript.

This project would not have seen print without the intelligence of freelance editor Judy Vago, and the gracious encouragement of Gabrielle Lord.

First published 2000
Copyright © 2000 Clinton Smith

The author asserts his moral rights in the work.

This book is copyright. Except for the purposes of fair reviewing, no part of this publication may be reproduced or transmitted in any form or by any means, electronic or mechanical, including photocopying, recording, or any information storage and retrieval system, without permission in writing from the publisher. Infringers of copyright render themselves liable to prosecution.

ISBN 1-877161-31-4

Published by Hazard Press Ltd
P.O. Box 2151, Christchurch, New Zealand

Printed in New Zealand

Chapter One

The thing was ancient, a Grumman amphibian that could have been flying before he was born. Chipped paint, worn tyres, oil-streaked engine cowlings… The aircraft was parked at the top of the ramp, half boat, half museum exhibit.

It wasn't the flight that worried him. He'd survived flying coffins in his time. It was the grey feeling in his gut – as grey as the slate-coloured sky, as grey as the sluggish sea that licked and sucked at the ramp like oil.

The sullen clouds were spoiling for a storm. A freshening wind tugged at the pennants on the brightly painted shed that was the terminal. The passengers were boarding. Four others only. Was it some kind of charter flight? He fell in behind the tall, long-haired woman, his eyes dropping to the movement of her hips as she stepped over the raised door-sill into the hull. She was in superb shape for her age. Nature had blessed her with a perfect rear – or a perfect aerobics instructor. She must have been fifty but had a body and skin most thirty-year-olds would have killed for. He stooped through the door himself, hand cradling the shoulder-bag he used as his camera case.

The interior of the aircraft was unlined except for a strip at window level. He was told where to sit and hunched in the excuse for a seat, opposite two webbing-covered boxes marked 'Great Barrier Island Store'.

Through the door space in the bulkhead he could see into the cockpit. Worn panels, primitive controls – like the cabin of a vintage truck.

One prop kicked, then another. The cabin shuddered, drummed with noise. Connor liked machines and this veteran example was intriguing. You got around on video shoots and he'd flown in everything from Iroquois to C-130s. But this was something new. So why wasn't he enjoying it?

It wasn't the grey sky or the flight across the gulf. It wasn't the assignment, which was lucrative enough. Something was wrong. Instinct told him to get out of the crate while he could. He pushed the feeling down. He was starting to imagine things.

Run-up over, they trundled down the ramp. Water thumped and sloshed against the hull. Through the flecked window, Waitemata Harbour was a smudge. Now the wing was the only reality, dipping and dunking its float.

The whine of the engines changed. The pilot's hand moved from the throttles to check twin, red-handled levers. Prop pitch? Mixture? Carb heat? Connor wasn't sure.

The altimeter was set on zero. Odd. Of course, sea level. That made adjustment simple. He looked back along the double row of mostly empty seats.

Just five passengers on a run that stopped at Barrier Island – a place he'd been told was very popular? Made no sense.

He frowned and pulled out the brochure – the brochure for a resort no travel agent knew. Thick glossy stock, four-colour photographs. It looked convincing enough, but his stomach told him he shouldn't have come.

He went over it again. The unexpected client with the super-heavyweight-class body. The man, who said his name was Blore, had the broad, deep-toned face of a Pacific Islander and his intimidating bulk made Connor's Sydney office seem like a cupboard. As he sat, his thighs stretched his suit pants thin like sausage skins. The chair creaked but held, though the wood frame parted slightly on one side, exposing twin dowels.

'It's a playground for the rich.' The voice from the huge frame was oddly soft. 'Bit north of Great Barrier Island. Know the spot?'

'Can't place it.'

'Fifty miles from Auckland – last stop before Valparaiso.' The man aired a crescent of amalgam to confirm his little joke. 'There are smaller islands in the group, some of them private, like ours. Trouble is, we're the world's best-kept secret.' He placed the brochure on the table between them. 'We're looking at several ideas for promotion. But first thing's a video for the travel trade.'

Connor picked up the brochure. Eight pages of tempting views. Delicate ferns beside a stream, a forest glade. 'Those pines indigenous?'

'No. The place used to be covered with kauri. Superb wood. Slow-growing, though, like your Huon pine in Tasmania. The sealers and whalers logged it for sailing ships. Now a lot of islands are bare except where they've planted pines. Great Barrier's mostly state forest.'

'Good weather?'

'Warmer than Auckland. But you get big storms out there.'

Connor glanced at the cover again. It showed a sheer rock peak of grey-brown stone projecting from a sparkling sea. The caption proclaimed: 'T55 – Hedonist's Hideaway'.

'Funny name for a resort.'

The man smiled but said nothing.

'You've done a good job on the brochure but it still looks pretty remote.'

'That's its charm.'

'Who put you on to me?'

'Fellow at VideoFac called Brian. Said you'd handle the whole project.'

The name meant nothing but Connor continued. Perhaps the man had got the name wrong. 'That's right. Concept to dubs. I hire in people and facilities, though I've an off-line set-up here.' He pointed beyond the sloping glass window of the sound booth. That's the editing suite. I'm basically Beta SP.'

'I'm not up with the technical side.'

'What money are we talking?'

'Our budget's pretty flexible. But before we discuss that in detail we need to brief you fully on the island – let you talk to our people, look around...'

'Without seeing my reel?'

'I'm sure it's good. Why not bring it with you? We could fly you there this Wednesday. Expenses paid, of course.'

'Sorry. Got an SRA job Wednesday. They've scheduled special trains and we'll have our arses hanging out. Twelve-hour day with fourteen set-ups. Could manage it next week.'

Blore rubbed his teeth with his thumb. 'Bit of a problem there. The island staff's on holiday next week. It really has to be this Wednesday.'

'Sorry about that.'

'Pity.' He jacked himself out of the chair and it creaked like a cane lounge in a slimming club. His bulk filled the room. 'Great shame. Great shame.' He fumbled for a business card. 'Well, if something loosens up...'

'I'll let you know.'

'Good.' He extended his hand and Connor's knuckles became painfully acquainted.

Something loosened up, all right. The SRA shoot was cancelled. No explanation. Three days' shooting – canned. He tried to talk it over with Tess.

She shrugged. 'Coincidence, that's all. Jobs get stopped.'

'They normally say why.'

'David, honestly…' Her arch look. She was eight years older and he never felt quite her equal. She gave the impression she'd married him to acquire a pet. At first he'd found that amusing but it wasn't any more.

She chased a last mung bean around her plate. 'It's probably internal politics. Why be so suspicious?'

The word was one of her weapons. He suspected she was seeing someone else, although a year ago she'd denied it. Confronting her had soured things further. Now she rubbed it in – sure of her independence, attractiveness, wit, of a mind faster than his that knew how to belittle him, tease. For a year she'd gone through the motions, playing the game of affection too well – satirically, never letting up. Their marriage was becoming a facade.

She said, 'If you distrust absolutely everything you'll end up sitting in a corner with your knees under your chin. And I'll visit you once a month on Fridays.'

This was another of her themes: that he was too fearful to contend. She knew him well, and where to insert the knife.

He let her comment slide. Reacting made things worse. 'He's throwing around free tickets and didn't even ask to see my reel.'

'He's probably not used to Sydney and doesn't know how things work here.'

'How'd he get on to me anyway?'

'You said he asked someone at the video place…'

'There *is* no Brian at VideoFac.'

'That doesn't prove anything. He got the name wrong, probably. People are hopeless with names.'

She moved behind his chair and started kneading his shoulders with firm hands. That was where the stress started, she said – forehead, muscles behind the neck, between the shoulder-blades. She was always telling him to relax, aware it made him tense. 'Cautious Connor. What are you worried about? Someone offers you a job and you think it's a conspiracy.'

'It fits too well. Smells like a con.' He knew it sounded lame, defensive.

'David, it's a *job*. Why not take it? You can certainly use the money. It's been a while since you've had anything come good.' She'd said 'you', not 'we' – another subtle dig. Her chiropractic practice made more most weeks than he billed in a month and she never missed a chance to emphasise her success.

'So you think my imagination's working overtime?'

'It's on a twenty-four-hour shift!' She kissed the top of his head as one might kiss a small child. 'Got to go.'

'Will you be late?'

'Could be. Bye.' She reached the door, looked back condescendingly. 'Do try to understand that life... is for living.'

The twin radials roared as the relic slapped its way across the bay. They still hadn't cleared the water. Perhaps they were going to surf there.

The hull stopped strumming beneath him. The spray, streaming across the window, cleared. They'd lifted off – boat imitating bird. Unexpectedly, the wing float swung up and out, its strut nestling into a groove under the wing as it became a wing-pod.

Ahead, the co-pilot was winding a crank with a shaft that went vertically into the bilge. Wheels? Trim? Everything about this flight was odd.

The needle inched around the altimeter as the chop below became a pattern. The fuselage was straining every rivet, despite the shallow rate of climb. The aircraft lurched in an updraft and the wing above his window flexed, then came back to true, the float on the end of it shuddering.

He hadn't seen the big man again. He'd rung to say he could make it Wednesday and had asked again about the budget. The man named a sum double what he'd expected – enough fat for a full crew plus airfares. The thing sounded like a windfall.

His tickets arrived by express courier. It hadn't been the best of mornings. He'd been depressed about a wife he wanted physically but didn't trust, and about his future. He mostly ground out corporate videos but longed to make docos for TV. He was a man, now thirty-five, with a home-based post production set-up. A man who'd need a crippling overdraft if he intended to keep up with the industry. It was crunch time. Get-with-it or get-left time.

He'd wished he could rewind the last few years, stop-frame a few mistakes, cut sequences and rewrite the ending with a positive, up-beat slant. Tess was right, of course. He was stale. And for years he'd coasted on hope. Something had to change, and soon. Meanwhile, he had a job. The trip would do him good.

Through grey stratus, watery sun cast a glimmer on the sea below. A tip of rock, partly covered with scrub, vanished as the wing-pod became a float. Below, tiny islands studded the sea, some no more than jagged knobs that rose abruptly from the water, surrounded by a frill of white foam, their peaks covered by tenacious shrubs and trees.

The smaller islands became a huge one, impossibly green, with wooded lower slopes and peaks receding into mist. By an inlet that formed a harbour, a meadow sloped to the bay.

They were coming in to land. The hull beneath him skimmed the water, kissed it, drummed along the tops of the crests then settled deep, pushing a steep wash from the bow. In seconds, the water had slowed them to a drift and they were floating in the calm of the bay. The engines were throttled back to a chug as they headed toward a shallow beach. The co-pilot was winding the crank. It had to be wheels. The side floats joined the wings again as they trundled up onto dry sand.

There were fifteen minutes of bustle as boxes were handed out on the beach. More freight came out of a hatch on top of the nose. Milk-run over, the aircraft waddled back into the sea and taxied to its take-off point. So much for Great Barrier Island. Next and last stop – T55.

He glanced behind him, relieved to find he was not alone. The four others were still aboard – two men and two women. He felt better. But not much.

The small woman beside the tall man was mostly hidden behind a paper. The international *Guardian Weekly,* which meant she was either intelligent or bored. They seemed in their early forties. Who were they? Visitors to the resort? They looked as if they could afford it.

Hanford Sinclair glanced at his wife, the pert face, the elfin body, half covered by the paper she presumably found more interesting than the flight. Women were alien creatures. Pity one needed them so much. He turned back to the window. They were climbing faster with the lightened load. He'd been surprised at this bucket of a plane. Hardly the traveller's antidote to jet-lag. Why not a chopper? It was only an 80-kilometre slog. What was bloody Thommo up to? Still, Auckland wasn't the Bahamas.

The letter had been unexpected. Few of his old school friends kept in touch. 'Dear Horse,' it began – 'Horse' referred to Sinclair's penis, the length of which had earned him the nickname at boarding-school. It seemed that

Thommo, the shifty bugger, owned this island off the coast of New Zealand and was inviting them to his tourist trap to mark its successful third year. Quite right, too. About time the bastard came good.

There was a brochure with the letter, showing views of the resort. Ranch-style guest house, book-lined study with club chairs. Over the page was a sunny bay where a slab-sided cruiser, half a million dollars big, nestled at a jetty. It looked like one of the floating kingdoms moored by the stern at Monte Carlo. There were para-gliders, people playing tennis. Tennis was his joy. And it would be good to see Thommo again. How long was it? Ten years? He'd thrash the bastard, six love, six one, six love.

Connor turned to the front again, but not before glancing at the other woman – the older one who'd climbed into the aircraft before him. She was combing her hair with long, practised strokes.

He'd first noticed her at the airport lounge, standing on the scales – Relic Airlines weighed both passengers and luggage – as if the cast-iron, juddering platform was the stage on Oscar night. He would have noticed her anyway because she invited attention. A strong, high-boned face framed by thick, brown hair with wisps of natural grey that looked far better than artificial streaks. Tall, erect: the perfect body. She obviously loved herself to death. So would any woman of fifty who looked at first glance like a super-model. An oldie but a goodie, he decided. Pity about the ego.

Grace Merrick wanted her hair to look perfect when she arrived. There might be photographers. You never knew. Fantastic, really. A week at a luxury resort overseas. Just for filling in an entry form that the salesgirl almost begged her to complete. 'You could win a marvellous holiday, honey.

Think – a week by that fabulous pool.'

The pool was fabulous indeed, displayed in the brochure in colour. It could have been in Greece: white marble columns supporting thin air, gleaming in the sun with an endless Homeric sea behind. She loved sunning her body and swimming. Be a change from Malibu Beach.

To celebrate, she'd driven to Santa Monica and had a meal at the Ivy by the Shore. She'd sat in splendour, like a queen. That was how you lived when you had money. She was born to have money. So why had she always had to scrape? Of course she'd done miracles with little. A matter of self-pride.

Someone tapped her shoulder. She glanced across the aisle to the man on the opposite seat – a podgy man in a flashy leather jacket.

'You going to the conference?' He was forty-plus, sounded East Coast – sallow, eyes red-rimmed.

'What conference?'

'Mido conference.'

Grace Merrick surveyed him, as one might look at a foreigner who didn't speak the language. He was a nobody. She shrugged, then turned back to her window. Also, he looked ill. She didn't like sick people.

'Thanks for nothing,' Dyson muttered. Who did the broad think she was? Fucking Queen of England?

Dyson had first heard of this island bullshit in the conference room when they presented the new Chunkies commercial. He'd been with the Sydney agency a year on the strength of his experience in New York, had snowed them about being a gun on new business – what a joke – then scored the Mido petfood account. But the meeting wasn't looking good. The new commercial was a dog.

The creative director coughed nervously as the last frame

went to black. 'Licking shots were a pain in the butt. Had to put prawns in her ears, pâté down her dress…'

'That's obvious,' the Mido MD said. 'Looks like she's being attacked.'

His brand manager jerked puppet-like to the cue. 'That bothers me, too. It negates the aspect of reward and affection that was a part of the demographic.'

Arsehole, Dyson thought.

The CD defended, his gold earring drawing attention to the redness of his ears. 'As far as I'm concerned…'

It went from bad to worse until the agency MD did the good-guy-bad-guy shuffle, dropping Dyson in it to save the situation.

'You've got two days,' the MD said. 'The sales conference starts Wednesday and Adrian's going to be there to present it – aren't you Adrian?'

'If someone tells me where.'

'Somewhere you can't get away.'

'Must be an island.'

'Not wrong.'

Dyson cranked out his stock look of ingenuous pleasure, a tired attempt that hadn't worked since his Young Turk days. 'An island? You're putting me on.'

The nose of the aircraft had dipped and the whine of the engines was now a purr. Connor pressed his forehead to the perspex, trying to look down. They were flying over specks of land, volcanic rock spikes weathered and bare, which suggested the waves below could be huge.

He glimpsed part of a larger island, mostly covered in forest, with open scrub beyond. There were animals of some kind on it. Not cattle. He tried to make them out.

They were losing height quickly now. The wing-pod lowering, locking into position. They powered in, flaps out, bucking against the wind. Here, far out in the Pacific, the waves looked too big for a landing. He braced himself and waited.

The sea flattened to a chop. A harbour? The lee of the island? The hull touched and aquaplaned, settling fast. One pilot was turning the crank, which signified a beach. He'd expected at least to get his feet wet. His body felt stiff. He longed to stand and move again.

Well, he thought, this is it.

He unbelted and waited for release.

Chapter Two

The five of them stood freezing on the beach – a crescent of pebbly sand that would soon be covered by the tide. Behind them a rampart of sheer rock towered against a melancholy sky. The wind whipped at their clothes and the gulls, flapping overhead, flew half sideways, correcting for drift.

The flight crew worked fast, handing out the baggage, concerned about the rising chop. They reboarded, closed the hatch in the nose and headed out against the wind, the wheels moving slowly up to nestle in circular depressions in the hull.

The passengers watched as the aircraft rounded the headland, the prop blast turning the sea behind it into sleet. The moment it was out of sight, the roar of its engines grew faint. Connor stared around him, flapping his arms for warmth.

They'd been abandoned on the most solitary place he'd seen – the cliff-face stuck like a dagger into a body of endless sea. On the strip of threatened beach, with the bitter wind chilling them right through, the only sign of habitation was two rusting drums half buried in the sand. The salty air carried the stench of the seaweed that lay in broad strands beneath their feet. The double thump of dumping waves was a warning. They couldn't stay here long. Soon, sea would cover the beach. But there seemed no way off the narrow rim of sand. It went no further than the rock face on each side.

He glanced at the people with him. On this pebbly shelf

threatened by the breakers and the gale, their urban postures and attitudes seemed surreal.

The tall man arched one eyebrow and yelled above the wind. 'All come for the party, have we?'

He must have been six foot three, good-looking, thin but wiry. In this mournful spot his expensive, casual clothes looked quaint. The accent? Connor couldn't place it unless South Africans studied at Trinity. As for the eyebrow, he'd practised hard.

The other man, paunchy and bag-eyed, had the rat-wariness of a New Yorker. 'You mean the conference?'

'Conference?'

'Sales conference. Mido Petcorp?' His spray-stuck hair, which had been plastered across his bald pate, now flew out from his head on one side in strands. He looked ludicrous and knew it.

The tall man made a face and placed his hand on the tiny woman's shoulder. 'Don't tell me it's the wrong island.' He turned to Connor. 'Can you enlighten us?' The hand went out. 'We're the Sinclairs.'

'Connor,' he said, and shook.

'Dyson,' said the paunch. He turned the other way so that the wind would blow his hair back onto his scalp. Instead, it blew across his face. This was no place for keeping up appearances. 'Well, T55's where the conference is. Stupid bloody name. They need an image campaign. We agree on T55?'

Connor said, 'That's what they told me.'

Sinclair called down to his wife, 'Correct address, apparently.' He turned to the other woman. 'You, madam?'

'Grace Merrick's the name. I was told I'd be met.' Her voice had a Californian lilt.

Sinclair switched on the charm. 'Are you coming to a conference or a party?'

She looked him straight in the eye. 'Mind your own business.'

A ball-breaker, Connor thought. Tess in another fifteen years.

Sinclair regarded her with equal disdain long enough for it to register. He turned to Connor. 'You?'

'Supposed to be coming to a resort. For a location survey.'

'I see.' The tall man scratched his hair with fingers two octaves long. Unlike Dyson's hair, his crop was abundant – power-hair, musician's length. And the wind revealed no gaps. 'Are we all coming to a resort, then? Be helpful to get that clear.'

'So where the hell is the transport?' Connor asked.

The others nodded, even Merrick.

Dyson pointed. 'Jeez. Here come the bell-hops.'

Sinclair stared from his great height. 'They're not serious.'

Four men had appeared from nowhere and were trudging along the beach. They wore camo-patterned drill trousers cinched over combat boots, battle-jackets, black balaclavas – all they lacked was camouflage cream. Their bodies were square, like blocks – barrel chests, no waists.

A woman was with them. Her skirt blew against her in the wind, revealing well-toned legs. She had an intelligent face. She didn't smile. 'Welcome to T55,' she said.

The troops also had not smiled. He doubted they'd ever smiled – even on their mother's knee when full of wind. The woman said, 'Follow me, please. Our apologies about this but they couldn't land on the bay side today. The weather's treacherous here.'

The huge men picked up the luggage as effortlessly as forklifts and trudged back up the slope of the beach, boots crunching on the shore pebbles, then sinking deep in the sand. Sinclair looked quizzically at Connor, who shrugged and zipped his thin windcheater to the neck. No point in freezing. They plodded off, following their luggage.

Dyson caught up, waddling flat-footed, trying not to get sand in his shoes. He jerked a thumb at the men. 'What kinda horse-shit's this?'

At the end of the beach the headland curved inward to become a convex chimney. Now they understood how the reception committee had suddenly appeared. Here, almost indistinguishable from the cliff-face, were rusty steps expansion-bolted into rock. The troop climbed first, like automatons, as if the bags were full of helium. The structure had been adapted to the site, had a fireman's-grid landing halfway up and seemed to lead to a ledge.

Connor climbed after the last man. At the landing he looked down. Sinclair ahead of his wife, his calliper legs taking two steps at a time, then the puffing Dyson, clinging to the rail, and Merrick, ascending regally as if all the world were applauding.

At the top was the lip of a small cave with a shaft of light at the back. The light came from a sloping tunnel cut up through the rock. Either side of its central steps, gutters trickled with slime. He could hear the men already in the tunnel, multiple boots on cement.

The woman was standing near the entrance, waiting for them all to reach her. She was perhaps thirty-five. Upturned nose, strong chin, practical hands with short nails. Connor noticed such things. You could tell a good deal about people if you looked at them in sections. She looked back at him searchingly, a curious look, as if she knew him. He was about to ask her a question when Sinclair came crouching into the cave and spoke first.

'Now look, there seems some confusion.' His voice echoed off the rock above them.

The woman raised her hand slightly. 'Please, no questions now. We have to arrive before dark.' She had an educated voice with a continental tinge. 'It'll all be explained at the house.'

'Is Thommo there?' Sinclair persisted. 'Thommo Farnsworth. This *is* his island?'

The woman didn't reply.

Connor's flesh began to creep.

The others crowded into the cave. 'Please be careful of the steps,' the woman said. 'There's a railing on the right. Take your time.'

She went up the steps ahead of Connor and, for the second time in an hour, he had the chance to contemplate a woman with almost perfect flanks. The way her skirt clung to her hips made him wish she were wearing jeans. Five years' marriage to an attractive woman had not stopped him studying form. It was automatic in him, as in most men his age, to assess the volume and proportion beneath the clothes. To this predictable ability was linked a cameraman's eye that saw with framing and a lens in mind. Don't dream, he told himself. Stay on top of this.

'Christ,' Sinclair said, 'this is bloody well insulting. I tell you, I'm not impressed.'

The rail was a rope hawser, attached to the rock by metal eyelets. Connor hauled on it, feeling it jerk as it was grasped by the others lower down. He was starting to get out of breath. The light ahead was an opening in the rock. They had been climbing for several minutes and there were perhaps fifty more steps. He could hear the overweight Dyson's phlegm-tinged, liquid gasp and the clicks of Mrs Sinclair's high heels. What did she think this was? A state function?

No-one spoke, now. No-one had the breath. All had slowed to a shuffle. Dyson, far below, was groaning and pressing his hands on his knees to help his aching legs take the steps.

The light ahead widened into a circle of sky as the tunnel abruptly ended and they emerged into a cleft between two rocks. Beyond was undulating scrubland. The militia were still in sight 100 metres across the field. How they'd gained so much distance carrying the cases Connor didn't know.

'Jeez, how much further?' Dyson gasped.

The woman, Connor noticed, was breathing fast, but not as fast as he was, and she'd gained distance on him during the climb. She was fit, all right. She said, 'From here, it's level, then downhill. Another fifteen minutes at the most.'

Sinclair's wife said to him in gasps, 'You sure this is meant to be fun?'

Sinclair had propped his length against a rock. 'All I'm bloody sure of,' he panted, 'is that I could use a brandy and soda.'

'I was freezing,' Merrick said. 'Now I'm sweating.' She seemed to be expecting praise.

The woman was walking ahead again, and Merrick was next behind her. Despite her age she didn't seem tired at all, her strong body striding out like a bushwalker on a day-trip.

They were walking beside a fence. Heavy gal wire, box-frame strainer assemblies with diagonal bracing which was professionally done, and close-spaced line wires. It was six feet high and wasn't designed for cattle. Odd, Connor thought. They could have saved work by using prefab rolls. He knew a bit about fences. A bit about many things. If you made enough videos you learnt about farms, factories, fences…

The foot-track meandered beside ruts that would have gutted a four-wheel-drive. But there were impressions in the ground so something had been along here. Only a tracked vehicle could have handled those craters and pitted ruts. A bulldozer? On an island? Unlikely. Besides, earth-moving equipment would have been used to level the track.

They were nearing a pine-covered hillside – secondary growth but old. He glanced back. Sinclair's wife held her party coat against her chest. Her shoes were ruined, her voice plaintive on the wind. 'Hanford, you may have to carry me.'

'Always have.'

The foot-track diverged from the wider track and headed straight into the forest. The squad diverted along it, single file, with the animation of a burial detachment. They followed, slipping on the carpet of pine needles, the old trees sighing overhead. They walked through its wilderness, the light fading with the wind. Connor checked his watch. Near five. It'd be dark in an hour.

The flabby American caught up with him on the downhill slope. He pointed to the platoon ahead, 'Bet they eat their spinach,' then brandished a flask. 'Medicine. Want some?'

'No thanks.'

He replaced the cap with care. 'At least they sent the Sherpas. Should be apologies all round when we arrive. And complimentary drinks.'

'Don't hold your breath.'

They must have cut straight across the island. The forest ended on a vast expanse of sea. Manicured grass sloped down to an inlet protected by the jagged boulders of a breakwater. As each wave hit it there was a crump, then the heavy swell exploded over the rocks, foamed between them and sent up spouts that showered the pocket-sized bay. In its lee, under the brooding sky, a large boat ground its fenders against the jetty. It would have been a sixty-footer. Not the gleaming pleasure cruiser from the brochure – more a cross between a fishing trawler and a patrol boat. Flush foredeck with hatch, stubby wheelhouse with raked, anti-glare glass. Behind the deckhouse with its side companionways a Christmas tree of pods, revolving dishes and antennae looked business-like enough to microwave anyone on board. At the rear was a stub mast like a Samson-post with the spar of its derrick horizontal, forming the ridge-pole for a tarpaulin attached neatly to frames on each rail.

The bay was different, too, from the idyllic place shown in the brochure. This scene, against the darkening sky, looked ominous.

Set back against the tree-line was what could have been a provincial town hall. It had stone foundations and a satellite dish on the roof. A town hall? He revised his opinion. More like a nineteenth-century jail – double-storeyed and huge – nothing like the chalet in the brochure. Despite the portico entrance, it looked as utilitarian as a blockhouse. But on the rise of the hill in front, exactly as advertised, was the curved neo-Randolph Hurst swimming pool – marble-edged and circled with ornamental columns. The shots had made it look magnificent. But they were taken on a sunny day. Framed against this sky it looked more like a white Stonehenge or a witches' circle. On two columns the Ionic volutes featured an adornment absent in the brochure – surveillance cameras with small, inquisitive lenses.

The troops and the woman stopped, waiting for the stragglers. Sinclair and his wife were the last. Hampered by her shoes, she'd finally removed them. She minced up, holding them in one hand.

The woman said, 'You'll want to settle in, have a rest and freshen up.' She still spoke to no-one in particular, as if she dared not become involved. 'Then tonight, at seven, you're invited to dinner at the house.' She pointed a little down the slope. 'You'll be staying in separate cabins, over there behind the pines. Please follow the man carrying your luggage. He'll take you to your huts.' She walked off quickly. She'd never announced her name.

'Jeez,' Dyson said. 'Thought we'd be staying in the mausoleum. Can smell the decanters from here.' He limped off, following his luggage. From a column, a camera tracked him. Connor watched it with suspicion. It wasn't a bank-issue job with a fixed wide-angle lens. It had remote pan, tilt and zoom and someone was giving it a workout.

A resort for millionaires? He'd seen nothing to suggest it. Most of the brochure's bright scenes appeared to have been fake. This place was far more bleak.

Grace Merrick frowned at the pool. 'I guess it looks different when it's sunny.' Her voice was wistful, disappointed.

Sinclair, scowling too, reached into his coat for his brochure. He looked at it, then at the house. 'Curiouser and curiouser. Nothing like this at all.' He waved the brochure at Connor. 'Did you get one of these?'

Connor gripped the edge of the page. 'Shit.' Alarm bells went off in his head.

The brochure was different from the one in his bag. The cover was the same but the scenes of forest and ferns had been replaced by photos of tennis courts and sporting scenes.

'They've printed one-offs!'

'Pardon?' Sinclair gave him the look of an agreeable aristocrat fraternising with the lower classes.

'Look.' Connor pulled out his own brochure and turned to the same spread. 'See? Different.'

The tall man stared from one to the other. 'It can't be. Unless one's a reprint.'

'You play tennis?'

'B grade.'

'Do you para-glide?'

'No. But Anita's tried it. Why?'

'And I'm interested in conservation. See this? Forests and

ferns. Same page. Know what it would have cost to do different sets of four-colour separations, then…'

Sinclair clearly knew well. 'It *has* to be a reprint.' He turned to Grace Merrick. 'Could I trouble you for a look at your brochure, madam?'

She looked at him as if assessing an over-ripe fish, long enough for Connor to wonder who would out-patronise whom. Finally, she rummaged in her handbag and produced a much-thumbed, much-folded brochure. She thrust it at Sinclair, not looking at him.

'Ta.' He unfolded it.

Once again, the cover was the same. But the inside spread was unlike either of the other two versions. It showed three views of the pool from different angles, with vacationers swimming and lounging. There were no tennis courts, forests or streams – just shots of food and pristine beaches by the sea.

Sinclair gaped.

Connor said, '*Three* reprints?'

'Impossible.'

'It can't be colour copying. It's too good. Unless it's done with some photographic process.'

Sinclair held the paper half sideways, feeling it and squinting. 'No. Bleeding thing's printed all right. Four-colour offset by the look of it.'

He turned on the man holding his baggage. 'What the hell's going on here?'

The trooper stared past them both.

Sinclair scowled at him from his great height. 'You deaf or something? Well?'

The man stood like a stanchion, unblinking. He had the scar of a repaired hare lip and thick arms bulged his battle-jacket. Either he was ruining his testicles with steroids or his parents had both been mammoths.

'Bloody hell,' Sinclair fumed.

His wife pulled at his arm. 'I'm sure this man knows nothing about it. It won't help to make a scene.'

'It's blatant misrepresentation. Or someone's playing games. If Farnsworth's trying it on, I'll sue the bleeder.'

The man in front of him could have been deaf. He stood effigy-like two beats longer, then wheeled on his heel and stomped off, carrying the Sinclairs' cases.

'Do come on,' his wife said, 'or we'll lose our luggage next.'

He thrust the brochure back at Grace Merrick. 'Bloody hell. I'll have someone's knackers for this.' He followed his wife and luggage in anger down a track toward a grove of pines.

Grace Merrick put the brochure back in her bag. 'Why all this fuss?'

'The brochures are different.' Connor told her.

'Does it matter?' She seemed unconcerned and he was in no mood to enlighten her.

'Guess not.'

She looked at him accusingly. 'I need a shower. Then I need food. That's all that matters to me. Are you a New Zealander?'

'Half. My mother was. I married an Australian. I've always lived in Australia.'

Her hand smoothed her hair away from one eye. 'I'd like to visit Australia one day. I've read about the Opera House.' She strode off, following her luggage, the imperious tourist, oblivious to the signs around her.

Connor's baggage corporal was waiting, eyes defocused. None of them had looked at him directly – as if they were wardens, escorting the condemned. The man turned, his back a moving wall.

Connor trudged behind him, dread washing through

him like poison. All the inconsistencies here could just possibly be accepted as benign. But the brochure business was bizarre. Cold sweat had dampened his shirt. One-off brochures? Who the hell would do that? Who would do that to *him*? And why?

The cabins were close together in a partly cleared grove of pines. Split-log timber huts, greened by copper sulphate preservative.

There seemed to be just four. For four special guests? Sinclair and his wife, Merrick, Dyson... him? He pushed the thought away. It was insane.

Each hut had a small uncovered porch, a single window and door. Connor's man walked up the three steps to the porch, crossed the boards, which groaned beneath him, opened the door and went inside. He reappeared without the luggage, stomped down the steps again, brushed by Connor without eye contact and headed for the house.

Connor was shivering. He felt sick but fought the sensation down. He hung on to the railing of the steps, feeling the rough wood under his hand. What was going *on* here? He felt completely out of his depth.

The nausea faded, leaving him cooling in his sweat, his shirt clinging to his skin. God, why hadn't he left the aircraft at Great Barrier? He sucked in deep breaths, waiting for his body to respond. Finally, shakily, he climbed the steps and went inside.

The place had everything one would expect from a cabin at a rural resort. Double bed with printed patchwork counterpane, scatter-rugs, built-in wardrobe, bench with shelves underneath and mirror above. His bag was on the bed. He drifted around the small room, not sure what he was doing.

Through an alcove was a shower, toilet and basin. Modern fittings. He'd stayed in motels worse than this.

There was even a phone in the main room. He'd scanned a brochure at the terminal that said Great Barrier Island was so primitive the communal phone had to be cranked. This was a touch-button job. He picked it up, heard a dial tone. Microwave link? Or intercom? Beside the phone was a folded card with a crest and typed words beneath. He bent to read it, heart thumping.

> Welcome to T55, Mr Connor.
> You are invited to dinner
> in the main house at 7.00pm.
> Dress: casual.

He shut his eyes and leaned against the bench, the bile climbing in his throat. He staggered to the toilet and threw up.

Connor crouched against the cold tiles, dry-retched, then slumped by the toilet, exhausted. The toilet paper, motel style, had the corners of the first sheet folded in. He ripped off a length and wiped his lips.

'Cautious Connor,' Tess called him. Not cautious enough, it seemed. Why the hell hadn't he followed his instincts and got out of this while he could?

He got up, leaning on the cistern, then braced himself against the wall. Blood drained from his head. He bent half double, holding on to the towel rail. When the dizziness passed, he stood propped against the wall, then shuffled out, intending to lock the door. There was no lock, just a catch. He felt he needed air. He went out on the porch again, the wind like ice through his drenched shirt.

Almost dark. For some reason he looked up. High on the trunk of a pine, a box, painted bark-brown, whirred and extended its glass eye for a close-up.

He went inside and shut the door. The wind moaned

around the hut. Chilled to the bone, he stripped and stepped into the shower. The water was mercifully hot but the pressure uneven – pumped from somewhere. His hands were unsteady. He fumbled the taps and dropped the soap.

Yes, his gut had known in advance – as his mind knew now – that this set-up wasn't just peculiar but desperately wrong. A resort with goons and robot cameras? More like an interrogation camp.

Did the others realise they'd been trapped? Merrick certainly didn't. As for the loser with the hair, Connor doubted it. But Sinclair wasn't dumb.

He hunched in the shower, water peppering his head, arms clenched across his chest, rocking under the stream. The water was hot enough to sting but his insides felt like ice.

Perhaps it was true. Perhaps you did attract what you most feared. He wasn't physically brave – had arranged his life to be safe.

Now in this cold hell of colder prospects his safe life had disappeared.

Chapter Three

With night came the black of a moonless, starless sky and the darkness of an unseen ocean. It was a darkness full of sound. The thunder of the sea, smashing against the distant headland; the constant *crump* as combers pounded the breakwater. The wind had become a gale, moaning around the hut, sighing into the window frame and rattling the door. With each gust the building shuddered as the timber bracing beneath it took up. Connor could hear the pines creak as wind whistled through the close-spaced grove, the interlocking branches scraping as they bent to its force.

He sat in the bedside chair as he'd been sitting for an hour, the outside tumult echoing the hammering of his brain. Shock had drained him and each shudder of the hut rippled through him.

He checked his watch for the tenth time. Almost seven. He'd already changed into warmer clothes and placed his thick padded jacket on the bed. Typically, he'd got ready well in advance, then sat trying to get himself together. An hour to think – to contemplate a resort that wasn't a resort, dinner with hosts who weren't hosts but people who coaxed people to this spot on false pretences. Why him? Why him? He still had no answer. At least the nausea had gone.

He got up, dragged on his jacket and zipped it up. When he opened the door the wind blew it back against his thigh, forcing him to step around and haul it shut from the outside. The creaking of the tortured trees was unsettling, the stress on the old branches huge. Lights on short posts beside the path emphasised the darkness. He could see the house lights on the hill, blinking through the swaying branches. As he went down the steps, leaning against the wind, a piece of branch struck the railing beside him and clattered on the decking of the porch.

He could see no-one on the path. Where were the others? He walked into the gusts, hands deep in his jacket pockets.

Beyond the horseshoe of pines the path lights stopped. Now there were only the house lights to guide him. The sea was deafening here – must have been enormous. He wondered if the strange boat was still in the bay. He had visions of it stoved in by the jetty, wallowing, submerged to the scuppers.

An unexpected light danced on the ground ahead, revealing an oval of green turf almost flattened by the gale. The beam came from the red surround of an emergency lantern; behind it, the shape of a man. The torch swung around and up the path as if urging him on. He continued past the light and, ahead of him, another beam shone out. There were men positioned all the way up, at about ten-metre intervals. They stood like stones, ready to wave him on. In this mad weather the thick-set figures, immobile behind their torches, were eerie.

As he neared the house its brightest light became a square, the square of the lighted porch – a portico with columns either side and a ceramic-tiled entranceway. When he walked across the tiles, heavy doors opened automatically, revealing a plain, carpeted foyer with another set of doors at the end. The doors behind him closed with a hiss, muting the thunder of the sea. The gale was replaced by air-conditioned warmth. Voices came from an archway to the side. He entered an ante-room that could have been the lounge of a provincial hotel – occasional chairs, bookshelves, painted seascapes on the walls. The others were already there, holding drinks. None looked as if they'd struggled through a gale.

Dyson wore a tailored jacket that draped his flab with some success. He turned as Connor entered. 'Thought we'd lost you. Drinks on the table.'

Sinclair sported an expensive suit, the patrician in fighting garb. His wife's small shoulders were warmed by some rare thing, ecologically unsound. But the older woman trumped them all in a scoop-necked, black woollen sheath that, as she knew, looked magnificent on her.

Connor, in his Nato-style jacket, felt hot and out of place. He took it off. 'I thought this was informal.'

Sinclair stroked his silk tie, checked the knot's relationship to his collar, his droll gesture for the evening. 'We're showing the Kaffirs how to behave.' He pointed to a door at the side. 'The repair department's in there.'

He went through the door to a washroom. Hanging space. Folded towels on a shelf – towels monogrammed with the crest that had been on the card in his room. It looked like a cogged wheel and he had no idea what it represented, but it wasn't Rotary. He hung his jacket with others on a peg and tried to smooth his hair. He'd worn his crew-necked jumper and now felt uncomfortably hot. The strip-light above the mirror made him look drawn and pale.

He went back to the other room and checked the drinks on the side table. Champagne, Steinlager, Scotch. He chose orange juice, thinking of his stomach.

Beside him, Dyson was ear-bashing Sinclair's wife: '…called Mystery Marketing. Designed to keep you guessing. Dumb idea of their MD so beyond criticism, get it?' He put his empty glass on the side table and poured another straight Scotch. 'Haven't seen a single rep here, and I know the arseholes by their first names. You practise with last year's group photograph.'

The small woman spread her hands and her ring finger sparkled expensively. 'Well, I assure you, Mr Dyson, we're as much in the dark as you are.'

He leered. 'You can call me Adrian. And you're...?'

'Anita.'

'Lovely name.'

Connor had spotted another camera, mounted near the corner of the ceiling. 'D'you still have no idea what this is about?'

Anita Sinclair shook her close-cropped head. 'Not a clue. All we can do is hope for the best.'

Her husband looked at his watch – a Cartier tank. 'Twenty past seven.'

His wife said, 'Their surprise party's becoming boring.'

'I'm hungry,' said Grace Merrick. The statement was loud, imperative. No para-chefs fell through the ceiling to feed her, although that was what she seemed to expect.

Connor followed Sinclair, who had crossed to peer at a painting. It depicted the bay on a boisterous day and had a good feeling for sea and sky.

'I like it,' Sinclair said. 'I'm not sure why.'

'He's painted the atmosphere, not the scene.'

'Yes... I see what you mean.'

'You have to paint the light. Not the objects. That's really the secret of it.'

'You don't say. Very interesting. Painter yourself, are you?'

'Amateur. So you've no idea what's happening here?'

'I'm afraid the jury's still out.'

'Reckon we've been kidnapped. Thing is, why?'

'Frankly, old sock, I don't give a stuff about why. Right now, I just want their guts for garters.'

'Would you come this way please?' Everybody looked around. The woman who had met them stood in the doorway. She now wore understated earrings and a plain blue dress but her look of concern hadn't changed.

Sinclair took his wife's arm. 'Into the valley of death…'

Dyson gulped half the contents of his second glass and topped it up to go. 'Now, with luck, we get answers.'

'They'd better feed us,' Merrick said.

The second set of doors beyond the entrance hall had been opened. The woman was leading them into a cavernous room and across a sea of black marble. It was a kind of dimly lit museum with padded leather benches in the centre and scattered exhibits cleverly spotlit by tiny directional lamps. Niches glowed in the walls. They were large and each held a display. It was a gallery of back-lit items devoted to a single art: war. Each niche contained a collection of military hardware: an array of automatic weapons, field computers and fill-input devices, shoulder mounted anti-tank launchers… Connor walked past them, dazed at the complete change of atmosphere. The larger items were mounted on plinths that outgleamed the floor. He paused beside a cylinder that looked like a flying torpedo. A plaque on the ebony mounting read AGM 136A Loitering Anti-radar. No wiser, he checked others. RBS70. AT4 'Spigot'. SA-7 'Grail'.

'Creeping Jeezuz,' Dyson said. 'It's a bunker for World War Three!'

A military museum? The items were too recent for that. The lighting, colour and finish, the black marble flagstones… the display was stunningly well done. It had the design sense of an elegant emporium and the atmosphere of a mosque.

Connor walked to one of the niches. Each had a printed information card. 'The AJAX/APILAS system,' he read, 'is a rocket which in its mine configuration arms at five metres. The calibre is 112mm, the weight 4.3kg, the weight of the explosive is 1.5kg and the MV 290 m/sec at 21 deg C. The round will penetrate in excess of 700mm of rolled homogeneous armour. Acoustic/seismic sensors switch on the system and the IR array provides range, bearing and bearing rates. The processor fires the weapon on the correct lead angle. The range...'

'Hanford?'

He turned to see Sinclair sit heavily on the edge of a bench, shaking his head, eyes shut. His wife, astonished by her surroundings, was now astonished by their effect on her husband.

'Hanford, what is it? Tell me.' She perched beside him in dismay.

But Merrick's reaction was strangest. Face horrified, mouth open, she was backing out of the room. Actually walking backwards as if she had forgotten she could turn. Three huge men appeared behind her, blocking the doorway. She backed straight into one, shrieked, then spun around.

The next part happened fast. Her hands splayed into claws. Then she was tearing at the face of the central man, grunting with frenzy, trying to thumb his eyes.

The man's hands came up, clamped her wrists. But she wrenched an arm free and scored a gash in his cheek with her nails. An elbow jolt to her chin snapped her head around and dropped her. Connor heard the thud as it connected with the side of her jaw. She was lucky the blow had been measured – the man's arm could have snapped her neck.

She went limp, stunned, and slid down his body to the floor, toppling backward on the flagging. Her head would have smashed on the marble if a second man hadn't moved his boot there first, as if practising for a drop-kick, then lowered her head to the floor.

She lay half on her side, legs splayed, skirt riding up around her thighs, her long steel-brown hair spread over the dark mirror of the tiles. Limp and senseless, she seemed more appealing than she had ever been when conscious. On the dark wall above the door a lens glinted and hummed as it zoomed in.

Now it was Dyson's turn to be nervous. The violence had him boggling. He backed behind an exhibit as two of the men hoisted Merrick like a sack, dead-lifting her as easily as most people would lift a rubbish bag. The first man put her across the shoulders of the second, who held her in a fireman's lift. The third man waved toward the far door where the woman stood. The gesture said, Get moving.

The woman said, 'Don't make trouble and you won't be harmed. Please come. Dinner is served.'

Dyson gulped the last of his Scotch and put the glass on the nearest flat surface – the wing of what looked like a very large and modernistic model aircraft with plastic domes in unusual places on the fuselage, labelled Multi-Mission STOL RVP. He didn't read the label. He looked around, bewildered.

Sinclair's eyes were open now, staring at the floor. His wife clung to him, shocked by the action at the door. She looked up as the man passed, carrying Merrick. The older woman was out to it, her arm dangling down his back, one shoe off, eyes open but glazed. The troopers by the door shut it with the reverence of rabbis locking a synagogue.

'What *is* this?' Anita Sinclair moaned. She looked bird-like, terrified.

'Mould,' Sinclair said, staring down. He wasn't referring to something on the floor, which shone with such dark lustre that one could have assembled mother-boards on it.

'Mould?'

'Before your time.' He got up and sighed, patting her Tinkerbell body. 'Sorry, dear. My fault, I'm afraid.'

Mould? Connor vaguely knew the name. Something to

do with a shoot? In the old days – with Rex?

'Okay, okay,' Dyson laughed, 'you had me by the balls but I've got it. This is like… one of those mystery weekends where you have to guess whodunnit. You people are like actors, right?'

Sinclair said dryly, 'Try again.'

'Come onnnn… It's a put-on. Jeez, I've been to weird conferences in my time but this one takes the cake. I give in, okay? You got me. Enough already. Like, give me a break.'

'Who's Mould?' asked Connor.

'You don't know?' Sinclair replied.

Suddenly it clicked. Connor felt as if a metal skewer had slid into his gut.

'Please come now,' the woman said. 'You'll find place-names on the table.'

Chapter Four

They entered a room with thick carpet and wall-length windows framed by heavy drapes. The only light came from candles flickering on the long central table, which was set for three courses and flanked by high-backed chairs. But there was no chair at its head. Instead, on the floor to the side, there was an oxygen cylinder fitted with bacterial filter and mask.

Merrick was slumped in a chair, her swelling jaw turning blue. Behind her chair, like a sentinel, stood the man who had dumped her there, blood beading the pale underlayer of skin exposed by the rip in his face.

'Caught,' Sinclair said to Merrick.

The woman moved her head in despair.

The windows faced the bay because the roar of the sea was audible here, but muted, as if filtered through acoustic-thickness glass. Connor glanced up into gloom. For once he could see no cameras.

He found his name-tag. David Ashford Connor. Did nothing escape these people? He loathed the Ashford, never used it. He pulled out the chair and sat. The woman stood by the side of the door. The two troopers joined her and stood stiffly like second touring company extras in an opera.

Connor looked up at her. For the first time she met his glance. She quickly, almost shyly, looked down, but it was enough to telegraph what she felt. She didn't like what was being done here. Hated it. And pitied them.

She did not glance at him again but the look had meant a great deal. It meant someone on 'the other side' was sane

– he was no longer alone. He felt a hot stab of gratitude that made the silver in front of him blur.

He heard the voice once more. 'There's a message under your cards. Not yours, Mrs Sinclair. You're our guest.' She turned and left the room.

Connor reached for the wooden card-holder, up-ended it. A small piece of paper stuck to the back bore a single word:

DEFAMER

He knew exactly what it referred to. He rubbed his eyes in despair and said under his breath, 'Oh, shit.'

Across the table, Merrick's guard had lifted her holder up for her to see. The eyes in the swelling face read what was written. She sucked in her breath and held it, which at any other time he would have enjoyed. He put his own card down before the others could see his hand was shaking.

Sinclair, to Merrick's left, jerked. 'Outrageous.'

He flung his card-holder at the wall.

Dyson, seated next to Connor, held his holder at arm's length, squinting. 'Can't read that.' He held it in front of Connor. 'What's it say?'

'Embezzler.'

'Come again?'

'Embezzler.'

'Yeah?' He put the card back on the table, name side up, coughed a wet cough, the phlegm rattling in his chest, and reached for his glass. It was empty.

Anita Sinclair, who'd checked under her card and obviously found nothing, looked at her husband, bewildered. 'What did yours say, Hanford? Hanford?'

Sinclair sat like a ramrod. She pulled at his arm. He didn't respond.

The chair on Connor's right was still vacant. Someone

was apparently to join them. There were voices at the door as the guard of honour parted to admit what looked like a medical contingent. First, a Chinese man wearing wire-frame spectacles and a doctor's solemn air of over-competence. Then an Asian nurse, pushing a wheelchair. In the chair was a very sick man. He might once have been handsome, even imposing, but age and illness had made the face a caricature. Bulbous, hooded eyes set above dark crescents of waxen skin, sensuous lips, huge earlobes and, beneath the jawline, shapeless rolls of fat. The thin hair, probably dyed, was slicked back along the bumpy scalp. One shoulder-blade stuck out further than the other, forcing his head forward.

One of his feet fell off the footstand and dragged on the floor. It was bloated and the skin at the ankle resembled a plastic bag full of mince. The nurse stopped pushing and stooped to replace the foot on the chair. Clearly the only improvement he could expect would come from his embalmer.

The sick man nodded at Connor, smiling. 'Don't recognise me, Mr Connor?' A deep voice, richly accented. Russian? 'I admit I'm not what I was.'

Sinclair's voice, icily satirical. 'Nicolae! You're not looking well.'

'I fear my tennis days are over.' As they wheeled him behind Merrick's chair, the deep voice came again. 'Hello, Grace.'

Merrick stared at the candle ahead of her, eyes glinting in the light. She didn't turn her head. Tears made snail-tracks down her cheeks.

They wheeled Mould to the head of the table. He muttered something to the doctor, who bent his head to listen, nodded, then spoke to the nurse in Cantonese. As the two of them walked from the room, they passed a woman coming in.

Connor glanced at her, then looked away. She had the flat, compact body of an Indo-Chinese but her horribly burnt and reconstructed face made it impossible to guess her age. On the left side, the skin had been dragged pearl tight across the bone. The other side was a mess of deep craters. One eye constantly blinked while the other stared, its eyelid barely moving. She crossed to the chair on his right and sat in it without a sound.

Mould lifted one hand slightly, displaying fingers like bananas.

At the sign, the men at the door stood aside.

More of the platoon entered, carrying plates of food and wine-buckets on stands - still in their military greens and with their cataleptic expressions. The floor gave slightly as they walked behind the chairs, doubling as waiters, efficiently stage-managing the meal.

Mould, now settled at the end of the table, raised his massive head. He smiled slowly, savouring the scene, as a trooper respectfully filled his glass. His bloated fingers closed on the stem and he raised the glass to each of them in turn.

'Welcome. Welcome.' The smile became beatific. 'I'm sure that none of you comprehend what... years of... patience, preparation... of pleasurable anticipation... have preceded... our gathering here tonight.'

Anita Sinclair stared at him, appalled. 'Would you please tell me what's going on?'

'Of course, dear lady. That's the purpose of the meal.' He gestured at her plate. 'Smoked moray eel. Local produce. To give you a feeling for your... surroundings. Though we're also partial to... Eastern dishes, aren't we, Duyen?' He turned from the woman with no face to the rest of the company. 'May I introduce Duyen Vo, my assistant. Among her many attributes is the... ability to cook a marvellous dessert made from sago, coconut milk and bananas.'

Merrick glanced at the woman, flinched and looked quickly back at her plate. Mould noticed. He seemed to miss nothing.

'I admit, Grace, she lacks your... smoothness of complexion, but intellectually you are to her as... how do they put it? As a nail is to a requiem.'

Merrick was weeping. She made no attempt to dry the tears. They dripped off her chin onto the lush skin above her neckline and ran down the swell of her breasts. She looked tragically beautiful enough to launch at least five hundred ships.

'Why so sad?' Mould persisted. 'Because the dream ended so soon? I'm afraid there's no gold at the end of the rainbow. Look at me.' His hand touched his chest. 'Ultimately, we're all defeated.'

Connor watched the man with grim interest. He seemed in the last stages of heart failure, but his charisma charged the room. The voice was strong, the mind clever, educated, wry. He was formidable. A person capable of anything. Those odd, drooping lids. He seemed forced to lift his chin to see out beneath them.

His assessment was interrupted as a hand slid a plate in front of him. On the bone china, elegantly arranged, were medallions of meat with lemon, avocado, lettuce... He'd been served from the left. He wondered if they'd take away from the right. He wondered with his hands in his lap. They were still shaking.

'Hey, fellah,' Dyson said. He was pointing to his glass, twisting around to the trooper behind his chair, who stood ready but did not pour.

Mould smiled. 'Sorry, Mr Dyson. My joke.' He nodded and the wine-trooper filled Dyson's Waterford crystal glass with a Leeuwin Estate chardonnay. The bottle, suitably frosty, had a napkin tucked around its neck.

'Australian wine,' Mould said, 'as Mr Connor's noticed. Although we're dining on local fare, one shouldn't carry things too far.'

'Cut the crap,' Dyson said.

Mould's rubber lips twisted. 'Certainly, Mr Dyson. Shall we start with you?'

Dyson shuffled uncomfortably and mumbled, 'What the fuck does that mean?' He watched the glass fill, reached for it and swigged it. Connor could smell his body odour, the acrid smell of his fear.

Mould gestured at him. 'Adrian Dyson, gambler, bisexual and soak. Thirteen years ago he was someone you'd believe in, as all good con-men are. He was with Seeker and Gretchem, New York, in charge of the Conquistador Fragrance account – international media budget $34 million.'

'Cute. Like we have to spell it out?'

'But he began to lose heavily at draw poker. Always thought he'd have a royal flush in the first hand dealt – though the odds are 649,740 to one. He progressed to five-card stud. The pots, and players, became bigger. The more he lost, the more he drank. And the more he doubled his stake to win it back. Finally… he owed serious money to some… very humourless people. You ask where the money came from?'

No-one had.

Sinclair, nibbling eel with distaste, scanned the room, his sharp eyes slits. His wife sat as if affronted. She hadn't touched her plate.

Mould's breathing was now laboured. His hand caressed the taps on the oxygen bottle as someone might play with their nails or feel for a familiar item in the dark. But he didn't pick up the plastic mask. He waited, gathering strength.

Grace Merrick retrieved a small handkerchief and wiped her face and chest. That done, she blew each nostril in turn, as if she'd read that it was medically advisable.

Mould, breathing more easily, continued. 'The money came from the Conquistador budget – siphoned off over time. He had an accomplice in the... media department, with whom he cultivated an unnatural affection. And another in the accounts department who... was bribed to divert money into a promotions company that... Mr Dyson, in fact, owned.' He paused, his breath labouring again. 'The media charts the client saw never quite agreed with the spend. Over six years he... appropriated $2,900,000. When the agency found out, they took the easy option. Dyson was let go. The client? Never told.'

Dyson said, 'What's it to you?'

'I own sixty per cent of Conquistador.'

'Baloney.'

A dry laugh came from Sinclair. 'Been branching out, have you, Nicolae? Into something that smells sweeter?'

'Careful, Hanford. We'll come to you.'

Merrick was feeling her jaw. Dyson's sins were unimportant to her. Her face was now grim with rage and she looked primed to explode.

Mould turned back to Dyson. 'Your new start in Australia was based on your pitch for Mido. A simple... credentials presentation. Easy, wasn't it? Because I also own two-thirds of Mido Petcorp. Now, perhaps, you see how... carefully I've followed your... pathetic, dirty life.'

Dyson didn't reply. His body seemed to have shrunk.

'So there's no conference, Adrian. You don't mind my calling you Adrian? I feel I know you so well.'

Sinclair pointed a long finger at Mould. 'Why don't I give *your* history, man?' He stared around at the other guests, assuming the high ground for his turf. 'Mould isn't his real name, which sounds like someone choking. His cronies are dictators, guerrillas... any mass-murder organisation. He sends Third World countries into deficit by flogging them military hardware. And he...'

'Behave yourself, Hanford.' Mould wasn't amused. 'You're in no position to take liberties.'

Sinclair ploughed on. '... and he thinks he's nature's little helper. Because people are wrecking the planet, the bugger wants to waste them. Elimination ecology. Not zero population growth, oh, no. For this flash bugger, zero means extermination.'

Mould moved one finger and Sinclair's mouth met the avocado on his plate. The man behind his chair had pressed his face into it.

Dyson guffawed, delighted that someone else was now the target.

As the gaunt man lifted his head, wiping slime from his cheek, his plate was removed – from the right.

'My staff are instructed to use just as much force as needed,' said Mould.

Anita Sinclair bounded from her chair and stamped her foot. '*Stop* this.'

Mould raised his hands placatingly. 'Mrs Sinclair, don't be a brat. I'm not your coloured maid. Try to... understand your situation. Normal conditions don't apply here. I can do... anything I wish – can have you gang-raped if it pleases me – though I fear you'd find that gratifying.'

Dyson leered at Sinclair's wife. Even Merrick now seemed to be listening. Her face registered disgust.

'Perhaps,' Mould went on, 'I could have you... necklaced on the front lawn and we could pretend we're in Soweto. You're welcome to choose your fuel. We have Dieseline, Avgas or petrol.' He said it softly, with great charm, but his fish eyes thrust it home. 'Now,' he rumbled, 'sit down.'

Anita Sinclair sat down as instructed, both hands over her mouth, eyes wide. Her husband's hand went to her knee – warning her to do nothing. The imperturbable troopers were preparing to serve the main course. One removed her untouched entrée.

'Our local industry,' Mould went on suavely, 'is deer. They were originally imported from England. The islanders sell the meat to the Germans and the antler skins to the Asians. We still keep a few deer on this island. For meat and target practice. Our second course is venison. Home grown.'

Anita Sinclair still gawked. Mould's diverting local highlights had not soothed her.

The sick man gave her a chilling smile. Connor had seen the same smile on a half-open tin of sardines. 'Please don't concern yourself, Mrs Sinclair. I've no quarrel with you. You don't know how… fortunate that is.'

'Why is my husband here?'

'Adultery with unforgivable lack of gallantry.'

'Adultery?'

'With my wife.' Mould's fork stabbed his last piece of eel.

Dyson choked on his drink, then grinned at Sinclair. 'You fucked his wife? No shit?'

Mould looked again at Anita Sinclair. 'It happened before you met him.' He put the fork down and pushed his plate away. A trooper removed it with deference.

She scowled back at him. 'Adultery? Is that so terrible? People are sexual beings.' She straightened slightly as she said it, tossing her head, moving her shoulders back a little so that her small, perfectly formed breasts were momentarily outlined against the thin material of her dress. The movement suggested that she was aware, suddenly, of her own sexuality. It told Connor without doubt that she'd never, for a moment, forgotten it.

'Unlike your husband and you,' Mould said, 'I don't

regard adultery as a hobby. I like it far less when… the adulterer sacrifices his lover to save himself. Your husband's… how shall I say it – unswerving self-interest – killed my wife.'

'Jeez,' said Dyson.

Merrick stared at Sinclair with distaste.

Anita Sinclair turned to her husband, who was dabbing his face with a napkin. He looked down at his plate, frowned, puffed out his cheeks. He was caught between a rock and a hard place. Anita looked back at Mould and said, 'A woman was drowned…'

'Ask him how.'

Connor glanced at the door. Two guards were still on station. The faceless woman next to him was forking eel to the gash that was her mouth. Mould said nothing more. Sinclair's crime, it seemed, wouldn't be spelt out.

Dyson jerked a thumb at Merrick and Connor. 'What about them?' Mould's eyes swivelled upward under the half-mast lids and bored into Grace Merrick. 'Ah, yes.'

'It was your fault,' Merrick shouted. She was closest to him and almost screamed it in his face. Her jailer, still behind her chair, stiffened, ready to restrain her. The blood from his laceration had trickled to his collar but he'd not once put his hand to the wound.

'So what'd you do, Golden Girl?' Dyson asked.

Merrick jerked up as if she wanted to slap him.

Mould said, 'Her crime was too revolting to describe. After all, we're trying to eat.'

Merrick's fists beat the table, pounding, pounding. Mould raised his voice. 'Stop it or he'll hit you again.'

The fists stopped in mid-air and stayed there, the knuckles white.

Dyson looked disappointed, his taste for dirty washing again denied.

'As for Mr Connor,' Mould's eyes were now resting on him. 'He did a documentary about the South-east Asian arms trade together with an associate who'd been a military attaché well connected with certain people in Somalia, Borneo, Angola. The publicity generated destroyed... friendly associations in certain governments that were... crucial at the time. I swore you'd both pay. You will.'

Connor saw a chance and seized it. 'Hang on. The director was Rex Connor.'

Mould's rich voice cut in. 'I know that, Mr Connor. I've gone into the subject like a pig after a truffle.'

Connor pointed at Mould. '*Rex* Connor. I'm *David* Connor. No relation. If you want revenge, you want *Rex* Connor.'

Mould gazed back with contempt. 'You think my surveillance is so poor that I'd fall for that?' He turned to address them all. 'I know more about you – all of you – than you know about yourselves. I've studied your... lives like chess moves.' He turned back to Connor. 'Because Rex Connor's a vegetable, and you think I can't get at him, you're trying to shift the blame onto him. But I know what you did to impress your hero Rex. You did a deal with certain operatives who gave you information and propaganda footage that allowed you to make three more programmes aimed directly at me. And you were paid very well by... certain people who later died most painfully to – how shall I put it – be economical with the truth.' His eyes blazed. 'You crucified me, Connor, did a job on me that cost me millions. You richly deserve your... seat at this table. As for your idol, Rex, I've something in mind that should... reach him.'

The woman in black yelled, 'He's mad.'

'Not mad, Grace,' Mould said. 'Just dying. You can do anything, you know, when you're dying.' He beamed at the other guests. 'She thought she'd won a soup-packet contest for a marvellous holiday abroad. Naturally, she's disheartened.'

'So,' Sinclair dabbed the last of the food from his face with his monogrammed napkin, 'what do you have in mind? Blood sacrifice?'

Mould ignored him. 'Now, with the second course, we've a rather good red.'

The venison was garnished with a rich brown sauce and had perfectly baked small vegetables on the side. Connor's stomach was a bag of acid and the only solution was to eat. What had come over him, trying to put it onto Rex? Cautious Connor. Craven, more like it. Christ. He could smell his own fear. Sweat streamed down his back.

The meat was unpleasantly gamey – worse than kangaroo. But the Chateau Rothschild made up for it. Criminal to gulp it but he needed the sedation.

The sick man pecked at his plate, fighting his body with his will. But this was his night and he seemed intent on living it to the full.

Dyson leaned against Connor, stewed, body rank. 'Pass the bread rolls?'

The comment was so mundane it stopped conversation. Dyson might be in big trouble but his digestion seemed unimpaired. The woman with no face lifted the basket and passed it via Connor. Dyson put a roll on his plate, then seemed to forget it was there, his display of hunger or defiance wasted.

Mould smiled. 'Does everyone have bread? Bread, Grace?' He lifted the basket with elaborate care and handed it to Merrick. She thumped one fist down on the basket. Bread rolls danced out, rolling over the table and scattering on the floor.

'Manners,' Mould said, tut-tutting. 'She's prone to tantrums, poor thing. So – to the purpose of this gathering.'

He fondled his chins as one might stroke a cat. 'I've studied my bugs for years. Now I'm ready to mount them on pins. But I'm not so stupid as to... think that they'll stay still while I stab. So I'm proposing... we play a game... a game I've personally devised – based on a Romanian poem.'

Dyson, voice thick with drink, had reached the stage of conspicuous bravery. 'You know what they say about Romanians? A Hungarian'll sell you his mother but a Romanian'll even deliver.'

'True.' Mould groped for the mask, held it over his face and breathed in. His other hand regulated the valve. The hiss of oxygen increased.

Sinclair was back on the attack. 'You have us here on false pretences. You're detaining us against our will, you're intimidating us, making threats – indictable offences.'

The mask was lowered, the tap turned off. 'Don't bluster, Hanford. It's so childish. Even if you could convict me, I wouldn't live to be tried.' He addressed the room again. 'My little game involves both carrot and stick.' He tapped both hands on the table and turned to the Asian woman. 'As I... tire easily, Duyen will give the details. Ms Vo?' His hand bade her rise.

The woman stood up and faced them. Everyone looked at their plates.

'There will be game between four accused. Play will be compul... compulsory. Winner get $20 million US.'

Mould beamed at Dyson. 'Should please you, Adrian. Take you *days* to fritter that away.'

Grace Merrick's jaw fell slightly. The amount seemed to have transfixed her more than anything that had happened in the room.

Mould saw it. 'Yes, Grace. A good round sum. Might even permit some... travel.'

Vo droned on. 'Three rounds to game. First round play

here. Second play when you go back to home.'

'Naturally,' Mould chipped in, 'my thoughts will follow you all. Also my eyes and ears. I have an excellent organisation – projection of force, we call it.'

'Third round – you come here again.'

'Hold it,' Dyson said. 'Hold it.' The information was still seeping through him. 'You said twenty… million? *Million*?'

Mould nodded. His hand retreated to his chins, pinching the folds gently, smoothing, stretching the skin. 'A lot of money. To some. You see, I've been dealing for forty years. Basic hard-target systems at the start. Weapons are a great commodity. Rugged. Long life-cycle. Generally several owners. The market? Colossal. Ms Vo? Your last information?'

The woman still stood there patiently. 'World military expenditure and arm transfer figure for develop nation well over one trillion.'

'So lucrative,' Mould interjected. 'For instance, an antiquated battle tank – say a Soviet T54 or 55 – could be… sourced a while ago for under $50,000 and sold for four times that amount to certain South American governments. We did quite well on those old tanks – even named this island after one to… commemorate our success. These days we deal more in… ground stations, missile systems, peripherals… Lately I've funnelled the profits into corporations. Weapons into ploughshares, you might say.' He paused, fighting for air, clutching for the mask. The assembly watched the ritual of the taps, the hissing gas.

Sinclair was trying to look bored, examining his nails over-casually.

At last Mould lowered the mask. The impressive head came up again slowly. 'Bargaining was my joy. But constant travel beat me. Now it's all in the past. But we still manage the occasional deal. Momentum… True, Duyen?'

The woman with no face said, 'We still do deal.' Her voice

was harsh, like a crow's. She sounded disgruntled. Mould made an exaggerated gesture of despair. 'My sorcerer's apprentice lives to… apply her knowledge.'

She said, 'He sick. He not care.' Her unblinking eye showed no emotion. Though it moved, it could have been glass.

Mould chuckled and his belly acquired an animation of its own. 'One thing he cares about – his hobby. When I offer you my… jackpot, there's a reason. More amusing if you're… involved several ways. And before I die,' he beamed again, 'I intend to savour that involvement. That is, I intend to play.' His body quaked again. 'With *you*.'

Dyson was sweating – from alcohol and interest. 'For that kind of bread, I'll do hanshtands.'

'Most encouraging, Adrian. But you'll have to do more than that.' Mould placed his hands together, fingers touching, like a bishop working up to a homily. 'Twenty million is serious money.'

Sinclair snorted. 'I'm not interested in your sweetener.'

Mould raised his hands in mock despair. 'Alas. It's a sum that appeals to all except the very wealthy Mr Sinclair.'

'So how do you persuade *me* to play?' Beneath his satirical front, Sinclair fumed.

'As our lofty Mr Sinclair is… flush enough to ignore the carrot, I need to rely on the stick. For instance, his egotism's based around his business… which he'll do anything not to compromise. I doubt his wife would make a good hostage. I think he sees her more as a receptacle.'

Anita Sinclair huffed. 'How *dare* you?'

Mould was back behind his mask. Dyson finally reached for one of the rolls that now rested against an upturned silver pepper-pot. He broke it in two, muttering to Connor. 'Can you believe this arsehole?' His fingers had chipped nails.

Mould's mask was lowered. The cold eyes swivelled. 'And

so we come to the good-looking Mr Connor. Nothing's gone right since his great days with Rex Connor. And now his business is waning. Not that it ever waxed... though he did have hopes. But life's generally... disappointing. So no grist for intimidation there. He has an impressive wife who's growing bored with him but he's... still sexually tethered to her. Not much to work with, but enough.'

Dyson jabbed Connor with his elbow and said in a stage whisper, 'Got a voice so deep you can smell the shit on his breath.'

Mould ignored him and turned to Merrick, a curl to his lip. 'And dear Grace. Well, she... has a sister she doesn't give a damn about. And a worthless brother she... dotes on, because patronising someone in the name of... filial love is... marvellous for the ego. And Grace has a... monumental ego that's survived all the events of a... vain and disastrous life.'

Merrick had her fingers in her ears. 'I don't listen to madmen.'

Mould's chest heaved. His hands were on the valves again. 'Now for the... entertaining Adrian. His wife has... long ago divorced him but he has two... sons who know not to lend him money, whatever the cunning excuse, and a... twenty-year-old Chinese youth he sleeps with. Bum-boy. Is that the term?'

Dyson flushed, put two fingers up at Mould and jerked them. 'Shove it.'

Mould lifted the hissing mask. 'You're an... endearing creature, Adrian. I'll enjoy watching your... progress in the game.' His skin was becoming ashen. He placed the plastic over his face.

'Shove it,' Dyson said again, without force. He looked stunned, destroyed.

After several deep breaths Mould removed the mask and spread his hands. 'So there you have it. Hostages to fate.

There's no joy in attacking your possessions. You're all churchmice except for Hanford. Tell me, Hanford. How'd you like me to… wreck your business? I deal with colourful types… all partial to contra-deals. Triads, the Mafia, the IRA, the ARM, the Khmer Rouge, the Jihad… '

Sinclair glowered at his plate like a man who had received serious news.

'Now.' Mould took a sip of wine. 'Your respective solicitors have just been informed by the Perpetual… Trustee Company of Sydney that you're… the beneficiaries of a trust fund. In this fund three people will eventually… receive $2 each and the fourth… $20 million. Give out the documents.'

The faceless one distributed forms to them all. She had dainty hands, with the third finger missing on the left. If she were married, no-one would know.

'A simple deed of trust,' Mould went on. 'You can discuss it later with Sinclair. He studied law at the University of Cape Town. His pass was mediocre, his conduct scandalous – I doubt his tutor's wife ever recovered – but he… knows enough to see it's genuine.'

Sinclair was scanning it. He turned a page and his eyebrow rose.

Connor glanced at his copy. A medical history was stapled to the back, signed by a Dr Lee. Certain words stood out: inoperable scar tissue, congestive failure, Capoten, Lanoxin.

'So it's not all one-sided,' Mould said. 'But I insist you play the game. If you don't… Well… ' He looked at Merrick, 'your … brother might have trouble with the authorities.' His eyes rested on Sinclair, 'You might find it difficult purchasing gold for your… current issue.' Now it was Dyson's turn. 'Your sons might run into ruffians.' The eyes now bored into Connor. 'Your wife might have an… accident in the car.'

Sinclair's eyes were slits. 'Those are specific threats – in the presence of witnesses.'

'Worse. They're examples to prove a point.'

He nodded to the disfigured woman to continue.

'In each draw of game we pick winner and loser. Winner must enforce penalty or become loser in next contest. Mean loser of last game must enforce next penalty. All penalties based on special poem.'

Dyson was muttering again. 'What the fuck?'

'But if last game loser does *not* enforce penalty, he let off one time. Next time must enforce. Game has seven rules.'

Dyson said, 'Can we have it in English?'

She looked at Mould as if to check her pronunciation. 'Poem has three verse. And each verse make one round. Verse one we give to you tonight. Tomorrow game begin.'

Dyson leant against Connor, voice slurring, 'So what the fuck was that?'

'Is simple,' Vo said. 'Tomorrow you see how it work. I referee all games.' She sat down.

Dyson stared at Mould. 'You mean she deshides the winner?'

Mould said, 'No. *You* do that. You'll see how it works as we progress. Don't trouble your… heads about it now. Well, that ends the… formalities for the present. Please eat, drink and be merry – for tomorrow…'

He didn't need to finish the sentence.

Chapter Five

Outside the hot-house building the air met them like a gale off a glacier. The thunder of the sea destroying itself on rocks reduced them in scale to insignificance. They were escorted back to the huts through the storm, each led by a man with a lamp, the line of lights bobbing down the slope a witch's dance in the furious darkness full of sound.

A wire sang in the wind above them and somewhere far off a strip of roofing had shaken loose and was banging. There was another sound, unplaceable, as of a bandsaw biting through steel or the growl of some huge predator infuriated by the gale. It came twice only before it was drowned in the ocean's roar.

Connor stumbled on tufts of grass, smelling pines and salt air, following the erratic oval of light from the torch of the man in front. Ahead of him, the dancing ovals spread more widely as they neared the huts.

Boots on wooden steps. Lights winking on in the cabins. The man switched on the light in Connor's hut, the sudden brightness outlining his heavy jaw. He left without a word, as if he'd returned some domestic item to its shelf. Connor watched him melt into the dark, wondering whether he should talk to the others. He walked to the edge of the decking, looked round. The lights from the four huts and the marker lights on the path dimly outlined the swaying crescent of trees. He saw shadows on the blind of Sinclair's hut. Sinclair was the one to talk to. Despite his patrician act he seemed no fool. But he couldn't do it now. Too tired, too shocked. Tomorrow.

He crossed to the other end of the deck and leaned over the rail, looking back along the side of the hut in the slipstream of the wind. In the light from the next hut he could make out a green box on the wall of his cabin. It looked like a fuse box but had no lid. The hut on this side was Grace Merrick's. He wondered how she was feeling. She might be a virago but took top marks for spunk.

He went inside, shut out the wind, leaning aimlessly against the door, then sat on the bed beside his half-unpacked bag, staring vacantly at the familiar things from home. His old Braun electric shaver, the travel alarm, his leather notebook with the ring-binder... objects of identity and comfort, talismans without power to protect.

Reality was this island.

This trap.

He looked around the room. The hut was almost certainly bugged. So where could he talk to the others and not be overheard? They could have directional mikes outside like the ones he'd used on shoots. Mould wasn't mobile, so had organised his eyes and ears. He examined the room again. It looked normal enough. No cameras.

The thought made him check the bench cupboard where he'd left his camera case. There'd been no secure place to put it.

The shelf was bare.

'Bastards.' He felt hot anger. Although it was pointless, he looked in the wardrobe, under the bed, checked other cupboards. No sign. Gone. Appropriated or pinched? Over two grand's worth of Nikon plus filters, lenses and battery drive. His fear flooded back. The loss was the least of his worries.

The phone rang... shrill in the room... jarring.

He jumped.

He let it ring twice more, then picked it up, as one might handle a grenade.

A woman's voice said, 'Mr Connor?'

'Yes.'

'A call for you. Go ahead, please.'

'David?' It was Tess, close and clear, bounced from a satellite into the hut, the shock of her voice bringing associations of home, suburban normality. 'Tess? God!'

'I'm so glad you rang.'

'Rang?'

'Now don't make a production number out of it. Everything's all right. But the car's a write-off.'

He shut his eyes, speechless.

'David? You there?'

'Are you okay?'

'I'm fine.'

'What happened?'

'I was coming off the expressway at Cammeray, crossing Miller Street, and this truck came from nowhere – ran into me at the back. Spun me right around, then drove straight off.'

'You sure you're… '

'Fine. I'm fine. Just here for observation.'

'Where?'

'Don't be a sonk. You *rang* here. North Shore Hospital, of course. What are they feeding you? Magic mushrooms? Who told you I was here?'

'In… Are you hurt?'

'Observation, I said. Things are slower in Kiwi-land. Must be catching.'

'Just… tell me what's wrong with you.'

'Mild concussion and whiplash, they said. They're letting me go in the morning. So *don't worry*. I'm fine. Don't come back or anything silly. How's the island?'

'I've been… '

The line crackled and went dead. 'You there?'

He stood stock still, then flung the phone at the mirror.

The glass shattered. Slivers fell. Behind the mirror, framed by glittering shards, was the galvanising of the box on the wall. Mounted inside it was a slave-driven video camera with a medium wide-angle lens. Connor wrapped his handkerchief around his fingers and carefully picked out the special glass until he could uncouple the coaxial cable from the socket at the back of the camera. Then he slumped on the bed and rolled face down.

Grace Merrick, naked in front of the mirror, checked her body for damage. The swollen jaw with its bruise, the red eyes. She went to the bar fridge, emptied ice-cubes into a face cloth, caught up the edges and applied the cold-pack to her cheek. She held it there, twisting to see if there were bruises on her body. None. Apart from aching teeth she felt no pain.

She prodded the firm slope of her breasts, then turned to check the backs of her thighs. The bottom, compact, superb; the athlete's legs. Her strength and proportion defied time – as if her body were independent of her – a marvellous carriage she just happened to be in.

How dare they hit her! She'd kill them for that. She felt sharp hatred – tinged with curious elation. Mould, her once and transitory lover, was now a lump of blubber on wheels, while she was still in her prime. What resentment he must feel.

So he wanted to play a game? She'd play all right – to win. $20 million! Money she was born to have. She'd lost a glamorous holiday but gained the chance to win a fortune. She was strong, resourceful, could do it.

At last her time had come.

She strode to the shower recess and adjusted the water. Tomorrow, rain or shine, she'd swim in Mould's pool and he'd see the shrine he'd once worshipped still intact. She wanted him to ogle her through his cameras. Her body, her glory, would taunt him.

One never knew what one would do. One's emotions over-rode everything. As they had tonight when she attacked that huge man. As they had that day in LA...

September, with the Santa Anas blowing – the dry west wind from Utah, superheated by the Mojave Desert. She was driving back from Laguna, sandy and sundrenched with warmth, and stopped in the queue at the lights. Stupidly, she'd left her handbag on the seat. Then the black man with the rag-wrapped hammer...

No. She wouldn't think of that now.

The water was soft on her skin. She let it warm, caress...

The phone rang. Mould wanting to taunt her?

It continued to ring – a problem for the caller. She'd not be rushed.

She finished her shower, patted her body dry, tucked the towel around her and went unhurriedly to the phone.

'Hello?'

'Mrs Merrick? Your call is through. Go ahead, please.'

Call? She hadn't made a call. 'Hello?'

The line was crackling badly. She heard a guttural voice she didn't understand – a coarse Arabic dialect. Then...

'Grace?' Her brother. The line was bad. 'Grace. I'm in trouble. Real bad trouble.'

'Ed?'

'Grace. They won't let me talk long. So listen good.'

Connor lay awake for hours, listening to the howling gale, staring at the blackness above the bed, mind thudding with images. The storm-lashed beach. The cavernous weapons display. Sinclair's face covered in avocado. Tears trickling between Merrick's breasts. The camera behind the shattered mirror. And, dominating it all, the liver skin, the wheezing breath, the implacable half-eyes of Mould.

Finally, exhausted, he slept in a nightmare-ridden daze. He woke once, wet with fear, first thinking himself safe at home, then realising that his waking nightmare was a dread far greater than the one he'd left.

He lay in the half-light of dawn, no clearer, no safer, no more resigned. The phone call had aroused all his emotions, his concern for his wife alternating with his suspicion of her. Tess, used as an example – nudged to demonstrate the extent of his bondage? To prove that nowhere was safe? Did Mould intend to kill them by degrees? What was the nature of his 'game'? What were the other victims thinking? What did they intend to do?

The storm had half blown itself out. The wind was spent and the roar of the sea no longer included the thunder of furious waves. He lay watching the light of dawn diffuse the edges of the blind. His life situation, his wife's – all apparently known by Mould. A cocktail of conflict and distrust that took the top off his head.

Sinclair was up early, dressed in expensive Italian jeans and jacket. His wife was still asleep – exhausted by the events of last night. At least the gale had passed. A small mercy but he was thankful. As he stepped into the morning's soft light, the slope to the sea looked Arcadian – except for a lone stormtrooper near the path beneath a tree, standing in the 'at ease' position, legs apart, hands behind his back.

The guard began to pace. Sinclair lounged against the rail and watched. Mould's troops had no weapons he could see.

Forty steps right. Forty left. The military mind. Bizarre.

The man paced back, looked at his watch, felt the pocket of his shirt to check something was there. He stood 'at ease' again, staring sightlessly ahead. They had to be mercenaries. How many innocents had they killed?

All men, he suspected, did things they'd rather forget. The airing of his own episode had chilled him. He'd refused to go into it. Anita didn't insist. She considered, as he did, that a meaningless life should be not be over-analysed but treated as a feast... before all mouths closed, before one reached the table's end. No, what concerned her was their predicament.

She'd said, 'You've no right to get me into this.' As if he'd had an option.

The guard was pacing again, still the only person to be seen. Sinclair strolled down the steps. Would the man intercept him?

Sniffing the salt air, he ambled toward Connor's hut.

A knock. Connor, half out of bed, hunted for something to cover him. 'Who's there?'

'Sinclair. You decent?'

'Hang on.' He dragged on the towelling bathrobe that had been hanging on a hook in the bathroom. The sleeves were short and it smelt of chlorine. 'Come in.'

Sinclair pushed the door open and stooped under the lintel. He glanced at the upside-down phone, the broken glass. 'You had a call, too?' He looked into the camera lens. 'Hello, Nicolae. How's reception, you bitter bugger?'

Connor held up the end of the cable. 'Bad.'

He was relieved to see his hand was steady.

'Hard cheese for Nico. God, the bugger must've seen my wife undress.'

'Must have a control room up there.'

'Think he can hear us?'

'Haven't spotted mikes but there could be bugs if he's that interested.' He knelt to disconnect the phone.

'Bloody business. Should we talk outside?'

'No point. They could have some kind of scanner. You saw the war room. They're not short of gear. Did you spot the camera outside on the tree?'

'Just noticed it. I feel like a bleeding goldfish.'

'Well, I don't want any part of it all. It's nothing to do with me. All I did was edit some docos. I'm a plain, ordinary peaceful person who's never hurt anybody and I just want to be left *alone*.'

'Tough titty, old sock.'

Connor knew he'd made a fool of himself. He couldn't handle this, hated it. The agitation of his body confirmed what a physical coward he was, how he shied away from force or violence – the reasonable man faced with the unreasonable.

'They've put my wife in hospital!' He used it as an excuse, hating himself for being so frazzled.

'Have they indeed? Well, my call wasn't cheering, either. He's cut off the supply of bullion I need for the new issue. Unless the bugger lets up, I'll lose several million rand.'

Dyson's twang outside, a perfunctory knock. 'Hi.' His haggard face peered around the door. His shirt, open at the collar and stained, looked like the one he'd worn last night. 'Saw you come over,' he said to Sinclair. 'Council of war time, huh?' He sidled into the hut. 'Got a phone call last night. Bastards have beaten up my kids.'

He said it with anger. Then his face crumpled and he subsided into the chair beside the bed, grinding his fist into his other palm, face working, rocking back and forth. Whatever Dyson was, his concern for his sons was undeniable.

Sinclair studied his nails as if he considered emotion bad form. 'We've all had phone calls.'

'Jeez, we gotta do something. What the hell can we do?'

'What indeed?'

Dyson sighed heavily, still rocking. 'We can't take on the gridiron team.'

Connor nodded. 'I've counted ten.'

'I make it twelve,' said Sinclair.

Dyson said, 'So we're stuck with a madman who can track us anywhere we go?'

Sinclair lifted the document off the bench, where Connor had thrown it. He shook his head slowly. 'Incredible. A twenty million stake for a blood sport.'

Dyson looked momentarily hopeful. 'Mould's an arms shark, right? So this could be a weapons dump. Guys who love guns always have that crud around. It's part of their shitty mindset. If we could find some heat. Or get on that corvette down there…'

Sinclair pointed to the camera. 'Look, man! There'll be one of these in each cabin. Mould's probably listening to us now.'

'Then we're stuffed.'

'Should we get the woman?' Connor asked. 'What's her name? Grace?'

Sinclair did his eyebrow trick. 'The creature of indeterminate age, whose body suits her so well?'

'You're chirpy, considering our position,' Connor said.

'Why show the bugger I'm worried?'

'I'll get her,' Dyson said. He shuffled back out, glad of something positive to do.

Sinclair lowered himself onto the bench, which accommodated his long legs like a chair. 'Well, we can't cast *him* as our saviour. He didn't even notice the camera.'

'Looks chronically sauced.'

'Unpredictable at the crease. Mine own executioner. I don't know why Mould is bothering with him.'

'If we could let people know – get to the police.'

'It doesn't work that way, old sock. You don't know what you're up against. Bugger's a billionaire. The police won't stop him. He'll do a deal. He's been working this out for years. Six bleeding moves ahead of us.'

'Well, you've got money. You could do something.'

'Oh, yes?' A hollow laugh. 'I'm South African. Have you been there?'

'No.'

'Lovely spot. Great conservation ethic, which should interest you. They even build platforms so cranes can nest on top of power pylons. But they also have draconian restrictions on taking money out of the republic. So my neighbours are sitting ducks, given the current political changes. If they join the chicken-run, it costs them. But Yours Truly has an offshore business.'

'And you're shit scared he'll wreck it?'

'He'll pulp it.' He frowned and said quietly, 'I know the bugger. You can't imagine what he's worth – or the kind of intellect you're dealing with.'

Voices outside. Dyson and Merrick. The door opened and he stood aside to let her in. She wore jeans, a jumper and her hair was still damp. The impression of youth was uncanny. She looked magnificent and sat in the only chair as if by divine right.

Dyson squatted on the floor. 'She's had a call too.'

Connor turned to her. 'We've been trying to work out what can be done.'

'Nothing.' Her voice was flat.

Boots outside on the stairs. A step on the verandah. A piece of paper appeared beneath the door and they heard the steps retreat. Sinclair took a stride and, with one long arm, opened the door. The man who had been on point duty was on his way back to his beat.

'Mould's Stasi post,' Sinclair said. He scooped up the paper, then perched back on the bench, reading it.

'What is it?' Connor asked.

'A ditty – headed "Verse One: Round One". Must be the first instalment of Mould's parlour game.' He read it, then held it out. 'Lugubrious.'

Merrick snatched and read it.

'Will you read it out, for Chrissake?' Dyson said.

She made a point of not doing so, as if letting him know his place, then, lesson over, unexpectedly began to read:

> Dung in your mouth,
> Your weapon in another's hand,
> Exhausted,
> Flogged,
> Shamed,
> Stagger into another dawn.

Dyson had his hand out for the sheet but Merrick passed it to Connor.

Connor read it and handed it to Dyson.

'It's crap,' said Dyson.

'Looks like we start by chewing turds,' Connor said.

Dyson said, 'Been eating 'em at restaurants for years and I never got a twenty million kickback. Don't forget the dough-re-me. Jeez. Almost had.'

'Is that a camera?' Merrick was pointing.

Connor nodded.

'Does each hut have one?'

'Probably.'

Her face softened, her eyes defocused. So Mould had already seen her body. Revenge was sweet. 'Is he watching us now?'

'Not now.' Connor couldn't believe how smug she looked.

'Then I'll tell you something. He does what he says. It's scores and accounts with him. If he says he'll pay the money, he'll pay. In his business you do what you say. People idolise him, you know. I've seen how he manipulates people. He can do anything with people.'

'You know him pretty well, then?'

She ignored the comment.

Connor persisted. 'So you'll eat turds for him, let him flog you and…'

'Do I have an option, Mr…?'

'Connor. No-one's thought of one – yet.'

'I'd like to roast the swine.' The statement was hurled like a rock. Her vehemence was extreme.

Sinclair leant forward. 'His army'd turn off your gas.'

'But he's had my brother kidnapped,' she went on as if he'd never spoken, 'so there's nothing I can do. Except play his rotten game. And I intend to get the money. Now you know.'

'I don't give a stuff about the money,' Connor said. 'And I'm getting sick of you all saying there's nothing we can do.' He looked down at Dyson without much hope. 'What d'you say?'

Dyson scratched his belly and arm, as if fighting a colony of nits. 'If we could get to the authorities…'

Sinclair snorted. 'Before you can cry to mama, big brother'll break your dollies.'

'Mind trundling that past me again?'

'For God's sake, man. He won't dust your kids off next time. He'll flay them. "*Silent enim leges…*".' He looked at them for a glimmer of recognition. '"For laws are dumb in the midst of arms".' He waved the papers at them. 'Any of you read this? Ms Duyen Vo – referee. In event of her demise, a Major J. Blore officiates.'

'I've met Blore,' Connor said. 'Huge bloke with a soft voice. Haven't spotted him here yet.'

Sinclair was reading on. 'In the event of Blore's demise, Mould's step-daughter, whoever she is, takes over. So we're set like a jelly for referees. The referee is restricted to confirmation of the winner with no other authority to divert funds. Terms of choice unspecified.'

'Think it's legal?' asked Connor.

'Looks watertight.'

Dyson rubbed the back of his neck, exposing a soiled collar. He badly needed a shave. 'I guess… Well, I guess, like he says, when you think it through – if I don't go along, he'll go for my kids. I mean…' He shifted uncomfortably on the floor, scratching again. 'If you really think someone gets the dough in the end… '

'We're neck-deep in shit,' Connor said, 'and you lot'll jump any way he says – play his game like he's God?'

'The Godgame,' Dyson said. 'Some tag.'

'Look, two of you know the man. Isn't there some agreement we could make with him that…'

Grace Merrick stroked her hair. 'It's *because* we know him that we keep telling you it's pointless. He won't listen.'

'She's quite right, I'm afraid.' Sinclair said. 'No way he'll negotiate. Just wants us to tear each other apart.'

Connor stared at them, astonished. 'And you're going to *do* that – to each other?'

Sinclair put the documents down and rubbed his eyes. 'Got there, old sock. Knew you would. Even Aussies can work things out. Only chance we have is if he dies before it gets too bad.'

'Jesus Christ! I say we tell the police or Interpol. We've got to blow the whistle on this bastard.'

Sinclair sniffed. 'You're ten years too late for that. He's too powerful now to make it stick.'

Merrick stood up and stretched, all eyes drifting to her body, as she knew. 'Discussing it won't get us anywhere. I'm going for a swim.' She strode out of the room like one born great.

'Knows her own mind,' Connor said.

Sinclair said, 'Horrible thought.'

Dyson stood up stiffly, scratching his knee. 'Could use some hair of the dog. Anything in your freezer?'

'Milk and orange juice.'

'Same as mine.' Dyson opened the door of the bar-fridge just in case. 'No joy.' He rubbed his eyes. 'I feel like the mummy's curse.'

Sinclair said, 'If it's a cocktail, I don't like your chances.' He settled back on the bench and picked up the poem again. ' "Dung in your mouth, your weapon in another's hand… exhausted, flogged, shamed…" Where'd he find this dirge?'

Connor got the tidy-bin from the bathroom, held it up to the bench and began sliding broken mirror glass into it. 'Have you two considered where you could end up? Wouldn't it be smarter to take a stand before this goes too far?'

Sinclair peered at the remote-control camera. 'I suppose if we were bronzed Aussies we'd get a piece of coat-hanger wire and with a few bush innovations we'd be rid of Mould in a flash. You can see I've lived in your country. I understand your folklore.'

'Just what we need. A smart-arse.'

He turned around. 'Come off it, Connor. You're as gutless as I am. Why pretend? We don't have a single move. He made sure of that long ago. It's checkmate.' He stretched. His arms were so long he could have doubled as a curtain-rail. 'I told you. You don't know the bugger. A spat with Mould's like being caught in a meat-slicer. All you can hope is that nothing too vital gets chopped off. We're in the slicer, man – shoved in the moment we got here.'

'Jeez,' Dyson said. 'I feel sick.'

'Better get used to it.'

Chapter Six

The first contest began that morning, sooner than any of them had expected.

Breakfast was poolside – self-serve, arranged on white outdoor tables shaded by white umbrellas and watched by the inquisitive cameras on the columns.

The powerful wind of the night before had swept the sky to a china blue, which was reflected in glimmering sea that stretched unbroken to the horizon. The clear, bright day had the bite of vivid impressions, the kind to feed the vacationing soul. To Connor, the effervescent light seemed ironic rather than restorative. But despite his dread he had to admit the scene was stunning.

Though he'd barely slept and felt shivery, the sun was warm on his back and the choice of food would have appeased the most demanding crew on a padded big-budget shoot. Scrambled eggs, baked tomatoes, sausages and bacon. Stewed apples, kiwifruit, grapefruit and muesli. Warm toast. A tureen of steaming porridge. Plus tomato, orange and apple juice. Were they, he wondered, being fattened for the kill? He moved along the table, loading his plate. He decided against the grapefruit, his stomach acid enough.

The Sinclairs sat together at one table. Grace Merrick, alone at another, ate her grapefruit with elaborate care, like a star in a studio canteen.

Dyson hadn't changed his shirt or shaved. Personal grooming didn't seem his priority. The bags beneath his eyes were satchels and he looked desperate for a drink.

Connor wondered where to sit. Not an inspiring choice. Eventually he joined Dyson on the upwind side. As he pulled out the aluminium chair, its rubber feet juddered on the marble.

'Seen any of the hit squad?' Dyson asked.

'Not this morning.' He attacked his scrambled eggs and squinted down against the glare at the small bay. The big craft was still afloat at the jetty. In morning light its steel-blue paintwork had a decidedly naval hue. A man stepped out of the deckhouse and walked forward to take in slack on the bow-line. He slapped loops round the cleat, applied a final half-hitch, then padded aft to check the stern.

A glint from higher on the hill made Connor glance toward the house. Behind the long building the wooded slope rose by degrees to a crest that must have been the headland they had walked from the evening before. Two people were coming toward them from the portico – an Asian in a chef's white smock and hat, carrying a silver serving dish complete with lid, and the pulp-faced Vo.

The chef veered behind the food table and lowered his burden with professional ease. Vo drifted along the marble, her Eastern-style dress hugging her body like shrink-wrapping.

'Mr Mould wish you good morning,' she announced in her harsh voice, with its slight tinge of colonial French. 'So now, we begin.' The remains of her face were expressionless. 'Round One. Section One. Eat dung. Is easy first contest. No need explain. All understand.'

'By the way,' Sinclair leaned back in his chair. 'Excellent coffee. We've done well,' he turned to his wife, 'haven't we, dear?'

'Couldn't eat another thing.' The Sinclairs were toughing it out.

'You not involve,' the woman said to Anita. 'Him only. So…' She crossed to the serving trestle, picked up a table-knife, walked back between the tables and squatted on the marble slab, placing the knife in front of her on the stone. The slit in her dress showed a sliver of thigh. Her body was neat, even tempting. Connor wondered what psychological damage had been caused by her ruined face.

'Gimme a break,' Dyson said. 'Not spin-the-knife? What is this? Kindy? How 'bout a deck of cards? I mean, if we gotta go through with this…'

'This time, knife. Knife simple. No trick.'

'Twenty million bucks on the nose and we play kiddies' roulette?' He shovelled toast into his mouth, hand shaking – nervousness or the DTs?

'Knife decide winner and loser of each round. First will spin for winner.' She flicked the knife and it became a blur.

Grace Merrick paused, spoon two inches from her mouth. Sinclair whistled the William Tell Overture as a gesture of defiance while his wife adjusted the sleeves of her jacket. But both kept their eyes on the knife. Dyson, leaning forward, gawking, had even forgotten to scratch.

The two cameras overhead whirred and repositioned, probing expressions for the voyeur in the house. The pool-cleaner moved along the pool, hose vibrating. A flock of gulls on the lawn took off suddenly, cawing and flapping. Connor registered it all without lifting his eyes, as if the focus of the twirling blade had somehow expanded his perception.

The blade slowed.

The seven people seemed frozen in time like figures in a Jeffrey Smart landscape.

It had to be the final turn.

The blade went… past him and… stopped at… Sinclair – pointing directly at his table.

Sinclair raised a presidential hand. '*Je suis formidable!*'

Vo, still crouching, said, 'Winner, Mr Sinclair. Spin now for loser.'

Dyson said, 'Hang about. What's this winner-loser caper?'

'Loser eat dung. Winner make him eat or become loser in next game. Automatic. Refuse to play mean you lose next game. Understand?'

'Shitty set of terms and conditions.'

She knelt again, spun the knife once more and stood up. All eyes watched the spot.

Spinning.

Spinning.

Dyson's whole body was straining forward, his lips moving with some soundless curse or prayer.

The pool-cleaner crept further toward the deep end as the seagulls, bickering and fighting, landed further up the grass. A slight wind ruffled their feathers. The blue sky was developing puffs of cloud.

The knife slowed at last and turned its blade toward Connor but… didn't quite stop. Another inch.

It pointed just past Dyson.

'Mr Dyson loser.' Vo crouched to pick up the knife and returned it to the table.

'Jeez. Not my week,' said Dyson.

The chef approached with his salver and placed it reverently in front of Dyson, then produced a silver spoon and fork, wrapped in a cloth napkin, and positioned them on Dyson's right. Finally, crossing behind Dyson, he lifted the lid off the dish.

Small brown pellets that looked like rabbit droppings reposed in the centre of the dish. They were garnished with fresh-sliced lemon and mint in minimalist style. The chef, behind Dyson's chair, had the ghost of a smile on his face.

Dyson got up and retreated to the far end of the pool.

Vo said, 'Mr Dyson. You eat?'

Dyson's voice from a distance. 'Rain check. Get back to you.'

'I think that is no. Is no?'

'Does it cut me out of the twenty million?'

'No. But means game change. So if you not eat, must say. Is no?'

'Big fat no.'

'Then Mr Sinclair – is your job *make* him eat.' She produced a stopwatch, a grey Seiko with a blue cord. 'You have ten minute. Starting… now.'

Connor, still with his back to them all, heard two more chairs being shuffled, and Sinclair's voice, 'Go to hell.'

'You not make?'

Sinclair didn't reply. Connor turned to see the chef replacing the lid on the dish as Sinclair and his wife – beanpole and child – pointedly strolled down the expansive lawn that sloped all the way from the pool to the jetty.

One busy camera panned to Dyson, its small motor whirring. He was leaning against a column, trying to look unconcerned.

Merrick was back at the food table, loading bacon onto her plate.

Vo, unfazed at being ignored, stood squarely in front of Connor, her good eye blinking like a hazard warning light.

'I explain now how we continue – how game work. Mr Sinclair, as you see, not force Mr Dyson to eat dung. So now Mr Sinclair must receive next penalty up. Become next loser. And Mr Dyson perform penalty. This now end of Game One. Time of Game Two will be announce.'

Connor waited for her to finish the rigmarole.

'I want to speak to Mould.'

She pointed up to the nearest camera. 'Speak any time.'

'In person.'

'Not possible.'

'Why?'

'Mr Mould not want speak to you.' She didn't alter her

expression. There were few muscles left to alter it. Dead-fish eyes and the gash for a mouth. It was like talking to a burnt-out letterbox.

'This whole thing's idiotic.'

'Is your problem.' She turned and pattered back to the house.

Merrick had returned to her table.

Connor said, 'What do you make of it?'

'It'll get worse. Nicolae's good at putting pressure on slowly.'

'Some breakfast!'

'Disgusting. I refused to take any notice.'

Like hell you did, he thought. Your eyes were out on stalks.

'When you finish that, want to go for a walk? Reckon we should give the place the once-over.'

She raised her chin in a display of public pondering and finally said, 'It'd be good to walk.'

He perched on a chair and waited for her. She showed no inclination to hurry. He glanced back at the house. Vo was standing by the main entrance, conversing with one of the troopers and, occasionally, looking back toward the pool. Vo listened to him, nodded and began walking back toward them while the man pulled a two-way radio from its belt-holder and spoke into it at length. Connor heard the crackle of a reply. 'Don't look now but Miss Face is on her way back.'

'Ignore her. She's revolting. I don't know how she can show herself in public.'

Dyson, tired of propping up the column, had sauntered over to join them, scratching. 'Knew this outfit were a bunch of turds. What the fuck are they up to now?'

The next development couldn't be ignored. The sound of an engine and gear trains. Around the side of the house appeared a khaki platform equipped with six fat off-road wheels. Two of Mould's troopers sat in the front, one steering it with motorbike-like handlebar controls on a console behind its punt-like nose. The thing bounced over a storm gully in the grass and pitched down the slope, like a suddenly exposed beetle heading for a crack in the floor.

Vo was back with them. 'Next game happen in one minute.'

'Goody gumdrops,' Dyson said. 'Spin-the-knife again?'

'You loser last game. You decide. You want card? We use card.'

'Don't have a deck on me.'

'We get.' She looked up at a camera. 'Pack of card.'

Connor followed her example, peering up at the lens. 'And my Nikon back while you're at it, bastards.' He turned to Merrick. 'How'd you feel?'

'I don't scare easily.' She looked down at the jetty. 'And I intend to win. So be warned.'

Dyson was staring at the strange vehicle. 'Quite a buggy.'

Vo picked up on the comment, seeming genuinely pleased, as if her hobby-horse had been patted. 'Is Williams Fairey Supacat M2 All Terrain Mobile Platform. Very good for airborne troop.'

'Thought it was,' said Dyson.

The vehicle pulled up beside the Sinclairs. One of the troopers jumped down. He waved Sinclair on board. Sinclair shook his head. The man pushed him against the side of the vehicle and the other man on board grabbed him under the arms, hauling him up. Sinclair's long legs started kicking but the first man collected them like twigs and loaded them on the tray, then climbed up as well.

Dyson said, 'Looks like Big-shot's dropped himself in it.'

Sinclair was still struggling. One of the men drew back his arm. His prisoner decided to sit quietly. The vehicle started to move.

His wife ran, yelling, after it. The slope was steep and she didn't run for long before slowing to a walk. Connor thought she was sobbing.

The platform roared back up to the pool, did a skid-steer turn and the engine died. Sinclair was bundled off it and frog-marched to a chair.

Another trooper doubled out of the house like a gorilla on heat. The thigh pockets on his drill pants jiggled as he ran. He trotted up to Vo and handed her a pack of playing cards, then stood back as she opened the box, tilted the cards into her hand and offered them to Dyson. 'You mix.'

Dyson took the cards, looked around him. The three huge men weren't going anywhere. Sinclair sat morosely in his seat, his fine line of repartee silenced.

Dyson shrugged and did a practised hand-to-hand shuffle. Then he cut the deck, put the halves on the table, riffle-shuffled them and scooped them up. Although the air was cool, his shirt was wet under the arms.

Merrick was spearing herself a sausage. She apparently liked her food.

Dyson handed the cards back to Vo, who extended the deck to Connor. 'One card each.'

Connor took the top card, feeling like a fool. The back featured a view of Lake Geneva taken from Lausanne. He didn't look at the face.

Vo moved in front of Dyson. Dyson, sucking his lip, took the card, checked it immediately. His expression didn't flicker but his eyes widened one notch. His poker-face wasn't the best on the block.

Vo crossed to Merrick, who made no response at all, continuing to eat her sausage, staring into space until the referee, losing patience, dropped the next card on the table in front of her.

'Now all players have card. We know Mr Sinclair is loser

for this game by refusing to force Mr Dyson to take penalty. We choose, now, winner only. Please all show card.'

Connor muttered, 'This is insane.'

'Show card now.'

Connor flipped his card. The Jack of Spades.

'Mrs Merrick. Card please.'

She sat, impassive, determined not to comply.

The man nearest her picked up her hand, spread the thumb and forefinger, placed the card between and clamped her hand shut on it again. Then he held her hand up, twisting it around to display the card. Four of diamonds. She drew her arm back angrily the moment he let go. Connor envied her guts.

The woman's eyes flicked to Dyson. He looked slyly pleased, turned his card around. King of Clubs.

'Mr Dyson win. Mr Dyson, as loser before, now also can choose form of penalty. Line was: "Your weapon in another's hand".'

'What weapon?' Dyson said.

'Produce weapons.'

The man who had brought the cards stepped forward and undid a pocket on his thigh. He pulled out several objects and placed them on a table. A nail clipper with curved handles and a folding bent wire spring. A cartridge-type twin-blade safety razor with swivel-head. And a slim, lock-blade pocketknife made entirely out of stainless steel with the number 1000 in worn blue paint barely discernible on the side.

Vo picked up the knife. She opened the blade with some trouble. It was less than five centimetres long. 'These all possible weapons we able find in Mr Sinclair's hut. Is clear that knife is Mr Sinclair's weapon for our game.'

Connor knew what was coming.

'Mr Dyson will use knife on Mr Sinclair. He say how.'

Dyson shuffled. 'Er... how about I clean his nails with it?'

'Suggestion veto. Must cause pain. Must stab, cut or wound.'

'Who says?'

'I say. I referee. No half-measure allow. Must stab to length of blade.'

Dyson looked at Connor. 'This sucks.' He turned back to Vo. 'Thought I had a say in this?'

'You have say. You decide where to stab. Can stab throat, eye, arm... You say.'

'What if I don't?'

'If refuse after switch, you automatically become next loser. Next penalty in game always worse. You want twenty million?' One end of her mouth lifted in a grin. The other side remained flaccid.

The troops weren't grinning. Their faces were crash-dummy blank. One had his eye on Dyson. The other two were moving behind Sinclair.

Vo placed the open knife, handle outermost, on her palm and held it out to Dyson.

Dyson looked at Connor again. 'Jeez.'

'This is sick,' Connor blurted.

Anita Sinclair had finally made it up the hill from the jetty, running the final few steps. 'What are they doing to him? What are they...'

One of the troopers grabbed her wrist and held her on the spot.

'Let me *go*,' she demanded.

He ignored her. She struggled on the end of his thick arm like a lamb caught by the hind leg in a fence.

'Decide place,' Vo said.

Dyson looked as if he might go belly-up. He steadied himself with one hand against a table. 'I don't like blood.'

Vo's lopsided grin again. 'Better him have pain than you,

yes? So tell place. *Now.*'

Dyson screwed his eyes shut, then wiped the sweat out of them with his sleeve. 'Er, how about the, er, calf?'

Vo frowned and looked at a trooper. He lifted his leg and pointed to his calf.

She nodded. 'Is okay. Prepare.'

The trooper behind Sinclair grabbed his arms and twisted them around the back of the chair. The other knelt in front of him, planted a boot on Sinclair's boat-shoe and pushed up the leg of his tailored jeans, exposing a sinewy lower limb.

Sinclair looked up at a camera. 'Mould. My God, I'll have you.'

Vo's half smile was still in place. 'Not worry, Mr Sinclair. We have doctor and full-scale clinic. You well look after. Now. Are ready, Mr Dyson?'

'No.'

She pulled out her stopwatch. 'Not stab in thirty second, you become next loser. Automatic. Him or you. Understand? Starting… now.' The watch clicked.

'No banana. Can't do it.'

'Elapse time, five second.'

Grace Merrick stood up with studied calm, still chewing, and strolled away in the direction of the tree-line, as if heading for her hut. No-one bothered to stop her.

Anita screamed to Connor, 'Help him!'

The man holding her glanced at Connor. His cold eyes said quite plainly, 'Try something and I'll rearrange your face.'

'Ten second.'

Dyson moved forward and knelt beside Sinclair's exposed leg like a supplicant before a prelate. He looked up at Sinclair with a labrador's expression. 'Jeez. What can I do?'

Sinclair said through gritted teeth, 'Make it fast.'

'Twenty second.'

Connor began trembling inside.

Dyson's hand tightened on the knife, knuckles white. From Connor's angle the blade was half obscured by his thumb.

'Twenty-five…'

'Jeez.' His arm thrust forward.

Sinclair's body went rigid, jerking. '*Yaaaa!*'

The knife, visible now, was still in Sinclair's leg, buried to the hilt, the small handle vibrating slightly with his pulse. Dyson had stabbed, then let go.

From the lower, cutting edge of the knife a crimson ribbon bubbled down white flesh and soaked into Sinclair's sock.

Sinclair threw his head back, cursing.

His wife had slumped to the ground in a faint. The man let her arm drop and joined the other two troopers beside Sinclair. They left the knife where it was and lifted the wounded man into the transporter, hands beneath his back and thighs, as one might hand up a child.

Sinclair screeched back to the cameras, 'I'll have you, Mould!' They fired up the platform and gunned it around the back of the house.

On the slab in front of Sinclair's vacated chair, brilliant in the sun, was a pool of blood smeared by footprints.

Dyson was sitting beside it, clammy in his sweat. 'Jeez, I had to. They forced me. Jeez.'

The whirring cameras stopped moving. Mould, for now, had seen enough.

Connor, still shivering inside, helped Anita Sinclair into a chair. She had come around to find her husband gone. She looked up at Vo, still partly out of it. 'You've taken him. Where've you taken him?'

'To clinic,' Vo said.

'Don't believe you.'

'Come see, then.'

'We'll have you torn apart for this.'

Vo tittered through the hole in her head. 'What you think is this? You think is *your* country? Think you can lock us in security HQ in John Vorster Square? Oh, yes. I hear they had many interesting technique.'

'Hanford'll have you all behind bars.'

She chuckled again. 'You very small woman and you long way from home. Could die here and no-one know. We good at covering tracks – to make people disappear. So if you want not to get hurt, suggest you shut face.'

Chapter Seven

As Vo walked back to the house Anita Sinclair stumbled unsteadily after her, determined to see her husband at once. Connor followed, concerned the tiny woman might fall. He caught up with her and offered his arm. 'Hang on to me.'

She looked up at him, pale and distressed. 'You'll come with me?'

'Of course.'

They walked behind the Vietnamese woman. From behind, he noticed, she looked normal. But as they reached the front of the building and she turned back to face them, she was transformed back into a gargoyle. She pointed to the side of the building with her gap-fingered hand. 'Clinic round back. Door open.'

Behind the mansion were a cluster of outbuildings. They skirted a vegetable garden and walked around the flat-bed vehicle to enter the door behind it.

Inside the corridor, to the left, were cross-over plastic swing doors. They pushed through them into an operating theatre, elaborately equipped. Sinclair was on the table in the centre, the nurse from the night before slitting his pants to the knee. A camera near a corner of the ceiling was focused on the scene. It moved to cover them as they came in, zoom lens retracting.

Anita gasped, 'Hanford?' and would have hurried to the table but a trooper wearing a smock and canvas overshoes waved her back.

Sinclair turned his head to her. 'I'm all right. Don't watch this.' He looked at Connor. 'Take her away. She doesn't like blood.'

Connor moved to usher her out but she shook her head fiercely. 'I'm staying.'

The doctor turned. 'Why you here?'

Connor said, 'Vo said she could come.'

'Then stay by door. Is sterile area.'

The nurse held Sinclair's ankle as the doctor gripped the knife and pulled.

Sinclair grunted as it came out. 'Shit.' There was surprisingly little blood.

The doctor looked at the blade, then dropped it with a clatter into a dish. The nurse began to swab.

'Too deep. Should irrigate,' the doctor said. 'Syringe with saline solution and catheter.' He turned back to Sinclair's wife. 'Blade was clean but we need to go into wound and flush. You may prefer not to watch.'

Connor looked down at her. 'He'll be okay. Want to go?'

She shook her head again, becoming rigid on the spot.

Sinclair lay back, looking up at the camera in the corner.

'You fortunate, of course,' the doctor said. 'Now if it had been here, the popliteal artery,' he tapped Sinclair just under the knee, 'you be bleeding like a pig. And if here, the femoral at the groin, you be dead in four minutes. Interesting, the body.'

Sinclair said, 'Always provide a commentary?'

'Medicine should be free of mystique. Is also good bedside chat.'

'Calming the patient, are you?'

'I like thinking aloud. Helps nurse, too.' He pushed Sinclair's foot down, checked for bleeding, pricked the leg. 'You feel that? And that?'

Sinclair nodded.

'Most fortunate. No significant muscle damage. No

nerve damage. No severed artery. Just clean and stitch up.' He turned to the nurse. 'We need Betadine. Plus shot in buttock. Plus tetanus. And, I think, catgut stitches for adipose tissue. And, by look of gash, three sutures to close skin. Three O nylon.'

'You seem a competent professional. Why are you working for a moral cripple?'

Dr Lee's impassive face cracked and he giggled. It wasn't a reassuring sound.

A nurse appeared with a catheter attached to a syringe. Lee took it. The nurse gripped Sinclair's ankle hard as the doctor said, 'You'll feel this.'

Anita turned her head back to the door. Her husband grimaced but made no noise as the doctor worked the plastic tube deep into the wound, the gash parting like a mouth as it went in, expressing a trickle of blood. Lee did not have a gentle touch. The tube was withdrawn and Lee worked away with swab and forceps. He said to Sinclair, 'You read my report?'

'I read it. I don't necessarily believe it.'

'Is true.' He finished probing and the nurse moved in to clean up.

'I'd prefer a second opinion.'

'You have eyes. You see how he look. Is diabetic. Has had multiple heart attacks. Now has congestive heart failure with poor kidney function, liver congestion, early gangrene in toes. And last week we perform abdominal paracentesis. Drain six pints. He find it tiring, of course. Removes protein from the body. He need cardiac bed to keep fluid from the lungs. But hard man to keep down. Normally would have local for these stitches but Mr Mould say no.'

'How much does it hurt?'

'Hardly feel. A prick and some pulling. Depends on tolerance for pain. I think your tolerance good.'

The nurse bore down hard on his ankle. The needle went in.

Lee said, 'Please not to jerk. You spoil my sewing.'

Anita Sinclair was wilting. Connor caught her before she fell to the floor and crouched by her on the cold lino, her warm body sagging against him. There was nothing sexual in it this time. She was barely there, face clammy-white. He put his arm around her and whispered, 'He'll be okay.'

Sinclair winced as the needle poked through his flesh again. 'Does Mould rate a local?'

'He in different category.'

'And what category am I in?'

Lee thought for a moment, impassive again. 'I would call it… Category P.'

'For peril? Or persecution?'

Lee tittered. 'For pawn.'

Dyson's hut had been cleaned, the bed made, and on the bench, like a reward, was an unopened bottle of Jack Daniels.

'Sweet Jeezuz.' He hunted for the glass tumbler and found it washed and replaced on the shelf above the basin. He sloshed bourbon into it and took a steadying gulp. The glow began to touch him, spreading, warming.

He heard voices and went to the window. The sun was retreating across the lawn and clumps of cumulus were drifting in from the east. Connor was walking Sinclair's wife to her hut. She seemed barely able to stand.

He saw, again, the knife puncturing the skin, ripping through the muscle below. Sinclair rigid with pain. Blood oozing…

He'd stabbed a man. Jeez! Not with words, this time, or strategies aimed first at stripping credibility, then confidence and, ultimately, income. But with a piece of steel cutting through flesh. At least it was overt. A variation on the ad game, where sixty per cent of work effort went into extracting knives from the back.

He took his third gulp, thought of his kids, and blubbered.

Halfway through his second glass he was starting to see dollars. Twenty million dollars. Whitewashed windmills. Tavernas. He and Chan – strolling with the Santorini locals to pig out on moussaka while the money, invested by querulous accountants, paid him... let's see... working on a conservative 10 per cent... over $500 a day.

He dragged his mind back to the present. The pines. The crescent of huts. Through the window he could just see the end of the pool on the hill. A woman on the diving-board. The strong body could only be Merrick. She did a perfect pike. Stuck-up bitch.

Merrick, Connor, Sinclair and him. A four-horse race. Good odds.

He went to recharge his drink, then noticed himself in the mirror. He had to pull himself together. Twenty million greenbacks weren't horse-shit. Win this one and he could give the ad game the big A.

Then he remembered about the mirror and peered into it. 'Thanks for the drink, you fucker.'

Connor opened the bar-fridge in his hut, poured an orange juice, gulped it and walked out on the deck. This whole bloody thing was insane.

He found himself walking about with no clear plan – walking up the path again to the mausoleum on the hill. In the state he was in, constructive thinking was impossible. He just knew that his body needed to move and inner agitation was moving it.

The wind had stiffened to squalls that were blowing the morning's fine patch out to sea. The sunlight was now far over the water, glimmering on the turquoise quilt through breaks in gathering cloud. Merrick was coming from the pool, wearing her terry-towel gown, wet hair hanging in strands. She had got off lightly so far and still seemed to be half playing the tourist. She looked every inch a celebrity as she walked past him without a nod.

He looked up at the house. None of the troopers was around. He reached the portico. No-one at the entrance. The doors slid open as he approached. He walked into the utilitarian foyer. Still no-one to stop him. Perhaps he could talk to someone – get them to see reason…

The doors to the war room were open. A single camera, fixed-lens type, glared at him from the wall. He ignored it and walked into the museum across the marble expanse, steps echoing in the cavernous room, entered the short corridor at the end. A door to the side was locked. But the dining-room doors were open. Sunlight from the long windows filtered into the room, painting the bare table with stripes. There was no other door. Just a wall-length drape at the end, behind the head of the table where Mould had sat the previous night.

It seemed odd – a room of such length with only one door. He padded over thick carpet to the drape and lifted one corner.

Wall.

He walked the length of the curtain, prodding, until he felt an architrave, then lifted the drape and ducked beneath, feeling for the knob.

The handle turned. He pulled the door open a fraction and peered.

A corridor, with doors further down on the opposite side. He opened the door against the curtain – and saw boots on the floor directly in front. Compound-soled boots with toes facing him.

Combat boots, size twelve.

He looked up to see the vast weightlifter's body that had sprung the dowels on his office chair. Shorn of his suit and in military rig, his huge frame looked less incongruous. He smiled and said in his soft voice, 'We meet again, Mr Connor.'

'Hello, Sunshine.'

'Having a stroll, were we?'

'Where's Mould?'

'This building's off-limits to guests except by invitation.'

'I want to speak to Mould.'

'Correction. You want to go outside.'

He grabbed Connor's wrist and pulled it, palm up, through the crook of his elbow, bearing down until Connor was dancing along on his toes. Connor didn't know why the man bothered with the hold. He was big enough to lift him with one arm.

'That will do, Blore.' The woman from the beach had been watching from a doorway as they passed. Her tone seemed to restrain the huge man instantly. Connor felt the pressure release.

'You sure?'

'Quite sure. I'll see him to the door.'

'Very good.' The man walked off, the floor vibrating with his weight.

Connor rubbed his elbow and bent it. It still worked. 'Thanks.'

'In here.'

He followed her into a room as long and lofty as the dining room. It was lined to the ceiling with bookcases and at the end, floor-length windows opened onto the forest. There were wing chairs, occasional tables and a desk near the windows to the side. It was a library of a kind, but not the kind in Sinclair's brochure. While some of the shelves held books and manuals, most contained ring-binder files. The names on the spines meant nothing to him: Redifon, Thompson-CSF, FFV, SATT, Fairchild Weston, Armscor. Shelves along one wall included built-in filing cabinets.

She shut the door after him and he followed her through the room to the desk. A large poster on the wall behind it showed a V/STOL Harrier flying over the Dover cliffs with some caption about test equipment and the Ferranti nameplate. She moved around the desk with its drawer-filled pedestals and sat in the impressive chair behind it. The computer terminal looked incongruous on the inlaid leather top. Apart from a neat stack of files and a vase of dried flowers the rest of the surface was uncluttered. Beside the vase was a model of a six-wheeled machine that looked like a cross between a reconnaissance vehicle and a tank. A sticker on the front read: AMX 10 RC – main battle tank firepower.

He sat opposite her, waiting for her to speak. If she could lose the frown, he thought, she'd be a remarkably attractive woman. But she didn't stop frowning, didn't speak, just looked at him as if wondering what to say.

'I'm David Connor.'

'I know.'

She held her hand across the desk. 'Gillian...' She seemed about to give her second name, then stopped.

The big room had been a lot to absorb. Now he could look at its inhabitant carefully. Perfect skin, slim, athletic body, glasses...

'Thanks for your help out there.'

'I'm sorry about all this.'

'Had the odd regret myself.'

She removed the glasses and smiled. The smile eclipsed the frown like a 12K HMI. The whole room lit up. Connor looked at her, stunned. She was beautiful.

'Is Mould listening?' He looked around the top of the walls for cameras.

'No.'

The fuses reset in his mind. Her smile had gone. But he was still seeing it. Or feeling it. 'The others are going along with this,' he shrugged. 'I felt I had to do something.'

She nodded. 'I know what you did to Mould was your job. But you really twisted the knife. It hurt him badly at the time and he doesn't forgive. Your partner would be here too if he hadn't had the… accident in the cave.'

'You know about the cave?'

She pointed to the walls. 'It's my job to know about things. Including you. You, and the others, and most of the world's weapons systems and a whole lot more. Meet the oracle.'

'Must be busy.'

'I've got a staff of six.' She gestured to a panelled door at the side.

'Blore one of them?'

'He's Vo's department.'

'Which is?'

'Procurement and Dispatch.'

'You run an unusual set-up.'

'Nature of the job.'

'Can I see Mould?'

'No.'

'Why not?'

She looked at him as if assessing him, her blue eyes utterly frank. He wanted her to keep on looking.

'I'm taking a risk even talking to you.'

'Put yourself in my position.'

'I did. That's why you're here.'

The phone rang. She picked it up and answered.

'Right. I'll handle it.' She stood up and came around the

desk. 'If I can get him to talk to you, I will. But I can't promise. And it may not get you far.'

'I'd appreciate that very much.'

'But for now, do as they say. It may not be pleasant but it's the safest way.' She stood up. 'I'm sorry about your wife.'

'Is he on the level when he…'

'Please don't ask me anything. I've really said all I can.' He felt that her abruptness was to mask her sympathy for him. He followed her back through the long room. 'Go out the way you came. You'll find Mrs Sinclair in the foyer. She probably wants to see her husband. Tell her she can't. And please get her out of this building.' She opened the door. 'I've done something for you. Now you do that for me.'

She closed her door the moment he left.

He crossed the empty corridor and found the door behind the drape. He opened it and was back behind the curtain just before another door opened opposite. He heard the bleeps of a fax, the sound of a laser printer, then the voice of Vo, as if she were calling back to someone in the room.

'No, no. Is Python 3 AAM. Was use in Bekaa Valley. Same as AIM 9L Sidewinder. Three-target mode: boresight, uncaged and radar slaved. What? Is 15km. Warhead 11kg. And what else? MO8? No. We ship to Bandar Abbas. Magnetic pressure and acoustic. Diameter 533mm. On thirteenth. Tell him no. We reconfirm.'

He inched the door closed, extricated himself from the curtain and walked to the other door.

Anita Sinclair was wandering around the weapons display, a child lost in a marble tomb. Her eyes widened when he entered.

'You've been in there?'

'Yes. But we'd better get out. Let's go.'

'I want to see Hanford.'

'You can't now.'

'How do you know?'

'I've talked to them. Come outside.'

He led her, still protesting, into the sunshine. The doors slid shut behind them.

'What happened in there? Who'd you speak to?' Anita implored.

'Let's get away from these cameras.' Connor started to walk up the hill toward the tree-line.

She hesitated, then caught up with him. 'I still can't believe what that man *did* to him.'

'It was only a pocketknife. And the least harmful spot the guy could probably think of.'

'It's incredible.'

'I know.'

'They could do it to *me*, next,' she said.

'They won't hurt you.'

'Why not? Hanford told me they'd put your wife in hospital. So wives aren't excluded.'

He had no answer to that.

Her small face was taut. He was sorry for her but felt she was less concerned for her husband's health than with the revelation that he could be vulnerable. And, through him, her.

'Did you know they've blocked Hanford's partners from buying bullion? His issue's in September. The dies are struck and everything. He'll lose millions if he can't get the bars.'

'He said something about it. What's his line?'

'He puts out issues of old coins. Copies – in silver, coated with gold and very cleverly promoted. He always tries to link them with some national festival or event. They're quite valueless numismatically but people don't really understand that. They think they'll appreciate. He charges thousands for each issue. Ridiculous business really – but lucrative. And the brochures make it look rare and distinguished.'

'You mean it's practically a con?'

'I think that's rather harsh.'

They walked in silence for a time.

'And what do you do, Mr Connor?'

'Make corporate videos.'

'Sounds interesting,' she said, her mind elsewhere.

They reached the trees and entered the forest, heading for the island fringe. He'd seen no-one following and the forest was too big to be wired. They walked for perhaps five minutes, smelling the pines and the sea, until they saw the ocean again. He looked around and up, then listened. 'Okay. Doubt they're receiving us out here.'

They stood beneath the last tree almost at the edge of the cliff-face.

'So what happened in there?' she asked.

'I got sprung by one of their goons. Then I was rescued by the woman who took us in to dinner last night.'

'And?'

'Nothing. She didn't want to talk.'

'Must have said something.'

'She said the safest thing is to go along with the game.'

She made a face. 'Not much help.'

They stood looking at the sea in silence.

She said, 'I just... feel so lost about all this. You must feel terrible too. I suppose you're worried about your wife?'

'No. Mould's proved his point and she's not hurt. They won't touch her again unless I stop playing his game. I'm pretty strung-out, though – actually went in there to try and talk to him.' He said it mostly to himself. 'Didn't think I was game enough to *do* that.'

'God knows what we'll end up doing.'

'Don't even know what I would have said to him. This thing's really freaked me out. I'm not with it.'

'None of us is.'

But he couldn't leave the thought alone. 'I mean, what

the hell *could* you say to him?' He scuffed his heel in the grass. 'Try to make him see reason?'

'According to Hanford, he's not a reasonable man. He's enormously intelligent, completely cold and one-pointed.'

'A shark, your husband called him.'

'Exactly.' She shivered and clutched her elbows across her chest. 'You can't be reasonable with a shark. It doesn't understand.'

He knelt and felt the pine needles. 'It's dry.' They sat down. A patch of filtered sunlight blessed the spot but looked as if it might be the last for some time. 'We can't just all agree to… slowly kill each other.'

She sat near to him, facing the ocean. 'The Roman gladiators had to.'

'This isn't ancient Rome.'

'You sure?'

He felt suddenly irritable with her. 'Just because you people are loaded doesn't mean you understand everything.'

She put a hand on his sleeve. 'Please, I didn't mean it like that. It's just that, well, Hanford and I have… an unusual life and we've… seen a great deal in a rather… explicit way.' Surprised at her touch, he looked at her hand. One of her tiny fingers wore an emerald that almost covered the knuckle. 'Wealth's as corrupting as power. It removes the restraints, opens doors to extraordinary places.' The hand had been withdrawn. She was looking at the ocean. 'It alters you until you're not sure what you want or even who you are. I envy your simpler life. At least it leaves some residual decency.' He was studying her as she spoke. She wore a plain, square-necked dress that probably had a designer label, and a gold chain around her neck. He doubted there was a bra beneath. Not that she was in need of much support. He remembered again how she had been at dinner last night, how she'd felt leaning against him in the clinic. He tried to concentrate on what she was saying.

'So, imagine someone with the power and influence *Mould* has. I know Hanford feels he can't do anything. I've never seen him at a loss before. All he can do is rant. To see him like that scares me to bits.'

'I don't like being someone's toy.'

'Mould wants revenge.'

'So what do we do?'

She shrugged. 'Accept it, I suppose.'

He slapped his knee. 'You amaze me!'

'Well, what *can* we do? Suggest something. Go on.'

'I can't – yet.'

'See? You think the others haven't thought about it?' She looked at him keenly. 'You don't understand Mould, do you?'

'Why?'

'David, is it? May I call you that?' She was peering up into his eyes. 'I think you're too decent. You have your honest job, your settled life in the last safe part of the world, your faithful wife…'

'Like fun. Got a business that's been going downhill ever since I lost my partner. Got a wife who mightn't be too faithful. And that's for starters.'

'But you see, Mould's nothing like you, or even Hanford. He's got his own country. Even his own army.' She brushed the back of her neck. 'Is something walking down me? Can you see?' She turned around, on her knees.

He pulled the yoke of her frock back and peered down her spine. Nothing. And no bra strap. 'Can't see anything.'

She leaned forwards, feeling around her waist, and the front of her dress hung slack, providing a top-shot of small, delicately uptilted breasts. It was so naturally done, it was possibly unintentional. But, as he had seen, Anita Sinclair was no child.

They sat, looking out to sea. First the turd. Then the

stabbing. Then the reunion with the twenty-stone Blore. Then the woman with the smile. Now Anita's body beside him. It seemed best to keep things conversational. 'The bastard doesn't understand me, either. He thinks his twenty million's a sweetener. Far as I'm concerned, he can jam it.'

'How could something like this happen in such a beautiful, peaceful place?' She paused. 'Thank you for being kind to me.'

He shrugged, picked up a pine needle, chewed the end. 'If I could have stopped them doing it, I would have.' He sighed. 'I'm not very brave, I'm afraid.'

'I think you're sweet. It's just that you're bundled up with people who aren't. Of course we don't see it like that. We call ourselves realists. That man who stabbed Hanford, the smelly little twerp, he's the worst, wouldn't you say? How does he strike you?'

'Bit of a cockroach.'

She nodded slowly. 'And Miss Self-image of California?'

'Suitable case for treatment.'

'Yes, isn't she extraordinary? Poor thing. Quite bats. And Hanford?'

'Aren't we getting close to home?'

'Indulge me. Hanford?'

'Smart. Supercilious. A user.'

'And me?'

'Want it between the eyes?'

She grinned. 'Perhaps a little lower.' There was no ambivalence to the statement at all.

He shook his head. 'Self-satisfied and amoral.'

She spread her fingers. 'So there you have it. A cockroach. A maniac. What was it... a user and his self-satisfied, amoral wife. Your opinion of others shows what you are. You see, I was testing you. No wonder we disturb you. Mould's far more like us than you are.'

He shifted uncomfortably. The woman's psychology eluded him. Even in this place she played games.

She said, 'It's true I'm amoral by your standards. But my father's Dutch. And in Amsterdam, where I grew up, people are refreshingly rational about sex.'

'I know. Seen your films. And the sex-shop windows with the shots of men with thirteen-inch dicks. And the girls in the windows on the…'

'Oude Zyds Achterburgwal. I never minded that. It's really quite picturesque at night. All the different-coloured lights reflected in the canal. Spreek u Nederlands?'

'Just Oz. So – what am *I*, then?'

'You're a good man in a bad spot – like someone at the wrong address. But I'm glad you are – for my sake. Shut your eyes.'

'Why?'

'Just do it.'

He shut his eyes, heard the pine needles rustle as she stood. Then there was only the sea and the wind.

Hands touched his face.

'Open eyes.'

She was kneeling in front of him, not smiling, so close her nipple brushed his cheek. Her clothes were neatly folded on the ground. She wore her rings, her gold chain and nothing else.

The tiny, perfect body, dappled in the filtered light, was more wood-nymph than woman. There was no hair on it at all, even between her legs. She unbuckled his belt, unzipped him, pulled him out. 'Nice.' Her head went down.

As she sucked, her hands yanked at his pants. He lifted so she could get them over his hips, hard as a rock now, wondering what he was getting into. Hell. He was being raped.

Then her fingers were in his mouth, in his anus, her mouth on his nipples, and before he could grip her, turn her, her small, muscular pelvis had thrust down, enclosing him. Moist, tight, bucking, as if the demands of her tiny body were more urgent than she could bear.

'I want it everywhere,' she said.

They became the beast with two backs, rolling, writhing, twisting, contorting in the agony of closeness, reinventing their shape with each lunge.

'Harder. Hurt me.'

The next few minutes were the most lurid Connor had experienced. The Dresden-china body, tiny, sinuous, taunting.

'Use your nails. Ahhh.' She twisted onto her front like an eel, her fingers guiding him around the world. 'In there. Ahh. Slowly. Ahh. Give me your hand. Ahhh. Ahhh.'

He didn't hear the huge man approach and position himself behind a tree.

Blore put the monitor for the tracer back under the ragged strips of the Ghillie suit and clipped it into his belt. Then he lifted the 8mm camcorder and fingered the rocker for the zoom.

When the pair finally slumped, exhausted, he lowered the camera and walked back, snorting and chuckling, through the trees.

Connor and Anita Sinclair talked a long time then walked hand in hand along the track to the corner of the high deer-paddock fence. He felt oddly liberated but still couldn't help referring to his wife.

'I've been faithful to her – in my fashion.'

She smiled. 'Forsaking some others?'

'This place is turning us into animals.'

'Not me. I've always been one.'

He ran his hands down her body, loving the sinewy feel of her. 'You're a worry.'

'I'm not. I'm a noble savage. And you're trying to make excuses for yourself. Enjoyment doesn't need excuses. You see the disadvantage of a conscience?'

'I'm not listening.'

'Oh dear. Another moral fraud.'

The guest-list for lunch included Sinclair – something neither of them had expected. He sat in a wheelchair, leg elevated on a support. When his wife saw him she said, 'Oh… Oh,' then fluttered to him and kissed his forehead. 'Poor, poor love. You all right?'

'I'll survive.'

She perched next to him, holding his hand.

Dyson entered then. He'd changed his shirt but Connor could tell from his face and breath that he was flying. He waved circles in the air at Sinclair. 'Remember, if I hadn't done it, they would have done it to me. Okay? Like that was the deal. Like if it'd been you, you'da done it too. Okay? No choice. Whole thing sucks.'

Sinclair said to the room, 'Don't light a match near him.'

'No hard feelings, huh?'

Sinclair raised the eyebrow. 'None at all. Remember that when it's *your* turn.'

'I might get lucky again.'

'Thought your fortune was generally outrageous.'

'Don't bet on it, fellah.'

The meal was curry with side-dishes, poppadums and carafes of white wine – a sit-down buffet with electric hot-crocks and a stack of plates at one end.

Connor, ravenous, took a plate and piled it with food.

As he sat to eat he noticed something at the end of the room. A monitor on a stand in the corner. It hadn't been there earlier.

Across the table from him Grace Merrick ladled chutney

onto her plate. Her nose was slightly sunburnt and her hair had been washed again.

Abruptly, music came from the monitor, a tarantella with a driving beat, played on original instruments. He looked up to see a title on the screen.

Blue background and orange words with drop-shadow: '$20,000,000 UPDATE'.

There was a voice-over – Mould's. 'Good afternoon, all.' The theme faded under. 'I can't be with you personally today but you're… all very much in my thoughts.'

The graphic dissolved through to Mould ECU. He could have been in bed – the shot was too close to be sure. The graphic and dissolve meant the place had more than a security-monitoring set-up. There'd be an editing suite as well. And, from the definition, it wasn't VHS. Looked like they'd assembled on Digibeta.

Mould continued. 'This afternoon's contest is concerned, as you may recall from the poem, with exhaustion. The winner will decide the penalty. The loser will undergo it. I'm sure you're becoming familiar with the format.'

Merrick said, 'Can't we turn it off?'

The answer stepped into the room. Three of the troopers. Blore was one.

The shot had widened slightly to show the head was resting against a pillow. 'As for the draw, it was decided when you sat down to eat. But more of that later. For now, please relax and enjoy your meal as we review the morning's activities.'

The theme faded up over a 64-frame dissolve – they really were getting cute – to a view from the pool, and the bay. The shot was grainier now, sourced from the cameras on the columns. They were looking at a high-angle shot of the seated Dyson as he was presented with his al dente turd. It cut to a close-up of his expression as he lurched sideways out of frame.

A dissolve to Dyson sulking by the column. A shot of Sinclair and his wife marching off. Another long dissolve to Anita Sinclair running up the hill, screaming.

Then Dyson, knife in hand, on his knees in front of Sinclair, pleading.

A shocking close-up of the knife going in.

Sinclair stiffening.

His wife fainting.

Connor's expression close-up.

Connor frowned. Seeing himself like that had shaken him. His own shocked face on the screen, backed by the ominous, jangling music.

The others in the room were transfixed.

Surveillance was one thing. But to be taped, edited and regurgitated, warts and all, was an intrusion none of them expected.

A white room with a central table. Sinclair being operated on. A close-up of the wound as they shoved the catheter in. A close-up of Sinclair's face, screwed tight with pain. A cut to his wife slumping to her haunches with Connor squatting, trying to support her.

The scenes went on. Dyson, sweating in his hut, knocking back spirits. A jump cut to him doing it again, with a second glass, and falling on the bed. A final shot of him sitting on the floor, the bottle between his legs, a glass in his hand, singing some song about a blow-up plastic woman.

The tarantella pounded on relentlessly as they watched Grace Merrick walking along the rocks in fast motion, her studied movements made ridiculous as she examined a shell or smoothed her hair. The speeded footage emphasised all her pretentious and studied gestures. She looked like a lost member of a synchronised diving team. It was damningly satirical. She watched but clearly didn't see the point. One of the troopers stifled a guffaw.

Then Connor saw himself, walking the length of the room they now sat in. An abrupt cut to him being manhandled out by Blore.

The shot changed to an out-of-focus forest. The scene came sharp. The camera zoomed in.

Connor looked at Anita Sinclair, who stared back at him, eyes wide.

The next three minutes of footage were a series of cuts – close-ups, zoom-ins or medium shots, all from the same perspective. The variation necessary came from the subject matter itself.

Dyson said, 'Jeez. It's pick-a-body-cavity time.'

Blore shook with silent mirth. The two other troopers were breaking up.

Merrick said, 'Disgusting. How dare he show us this? How could you two *do* such a thing?' She got up to leave the room and was pressed back in her chair by the quaking Blore. Dyson was leaning forward, rocking with laughter, slapping his thighs and whooping.

Connor half looked at Sinclair, who was watching the screen with academic interest, as if it wasn't the first time he'd seen his wife with a man. Anita's eyes were now only for her plate. She ate with careful composure. Face crimson, Connor watched his body convulsed with lust.

Now Sinclair was quietly chuckling.

Dyson said, 'Jeez. It's educational. She's better than the kids at the Mabhini in Manila.' He leered across at Anita, adjusting himself under the table.

Sinclair nodded. 'Amazing, isn't she? Feckless but ever willing. What more can sweet reason ask of a wife? Except a decent game of tennis.' The exhibition came to its climax. Sinclair sighed, 'Ah, *le petit mort*.' He turned to Connor. 'Isn't she a sprite? I like them android, don't you? So... provokingly ambivalent.'

Although the man appeared disinterested one never knew the heat under the coals. Had the situation been reversed – had Sinclair made it with Tess – Connor felt sure he'd be punching him out by now. Except he'd never punched anyone – not even in school when he was picked on. A life without a single fight. Unless you counted a bash at karate – incited by Tess who, during their first pre-marriage argument, had called him a wally and wimp. And that was structured stuff, not a roundhouse contest on hard surfaces against someone wearing boots. If he punched someone, he wondered, or tried the kicks he half remembered, would it stop them?

Mould was back on the screen. 'So, enough lechery. To business. Under each of your plates is a number between one and four. The number you will have depends on the order you came into the room or the order of the plates. Completely random selection. Number one wins. Number four loses. I'm sure we can all look forward to an interesting afternoon.'

The monitor went blank and started to hiss. Blore crossed and turned it off as Vo entered the room.

Dyson was holding his plate in the air, food sliding off it. 'Three. I'm fine and dandy.'

There was a chair at the end of the table where Mould had been wheeled the night before. Vo sat in it quietly and placed both hands on the cloth in front of her. Blore crossed to her side like a doting gorilla.

A trooper lifted Merrick's plate. Beneath it, Connor could see the number one.

Vo announced, 'Mrs Merrick – winner.'

Now his own plate was being lifted. A black four, painted on the base.

'Mr Connor – loser.' Vo leaned forward. 'Contest three of first round. Trial is physical exhaustion. Next contest begin this afternoon at 1500 hour. Mr Sinclair, in meantime, as last loser, must decide Mr Connor's penalty.'

Sinclair said, 'Must I, indeed?' He put his hands on the wheels of the chair and spun them opposite ways to face the loser more directly.

Connor felt the trembling inside him again. Now he knew why the tape had been played. Mould's 'game' was becoming not just punitive but diabolical.

'Well, old sock,' Sinclair smiled, 'tat for tits, eh? How ironic. Would have thought you'd been exhausted enough for one day, but I'm sure I can think of something… appropriate.'

Chapter Eight

Grace Merrick checked her watch – 3:15 – and peered through the curtains at the sky. Wind was sighing across the island, bringing the salt smell into the room. The retreat of the sun was unsettling – bright day dulling to a storm, suggesting that the gulf had no seasons, only samples.

The trooper still waited outside but she had no intention of hurrying. She checked her face in the mirror. The swelling had practically gone down. She spread her lips, found pale lipstick on her teeth, rubbed it off with her finger, then reached for the mohair sweater she'd knitted on size five needles during the empty nights in LA. Its warmth was immediate but the wind would still get through. She added the red rayon jacket she'd bought during her stopover in Hawaii.

When she left her hut, the blank-faced soldier trudged ahead of her, leading her toward a group of people halfway down the slope.

Sinclair was there in his wheelchair, leg propped on the board. Dyson sat on the grass, looking too sloshed to stand. There were three more troopers, huge and silent, and the slim figure of the dragon lady with her hideous, pulped face.

She heard an engine and turned to see the military dune-buggy bouncing down the slope with Connor beside the burly driver.

What would they do to him? After the filth on the tape, she hoped the arrogant Sinclair person would think of something painful. Incredible that the wife could be so promiscuous. Revolting slut. If sex had to be endured, a woman should lie passively and be worshipped, not squirm like a ferret.

Connor climbed down from the vehicle. He didn't know what was ahead of him. They'd checked his blood pressure, heart and pulse rate at the clinic as if his survival mattered. 'You are fit,' Dr Lee had said, 'as… what is your expression… a Mallee bull.' He'd cackled mightily at his grasp of Aussie idiom.

'Now,' Vo said, 'we begin. Mrs Merrick is winner and so must force Mr Connor, loser, to perform penalty given by Mr Sinclair. First, he explain this.' She looked at Sinclair pointedly.

Sinclair nodded. 'I've suggested that the concupiscent Mr Connor works off his remaining energy by becoming…' he paused melodramatically, '…a horse.'

Vo put her terrible head on one side like a bird.

'Please explain.'

The white sock on Sinclair's uplifted foot flexed as he tentatively bent his toes. 'I propose he carries this sot here' – he pointed to Dyson – 'piggy-back till he drops.' Dyson looked up at the mention of his name, then leaned forward before jerking slightly and swaying upright again.

'I propose that he goes around and around the same track until he can go no more. And if he stops…'

Vo turned to Merrick. 'So. You make him go. You enforce.'

'And if she doesn't?' Connor said.

Vo looked at him with her assortment of eyes, 'Next penalty is to flog. If Mrs Merrick not make, next contest, she is flog by Mr Connor.'

Connor looked at Grace Merrick. Perhaps something was behind the perfect mask, some quality that had eluded him. 'Suppose I have to be a gentleman?'

Merrick gazed back expressionless, as if peering at a bug. She said to Vo, 'I need something sharp, like a spear.'

Connor stared at her with disbelief. 'You're taking this very seriously.'

Merrick ignored him, still looking at Vo.

Vo said, 'No. We have already bring something you will use.' She gestured to one of the squad. The man reached up over the tray of the vehicle and lifted down a slim propane cylinder – a gas blowtorch with fine-jet attachment.

Connor was speechless.

'Here will do.' Sinclair indicated the course with his arm. 'He can go in a rectangle from here. Up the slope, across to the trees, down to that pond, across and back.'

Vo bent and prodded Dyson. 'Stand up.'

Dyson curled his lip. 'Put it where the sun don't shine.'

A trooper stepped forward and hauled him to his feet. The fleshy man protested, his legs soft, refusing to stand. Two of the men lifted him, taking an arm and leg each, and tried to load him onto Connor's back.

Merrick took the propane cylinder and peered into the end of the nozzle. It was about a centimetre in diameter, with a central hole and six pin-prick holes around that. She turned the knurled-brass knob at the base of its stalk. Gas hissed out. A trooper struck a match and held it to the end. The gas blew it out. He tried again and this time a jet of blue flame appeared. She held the cylinder away from her and watched Connor through slit eyes. He'd pay for his dirty pleasures with that whore.

Connor remembered the words of the woman with the frown. 'Do as they say. It may not be pleasant but it's the safest way.' Until he knew more, it seemed wisest to take her advice. He linked his hands behind his back.

Dyson's legs dangled either side of him. The man was dead weight, and stank of bourbon.

They strapped Dyson onto his back with a coil of jungle-green webbing. They took straps over his shoulders, down and under Dyson's thighs, then wound them around both their torsos until they were cocooned. There was no longer any need for him to hold his hands behind his back. The webbing made them inseparable.

Sinclair grinned from his wheelchair. 'Cheer up, Connor. You look like a water buffalo backed up against a thornbush,' he gestured dramatically, 'standing its ground against a lion.'

'Thanks a lot.'

'Actually a buffalo is far heavier than a lion. Can kill a lion if it's not careful. Be interesting to see you on the attack. What are you like at fighting, Connor?'

'Whad about me?' Dyson said. 'Whad-do I look like?'

'Like a very important parcel – in the Dead Letters Office.'

'Smart-arse.' Dyson was ready to roll. He geed-up Connor by digging his legs in. 'Hayr!'

Connor tried to elbow him in the ribs but the webbing stopped the blow. Merrick stepped in front of Connor and pulled the trailing end of webbing. 'Move.'

Sinclair held his hand up and waved to them, just bending his fingers from the palm.

Connor started walking up the slope. It wasn't hard at first. He was fit enough, had a set of weights at home and still occasionally rode his old surfboard. He also took his headphone-radio jogging three times a week and tried to eat sensible food – all mandatory for someone married to a health professional.

Dyson was heavy but they'd done a good job with the straps. He walked up the hill, almost to the swimming pool, then turned and trudged across the slope in the direction of the huts, to the trees. It was easy on level ground and he could relax on the downhill leg.

Dyson made clicking noises with his mouth, then began whistling a spaghetti western theme. Sinclair's task would soon be less ridiculous. The fleshy man was feeling heavier each step.

Connor reached the pines, turned and started down the hill toward the pond. It was like a small dam – perhaps seven metres square, fed by a stream, with dark water at the edges wreathed in weeds.

Dyson's head lolled. He was more pickled than a cherry in brandy. He started singing his plastic doll song again '…she's my life-size, wife-size, full-grown, blow-up plastic girl. Ain't nothin missin…' He was no Kenny Rogers. Something glinted from a tree. Connor looked up to see another camera panning. Mould was getting this from two angles.

He made it to the pond. Large fish cruised below the surface, tails barely moving. He walked around the perimeter, head turned to avoid Dyson's breath, and changed course for the buggy. One of the troopers had shouldered what looked like a Betacam camera. Dyson had stopped his racket, stupor coaxing him to sleep.

Connor was starting to puff now. He walked more slowly, conserving his strength.

The people on the slope hadn't moved. He wondered where Anita was. God. Perhaps Sinclair had confined her to the hut. He was glad she was missing this performance.

As he approached the group, Sinclair waved. 'Well done, old sock. Chop, chop.'

The breeze had died. The clouds were a blanket of grey. As he started up the hill again, the first heavy drops began to fall. The straps were gouging his shoulders and chest. Dyson weighed a ton, his head lolling to one side. A clap of thunder rolled across the sky.

He saw a trooper fetch a tarpaulin from the buggy and hold it over Vo. Another began to push Sinclair back up the hill toward the house. For a few steps the wheelchair kept pace beside Connor.

Sinclair called across. 'They're taking me to a drier spot. Not allowed to get the leg wet. So I'll leave thee in the storm. *Alter idem.*'

Merrick was still there, legs apart, red jacket zipped to the neck, hood on head, the blue flame near her feet.

Connor trudged to the top of the hill and turned again for the trees. As far as he could tell, the monkey on his back was asleep. He glanced at his watch. Four o'clock. How many times would he have to go around? Exhaustion, they'd said. Might have been simpler to refuse. Simpler but more unpleasant. Mould would see to that.

He was breathing hard and had back cramp. The rain was drumming on his skin, dripping into his eyes, transforming his clothes into dish-rags. He reached the trees and turned down the hill, Dyson weighing on his back like mortal sin.

Anita Sinclair walked onto the deck of her hut and huddled under the eaves. Rain was falling in sheets, spattering the planks, bouncing off the railing, the rising wind driving it into sleet. She stared beyond the ring of pines to see if the group of people was still there. Surely they would have found shelter? No, they hadn't moved. Then a top-heavy figure appeared, staggering, stumbling up the hill. A man on another man's back. And the man beneath looked all in.

The rain made it hard to see clearly.

David… carrying… who? Suddenly the shape fell and, developing eight limbs, writhed like a huge spider on the grass. It didn't get up again. Presently, another shape appeared, a hooded shape carrying something round with a jet of flame at the end that seemed impervious to rain. The shape stood close, pointing the flame at the spider as if threatening to burn it. The thing waved its limbs, heaved, rolled, then painfully rose and was transformed again into… a man strapped to a man. It staggered on and she expected it to collapse on the ground at each step.

Connor's was gasping, his nose running. The webbing was slicing into him and his body burned with fatigue. If he fell again, the woman would scorch him. She was sadistic enough to do it.

He gasped, 'Christ.'

Dyson said, 'He's dead.' He coughed up phlegm and spat. The rain had sobered him a little and the fall had done the rest.

Connor made it to the top of the slope again, his legs trembling with fatigue. 'I've had it.'

'Ball-o-wax.'

'Shut up, arsehole, or you get it.'

'Least mine's safe.' Dyson jeered. 'Take another dive and Miss Self-absorbed of 1930'll be up your giggly.'

Connor fell again, on purpose, twisting to land on top of Dyson.

The breath exploded out of the other man and Connor hoped he'd cracked the bastard's ribs. Dyson was so winded he could only suck air and groan. Somewhere above the pelting rain they heard the hiss of the approaching torch. Then Merrick's red jacket was above them, the jet of flame from the cylinder pointing down. She was soaked, dank hair hanging from the side of her face and out the edges of her hood. Her thin-lipped mouth was set. 'Get up.'

'Can't.'

'Do it or I burn you.'

Connor gave it all he had, somehow got to his knees but couldn't straighten his legs. He propped, trembling, on hands and knees. 'Can't. Bloody… can't.'

She lowered the flame fifteen centimetres from his pants. He could feel its heat through the soaked material. 'Then crawl.'

He began to crawl like a baby, splaying his arms and legs wide so that the bulk of Dyson didn't topple him.

Dyson's legs dragged on the ground. He groaned and gasped.

Connor looked back into stinging rain. Merrick was right behind, watching. He prayed for the rain to choke the jets of her torch but she held the nozzle down and it didn't even sputter.

Dyson gasped ripe curses.

'Felt that, did you?'

Dyson had. Between gasps, he speculated on the sexual activities of Connor's mother.

Connor said, 'Want it again?'

Grace Merrick was starting to freeze. Her trousers and shoes were soaked and the inside of her jacket was dripping. She left Connor in the downpour, crawling down the hill like a tortoise, and squelched back to the people by the buggy, sodden grass sucking at her shoes. The two remaining troopers and Vo were still under the tarpaulin, their backs sheltered by the machine. It hadn't helped much. They all looked miserable.

'Why does he crawl?' asked Vo.

'Can't stand. How long's this go on? I'm cold.'

'Mr Sinclair say how long.'

Merrick looked up at the house to Sinclair beneath the portico. Sinclair gave a regal wave. She looked back at Connor. He'd crawled to the pond and stopped. She headed back out to him, shivering and angry, ready to apply the torch directly to his pants.

Connor saw her coming and crawled to the edge of the water.

'She'll get you this time, sucker,' Dyson said.

Connor waited until Merrick was three metres from him, then crawled into the pond and flipped over.

Dyson went under, pinned by the weight. He struggled but couldn't right himself. His hand went over Connor's face, trying to drag his jaw off. Connor bit and the hand disappeared underwater fast. The drowning man kicked and clawed. Then Connor's head was underwater too.

Merrick waded into the pond as Connor's head broke water. He went under again as Dyson rolled him under into mud. She played the flame directly on the first bottom that surfaced. The sodden material steamed. In the centre, a small brown spot appeared.

Dyson jerked like a sprung trap and rolled.

Connor surfaced to suck air, staring at a blue flame edged with yellow where rain ran into the nozzle.

He kicked up weakly at Merrick's belly, enough to push her off balance. Her arms went wide and she splashed into the water, still holding the torch high.

He couldn't do more with the thrashing Dyson shackled to him. With his last strength he crawled out of the pool – crawled fast, knees out of his pants, hands made into fists, knuckles skinned. Dyson roared with pain as Merrick rose from the pool, half Aphrodite, half drowned cat, and kept coming, propane hissing out of the cylinder.

Connor knew that however fast he crawled, sooner or later she'd fry him.

Sinclair was enjoying it all hugely. They'd even provided him with binoculars. Connor was near collapse, but he was young. Wouldn't hurt him.

He raised the binoculars again as he'd done most Januaries at the Metropolitan Handicap at Kenilworth, though usually to look more at the young women falling out of their fashions than at the horses on the track. It was difficult through rain but the powerful lenses were good. Dyson's wide-eyed, contorted face flashed across the lens. He steadied on the scrambling Connor just before the fat man toppled him over.

Connor spat mud, wrenched his head around, rain pelting into his eyes. He was face down on his elbows, arms shaking with fatigue – couldn't struggle on, even if she tried to kill him.

Merrick's leg – right beside him. No strength to look up. The propane hissing nearer. Now the nozzle, sword of flame, yellow-edged, blue-centred...

Christ, she was going to do it. She was going to burn his bloody flesh off.

She was lowering the flame. It touched the back of his jeans. Steam rising from the material, the fabric charring...

Connor bellowed, face etched with agony, the pain releasing reserves that gave him for that moment extraordinary strength. He rolled, thrust his legs at Merrick's closest foot. His left foot behind hers, blocking it, right driving at the shin, below the knee – the jiu jitsu trick of fallen men. Merrick shrieked, toppled back, arms flying wide, the torch sailing through the air and down the slope. She fell heavily and slithered. She'd tried to save herself but landed on her elbow. Wouldn't have done her any good. First rule of a break-fall was to keep the elbow straight.

Sinclair leant forward. Bloody good. The young dissenter had turned it around. He wondered if Merrick's sadism was sexual compensation but doubted it. She was fuelled by high-octane adoration. Vesta, no less. The torch proved it. And she'd even requested a javelin. He wiggled his toe, delighted with the classical comparison.

Connor managed to crawl three more laps. For an hour each movement had been agony and now his limbs wouldn't function. He felt his back was about to break, his elbows to pop from their sockets. Both hands were bleeding and his knees had been scraped raw.

Dyson urged him to keep going, beating him about the chest, trying to walk for him, frightened of the woman with the torch.

Connor barely felt the blows. He couldn't raise his head. One arm buckled. He collapsed onto his elbows and Dyson's head hit the ground.

He tried to keep crawling on his elbows, the frantic Dyson trying to prop him up.

They both collapsed. This was it.

Duyen Vo was thinking of Tet. Of peach blossom and fireworks and the curl of smoke from incense in front of the family shrine. Of rice terraces, noodle soup and visits to the graves of her ancestors. Of Danang, green water and kingfishers, of struggling to learn Russian. Of Hue and live M-16 rounds and landmines sold in the bazaars. Of the explosion near Doai when fragments of her father's bone peppered her like bullets. Of the long months of agony after the napalm attack. If it hadn't been for Nicolae she surely would have died. As the bright images became darker, she tried to concentrate on the game.

Merrick's legs beside him again. The flame on the back of his thigh...

The wet cloth smoked. The brown patch steaming into the material, then the material parting with a line of red at the edge.

Connor's leg barely jerked.

He could smell his burning flesh.

She cooked him a moment longer, then threw the torch on the grass and stomped off toward the trees, limping a little, rubbing her knee.

His body was a kingdom of pain. He saw nothing, wanted to die.

Vo was soaked and the pants of the cameraman were plastered to his thighs. The other trooper was disguised as a waterfall. They waited, dripping, for instructions as the head of Procurement and Dispatch watched Merrick limp off through the trees.

Her live-dead eyes swivelled back to the heap in the rain. Finally, she nodded. 'Is enough. Take to clinic.'

As the two men went to get the bundle on the grass, she squelched back through the downpour to the house, reached the portico and stood dripping in front of Sinclair, a puddle forming around her on the tiles.

Sinclair frowned. 'I didn't say finished.'

'Is finish.'

'You said I could say when it stopped.'

'Mr Connor no longer respond. Poem say exhaustion – not death.'

He looked at her drowned-rat hair. 'Got a little damp, did we? An umpire's lot is not a happy one.'

Vo's soaked dress revealed a body good enough to deserve a proper head. As his eyes travelled appraisingly south, her gaze iced over. She stepped behind the wheelchair and started to push him into the pelting rain.

'Hang on. Mustn't get my leg wet.' The leg was already beyond the roofline, getting soaked. He grabbed the wheels and clung. 'Bloody hell.' The chair propped and went no further. He reversed himself back into shelter.

Vo glanced at a nearby trooper. He clicked his heels in instant assent. Then he walked forward, gripped the wheelchair like a pipe-wrench and wheeled it straight out into the downpour, pushing the now-drenched patient all the way down the slope to the pond. He even walked into the water behind the chair himself until Sinclair sat waist-deep, his white bandaged leg submerged, toe sticking up like an ice floe.

As the man turned and started back, Sinclair struggled out of the chair, standing on his good leg, trying to hop in the water. He fell with a splash that rivalled the beam-on launch of a Bengali scow.

Vo gave a lopsided smile and went inside.

Connor opened his eyes and saw the chrome handle of a jute-coloured metal drawer. Above it was a stainless-steel shelf. On the shelf was an empty glass with a spoon, and a kidney dish from which projected the end of an empty syringe. He realised he was in bed and tried to move his legs. Pain shot through him as if he'd been poked with a cattle prod.

Something white was resting beside his face. He turned his head with effort and it was a minute before he recognised the object as his bandaged left hand.

He shut his eyes.

'Mr Connor?' A woman's voice with a European accent.

He must have drifted off, because someone was now sitting beside the cabinet and there had not been a chair there before. He turned to focus on her. The woman from the library. Gillian. She wore a white blouse and jeans but he was not well enough to appreciate the sight.

'Mr Connor?'

'You.'

'Please try to listen. I know this isn't a good time but it's the only one I can arrange. Mr Mould's prepared to see you. That's if you still want to talk to him.'

He tried to twist over and face her. It felt like sliding over rolls of barbed wire. He nodded. 'Thanks.'

The woman sat looking at him for a moment, then got up and left the room, leaving a faint trace of musk. The Asian nurse entered, pushing an empty wheelchair. The small wheels at the front of it rattled as she positioned it next to his bed.

'Now we sit up,' she said. 'Sit!'

He managed to do it, every muscle in his body shrieking, and got one leg down off the bed. His knees and elbows were bandaged and, as she helped him into the chair, pain shot from the top of his thigh right up his side. She propped a pillow behind him and wheeled him through the door.

As they entered the corridor he saw Vo walk into the next room. The nurse stopped pushing and parked him just outside the door. 'We wait.'

Two troopers came toward them from the opposite end, blocking the passageway with their bulk.

The nurse pointed. 'Ms Vo in there.'

They strolled down the corridor again and stared out the window, waiting.

Connor could just hear the voices in the room, the rumbling wheeze of Mould, the crow-like accent of Vo. He tried to make out the words.

Vo's voice: 'Fifteen medium-use PT-76 with, say, ten full operational.'

'Still a hundred or two in your country... and there's India.'

'...want B-type.'

'B?'

'As D-56TM fully stabilise gun and NBC system.'

'End-user certificates?'

'Okay... request in three month outside.'

'Be vague. Let it sit. You're dealing with the... Arab mind, not the Ulster Volunteers.' A pause. 'You're...' A long sentence that was lost. 'Why persist?'

Her voice raised. 'What else I do with this face? Is all I know. You unfair.'

Mould's laugh, starting as a rumble, developing into a quake, ending in a cough. 'Technically, the three of you could run it. But there's one thing none of you have.'

'Now what cruel thing you say?'

'Charisma.'

'Charisma. What is that?'

'The... essential element. You're like... mortar rounds without fuses. It's going to fall apart. Less painful to face facts.'

'I... damn... you.' It was a heartfelt curse.

'All of us are damned.'

Vo came through the door, head down, good eye moist, and hurried quickly past the troopers, who walked back again and now entered the room. The wheelchair moved. The nurse was pushing him again.

It was a similar room but larger, with bare walls and medical equipment. The troopers were now stationed just inside the door and, as the nurse wheeled him in, they walked either side of his chair, like liners escorting a tug. The chair stopped in front of an elaborate hospital bed. The men halted and stood like columns beside him, so close that he could hear the belts around their guts creak when they breathed. If they thought he was in shape to attack their beloved leader, he had news that would surprise them.

In front of him a white-covered whale was propped on a sloping mattress. 'Well, Mr Connor. How was your excursion?' The deep voice was incongruous coming from someone who looked so sick.

Connor tried to get his head together. 'You fucking arsehole.'

'Perhaps you're too tired for conversation.' His skin was

so pale he looked like a talking corpse but his voice seemed stronger, the effort to talk a little less. 'I understand you've been speaking to Gillian. So what did you wish to... impart?'

He tried to think but his neurons had ceased holding hands. 'Listen, shit-for-brains. You were fucking up the world with arms deals and all we did was expose you.'

'No, Mr Connor. You exposed half of me. And half-truths are lies. You mistook your own crassness for smartness. You slanted it and took the money.' Mould's hand went to his jelly chins. 'You would have seriously offended even a reasonable man...' The chilling eyes beneath their drooping lids. 'And I'm *not* a reasonable man.'

'Vindictive fuckwit.'

'Yes, I enjoy... tweaking your fears. You've never put yourself on the line. Such a carefully... sheltered life.'

'You're not the full quid, mate.'

'And what does that expression mean?' The blubber smile.

'A few coupons short of a toaster. Cracked.'

The lids remained at half mast. The eyes beneath them did not flicker. If Mould had any spontaneous reactions they had long ago been garrotted by his brain. 'I have the... power to dictate your life. A deeply satisfying power. I enjoy dangling you over the snake-pit, it's as simple as that. And your... chance to be rich remains.'

'You can shove your stinking money.'

'I thought you wouldn't want it. You're almost too reclusive to want anything. This afternoon was good for you. It let you know you're alive.'

'Rank bastard.'

'I understand you, Connor, and your petty, suburban existence. I know about everything from your use of ZSC fungicidal talcum to the last time you renewed the... tie-rod ends and caster bushes on your car. I know your favourite programmes on SBS, even what your wife's doing now…' Mould grinned until his eye-teeth depressed his lower lip, '…and where she met him.'

Connor jerked forward in his chair and made a lunge for the bed. Halfway there he hit a brick wall that slammed him back in the chair so hard that it reversed in a crazy parabola, rebounded off the doorframe and did a quarter-turn twist that jerked his head over the back of the seat and almost flipped him onto the floor.

Four camo-clad legs and four fists filled his vision. They were dying for him to try something more.

He sat as still as the second-last bidder in a rigged auction. But his stomach was burning through his chest and his muscles were in spasm.

Mould's deep voice came from the left. 'Your suspicions are quite right. The current man is Lester Stuthridge, a cotton consultant from Moree, New South Wales. If you want his collar size or basic metabolic rate, I can… have them for you in five minutes.'

The chair jerked from behind. They were pushing him forward to the bed again. His exertions had sprung the bandage around his left knee and the paraffin gauze beneath it was blossoming red.

'How do I know you're telling the truth?'

'Lester Stuthridge has… two preoccupations. One's your wife and the other's the exact composition of the chemical cocktails he… uses to spray boll worms. His thoughts are limited to the amount of endosulphan he'll use on his… *Heliothis armigera*. The grandest sight he's ever seen, apart from the… small birthmark on your wife's inner thigh is a… crop-duster filling up with Dipel ES.' Mould quivered slightly with amusement, as if he didn't want the pain that might accompany a satisfying chuckle. 'Cotton-growing isn't my forte, so I could hardly have dreamed all that up.' Mould watched him for a moment with that same speculative look. Connor's head was down, his bandaged elbows on his knees.

Mould continued. 'Like to hear the good news? I offer you...' he raised a bloated index finger '...the elemental life.'

'You what?'

'I offer you trial by fire. Rare now. People aren't challenged any more. For most people suffering's a programme on TV. Even... revolutions are called "unrest". The word "disruption" is considered unclean. Reasonable people like... you have tried to legislate against pain until the... planet stinks with fear.'

'Got quite a turn of phrase – for a sadist.'

'Stock-in-trade. I've been charming the pants off degenerates for years.'

'Guess it takes one to know one.'

'It helps.'

'You're mad.'

'Oh, no. I have my credo.'

'Which is?'

'As Hanford told you, I'm concerned about world population. There are fundamental reasons why governments will never face it squarely. Population's the tumour. And the surgery's war.' Mould panted slightly and the nurse raised the mask. He took two deep whiffs of oxygen and a little colour suffused his cheeks.

Connor laughed without humour and his ribs seemed to stab through his chest wall. 'So you promote mass extermination...'

'Where I can. Because I'm interested in ecology.'

'Pull the other one. If you were such a greenie you'd be using your loot to plant forests.'

'I do more than that.' Mould hunched toward him, eyes suddenly intense. 'My interests include... parts of the Amazon Basin, Madagascar, Sarawak and Sumatra... either purchased through holding companies or protected by… bribes to governments. In cases such as Sarawak where the… government controls all forest areas, you have to massage officials to get… anywhere at all. In Indian parks such as Nagarahole and certain areas of Siberia I fund undercover wardens. Other areas are… patrolled by mercenaries briefed to shoot loggers or poachers on sight. If anyone saves the tiger, it'll be me. I'm also… doing what I can for the jaguar, anaconda and lemur. Then there's the situation in Somalia…'

'Oh no, don't let's forget about Somalia.'

'I fund bio-diversity projects in a score of zoos around the world. I've set up trust funds for the Arabian oryx, for the Mhorr gazelle…'

'But people don't matter, huh?'

'Tabloid thinking. Use your brain. Thousands of species are… disappearing from loss of habitat. For instance, some… parma wallabies were taken to Kawau Island, near here, in 1870. In Australia, feral animals practically… wiped them out. They were thought to be extinct. But Kawau, otherwise an ecological disaster, has helped… preserve the genetic diversity of that species. See how threatened creatures are? All except the human. If you… died tomorrow, you'd benefit the earth… save it forty years of… pollution, a mountain of garbage…'

Mould stopped talking, his face grey. The passion of his outburst had weakened him. He lay back in the sloping bed, and gasped, 'Get this… elephant off my… chest.' The nurse placed the oxygen mask over his face. He took long gasps, then waved one hand dismissively. The interview was over.

They wheeled Connor back to the ward, made him get back in the bed and the nurse gave him Chinese tea to drink out of a Pyrex glass.

Tess. Was it true?

Instinctively, he'd known. How many others had she had... on the table with the breathing hole in her chiropractic surgery, among the towels and the charts and the hanging plastic replica of the spine? How many of her patients had wanted more than manipulation and activator hammers and sudden, excruciating jerks? And how had the feeling between them dwindled? The unmeasurable decrease over years that reduced love to habitual responses and, finally, to betrayal.

He gulped the tea. The nurse was squatting by his knee, unwinding the bloodstained dressing. She said in a flat, dry voice, 'Hold still,' confirming that there were three sexes – males, females and nurses. 'You come to clinic tonight before bed – we change bandages, okay?'

He nodded and lay back, watching her walk away to the medical cabinet – bandy legs and flat bottom in starched white uniform and stockings.

He thought back to the diatribe of Mould. Forests in Madagascar? The greening of the mercenaries? He even partly agreed, which made the situation more absurd. Was the man on the level? In a twisted way it made sense. Governments ducked big issues. The standard technique for remaining in power was to say the right words but do nothing. Mould was clearly not mad. Malevolent perhaps, but... For God's sake, he told himself, don't side with the bastard. He's doing his best to kill you.

He wished the woman from the library would come back.

When he woke he was back in the hut. Probably the tea had included a mild sedative. As he tried to sit up and inspect himself for damage, a stab of intense pain came from beneath the bandage on the back of his right thigh. His body ached in every limb. Even the slightest twist destroyed him. Blood had soaked through the bandages on his hands and knees. He discovered that his chest and arms were a mass of welts and bruises. He finished the inspection and peered around the room. Twilight filtered under the blind. The mirror on the wall had been replaced. His camera case was back, sitting on the bench.

He put an experimental leg on the floor. Then a second. He tried standing. It was painful as hell but not as difficult as he'd expected.

He forced his damaged muscles to walk and made it to the bench, leaning on it for support while he checked inside the camera case. Nothing had been taken except the film. The cloth he used to tuck around the camera had been cleaned and neatly folded. Everything ran efficiently in this worst of all possible worlds.

A piece of paper with the verse of the poem was on the bench, its edge precisely aligned with the edge of the wood. He read the last lines again.

> Exhausted,
> Flogged,
> Shamed,
> Stagger into another dawn.

Mould's taste in poetry was as uncompromising as his views on conservation. The flogging next.

Connor felt woozy, made it back to the bed and sat down. At this rate Mould would kill them all while stuffing them like geese.

Only one thing mattered now: that he didn't draw the short straw twice.

Chapter Nine

Vo phoned to say dinner was in the dining room and to ask whether he wanted to be collected. He told her no. As he limped up the hill he regretted it – felt as if his joints were scraping on raw bone. He heard voices behind him and looked around. Sinclair, on crutches too low for him, was being shepherded along by his wife.

Sinclair caught up and said archly. 'Evening.'

His wife glanced over with concern. 'Poor David. You all right?'

'I look it?' He glared up at Sinclair. 'Thanks a lot.'

'Enjoy my little cure?'

He made it to the dining room, feeling helpless and trapped, unsure whether his joints would work properly again or if he'd need a graft on his thigh. The bandages constricted him and needles of pain jabbed into him as he sat.

Dyson shifted, wincing on his chair, looking surprised to see him. Despite a singed rear and abraded face, his pouring arm seemed unaffected.

Merrick sat as erect as a pylon in a dramatic black top – polo-necked but armless and backless. She had a sniffle but still contrived to look magnificently bored.

The gathering was joined by Mould as the medical detachment appeared and wheeled him, with oxygen and paraphernalia, to the end of the long table. They left him there, a shape under a rug, like the next autopsy in a morgue.

The first course was pumpkin soup. Connor could barely hold his spoon. The bandage had spared his thumb but he couldn't completely bend his fingers and his strap-damaged shoulder made even lifting his arm an event. He missed his mouth first go and had to focus on the docking procedure.

The nurse filled Mould's spoon for him but he brushed her away. Though visibly weak, he was determined to feed himself.

Vo, in the chair near Mould, was also having soup-schmerz, her half-animated face not performing well.

Gloom had collected in the darkened corners of the room, its cause more basic than the unfortunate choice of soup.

Mould looked at each of them in turn, savouring their depression. A smile formed above his chins like a contented wound. 'You're very quiet tonight.'

Sinclair said, 'What d'you expect?'

'Sobered you, have I, Hanford? How satisfying. May I extend my congratulations to all present. You've... entered into the... spirit of the game. And I'm sure you're... eager to begin the next contest without delay.'

Sinclair surveyed Mould like a French chef confronted with a haggis. 'We get a chance to heal? Or do you intend to flog a dead horse?'

'Depends on the loser.' The wound of Mould's mouth widened.

Bastard, Connor thought. You're loving this.

The long curtains became a lighter red as lightning flickered in the room. The thunderclap was immediate, loud enough to shock, rattling the windows, adding to the sense of foreboding.

The soup plates were removed. No-one spoke. It was as if Mould's supremacy had forced them to await events with the resignation of rabbits in a trap.

Sinclair held up his glass and a trooper recharged it. His indignation still allowed him to savour the excellent chablis.

Dyson looked at his tormentor. 'So what's your next shitty little shindig?'

Mould lowered his spoon and raised his head. He had everyone's attention.

'This evening we have the flogging. First our main course of trout, followed by crêpes with... lemon, fig soup and cream. Then coffee and liqueur – served in the gymnasium. Cigars will be provided – that's if... the ladies don't object. I'm fond of cigars, though I shouldn't have more than a puff as I'm... near to losing both feet.'

Sinclair took another sip. 'Nothing like a post-prandial flogging.'

'I agree it's a packed schedule. But when death's imminent there's no time to pace one's pleasures. So let us proceed. Mr Connor?'

'What?'

'As previous loser, you call the tune for the next game. How do you see arrangements?'

'You mean – I'm supposed to decide how it's done?'

'That's right.'

Connor looked at his bandaged hands. 'How about three strokes with a wet dishcloth?'

'Some hours ago, Connor, a blowtorch was cooking your skin. Suppose Grace loses. Wouldn't you prefer something more severe?'

Connor looked at Merrick, who stared back with an expression of contempt. Anger surged through him. 'I'd like to see her whipped until her back looks like fresh liver.'

Mould raised both hands. 'Excellent.'

'Jee-zuz,' Dyson said.

Sinclair stared at Connor with disbelief, then shook his head.

'Now, now, Hanford.' Mould was beaming. 'What if Adrian loses? The gentleman who stabbed you. Wouldn't fresh liver seem appropriate?'

Sinclair nodded with a twist of the mouth and looked at Connor. 'Oh, wise young judge,' he intoned.

Dyson's face reddened. He glared at Sinclair. 'And what if *you* get flayed, big-mouth arsehole? Personally, I'd pay to see it.'

Mould beamed at them all. 'Right there, you have a demonstration of how violent we are. But we package our savagery with fine words and label it civilisation.'

'I didn't realise,' Sinclair said, 'that the flogging included the ears as well as the back.'

Mould smiled. 'I enjoy your *bon mots*, Hanford. Pity your character isn't the equal of your wit. Time for the trout. And if they taste sour it's your fault for disturbing their afternoon.'

Thunder rolled again across the sky and sharp taps began at the windows. Hail.

The gymnasium was at the end of a corridor. It had glass skylights that rattled with hail, a polished timber floor, and was at least ten metres square. Hanging lamps cast a bright glow on the Nautilus machines and weights.

Connor had produced exercise videos and knew enough to assess what he saw. There were bench-presses, hack slides, racks of assorted barbells including E-Z curl bars, a neck harness, two Keiser air machines, inversion boots, even a power-gripper. Mould's gym was elaborate enough to make a hard-core bodybuilder have an attack of the prone hyperextensions.

As they entered, a trooper switched off all lights but one at the end of the room. The space shrank to the illuminated circle that reflected off the full-length mirrors on the wall. The light was directly above a rack that supported an overhead horizontal bar. On a small table to one side were coffee things and the promised box of cigars.

This, it seemed, was an occasion, for Mould honoured them again with his presence. His wheelchair was pushed across the darkened room to the focal point of light. Then a trooper passed around coffee, serving Mould first. Roman chairs were the only seats and no-one seemed concerned about their abdominals. So, except for the two men in wheelchairs, all stood.

Blore, who had wheeled in Sinclair, lumbered to the table, picked up a salver holding rum balls and began offering them around.

Connor took a bite. It was good. As he was about to screw up the paper cup he noticed a circle drawn on the inside of its base. Others were discovering their own inscriptions.

Vo said, 'You see now you have entered in draw.'

'Jeez, when do we have a proper bet?' Dyson moaned.

'Mr Connor not specify way we draw. So we oblige to provide way.'

'Shitty arseholes. If we gotta have a massacre, let's do it right. Have a bet, for Chrissake. Not like this. Cupcakes! Christ!'

Vo took his cup and half smiled. 'Fortunate for you, have chance to specify next draw.'

'Huh?'

'Nought is neutral. Cross loser. Star winner. And you, Mr Dyson, draw cross.' She held it up and showed it. 'Who has star?'

'No way,' said Dyson. He scuttled for the door and two of the troopers took off after him.

Vo raised her voice above the slam-dunk squeak of tortured boot-soles. 'Who has star?'

Merrick held up her cup.

Dyson was now in the half-gloom at the rear of the hall, dodging around the equipment like a jelly on the loose as the troopers converged from opposite sides. They cornered him against a pulley machine and hoisted him effortlessly in the air, proving that the gym was more than a recreational amenity.

Dyson's profanities filled the room.

Now they had him in the aisle and were hauling him along by the armpits. His feet dragged behind them, scraping on the floor. A third trooper was attaching handcuffs to the bar. Connor stepped back to save his coffee as Dyson was manhandled to the rack. They stripped him of jacket and shirt. His bare arms were forcibly raised. As they didn't reach the bar, the third man lowered it three notches and there were clicks as they manacled his wrists.

The men moved away, exposing the dangling victim.

His ripped shirt hung over his belt and his heels didn't quite reach the ground. The overhead glare threw the bulge of flesh around his waist into relief.

'Cummon,' Dyson cried, 'Gimme a break. I'll pay back the money, okay?'

'What touching faith you have in your ability,' Mould said.

'Oh Jeez,' Dyson moaned.

Propped on his crutches, Sinclair examined his cigar. His eyelid went up. 'Davidoff Number One.'

'You approve?' Mould asked.

Sinclair smelt the cigar and nodded. Davidoff, a Russian genius, had made the selection of Cuban tobaccos an art form. 'Some consider them too tightly wrapped.'

'Some people quibble over anything.'

Sinclair was handed a cutter by the hulking Blore. He used it and Blore held a match to the cigar. The tall man moved Blore's hand back so that the match was half an inch from the end, then turned the cigar as he sucked, drawing the flame evenly in. Connor, not versed in such niceties, lit his cigar as one might light a fire.

Then he noticed, on the floor, a length of braided leather – part of a stockwhip.

Dyson's abuse echoed off the walls.

Mould looked at Blore and pointed to his ear.

Blore stepped forward, felt in Dyson's trouser pocket, withdrew the ad-man's handkerchief and stuffed it in his mouth. Then he removed a roll of insulation tape from his battle-jacket pocket. He plastered Dyson's mouth with it, winding it around his head several times. Now Dyson could only kick and his swearing was restricted to his thoughts.

Another trooper handed the stockwhip to Merrick – brown leather, cut off three feet from the handle, shorn end lashed with white sail-twine.

Merrick felt the weight, then ran her left hand along the whip. Watching her, he thanked his stars that his rum ball hadn't been sitting on a cross. She looked a formidable antagonist in the backless top – tall and super-fit with swimmer's muscles beneath the bronzed skin – powerful enough to slice Dyson into fillets. And the unfortunate Dyson had no option. He was condemned to be cut to bits. He had the freedom, prospects and ability to protest of a pig with a slit larynx in the bathroom of a Cuban high-rise.

Mould looked up at them from his throne. The white cotton rug over his swollen frame absorbed the light and seemed to glare, making him appear more slug than man.

Vo said, 'If you need more coffee, now say. Because shortly we begin.'

'I'll have more,' Merrick said.

A trooper topped up her cup.

As Anita Sinclair lowered her cup it rattled uncontrollably on the saucer. 'This is nauseating. I'm leaving.'

'No-one leave room,' Vo said.

Mould pointed to the cigar box. Blore got him one,

snipped the end, placed it in his mouth and lit it for him. He took one long puff and breathed out, adding more smoke to the shaft of light. The hail no longer rattled the skylights. Now they drummed with rain.

Vo nodded to Merrick. 'Begin.'

Merrick ignored the command, sipping her coffee with slow self-possession.

'Begin. You hear?'

Merrick took another sip, then turned slowly to face her. 'I'll begin when I've finished my coffee.'

'Begin now.' The gargoyle stamped her foot.

Merrick put her coffee cup down on the table, raised the whip and extended the handle toward Vo like a pike. 'I'll begin when I'm ready. I'm not yet ready. *Do* you understand?'

At the move, Blore jerked forward as if ready to defend Vo with his life.

'Don't press it, Grace,' Mould said. 'You'll suffer less.'

Merrick wheeled on him, shaking the whip. 'You may be able to victimise them. You may be able to torment my poor brother. But you'll *not* do it to me.'

'Pride, Grace, is very... expensive.'

'I don't have your power,' she thundered. 'I don't have your money. But what I have is myself. That's what you can't get at. That's what you can't stand. You can't get at what I am inside!'

Blore moved in, ready to block Merrick. She whirled around and raised the whip. He made a come-on gesture to her, sneering.

Connor finished his coffee with a gulp.

Mould motioned Blore back. 'Let her have her little moment, Major. No harm done. And we don't want to humble so magnificent a creature. At least not now, when she has duties to perform. *Do* finish your coffee, Grace.'

Merrick placed the whip on the table and picked up her cup again.

Mould said, 'I thought we mentioned Armagnac.'

Vo said without turning, 'No Armagnac. Fetch.'

A trooper trotted into the gloom behind them.

Merrick put her cup down with deliberation, then snatched up the whip. She advanced on Dyson before the others had quite noticed she was beginning. Connor glanced back at Anita, who was trembling and seemed ready to run. A smack of leather on skin. He turned to see Dyson flinch, heard his stifled groan.

The troopers retreated out of range as the whip came back. She swung it in an arc, flicking it as it landed.

The first blows had coloured Dyson's skin with an angry stripe of red. The later ones crossed it at an angle. His body writhed with the pain but his cries were muffled by the gag.

Connor's body was so tense his ribcage seemed unable to expand. He struggled to breathe. He had never seen anyone whipped. It was as if he felt each blow connect, identifying with the trussed blubber on the frame. He stood, jaw clamped, fighting his wish to pull the woman away. He knew that intervening would be useless, knew that Mould's huge men were just waiting for him to do it.

Worst of all, he found the scene arousing... Merrick's perfect body, silky flesh, the muscles of her back and arms. The presence of pain. The energy level in the room...

At first there was no damage, just red welts.

The end of the whip sometimes hit the rack, sometimes curled around Dyson's stomach. But as Merrick became more expert, it fell steadily across the same area.

Dyson's legs danced with each blow and the handcuffs bit deeper into his wrists. He was yelling but the sounds came through as a whining moan. His nose and eyes streamed, his face was a pop-eyed red and his back was becoming striped with the purple of broken capillaries.

A trooper with a silver tray was now offering around Armagnac.

Although Connor had little sympathy for Dyson, he found it hard to watch the leather connecting. He took a liqueur glass, gulped, and the stuff made his throat a furnace.

Merrick had really hit stride.

Mould's heavy-lidded eyes were fixed on Dyson's rapidly pulping back. He rocked gently in his chair, savouring each blow, on his thick lips a beatific smile.

Sinclair was also relishing the sight, his cigar conducting the beat. The wine had done its work. He looked benign, had an expression of aesthetic appreciation. 'Bravo!'

Mould handed his cigar back to Blore. 'A shame. But when one has veins like spaghetti...'

Connor realised what he was seeing. The oppressed were now the oppressors, the quarry siding with the huntsman. Mould, sitting there gloating, while his victims supervised their slaughter.

Merrick switched hands and continued whipping with her left. The room reverberated with the flick of leather on flesh. Dyson's back was now gouged and smeared by the slithering of the whip. Blood from the flicking lash was peppering the mirrors and the frame.

Dyson wasn't young and a heart attack was a possibility. Connor turned to Mould. 'Enough's enough.'

Mould's reptilian eyes were fixed on Dyson's lacerated back. 'This is *my* revenge, Connor, not yours.'

'No need to bloody kill him.'

'If you knew how much the body can stand...'

'You malicious bastard.'

Blore glanced down at Mould, eyebrows raised, but Mould shook his head.

Connor knew that if Mould had nodded, Blore would have taken him apart. He wasn't ready for that, was surprised he'd spoken at all. All his life, when out-gunned, he'd backed down. And this was hardly the place to stick one's neck out.

Mould was now looking past Dyson to the mirrored wall where he had a full-length view of the man's agony. Another Mould touch, Connor thought. Everything precisely planned.

Merrick changed hands again. Her bare back was moist. Dyson's face oozed like a beetroot dipped in brine. His back was swelling into thick weals and the crossed stripes made him resemble a rare steak off a griddle.

Sinclair stretched for a second Armagnac. 'Still can't see his backbone. Come on. Let the pig gape.'

His wife cried out in disgust, 'Hanford! You don't have to condone it.'

Connor felt like kicking away his crutches. 'Bastard. Whose side are you on?'

'He's the man who stabbed me, remember? Quite reasonable to tone him up a bit.'

'Could be you.'

'You sententious idiot. *You* were the one who ordered fresh liver.'

'You're pissed.'

'Grow up, Connor. You're in a bucket of rats. Face it. Old Nick's a psychological engineer.'

Dyson's back was crimson. The whip had covered the flesh in cuts and blood was soaking the waist of his hanging shirt. The whip glistened red. With each stroke his raw flab seemed to quiver. His wrists were bloody from straining against the handcuffs. His body slumped, unable to stand, and hung.

Anita Sinclair was on her hands and knees, her head between her arms, the sound of her retching a counterpoint to the slash of the whip.

Merrick wasn't stopping. She was breathing hard and

intent, as if avenging all slights to her sex on one sacrificial body.

Mould finally raised his hand and the troopers moved forward to stop the action. Merrick seemed reluctant to finish and gave a final stinging cut before they prised the blood-slimed leather from her. As the lash came back it flicked out toward Connor and spattered some blood on his shirt.

'Well done, Grace,' Mould said. He moved his hands half together as if to clap but appeared not to have the energy. 'You did well. She's not squeamish, is she, Connor?'

Connor looked at his shirt as the remains of Dyson were unhooked. 'What's that supposed to mean?'

'You didn't watch much.'

'Because he's still *human*.' The cry was from Anita. She was slumped behind a puddle of vomit.

Mould looked back at her with distaste. 'A waste of fine trout. What do you mean by human? A member of the species that's making the world... uninhabitable for itself?'

Sinclair twisted his cigar. 'Forget the broad perspective or you'll make our young adulterer confused. Try to stay just plain bad. Then we'll all know where we stand.'

Anita was wiping her mouth. She'd managed to stand up. 'Can we go now?' Her tone expressed loathing. Sinclair looked down at Mould. 'Well?'

Mould's eyes didn't move or blink. He replied very softly. 'Don't get too cocky, Hanford. There's considerable pain ahead for you. Unless you're very, very lucky.'

'I may never lose again, old sock. I'm not in the habit of losing. I'm a resilient bugger and I might just have you yet.'

Mould looked straight ahead at the blood-flecked mirrors. 'You lost when you abandoned my wife.' His deep voice was ragged with hatred. He motioned to Blore. The after-dinner entertainment was over.

Chapter Ten

As Connor left the gymnasium he was told by Vo to report to the clinic. 'Dr Lee say you need to have dressing change. Be there at 2100 hour. Go round back.'

At nine o'clock, as he passed the vegetable patch, he heard screams curdling enough for a sound effects track. He entered the building and pushed through the plastic swing doors.

Dyson's scourging was being followed by the crucifixion of a saline bath and back scrub. They were holding him naked and spreadeagled on the edge of a large plastic tub, his arms and legs anchored by four of the biggest troopers.

Dr Lee turned to Connor as he came in. 'Please wait.' He propped himself between a scrub sink and a trolley and watched them lower Dyson into a solution which, from the racket he was making, must have burnt his raw flesh like acid. He sat in the tub yelping as Lee's nurse swabbed his back.

Lee frowned. 'General anaesthetic is usual but Mr M has vetoed.' He left the tub and wandered to the scrub sink as the swabbing went on.

'Enjoy working for a sadist?' Connor asked.

The doctor shrugged. 'Everything relative. Far better than selling offal and goats' heads in Kashgar.'

'Must be good pay.'

'Very good. And conditions. Good wine more pleasant than fermented Mongolian mare's milk.'

'Quite the comedian. Suppose you find us lots of fun?'

'Frankly, yes. We all welcome break in routine.'

The screams stopped because Dyson had passed out.

That made it easier on the ears, and faster. Lee helped scrub the rest of the wound, then got them to lift the unconscious man onto the surgery table, where he applied cream with a spatula while the nurse set out pads, dressings and paraffin gauze.

Connor said, 'He doesn't look good.'

'Not just because of this. His Gamma GT reading would be unusual.'

'Meaning?'

'Liver damage.'

The dressing was mostly in place before Dyson came to. Lee smiled at him. 'Almost finish.'

Dyson moaned, the pain of his raw back blocking out everything.

'No worse,' Lee assured him, 'than motorbike accident. Nice and clean. No picking out gravel. No bone exposed. Soon you have scars like road-map. You be marked man.' He chuckled in falsetto.

'Fucking creeps.' Dyson moaned. 'Jeez. Oh, Jeez.'

'You fortunate we have completely equipped clinic. You may find that useful in near future.'

'You're bad as them, you fucking freak.'

'I'm angel of mercy – all that stand between you and terrible septic complication. Tonight you sleep on your tum-tum.' Lee giggled at his grasp of the vernacular and the nurse also tittered. 'Then, in two days, if you still here, though I think you somewhere else, we re-dress back. And no need to say to wear light shirt.' He chortled with delight again as if he found himself unbearably funny. The nurse laughed so much she nearly dropped her adhesive plaster and the two troopers slapped their knees.

'Fucking swine,' Dyson screamed.

The beaming doctor turned to Connor, 'Now is your turn.'

Next morning the rain became blue sky, warmed by a third-grade star that shone without concern for the microcosm below. At nine o'clock precisely, Anita Sinclair arrived at Connor's hut. She stood with her overnight bag like a child visiting her aunt. Connor found her presence disconcerting, with her husband one hut away.

'So what's this?'

She drifted in and opened the empty drawers under the bench, 'Can I put my things in here?'

'Does your husband know what you're doing?'

'He helped me pack.'

'He doesn't care if you move in here?'

'Why shouldn't I? There's nothing over there except his boring holiday reading. A book on Samuel Johnson and Schweitzer's autobiography. I'm not interested in the lives of others. I'm interested in my own.'

'So you've come over to screw the incredible bandaged man?'

'It's the one pleasure left in this hell-hole. Besides, your corruption was sweet. Attached males are fun.'

'What's *he* think of it?'

'Really, David,' she huffed. 'He considers infidelity civilisation's great achievement.'

'Answer the question.'

'Ask *him* if you're so concerned.' She turned away and got on with her unpacking.

'I will.'

Sinclair was on the porch, testing his leg. He still had no shoe on it but the crutches were leaning against the railing. As Connor approached, he took several steps unaided, going 'Oo-ah' as his weight came down on the bandaged leg, then turned with mock surprise. 'Connor, no less. To what do I owe this bliss?'

'You know damn well. Anita's trying to move in with me.'

He shrugged. 'She finds the demands of that small body difficult to control.'

'She's your wife.'

'Part person. Part possession. Tragedy of womankind. All evil, ready to be rooted. Wear her like a crown.'

'I didn't suggest it to her.'

'Grow up, Connor. I'm sick of your asinine prudery. You're now in an environment where consideration's read as weakness. And yet you walk unbraced.'

'I'm learning fast.'

'About time. As for my preferred sexual partner, grab what you can get. And don't be surprised if I require the ocular proof. Oo! Ah! Bleeding leg. Three steps and I'm stuffed.'

Connor reported the conversation to Anita, who was hanging a dress in his cupboard. 'He's even threatening to watch.'

She shut the drawer and shrugged. 'He likes to.'

'You let him?'

She turned, hands on her small hips. 'I sleep with whom I wish. This is *my* body, not his.'

'You let him watch?'

'Why not? God, you're stuffy.'

'I thought…'

'You thought I was like you because I cry and get upset. It hasn't struck you that I can suffer – yet *not* be like you at all.'

Connor peeled the bandage off his hand. Despite the impregnated paraffin gauze, raw skin was stuck to the dressing. 'I'm missing something here.'

'Just because one's selfish and rich doesn't mean one doesn't feel.' She sounded like a Parisian communicating for the first time with an Eskimo.

'I'm not used to wife-swapping.'

'But you haven't swapped her, David,' she reminded, 'just screwed someone else. When you look at all sides of a question, it's pointless to strike attitudes.'

Connor banged out onto the verandah and yelled to the air, 'You people!'

She came to the door, voice flat. 'If you can't take your own medicine and want me to go…'

'I… want more tape for these bandages.' He walked stiffly down the steps toward the house.

Grace Merrick, who had been swimming in the pool, was coming toward him across the lawn. She wore a black one-piece bathing suit that glorified her figure. Connor felt like flooring her with a punch, then decided to let his hands heal first. He expected her to swan by, head in the air. Instead, she stopped some feet away and spoke.

'Have you seen Dyson yet?'

'No. Seen the burn on my leg?'

She ignored the comment. 'The poem says there's another trial before we can leave. We can't have it without that loathsome man.'

'That's *your* lookout. You flayed him.'

Her eyes glittered with anger. 'You hypocritical, holier-than-thou. I did what you said you'd do to *me*.'

Connor took a step toward her.

She didn't budge. 'I have a nasty kick.'

'Matches your personality.' He limped past her toward the house.

Despite himself, he couldn't resist one glance back at her, to see if her departing rear was as notable as her front. It was perfectly firm and brown and moved like rubber on springs. But he wouldn't penetrate that perfect carcass for all the ride-on mowers in Canberra. Fate had been cruel to Merrick, he decided, by blighting her soul with such a frame. A wiser god would have rendered her deformed from birth.

He managed to get re-taped but spotted no other patient in the clinic, although the nurse returned from another room bearing a male bedpan and blood-soaked cotton wool.

Anita was still in the hut when he got back. Their lunch had been delivered on a tray engraved with the ubiquitous cog pattern.

The tray featured roast duck and French champagne, and tied to its handles were tin cans trailing from string. Dessert was a small mock-wedding cake. On top of it a marzipan couple were frozen in a horizontal folk-dance.

Anita laughed. 'At least someone has a sense of humour.'

'The man's slowly killing us and you find it amusing?'

'No, David. You're slowly killing each *other*. Hadn't you noticed?' Just as abruptly, she began to cry. 'God, I want to get out of here.'

The tears he could relate to. He held her for a while, then made sure she ate the cooling duck. They both got a little drunk and she helped him undress. They stood, naked, holding each other, the top of her head on a level with his chest. He checked the towel over the mirror again and they made love with the drawn blinds blotting out the sun.

It began tenderly, a bandaged man and a willing sprite. Soon it was more urgent. She was wet with their sweat and writhing. The bandages on his hands didn't help and his raw knees hurt like hell, but it was worth it. She was astonishing.

Then they lay together, face down. He stroked her hair, her small, perfect breasts…

Someone coughed.

Connor twisted around as if stung.

'Good. You took the weight on your elbows.'

Sinclair was propping up the frame of the half-open door.

'One of the two marks of a gentleman. The other one?

A gentleman never pees in the bath. As you can imagine, true gentlemen are rare. Can I have some cake?'

Connor said, 'You're sick.'

'How was she? Fairer than the evening air? Sorry I can't join you. Got enough crutches to cope with right now.' He came in and cut himself some cake.

Anita turned on her back. 'Go away. Can't you see the poor thing's embarrassed?'

Connor started to get out of bed.

Sinclair raised his hand. 'Don't disturb yourself. I'll find my own way out.' He hobbled out of sight with his slice.

Connor lay back and shut his eyes.

'He's a shit – but we get on,' Anita said.

There was a knock at the door. Connor opened his eyes again. 'Christ!'

Half of Sinclair's crutch appeared through the door. He didn't bother to put his head in. 'Only me – with the news on the Rialto. The faceless one's just told me we have a free afternoon. Said I'd pass it on.'

Connor said, 'Great.'

The door swung shut.

Anita put her hand on his arm. 'Lighten up, David.'

'Lighten up, she says. Someone's slowly killing us and...'

'That's the point. Things are too terrible to stew about. The world's vicious. Cruel. None of us get out of here alive.'

'I can suck my own eggs, thanks.'

'No matter how well you live, the only real safeguard's despair.'

'Next time you come, bring an interpreter.'

She had a finger in the damp fluff between her legs. 'Next time I come'll be without *you*, unless you hurry up.'

Another one, he thought, with the body of an angel and the mind of a dung-beetle. He got off the bed and cut some cake – fruit-cake, crusted with thick, life-reducing icing. She arched her neck on the pillow. 'What torture are we up to now?'

'You mean the poem? "Shamed". Could mean anything.'

'And Dyson's choosing. Imagine. He'll want his pound of flesh.'

'God help the next loser.'

She was suddenly a little girl again, nurturing her famous despair. 'God help us all.' A tear ran into her ear.

Chapter Eleven

They were woken by the phone. Connor rolled stiffly out of bed to answer it, feeling as if his body had aged ten years. It was Vo, summoning them to breakfast beside the pool. Anita sat up in bed, looking like a pre-pubescent from a porn-art publication.

'Breakfast,' he said, 'by the pool in half an hour.' He hobbled back to the bed and sucked one of her small breasts right into his mouth. The towel had slid off the mirror. Neither of them cared.

They finally left the hut, scuffing the pine-needle carpet beneath the trees, heading for the pool where the white columns rose like Delphic ruins. Connor had travelled to Delphi as a youth, roughed it on the local bus from Athens, charmed by locals who dangled their hands in the aisle and danced their fingers around their worry-beads. The driver and the road soon explained why worry-beads were necessary. But the place, when he arrived, was so silent, so atmospheric, that he felt it renew him to the bones. T55 wasn't Greece but, today, was a champagne place. The bog-a-duck weather had passed and as he walked up the slope in the sun the fresh sea air had an essence that seemed to affect the light as well as the lungs. Above them, seagulls hung in the air as if suspended by strings.

By the pool was the usual smorgasbord and four small tables, each with two chairs. They filled their plates, then went to the table furthest from the pool. Connor pulled out a chair and Anita parked her pert rear. Her husband was at another table with only his crutches for company. Merrick, also solitary, had a table by the pool edge. Today she was queening it in pants and an elaborately knitted sweater.

Sinclair called across, 'Sleep well?'

Merrick said, 'You three are shameless. Disgusting.'

Sinclair looked across at her. 'Natural functions aren't disgusting. Only an unnatural approach to them.'

'I don't listen to degenerates.' Merrick glared out to sea.

Sinclair turned his attention to Connor. 'Seen Dyson?'

Connor, mouth full, shook his head. Sex, jeopardy and fresh air had sharpened his hunger.

Sinclair wiped his lips, put his napkin down precisely and stood up. 'Mind if I join you?' He poled himself over, exuding urbanity, dragged over another chair, cast his crutches on the ground and hopped a step to sit beside his wife, who promptly got up to get food. He looked at Connor brightly. 'Beautiful day.'

When Anita returned with lamb's fry and bacon he screwed up his nose. 'Hope they're not feeding us bits of his back.'

'Don't be revolting,' his wife said.

He refocused his attention on Connor, smiling, then turned to Anita. 'Queen and huntress, chaste and fair/ in your aluminium chair/ did sweetly you together lie/ like two piggies in a sty?'

'Give it a rest,' Anita said.

Merrick, who had eaten, continued to nurture her disdain. The cameras on the columns whirred and repositioned. Only the sound of their motors reminded them that they were being observed. That fact, Connor realised, soon faded from the front of the brain. Then he spotted Dyson, shuffling down the hill from the house. He looked haggard and stooped.

Sinclair observed the approaching spectre. 'He who was dead, liveth. He called loudly, 'Morning.'

Dyson didn't respond. He went slowly to the pool edge,

put a hand out to steady himself against a column and stared at the pulsing cleaner hose-pipe. His shirt was outside his pants and the thick padding of the dressing made it stand out from his body.

'Seems friendless and alone,' Sinclair murmured.

Connor agreed. It was Sinclair he couldn't fathom. The worse things got, the more flippant the man became. Not that his wife was much better. He felt out of his depth with both of them.

'Atten-chun.' The voice was Vo's. It came from two small speakers high on a column. Startled, everyone looked up. 'Today, last contest in series begin. When game finish, you all allowed leave island. Now, we draw for next winner and loser in way last loser, Mr Dyson, decide. Under shaker near this column, you find dice. All throw dice one time. Lowest number lose. Highest number win. Mr Dyson, as last loser, decide penalty. Begin.'

They all turned to look at the flagstones by the column. Sitting on the marble was a knee-high white cylinder. Presumably under it were oversized dice.

No-one bothered to investigate.

The voice went on, 'Will throw dice now.'

Merrick finished her last piece of toast, dabbed her thin but perfect lips, then looked at Dyson.

The ad-man stared back. 'Filthy shit-bag.'

She stood up with overdone self-composure, stretched her arms, gave a small yawn and said 'Ooo,' feasting on their attention. 'Twenty million dollars.' She said the words distinctly. 'You may not be interested in a fortune – but I am.' She swanned to the column and lifted the cylinder. Beneath it was a die the size of a fist. She picked up the die, displayed it to all, then up-ended the cylinder and dropped it in. It made a hollow clunk when it hit the metal base. 'Who'll go first?' She raised her perfect eyebrows.

'You're holding it,' Connor said.

She paused for a minute as if considering.

Her mouth became tight. Then she shook and shook the cylinder, one hand over the top. The die bounced and rattled. She kept shaking with all her strength.

Sinclair put a finger in his ear. 'You mind?'

Finally she threw – with her arms, her hips, the whole of her – as if sheer effort would ensure the highest score. The die bounced and blurred along the marble, rolling, twisting as it hit grooves in the flagging. It bounced against a column, fell back, one last flip... and was still.

Two.

Merrick's face was like stone. She stalked to her chair again and sat.

Dyson grimaced. 'Bitch. Better watch your arse.'

Merrick stood straight up again, walked to the column and picked up the die. She threw it in the cylinder and shoved the lot at Dyson. 'Do better.'

Dyson said, 'Kiss my ring.' He took it, wincing. He was unable to stand fully upright and any move seemed to pain him. He breathed in several times, standing still. His lips moved soundlessly.

Sinclair rolled his eyes. 'These people with a gift for intercessory prayer. Proves we're barely out of the trees.' He lifted his wife's drained coffee cup. 'More free radicals, beloved?'

The cylinder rattled again.

Connor watched the action, feeling hot nervousness suffuse his body. Dyson's back permitted modest shaking only. He did his best, flinching, then tipped the die out. It skittered a little way and lay still.

Five.

Dyson's mottled face leered at Merrick. 'So fuck *you*, bitch.' He shuffled to the coffee jug, dropping the cylinder in front of Connor.

Connor looked at it, then at Sinclair.

Sinclair smiled grimly. 'Be my guest.'

Connor shrugged, grabbed the cylinder, got up and went to pick up the die. The cameras on the columns followed as he loaded the tube and shook it twice, immediately tipping the die out. He didn't believe in arcane preliminaries.

Three. He was safe!

He wiped his hair back from his brow and the hand came away damp. He felt damp right down his back. He sat down, feeling huge relief, blood still pounding through his body.

It was Sinclair's turn. He didn't bother to rise. He took the cylinder from Connor and Dyson kicked across the die. This would be the decider.

All eyes and the cameras stared.

Sinclair loaded the shaker. He looked nonchalant enough but his hand trembled slightly as he tapped the cylinder with his fingers and stared up at the nearest lens. 'Enjoying this, Nicolae?' He put down the shaker, blew his nose, picked up his cup of coffee, had two sips and put it carefully down. Then he hitched up his sleeves and displayed his palms to the assembly. 'You'll notice the hands never leave the wrists.' He lifted the shaker, made an exaggerated fuss of jiggling it, and threw.

The die flew across the marble, teetered on one, then fell back.

Four.

People gasped.

Sinclair lurched back in his chair, relieved.

That got to you, Connor thought.

Dyson turned to look at Merrick, almost drooling. He'd won. 'So fuck *you*, cutie pie. You're busted. *Your* turn now, you auto-erotic hag.'

Merrick rose abruptly and, with one thrust, shoved him in the pool.

Dyson went in back first. Water sprayed the tables.

Almost immediately Dyson surfaced, roaring with pain as he was forced to move his arms to keep afloat. His shrieks became bubbles as his head went under twice but he finally made it to the safety of the steps. Merrick arrived there first. 'You filthy excuse for a man. Beware. Beware. I don't forgive.'

Dyson huddled on the steps, grimacing with pain.

She kicked at him but could not reach, then spun around, glaring up at the cameras.

The food table was beside her. She gripped the top and heaved it off its trestles. Crockery smashed on the tiles and food splashed and slid into the pool. She knocked over her own table, picked up a chair, smashed it against a column, then hurled it away. It landed on the grass, tipped on its back, legs pointing at her defensively.

Next she bent down, scooped up half a rockmelon and hurled it up at a camera. It missed narrowly and lobbed into the pool with a plop. The skirt of the pool-cleaner was already attempting to digest fried rounds of tomato. The rockmelon, Connor thought, was really going to puzzle it. Gulls shrieked overhead and dived on scattered bits of bacon.

Vo's voice crackled from the speakers. 'Next contest tonight. You have day free.'

It was over. Merrick drew herself erect, reset her face and smoothed back her hair – self-image re-established in that one ritual action. She walked regally off toward the huts, saying as she passed Connor, 'I must go and clean my teeth.'

Sinclair let out his breath. 'Talk about a mad woman's breakfast!' He flicked off his pants a triangle of toast that had landed, predictably, marmalade side down. 'Well, things could be worse.'

'They could?' Connor said.

'One could be married to *her*.' He looked up at the

camera again. 'Stiff cheese, Nicolae. I survived again.' Dyson lay face forward on the top step of the pool, moaning and plucking at his shirt.

Sinclair heaved himself onto his crutches and reached for Anita's hand. 'Mind if I borrow her back, old sock? Relief has quickened the old carcass. Could use a spot of cloaca.'

Anita helped her husband past Connor without looking up but brushed her hip against his thigh as she went by – a promise for the future.

Dyson was trying to unbutton his shirt with shaking hands. Connor scuffed through the broken plates and tried to help him up.

'Take it easy,' Dyson moaned. 'Christ. Ahh.'

Connor got him up and steadied against a column.

'Get this shirt off me. Get it off,' Dyson sobbed. Connor tried to work the shirt gently over his shoulders. The dressing was sodden and it looked as if any attempt to remove it would also remove part of Dyson's back. 'You'd better get back to the clinic.'

Dyson, whimpering and bent double, hobbled away toward the house.

Connor stared up at an inquisitive camera, jerked his middle finger up, then turned toward the sea.

The sun on the waves was dazzling. He squinted at the boat moored at the jetty. There was something odd about the foredeck. The large hatch was in two sections that both looked too heavy to lift. What was it for? It seemed too large – unless the boat ferried supplies from the mainland and the bow had been converted to a hold.

There was an orange near his feet. A perfect oval. Super-real. In fact, this whole incredible experience seemed more vivid than normal life. He retrieved the orange and started to peel it, feeling the sun and wind on his skin. With surprise, he realised how calm he was, now that the ordeal was past.

In a covert way he was glad that the buck had stopped at Merrick.

He realised he was in overload. His world had contracted to emphasise the moment. Perhaps Mould was right about the elemental life. This slope and this sea were existence. He was acquiring the focus men must experience in war.

It was some time since he'd thought of Tess. Tess in hospital, put there by Mould. Tess, her languid sensuality pleasuring another man. But what he wanted now was the firm, miniature body of Anita.

He split the orange into segments. It was sweet – the taste sharpened by his fear. 'Grow up, Connor,' he told himself. Wasn't that what Sinclair had said? And Anita had called him stuffy. They saw him better than he knew. He admired their wry nonchalance, which came from experience and poise he lacked. Then he recalled the rumbling voice of Mould – urging him to stop fence-sitting and contend. He'd be stretched, in this warrior's world, until whatever he was capable of emerged.

Gulls soared far above him in the champagne air. Somewhere inside he felt that his life had just begun.

Connor decided to occupy the morning by attempting to walk around the island. He wanted to check the layout and decided to stick to the coast for a first sweep. He clambered over the shore rocks and scuffed along a tiny beach. Fifteen minutes out, two troopers intercepted him, appearing ahead of him like statues on the rocks.

The men stood grinning, hands on hips. Neither moved or spoke. Connor stopped, turned to look out to sea, determined to tough it out. When he felt he'd made his statement, he started walking back the way he'd come. A minute later he looked back. They didn't seem to have followed.

Something was happening near the pond. A squad appeared to be setting a fire. Above a pile of sawn, dead branches they'd constructed a rustic spit. Two men, one with a sledgehammer, were driving metal Star posts into the ground. He was unsure but assumed an unpleasant motive. One man waved him back toward the huts. He turned and walked up the slope.

Inside his hut, on the middle of the bed, was a printed invitation:

> **Mr Mould**
> demands the pleasure of your company
> at 1800 hours, beside the pond
> for a farewell barbecue.
> Dress: informal.

Connor read the card again, feeling suddenly utterly tired.

Grace Merrick lifted her swimming costume off the towel-rail. It was dry.

She went back to the main room of the hut, carrying the costume and her waterproof sunscreen. She put both on the shelf, stripped naked and stood in front of the mirror. Mirrors fascinated her. And if there were a camera behind this one it was a bonus. Let him drool for what he couldn't have.

She cupped a hand under one breast and lifted it a little. They'd dropped a little over the years but the slope at the top was still enticing, the curve beneath the nipple still full.

She squeezed sunscreen into her palm, then started plastering it on her skin, covering herself all over.

Mould's right hand moved the small joystick projecting from the elaborate remote-control handset. From the under-lit square buttons across the console his finger selected one. The wall of scenes on the monitors didn't change. All were in monochrome except for the perfect colour reproduction of the 28-inch Sony broadcast-quality monitor in its frame of back-lit perspex. It was the best there was, but didn't compensate for the patches in his vision.

It showed the torso of Merrick, who seemed to be oiling herself all over… beneath the breasts, across her belly… He changed the scene to show Dyson, his shirt off, seated in the clinic, flinching and whimpering as the nurse attended to his back. Dyson was replaced by a top-shot of Connor on the toilet. His second time for the day.

Grace Merrick pulled the lycra up over her hips so that the scooped back revealed the perfect hollow that went down her spine to her buttocks. She put her arms through the straps and felt inside the stitched border to position her breasts more comfortably.

And now?

She donned her pants, jumper and shoes again. Was there anything else she dared take? Her bathroom drawstring basket would hold the soft cloth sunhat and her light jacket if she rolled it tight. Her pants belt could be used to secure the bag to her. Main thing was not to be seen.

She left her hut and walked through the pines, staying well inside the crescent of trees until they met the forest at the top of the slope, then continued deep into the wood. She didn't know where she was.

She listened for long seconds. No sound of pursuit, only the ocean and the chattering of a bird close above. She started down the slope, half slipping, grabbing tufts of grass for support. She could hear sea slapping against the rocks.

When she reached the shore she stopped to listen. Still no sound of anything but sea. And best of all, through the trees she could see the rock – a rock with green on top of it and shrubs at one side – the one she'd spotted the other day during her walk. It rose perhaps twelve metres above the water, looked climbable and was – how far away? At most three kilometres. She could make it if she took it slowly. From there a passing boat could see her. No-one would believe she could swim there. She'd won the 400 yards at college three years in a row. Everyone had idolised her. What marvellous years those had been.

She slipped off her pants and sweater, fastened the belt through the drawstring of the bag and slung it around her waist so that the bag hung down behind her.

Crouching low, she left the trees, glancing to left and right. No-one. It was hard to reach the sea across the brown, pitted rocks. They were encrusted, sharp enough to cut her feet. She felt beyond the last rock with her foot. The water had a bite and refrigerated her foot below the ankle. She gritted her teeth. She'd warm up. Anyway, she'd rather drown than let that fat swine lay a hand on her.

She placed her toes around the edge of the last rock, braced herself and dived.

The shock of the cold went through her. She kicked out strongly, doing the crawl. She was swimming across the chop, so breathing was no problem. She swam hard, warming a little. The oil would be helping. The bag flopped a bit behind her but didn't really get in the way. This was what she was good at. This was what she knew.

After perhaps ten minutes she trod water and checked her position.

The island was some distance behind her. In the troughs she couldn't see it at all. The waves were bigger here, two-metre rollers with the wind kicking spindrift off the crests. She rose and fell like a cork. It was a little frightening in the troughs with the next billow towering above. But as she rose on the crest, feeling the enormous power of the water beneath her, she could still see the island's soaring headland.

Sighting her destination was harder. She trod water, facing the other way. Nothing. It couldn't have moved...

It was a while before she saw it – far off and a long way behind her. She gasped. There must be a rip. It had pulled her far off course. Horrified, frightened suddenly, she floundered, swallowing a bitter mouthful of sea. She coughed, then turned and tried to swim into the swell. It was like climbing a mountain but she desperately plunged on.

After five minutes' swimming against the waves she checked her bearings again. She seemed to have drifted even further from the rock. The rip must be strong. She trod water, looked around again. Don't panic, she told herself. Panic kills. You can survive. You're brave. You're strong. You can get out of this.

But this wasn't the pool at college. This wasn't Malibu beach. This wasn't the heated pool in Seattle. This was open sea.

Blore walked into the operations room. 'She still there?'

'Yes sir.'

'Half an hour in one spot?'

'Tracer's static, sir.'

'What if she's taken off her shoe?'

'Hadn't thought of that, sir.'

'This isn't the P.L.A. You're paid to think. Get someone out there. Now.'

The wind seemed to be freshening. The spray on the crests stung her eyes. Once again she tried to see if there were another volcanic pinnacle she could reach. She saw nothing and, for all she knew, the next landfall was Tahiti.

Merrick turned her back on the spume and trod water. It was important not to waste energy. After all, no-one had to drown. You could always flop with your head in the water which increased the displacement or something so that you floated just below the surface but couldn't sink. Then, when you needed a breath, you simply pushed once with your arms and legs and raised your head out. You could survive for days like that. She'd try it.

The technique worked well, but the water was too cold. The chill, peripheral at first, was invading her body progressively. She needed to swim to keep heat in herself. Her fingers and feet were numb. All her warmth seemed to be pooling into the small cauldron of her belly. She concentrated on that. She was a fire, blackening from the outside, with the red coals still glowing in the centre.

Mad. Perhaps she'd been mad. She wasn't used to the scale of things here – the open sea. She'd always been too game.

She started to swim again, going with the tide. The island was now far behind her and there was no way to fight the sea and return. She could see perhaps half of the headland, the tops of the trees obscured by waves – waves overtaking her now, streaming past her on the crests, then dropping her into their troughs. Slowly, it dawned on her that she might die.

There was no point looking any more. There was no island, nowhere to swim to. So she swam with eyes shut. It hurt less that way. Instead of the sea, she heard her breath sighing through her. Instead of the sky, she saw behind her closed lids the child's face screaming inside the plastic bag. Screaming for breath as the condensation-fogged bag was blown out, sucked in, blown out… the last useless breaths. And now, for her, it'd be the same. Except it would be water sucked in, expelled, sucked in. How many more times could she raise her arms, kick her feet, move on like an automaton until the cold went right through her and she died?

Something bumped her side. Something solid and heavy, like the nudge of an inquisitive shark before it lunged and bit and tore, its scores of removable teeth rending the flesh, severing the bone, leaving nothing but a gash that stained the sea ink-red – trailed strands of offal in the water from a body like a punctured sack.

Terrified, she drew her legs up under her, forcing her head up, crying out. Not this way. Please, not this!

Then she smelt the diesel fumes and saw the doughnut of an orange lifebuoy with its salt-frayed edge of cording disappearing down the trough ahead of her.

Energy surged through her. The big boat was almost beside her – huge and solid, pitching in the swell, the red underbelly of its hull exposed at the bow as the sea lifted it by the waist, then thumping down again, spurting spray. A strong vibration in the water. The craft was quickly ahead of her and turning. She noticed the spar now, extended from the foredeck, trailing the rope with the lifebuoy. Men were leaning on the railing at the side, watching her without concern.

On the second pass she caught the lifebuoy and got herself inside. The big boat seemed dead in the water and had to go ahead again to stop rolling like a bathtub in the sea. As the slack took up on the line, she was jerked through the water, trailing a wake. She had to hang on hard if they were to haul her up. But her arms were still clamped around the buoy, which was lashed by a short rope to a heavy metal cable. She heard a winch as the cable took up and hauled her out of the water. The drag was painful but there was no way she'd let go. She saw the man Blore on the deck making winding motions, heard the winch motor rev, then she was dangling clear of the sea. Every man on board was staring at her. Staring at her beautiful body – the body they could worship but couldn't have. She angled her face toward the sky, as if martyred, to accentuate the arch of her back.

Chapter Twelve

Connor blinked, then sat up. How long had he been lying there? The sun had extinguished itself in the sea and the air was cold. He tried to see his watch. A quarter to eight. He took his leather jacket out of the wardrobe, shrugged it on, zipped the front, then went out onto the deck.

A line of lights was winking down the hill as they passed behind the greater darkness of the pines. A light was coming toward his hut. Now he could see the trooper holding it. A scar ran from his cheek across his scalp and he had one tooth missing in the front. He gestured for Connor to follow, then turned and trudged toward the lights, as immune to events as a district court sheriff.

The barbecue looked normal enough. Flares on poles set in a circle. A fire, ringed by stones, formed of thick logs that were now mostly glowing ash. A deer carcass was being roasted on a spit and the sweet aroma of it, together with the faint pine-needle scent from the trees, accentuated the horror of the coming night's proceedings. To the side, a long trestle table held bottles, glasses, salads and desserts. Two white-aproned troopers waited behind it to serve the compulsory guests.

Connor passed Vo, who stood talking to Blore, her ravaged face a moonscape in the glow. She seemed to converse in a code from *Jane's Defence Weekly* which, together with her accent, made her almost incomprehensible.

'…our French friend. Four AMX10 RC.'

'Shipping to?'

'Libya.'

'With 105s?'

'Anti-armour. And three Sikorsky CH 53G. Parts guarantee. Ex-FRG.'

'Who's ripping off the Heeresfluger? And the SRX engine ports?'

'6F11 ship tomorrow.'

The huge man nodded deferentially as if the tiny creature had him on a string.

Sinclair and Anita stood together, warming themselves by the fire. She wore a child's parka and ski pants over her child-gymnast's frame. The fire outlined her legs – Dresden china body with earthenware mind.

Sinclair turned and raised his glass. 'Drinks over there.'

Connor nodded and moved to the table.

One of the white-clad troopers, a good-looking Fijian, raised his eyebrows.

'I'll have the cab sav,' Connor said and, as the man poured it, he added, 'Cold night.'

'Be colder if we get a southerly. Straight off the Antarctic.'

'So what do you think of all this?' Connor hoped to draw him out.

'Good.'

'Why?'

The man chuckled. 'Light relief.'

Connor turned to the man beside him. 'And you agree with that?'

The second man, dark-skinned with the features of a sheikh, gave an inward smile. 'Mr Mould is our sultan and he has our soul's ear. He metes out utter justice. We are proud to be the dust of his feet.'

Sinclair called to Connor, 'Military mind – spans all nationalities. Individuality in intaglio. Can't suborn the buggers – I've just tried. So come here and get warm.'

He joined the Sinclairs, wary.

'Hello, David,' Anita said.

'Hi.'

Sinclair stared at the carcass. 'Another night of venison and anxiety?'

'Where're the other two?'

His wife pushed a log further into the fire with her foot. 'We think Merrick's run away. Saw her leave her hut at lunchtime. She looked furtive.'

'Can't run away on an island.'

'Perhaps she found a boat.'

'I've seen no boats – except the big one. Anyway she wouldn't get far. They'll have all kinds of gear to track us. Bet they always know what we're up to.'

'Cheer up, old socklet. We're not dead yet. And tonight, thank God, we're mere spectators.'

Twin lights stabbed through the dark. The whine of the skid-steer mobile platform, rocking and grinding down the hill. It stopped abruptly just behind them and, as the two small round headlights died, he could see a struggling white-clad figure on board. Grace Merrick was being manhandled down.

'Bastards!' she screamed. 'Bastards!'

The men frog-marched her toward the fire. She cursed, trying to kick out at their legs, trying to bite and twist but despite her strength she couldn't do much. They had both her arms behind her, palms twisted up, forcing her to stumble forward, half-bent. Her head thrashed and she swore and spat as they pushed her to the stakes – four star-posts driven at an angle into the ground. She wore the terry-towel robe from her cabin. It seemed to be all she had on.

They forced her forward onto her knees, then each man took a limb and pulled. She fell on her stomach, biting grass, trying to kick back like a steer. A fifth trooper brought rope from the vehicle. He knew exactly what to do. He doubled it for each limb, using a lark's head hitch around wrists and ankles, with a half-hitch to follow, although there was no way she'd get any slack. Then he took up the line around the posts with a clove and two half-hitches. When he'd finished she was spreadeagled, barely able to turn her head.

The troops filed to the food table for their roasts.

'I don't like this,' Connor said.

'What are they doing to her?' Anita asked anxiously.

'Ask Dyson,' her husband replied. 'And speak of the devil.' Dyson was behind them.

'What's going on?' Connor asked him.

'You'll see.' Firelight emphasised his sagging face. He was still half crouching but had changed his shirt and looked more alive. In his hand was a small metal box, with ventilator slits on two sides, connected to a rubber-covered handle by an insulated cord. From the handle projected two metal rods with brass lock-nuts in each of the ends. The nuts secured a length of stainless-steel wire, which formed a narrow loop like a prong. The wire was blue-grey on the loop as if it had been repeatedly heated.

'I'm just following instructions,' Dyson said. 'They asked how I wanted to do it. You have to say.'

One of the men was connecting cables to the back of the box. The cables snaked back to the buggy. The man trudged back to the vehicle and was lost in the dark. A small motor kicked, started up. A portable generator.

'Shit. It's a bloody poker-work machine,' Connor said.

Dyson licked his lips. 'She didn't mind scorching your arse. Or flogging my back raw. She's disfigured me for life. You can't imagine – I can barely stand. Even the guys on the windjammers didn't get flogged like that. She tried to dust me. She's brain-dead – got the IQ of a pitbull.'

Sinclair said, 'He has a point.'

'And it's not going to cripple her,' Dyson whined on. 'They wanted me to use a branding iron straight out of the fucking fire.' The racket of the generator drowned the rest of his words.

The faceless one beckoned Dyson from the stakes. 'Shaming begin now. Come.'

Dyson glanced at them, shrugged defensively, then yelped as it stretched his back. He shuffled to the scene of his crime, the cables following him like a tail.

'Where begin?' Vo asked.

'Just her arse. Told you before.'

'Message will go on bottom.' She gestured to one of the men. Dyson put the box on the grass and knelt beside Merrick. It took him some time to do it. He was obviously in pain and flinched with every move. A trooper handed him a pair of shears. He complained about his back. 'Can't stretch.' The trooper knelt on the other side of Merrick and there was the flash of light from the blade. He sliced into the towel robe, starting at the hem then pushing up to rip the material, cutting through the belt, continuing halfway up her back to the collar. He didn't part the material. Then he stood.

'Begin,' Vo said.

Dyson flicked the switch on the transformer box. The troops were close by, watching. Despite their professional disinterest, they wanted to see the woman's body. One had a video camera on his shoulder, recording the scene for Mould.

Dyson paused dramatically, then flicked the cut material to the sides.

Grace Merrick in the flesh was fantastic: a hedonist's dream. The firelight on her bronzed skin, the muscles of her legs, the curve of her back as she strained... An athlete's frame, every muscle beautifully formed and defined – the Girl from Ipanema preserved.

'One wonders,' Sinclair drawled, 'how such a magnificent body could house such a rudimentary brain.'

The wire probe glowed red. Dyson picked up the handle, bending from the waist, and blew on it. The glow barely dimmed. He held it up for all to see. 'Now the bitch gets hers.'

'You touch me and I'll kill you,' Merrick snarled.

'This one's for my back. I'm going to burn your butt off.'

'I'll kill you. I'll kill you.'

Dyson grinned. 'Cute arse. Shoulda been a boy. Got the balls for it, shitty, bull-dyke bitch.'

'You touch me and *you're dead*.'

'Stinking, stuck-up bitch.'

'You're dead,' she shrieked. 'Dead! *Dead!*'

Dyson looked momentarily concerned, then hit stride again. 'Like hell. This is payback. Moment you picked up the whip, you had this coming.'

'Too much talk,' Vo snapped. 'Begin. Burn bottom now.'

'Hang about,' Dyson said. 'Gotta get this right. Gotta art-direct this a bit.' He ran a finger lightly over Merrick's tightly flexed rear. At the touch of his finger her whole body bucked.

Anita turned away. 'I'm going back to the hut.' As she began to walk out of the firelight, Sinclair nodded and followed.

He was blocked by Blore's leg-of-mutton forearm. 'You stay – and watch.'

Sinclair, as tall as the man was solid, looked down on him with distaste but knew he didn't have a choice.

'Wait till you see the whites of their eyes,' Connor muttered.

'I can even see his blackheads.' Sinclair mimicked Blore's scowl, then turned around again to stand by Connor. 'What does one do, one asks oneself?'

'Nothing,' Connor said. 'Yet.'

The glowing wire descended. Dyson checked his audience, grinning, then turned back. The wire touched. Merrick jerked, bellowed. Dyson touched the probe to her again. This time the flesh depressed and sizzled. No blood – only the charred flesh and curling smoke. She was bucking so much that a trooper straddled her legs to hold her down. Dyson couldn't do it. He was pained enough using the probe.

The glowing wire lowered again and this time the smoke was considerable. He was holding the loop at an angle, drawing it along with an engraver's care – charring a dark channel in the flesh.

Merrick's bellows drowned the generator and everybody knew that, for her, the most diabolical part of the torture was disfigurement, not pain.

Connor felt sickened, angry. Merrick might have delusions of grandeur but to do this to a woman and to destroy such a body was depraved. For the first time he wished to help her. But he knew this wasn't the time. Feeling hot pity for the woman, he looked down, not wanting to watch.

When he looked up again, a straight, three-centimetre-long burn was carved in Merrick's left buttock. Dyson, biting his lip, now seemed to be inscribing a circle. He blew smoke away from his face, fighting her struggling body.

Merrick was berserk. Her struggles were terrible, her hands blue from tugging on the ropes. She'd slightly loosened one stake and a trooper had his hand on the top of it. Letters were forming in her flesh. V, then A.

Connor's hands were fists. Merrick or not, this was vile.

Vo looked on impassively as the camera recorded the scene. The event was so extraordinary it was impossible not to watch.

VAI…

Merrick's perfect left cheek was now embroidered with a black-charred furrow perhaps half a centimetre deep reading VAIN.

Dyson held the probe above her other buttock. The message apparently went on. The smoke and sizzle resumed. They could smell her burning flesh as she writhed and tore at the ropes. She no longer shrieked – her breath was hoarse.

VAIN BIT…

VAIN BITC…

'Full marks for critical judgment,' Sinclair said.

Connor glanced up at the tall man who was scratching his ear. If he found this distasteful, he was determined not to show it.

Dyson put down the handset and grinned at Merrick. 'Finished. Hope you like it.'

Merrick yelled, '*You… are… dead.*'

Dyson put both hands on one knee and winced. He groaned as he struggled to his feet, then shuffled back nervously as the trooper who had tied the woman up began loosening the ropes.

Dyson backed closer to the squad. 'You're going to restrain her, I hope? I'm in no shape to handle trouble.'

The men ignored him, collecting the transformer, pulling out the stakes. The man with the camera crabbed sideways, ready to record the next events.

Merrick was on her knees, beside herself with rage. Hands behind her, feeling for damage, red weals on her ankles and wrists. The next instant, despite her pain, she was after Dyson, the ripped robe flapping around her. It was almost off her shoulders as she grasped the protesting ad man around the neck and carried him to the ground with her rush. His back hit first and he screamed with pain. Then she was all over him like a panther. The robe fell down her arms and covered him like a sheet. Her whole body was exposed but in her rage she cared for only one thing – piercing his windpipe with her thumbs.

The sight of her full, firm breasts was spectacular but Dyson's bulging eyes showed he didn't consider it worth dying for. As he kicked and flailed she clung on until he rammed both hands under her chin, pushing her head back far enough to crack her neck.

Connor knew the way to break the hold – hands together, both arms driving up like a wedge. But Dyson was no judoka and his face now matched the redness of Merrick's wrists. Her arms were longer and stronger than his and she clung like a clam. Every twist he made, she countered. He hadn't breathed for probably thirty seconds. The troops laughed. They liked this a lot.

Dyson kneed her in the crotch. She wasn't expecting that and lost balance. He managed to roll her, twisting as her grip went, gasping. As he tried to scramble away she grabbed his leg and bit.

He kicked back with the other foot. She saw it coming but it connected. Finally he was loose and on his feet. She would have caught him except the robe tripped her. She fell on her side and he was away.

She lay in the circle of spectators, naked, branded, bruised, then stood up without a word, trying to pull the cut robe around her. She glared around, face filled with pain, then looked down and sobbed.

Vo stepped forward. 'Trial finish. All meet in house in half an hour.'

Connor walked up behind the half-bare woman and gently put his hands on her shoulders. She shuddered like a colt but didn't resist. As he guided her out of the circle, Vo stood in their path. As if the camaraderie of disfigurement had touched her, she stood back to let them through. Blore, ever attentive to Vo, signalled his squad to fall back.

He walked Merrick toward the huts. She was shivering terribly and trying to wipe her running nose with her hand. He gave her his handkerchief and she blew hard, one nostril after the other. He wasn't sure why he was helping her. He could still feel the burn on his thigh.

'Better have a very hot shower and put on something warm. Got any antiseptic cream?'

She shook her head, sobbing.

'I have. I'll get it for you.'

'What did he do to me? What did he *do*?' Her hand was behind her. Her bottom must have been on fire.

'He wrote words.'

'*What* words?'

'You'll see.'

'You don't have to help me.' She was trying to control her tears, as if they didn't conform to her self-image. 'I can take care of myself.'

He continued to walk beside her.

She turned to him, eyes manic. 'You know I'll kill him. He won't get away.'

'U-huh.' He saw her up the steps, then crossed to his own hut for the tube of Bepanthen. These last days he'd used a lot of it himself. As he reached her hut again he heard her yell of rage and knew that she was looking in her mirror. 'I'm putting the tube inside the door,' he called out, opening the door a crack and pushing it in, as one might push food through bars to a wild beast.

As he walked back to his hut he felt a flicker of irony quite at odds with his sympathy of moments ago. He'd have a scar on his thigh. But Merrick would have more – a permanent character reference – unless her plastic surgeon was a pip. Yea and verily, Dyson's back, and his thigh, were avenged.

Then his sorrow for her returned; his sorrow for them all. Mould, he suddenly understood, was removing their treasures one by one. His security. Sinclair's superiority. And Merrick's cherished appearance. Unless somehow they stopped this, he'd break them. They had to do something.

Grace Merrick applied the ointment, as if it might magically remove the furrows with the livid skin on their edges that spelt out the hideous words. The pain didn't matter. What mattered was that her body was destroyed. Dyson would pay. She'd tear out his eyes.

She was sobbing and trying not to. Her rule was never to cry before 9pm, but she couldn't stop.

A knock. She mopped her streaming face with a towel and looked around for something to put on.

Vo's voice. 'Be ready in five minute for final event of first round. You not come, we come and get.'

Chapter Thirteen

The last event of the evening was even more bizarre. The usual procession through the darkness to the bunker on the hill, following the silent troopers with their lamps. The gathering in the foyer.

Sinclair on his crutches, surly and trapped. 'For God's sake, what's this about? We've had the last trial.'

His wife added, 'They said we could go now.' She looked birdlike, eyes darting around the room.

'Had enough of this shit,' Dyson said. His open collar exposed red marks on his throat and his shirt was still flecked with blood. The troopers ignored all comments, standing guard in silence.

Finally Merrick was ushered in. She looked sucked dry, her face haggard, as if the moisture had been removed from her flesh. For the first time she showed her age. She wore a simple skirt and sweater. Connor knew she couldn't sit. He found it painful enough himself.

Dyson was ready for fight or flight but she didn't even look at him. Certainly the men on either side of her would have stopped her if she'd gone for him. But this pointed disregard was ridiculous. No attitude she could assume would ever erase the image of her, bare and bitter, writhing on the ground.

Connor had pitied her for the short time that she cried. But now, with her tears gone and queenly air resumed, she seemed pathetic.

A trooper opened a door off the reception room and they were herded down a corridor and ushered into the library. Two men took up positions either side of the door.

A single table-lamp illuminated the centre of the room. They clustered around the light, no-one sitting, no-one speaking. Sinclair stared at the lampshade, his customary banter long gone. Dyson didn't dare open his mouth, afraid of triggering an attack.

Anita glanced sideways at Connor, her eyes saying, 'Now what?'

He raised one bandaged hand to say, 'Who knows?' Except for her, they were all cripples.

A crack of light widened in the wall as the door opened at the end of the room. The shapes of bodies against the light: two troopers, Vo, and Mould's wheelchair, with Blore behind pushing him into the room. The chair stopped just out of the light. The troopers stood one either side of it. Vo was cradling a clipboard.

Mould looked better. The fluid tap must have relieved him. He contemplated his victims, head moving slowly with his eyes. 'Enjoy your barbecue?'

Merrick stared over his head, body rigid. She must have been hurting like hell.

Mould chuckled. 'Good, Grace. You're learning.'

Sinclair said, 'Spare us the gloating.'

'Not as cheerful, Hanford?' Mould's grin was sly.

'Isn't it time you died?'

'Poor Hanford's met a bigger fish. I can see how that must grate.'

Merrick was actually trembling, as if she could only just stand still. Blore had his eye on her, ready to block her if she went berserk.

Mould saw it. 'Relax, Grace. You still look splendid with your clothes on.'

She stood without speaking or moving. Connor could imagine what that was costing her.

'And as for the lovers… you'll be parted.' Mould looked

at Connor and Anita, smiling. 'You all leave here tomorrow at 0900 hours. Your return flights from Auckland have been adjusted and we've done our best with the connections. Itineraries are now in your cabins.'

Connor said, 'You're letting us go?'

'Not entirely.' Mould put two fingers to his chin. 'My eyes and ears will go with you. You're… beginning phase two of the game.'

Vo walked forward and handed each of them a piece of paper. Merrick's was first but she failed to put out her hand so Vo let the copy flutter to the carpet in front of her. Connor glanced at the laser-printed verse and closely spaced type, not reading it, looking back at Mould.

'You now have stanza two,' Mould said, 'and a full set of rules. I suggest you study them. They map your immediate future.'

Dyson was squinting at the paper. 'You mean we play the fucking game even when we leave here?'

'You do indeed, Adrian. A chance to suffer or grow rich – in the field. It'll add emphasis, spice to your life. And as you go forth, your money'll multiply. I refer, of course, to the interest set aside for you, which in the last three days has increased by over $1600. No, what you've just experienced was merely an introduction – minor things to get you in the swing. And you've co-operated well. So now, the good news. I've… removed the gold embargo, Hanford. Your new issue's safe. And Grace? Your useless brother has… just been released from jail. He's been obliged to stupefy himself with Stella, which took no great persuasion, and he's been placed in a… taxi on his way to the Khan Al Khalili market. Considering the unsettling driving habits of the Cairenes, whether he'll arrive is debatable. But then, he's no great loss.'

His tone changed. 'It's time to put away childish things. The game now becomes more serious. So, once again, I acquaint you with the rules. If you're not… clear about them, you could… hurt yourselves very badly. Duyen will restate them. Listen well. Ask questions if you have doubts.'

Vo lifted her clipboard and read slowly. 'Rule One. A draw will be… will be held for…'

Mould turned to her. 'On second thoughts, Duyen, perhaps you'd better give it to the Major.'

She handed the clipboard up to Blore. The huge man took it from her with the delicacy of naked devotion. He then placed two fingers of his shovel hand under the flap of his battle-jacket pocket and fished out a pair of half-framed spectacles. He flicked them open, applied them to his nose and softly cleared his throat.

Rule One. A draw will be held for the winner and loser of each game except where there's a switch. (See Rule three.)

Rule Two. A previous loser may be invited to refine the details of the penalty in the next game. (See Rule Five.)

Rule Three. A winner refusing to enforce a penalty automatically becomes the loser for the next game and the loser the next winner. This is termed a 'switch'. (See Rule Four.)

Rule Four. If this switch occurs and the winner refuses to enforce a penalty, that penalty is applied by Mr Mould. (See Rules Five and Six.)

Rule Five. A loser can only avoid a penalty once. If a penalty fails to be enforced on a subsequent loss, it will be enforced by Mr Mould.

Rule Six. Players discussing the game with anyone but the participants and organisers will incur a separate penalty enforced by Mr Mould.

Rule Seven. Only two penalties can be sustained by any one player in succession.

'Thank you, Major,' Mould said. 'We've been playing strictly to those rules. As you see from the poem, the penalties are becoming… specific. In other words, you've had your fun. Now you'll do as I dictate.'

Sinclair was studying the rules. 'I'm doing my best but I'm no Grand Master.'

'It's complex,' Mould said, 'but you'll see the logic as we progress.'

Connor said, 'What's this switch?'

Mould nodded. 'In brief, it means you can place yourself in trouble if you initiate a switch. If the winner refuses to enforce the… penalty after a switch, he or she attracts that penalty as well as becoming the… next loser. For example, it was fortunate for Adrian that he… stabbed Hanford – or he would have been stabbed himself, as well as becoming the loser in the subsequent game. See it now?'

Sinclair said, 'What's the penalty in Rule Six?'

'Perhaps, like the ladybird, your… house'll be on fire and your children gone.'

Connor said, 'So if Grace hadn't or I hadn't…'

'If you not be horse,' Vo said, 'next time you flog Mrs Merrick. If you refuse to flog her – then we flog you.' You see, penalty increase in…' She glanced at Mould.

He supplied the word. '…severity. It's a forcing bag.' He looked at Merrick. 'You'd understand that, Grace? I still recall your beautiful iced cakes.'

Merrick was shaking with rage. It was painful to watch. But her pride restrained her from cutting loose.

Connor was frowning at his rules. 'So if a switch happens twice?'

Mould smiled. 'Considering collusion? Don't. Whatever you try, I'm ahead of you.'

Sinclair was also studying the rules, his sharp mind working on the mosaic, looking for the best moves but not finding any. 'Very clever. You're a malevolent swine.'

'...Who finds revenge exceedingly sweet. And now...' He held out his hand and Vo gave him one of the sheets of paper. 'And now, for those of you still not familiar with it,' he glanced at Merrick, 'I'll read the second round stanza.' His deep voice filled the room.

> Beast slaughtered and wagon smashed
> Wife raped,
> Nearest kin destroyed,
> Crippled and halt,
> Stagger into another dawn.

He looked up and beamed. 'There remains just one more... event to conclude the formal part of the evening.' He turned to Vo. She felt below the back of the wheelchair and straightened, holding a plain ceramic jar.

'In this jar,' she said, 'are four ball bearings. Two are white, one red, one green. Green win. Red lose. Very simple.' Holding the jar high, she moved to Dyson. 'You take one.'

Dyson looked at Vo's blighted face, nervously licked his lips, said his inner incantation, then reached into the jar. He withdrew his hand and displayed a small ball between his finger and thumb. It was white. He grinned. 'Not my problem, huh?'

'Congratulations, Adrian,' Mould said.

Vo now stood in front of Merrick. The branded woman stood rigid, disdaining to look at anyone or to respond.

Mould said, 'It doesn't matter. One default makes no difference.'

Vo continued to Connor, holding the jar high. He let his breath out slowly, raised his hand and felt inside, picked a ball and withdrew it. Green.

Green wasn't good at all.

Mould clapped twice. 'Excellent. Mr Connor wins. I can see from his expression, that he… now understands that both winners and losers are unpleasant things to be.' He beamed again. 'That leaves Hanford to decide the matter as… Grace seems too tired.'

Sinclair placed his hand in the jar and held up his selection with cold anger.

The bearing was red.

Mould rocked forward and back slightly with enjoyment. 'Goodness, Hanford. Another regrettable loss. You've probably earned Connor a free trip to Cape Town. Perhaps the… lovers'll be reunited after all.'

Again he looked at them all in turn, his lizard eyes lingering on each face as if the pleasure of it were almost sensual. 'Now I suggest you all try to… get some sleep. Because your trials have… barely begun.'

Chapter Fourteen

Connor found himself booked with Dyson on a Qantas flight to Sydney – first class. Dyson's seat was across the aisle. Mould's staff apparently had some scruples.

He tried to ring Tess from the airport but her office answerphone was on. He left a message to say he was returning and he'd get home from Mascot himself. He'd left Thursday. It was Monday. The five days seemed more like a year. He sat in the Auckland airport terminal extension with its feeling of space and calm and light, watching the Japanese tourists, the patient mothers with impatient children, the self-important, callow businessmen shouting into six-watt, 800-Megahertz executive comforters while the antennae cooked their brains. Back in this womb of the familiar, it was hard to believe the island existed.

He looked at his bandaged hands. Thin plasters now. But beneath his jeans and jacket his joints were swathed in gauze. Dyson was with him, following with the inevitability of a pull-along toy.

'Can't bear to put a coat on. Agony. Sure I'm not bleeding again?'

'I don't give a shit if you bleed to death.'

'You were the klutz who ordered the flogging. Chopped liver. Remember?'

'Watch it, Dyson. I haven't forgotten your performance on the hill.'

'I'd had a skinful, for Chrissake.'

'Still have.'

'Horse-shit.'

'You smell like a pub carpet on January the first. Stay away from me.' Connor moved to another row of seats.

Dyson picked up his natty cabin bag and followed. 'Look, we gotta talk this over, gotta stick together. You're the only person in Australia I can talk to about this.'

'Breaking my heart.'

'We're in this together, remember.'

'Rack off.'

Dyson didn't move. He sat two seats away like a schoolboy in disgrace until it was time for them to board. Connor got up.

'Hang about. Don't have your address.' Dyson attacked his bag zips, looking for a pen.

Connor left him scuffling.

The house looked the same – the letterbox crammed with junk mail, the grass longer. She wasn't home. The kitten rolled on its back to be petted. He picked it up and it clawed him with joy. There was a message propped against the blender.

Quiche in fridge. Salad in bowl. Letters in studio. See you tonight. Love, T.

He unpacked his bags, poured an orange juice, then walked to the studio behind the house and keyed in the security code. The place smelt musty, unused. He picked up the letters she'd poked under the door, slid behind his desk and reached for the letter-opener. One overdue cheque. The rest – bills and reminders about subscriptions. The fax started up behind him. When he heard it slice the page he fished the stack of papers out.

One glance at the crest on the top sheet focused his attention. A circular cog, but not Rotary. He gripped the paper, heart pounding.

> Mr Connor,
> Welcome home. This to advise you that Grace Merrick will be consulted about the nature of the next game and we will forward further details within two days. Please make no arrangements that restrict your time until flight details are established.

There was no signature.

'Shit. *Shit.*' He crumpled the sheet, stood up, locked the studio and went back to the house. He needed to take off the bandages and have a proper shower. He needed... He didn't know what he needed. With the game hanging over him, the familiar things around him seemed alien. He had a strange impression that his life didn't fit him any more. He stood in the kitchen, staring at an *Australian Geographic* calendar with an illustration of the Numbat and Port Lincoln Ringneck in a scene lacking all perspective. Compared with the island, the silent house seemed as two-dimensional as the drawing.

Then Mould's words echoed in his head. 'I have something in mind that should reach him.'

Rex. Rex Connor.

Perhaps he could do something in time...

He dragged up the tilt-a-door, pulling it sidewards to prevent it sticking in its frame. His red 505 squatted in the garage, 170,000 on the clock. Would the solenoid jam again? The ageing wiring now had a relay to boost the amps. He got in, turned the ignition. The engine coughed and caught. Relieved, he waited for the roughness to settle, then headed north over the Suspension Bridge, toward the tree-lined northern suburbs, watching the traffic in the rear-view mirror to see if anyone was following. He took the back route, Arterial into Pentecost, with a right into Bobbin Head Road.

The sister on the desk in the nursing home had the pallid,

overfed body of a woman who served behind a counter in a cake shop. She kept shaking her head. 'No, Mr Connor's not here at present. I told you, his relatives have the care of him for the week.'

'What relatives?'

'His brother.'

'Brother?'

Her disapproving look. 'I'll verify if you wish. It'll be on his progress file.' She turned to a filing cabinet, slid open a drawer, her uniform ridging under her arms. 'Here we are.' She pulled out the file. 'James Connor. He's been visiting him for some time. We all know him.'

'Big man? Looks like a Maori?'

'No, looks very like Rex. They could be twins. He's been visiting for years – taken him twice before. We've never had trouble. Of course, with dementia patients there's a metal bangle on the wrist with our name and phone number, so it's unlikely we'd ever lose one.'

'You have an address?'

'We have an address for next of kin which we can't divulge under the Privacy Act.'

'That where he is?'

'We don't ask trusted relatives where they take patients. That's their business.'

The phone rang. She turned to answer it. 'Sunnytide Nursing Home. Yes, one minute please.' She walked to the corner of the corridor, all broad rump and white stockings, and called, 'Dr Brennan there?'

Connor snatched up the file and scanned it. The address was on the back. Reciting it mentally, he dropped the file back on the desk and was out of there before she turned.

He reached his car, jotted down the address, then opened the glove-box and lifted out his street guide. He located the cross-street, started the car and lead-footed it. The old

Peugeot struggled grudgingly beyond the stately speed it knew.

He couldn't enter the nondescript street. It was blocked by people and vehicles. The cloud of black smoke told him why. He left the car and walked. The place was a wood-and-fibro Housing Commission clone. Behind the low wall were three dead rose bushes and a square of unrelieved grass. Canvas hoses snaked across the grass and the tiled roof was about to fall in. The heat of the fire scorched into the lungs. There were two pump trucks with side-mounted panels and three teams manning hoses – 38mm with black diffusion nozzles. In the great days with Rex, they'd done a series on the Fire Department. The gear was different then. Now they had yellow and black fire-resistant uniforms and US-style helmets with visors and neck-flaps. A hose team was backing out of the front door, the nozzle set to 'fog', covering two search-and-rescue men. He could see them now as the mist of water settled the smoke. They had yellow CABO air-set bottles on their backs and carried something between them that looked like a sack. The clutch of onlookers gasped as the rescue crew reached the front fence and put their burden down. One man ripped off his black rubber headset and threw up.

Rex Connor was still alive but some of his body was burnt away. In his hairless, charred head with its oozing face, the black hole of his open mouth was contorted in a scream – a scream drowned by the crackle of the building and the shriek of the ambulance two blocks away. On what was left of his wrist, a metal bangle was still visible.

Connor got as near as he could. The smell of burning flesh was nauseating.

A fireman pointed at him. 'You! Out of the area.' He backed off, eyes streaming, chest heaving, walked a little way along the footpath and flopped. The scene was blotted out for him by tears. He was dimly aware the ambulance had come and gone. He squatted on the grass verge, sobbing. The sound of the fire had died to a hiss with the occasional crack of an exploding beam. The smell, that incredible smell, still hung around his nostrils.

Someone was shaking him. 'Okay, then, are you?' He looked up to see a helmet and, beneath it, a hand, ripping back the velcro tab on the high collar. 'Bit of a shock? Always is. Doesn't matter how often you see it.'

'He was… still alive.'

'Went to a refinery, once. Crude oil boiled over. Fireball – thousand feet in the air. Found this bloke in a portable hut. Clothing on fire. Horribly burned. Looking at me. Alive.' He took of his helmet, wiped the soot from his face.

'The smell…'

'Smell's the worst. Gets inside you. Can't forget it. I can go into a room where a fire's been and tell if someone's been burnt alive there.' He called to the station officer of the other crew. 'Position in hand. Released and returning to station.'

'He won't live?' Connor asked.

'No way. Best thing.'

'You sure?'

'No skin left. We're trained in first aid but doesn't help much. And we don't get counselling, either. Some blokes can't hack it. Depends on your type. You okay?'

'I'm okay.'

'I'd go home and have a few tinnies. Takes the edge off it.'

'Thanks very much. Appreciate you talking to me.'

'You're welcome.'

The front door slammed. He heard the rustle of parcels. 'David?'

She came into the sunroom. 'My God.'

He'd taken off the bandages and showered. He sat in his

shorts and a T-shirt, three empty beer cans beside him. He stood up and said flatly, 'Hello.'

'What happened?'

'I fell down some rocks.'

'You look terrible.' She came close and kissed him, frowning. 'Should have bandages on those knees.'

'I'm letting the air get to them. How are you?'

'Fine. Neck's much better. The car'll be another week. So? Was it successful?'

'I survived.'

'Why didn't you say you'd be so long?'

'Didn't know then.'

'You could have phoned.'

'It's an island. Phone worked once and went dead.'

'Thought you'd hung up on me.'

'Was the line.'

'You sure everything's all right?

He sat down again, trying to sound normal. 'I just went to visit Rex. He's dying.'

'*Dying?*'

'He was burnt in a fire. They say he can't survive.'

'That's awful.'

'So I'm feeling a bit…'

'When did this happen?'

'Today. Saw the firemen drag him out.'

She sat beside him, put her arm around him. 'David, I'm so sorry.'

As he told her the bare details, the silly tears came back again. He was thinking of the great years. He and Rex together, killing 'em. And the studio at the bottom of the garden, disrupted by the flamboyance, the noise, the untidiness of Rex, instead of as it was now – all neat and prim, waiting for clients that didn't come.

'Just terrible.' Tess was upset too. 'At least he's out of his pain. I mean, it wasn't much of a life for him. You think he suffered very much?'

He blew his nose hard. 'I'd rather be crucified than that.'

'What a terrible, terrible accident. The trouble with those things is there's no-one you can blame. D'you manage to see his brother?'

'Doesn't have a brother.'

'Must have had. Perhaps he never told you.'

'Perhaps.' No point in saying more.

When Grace Merrick arrived in New York the five boroughs were sweltering in heat. She took a cab from JFK. It was only $38 to Manhatten, including tip and the Midtown Tunnel toll. She arrived at her sister's, pressed number six and waited.

Her sister's voice. 'Hello?'

'It's Grace. I have two cases.'

'Welcome to alienation city. Hold it right there. I'll come down.'

After her sister had hugged her, she held her at arm's length. 'You look like you've had a holiday in Sarajevo. Who did you fly with? Air China?'

It was a three-floor walk up, with narrow stairs. The apartment itself was small but it had two bedrooms, which was more than Grace had had in LA. They dumped her bags in the second room and her sister fussed, 'Coffee?'

'I'd prefer something cold.'

'Okay. Thirty-five per cent reconstituted orange or ice-water with a twist?'

'Water.'

'Coming up.' She vanished into the fridge. 'Sorry. No lemon.'

She sat in the small sitting room with its view of exhausted pot plants on the fire escape steps through the single heavily barred window. The air conditioner in the kitchen alcove was noisily doing its best but the flat was little cooler than the street.

Her sister came back with a glass for each of them. She was younger, dumpy, her kindly face concerned as she busied herself making her glamorous big sister comfortable. 'And here's your key for the street door. These are for the locks on this door. Talk about home of the free and land of the brave.' She finally sat down. 'So! How *was* it?'

'I don't want to speak about it now.'

'That bad, huh? Look like you've seen a ghost.' She got no response. 'Well! Anyway, you're here now. And I've got it all worked out. First you grab some shut-eye. Then when you're feeling half human, we binge. I know a great place on Second. Pizzas you'd die for. Or if you want a knish, down on the lower East Side there's this place called…'

'I'm not hungry.'

'You're always ravenous. Come on.'

'I was fed like a queen on the plane. I flew first class.'

'Wow. So… Tell me all about it.'

'Not now. I need to sleep.'

'Dynamite.' She cocked her head on one side. 'Gracie? Something wrong?'

'I said I need to sleep. Was all I said.'

She reached behind her to the bookcase. 'This came for you. Hand-delivered. Know someone in town I don't?'

Grace Merrick opened the envelope. There was a single white piece of paper with Mould's crest at the top.

Ms Merrick,
You will meet me at The Cloisters tomorrow at eleven beside the Central Fountain in the Garden of the Cuxa Cloister. Your sister knows where it is.

It was unsigned.

She looked up. 'Do you know know where The Cloisters are?'

'The Cloisters? Miles away. On the hill above the Hudson. Fort Tryon Park. Run by the Met.'

'I need to go there.'

'Why? No-one goes there. Medieval stuff.'

'I have to go tomorrow.'

'Okay, okay, slow down. Want me to come with you?'

'No. I need to go alone.'

Her sister hit her forehead. 'Plot thickens.'

Martha and Frank had kept the mansion well. There were fresh outsized sheets on their outsized bed and new soap in the ensuite. The dogs looked healthy and no-one had broken in. Considering what he'd recently spent to stop them, Sinclair wasn't surprised.

They slept for hours. He woke to find Anita stroking his penis. 'Plug me.'

She rarely talked like that. When she did, it was a demand.

Now, seated on the balcony, she looked like an angel from the Upper Fifth as Frank put the tray with the drinks on the low table between them.

'Anything more, sir?' His Cape Coloured face above his white shirt expressed deference. What he thought was his own affair.

'Not now.'

'Martha's ready to check the menu when you say.'

Anita nodded and stared out over the expanse of trees as the man retreated.

Sinclair took his drink, walked to the railing and looked down at the pebbled walks, the carefully casual placement of the exotic African shrubs that mimicked a garden layout he particularly admired – on the slope at the left of the

Voortrekker monument in Pretoria. It was colder here in Cape Town but the succulents were doing well – sheltered and warmed by the reflection of the sun from the high, white wall with its elaborate lattice of razor wire and sophisticated sensing alarms.

'When'll he come?' Anita said.

'Haven't we discussed it enough?'

'What d'you think that appalling, sick woman'll decide on?'

Sinclair shrugged. 'I'm not a forensic psychiatrist.' He ran his finger slowly around the top of the crystal glass, dipped his finger in the wine and tried again. The high-pitched tone began.

'Hanford, it sets my teeth on edge.'

He stopped and pointed to the top of the wall. 'See that wire? If Connor tries to get over it, he'll cook.'

She sat for a while in silence, then, 'Think we should buy guns?'

'Why d'you want a gun, beloved?'

Her small face was tight. 'No-one's going to kill my horses.'

'Horses?'

'You know how I feel.'

'God, woman. You'd shoot Connor? A few days after you've corrupted him?'

'If I have to.'

'For three nags?'

'If he touches Starfire, I'll kill him.'

'Bleeding won't. Don't want police here with their Calvinistic yokel minds.'

'What about the cars? The dogs?'

'The cars are insured. And the dogs are doorbells, not pets – to keep Kaffirs and Connors out.'

'Well, I don't want my car smashed.'

'They've plenty more Break My Windows. You're in the only country that exports them outside of Germany. No waiting. We just get you another.'

'What about Vanderblore and Ravello? There's the Porsche, and the Saab and the...'

'Insured, dear. Insured. Who gives a stuff about a car or six?'

'Seven. There's the Morgan at Birkhamstead. They wouldn't sink the barge?'

'Barges don't have wheels.' He spread his hands. 'I know it's unpleasant. But I'm trying to look on the bright side.'

'There *is* one?'

'Well, at least no-one's going to pig-stick me this time or write messages on your cute little botty. The worst thing's physical attack. Property we can replace.'

'I think we should get guns. Everyone in the neighbourhood has them.'

'*Moi aussi*. I have an automatic. A Walther P5.'

'You never told me.'

'Bought it years ago in the Carlton Centre. Just wandered in and asked for it, like asking for a toaster. Fellow assured me it's unjammable. Didn't know guns jammed. Sold me ammo, too. I've never fired it.'

'You should go to the practice range.'

'And meet the neighbours? No thanks. Something strange about bonhomie when people are practising murder.'

'You really feel we're secure?'

'*Corpus Christi*. You've even got the traditional rape gate in the hall. We've never shut it yet. Seeing we're childless and promiscuous – I mean, is there anything more ironic?'

'Must you go on?'

Sinclair drained his last sip of wine. 'We're as secure as money can make an ordinary domestic building that's not in a compound. I can't put up a double gulag fence like the thing around the Caltex refinery. I don't want jail-house embrasures like that mess around the TV tower in Jo'burg.'

'When you want to skate around a point, you exaggerate.'

'Why not? It works.' He reached for the bottle. 'In this country, civilisation's unravelling. But then it's unravelling everywhere. If I knew anywhere it was ravelling, I'd *go* there. Good God, a new neglected positive.'

'You're not hearing me, Hanford.'

'Yes I am. I'm sensitive to subtext. And you know the answer as well as I do.' He filled his glass. 'We might stop Connor, but we won't stop Mould.'

The sun was long over the hill behind the house and the air was becoming a little cold. The last of the tourists would be emerging from the high green door of Constantia and would be straggling along the gravel paths to their coaches.

He glanced across at her. What was she thinking, that sprite, that fountain troubled?

Anita Sinclair was visualising the farm near Soetendal – was stroking, riding the most beautiful horse she'd ever owned. A blue roan with near perfect conformation. Lovely hind leg. Good length from hip-bone to hock and good width between the hip-bones. Perfect slanting shoulder and generous eyes. Not a mean bone in her. She'd kill rather than see that horse suffer.

'Back with the horses again?'

She nodded, eyes glittering, and stood up. 'I'd better see Martha about dinner.'

Dyson, carrying his suit coat, walked across the glass-roofed atrium, entered the glass lift and rode it to the fourth. He stepped out into the foyer with its fake yucca trees. Behind what looked like a space-age altar sat the agency's straggle-haired receptionist.

'Morning, Mr Dyson. Good trip?'

'Great.'

He walked under the three-metre-long crocodile inflatable hanging from the ducting outside Creative, past Dispatch, the dub room, the old finished art studio, now the billiard room, short-cutting through the bowels of the business toward his plush Account Service office and making a bee-line for the bar-fridge in the credenza.

After he'd poured himself a stiffener he took the video cassette and speech notes out of his briefcase.

'Jeez,' he said. 'What a farce.'

An account executive stuck her head in the door. 'Go well?'

He gave her a thumbs-up. 'Killed 'em.' He hung his coat up. 'Ted in?'

'Someone's with him.' Her shape detached from the doorframe. So she didn't know, at least. But he felt bad vibes, like his desk was on fire. How could the shit-bags at Mido set him up like that?

Message slips in a row on the pad. Calls from media reps, the in-house producer. He lifted the phone and dialled Production. 'Lucy? Adrian.'

'Hi! Get my note about rollovers?'

'Just walked in. Listen – know a David Connor? Does corporate videos.'

'What's the company name?'

'Don't have it.'

'Doesn't ring a bell. I'll check the production book and B&T. Get back to you.'

He strolled to the corner office. The agency MD's door was closed. Through the smoked glass at the side he saw the back of a familiar head – Archer, the Mido MD. Jeez. Jeez. The two of them there. Jeezuz wept.

He made signs through the glass. The agency MD saw but ignored him. Jeez.

'How long's he been in there?'

'An hour.' The secretary's eyes told him he'd turned into a tampon.

He scuttled back to his office and fixed himself another stiff one.

The phone rang. 'Lucy. It's Connor and Connor.' She gave him the number and he scrawled it down, too stunned to think much about it.

A figure walked quickly past the door. He knew the height, suit, stoop. Archer. He hadn't even looked in. Jeez. Oh jeez.

The agency MD came into his room, nose-hair bristling.

'Could have included me,' Dyson said.

'He didn't want to see you.'

'How bad?'

'Pulled the plug. Effective this morning.'

'What he say?'

'Very odd conversation. As if there was something he couldn't tell me. Got the impression he doesn't know much. Said it's no reflection on you. Said to tell you that.'

'Which means you offered to take me off the account.'

'Naturally. No bite. All I could suss out is it's something to do with their share structure. Blowed if I know what to make of it – unless someone high up thinks we stink.'

'Jeez.'

'So what happened at the conference?'

'Zilch. It wasn't even there.'

'Come on, Adrian. He said it went well – said your presentation was a blast.'

'I'm gonna puke.'

'Adrian, I'm missing something…'

'Who's got it? Clemenger? Pats?'

'They're inviting submissions. What I don't get is he said they decided to fire us months ago but had to wait until after the conference. It makes no sense.' He licked his finger and smoothed one steel-grey eyebrow. 'Adrian. You're not levelling. What's going on?'

Dyson said. 'What the fuck. It's done. You firing indians or chiefs this week?'

'Got any new business prospects?' They both knew what was coming.

'Just say it,' said Dyson. 'You've been wetting your pants since you came in.'

'All right.' The man scowled and his eyelashes held hands. 'You've milked this place. And I don't have to put up with it any longer. So I don't want you here tomorrow. I want to get this room fumigated. See Bernie about your package. You're collecting as little as we can give you.'

'Love you too, Ted. Anyone tell you you've got a terminal nose-hair problem?'

The MD jerked two fingers up at him and left the room. Dyson turned, trembling, to clean out his desk.

Chapter Fifteen

Grace Merrick walked through the curious building, staring at sculptures, peering into gothic chapels. It was simply a fabrication, she thought. Like America. She consulted the brochure. The Langon Chapel. She walked through the massive oak doors into the bare room with its barrel-vaulted ceiling. Which way now? Left.

The next room was equally bare, with stone seats around the walls and columns holding a rib-vaulted roof. Through the arched doorway a colonnade cast curved shadows on the flagging. Yes, this was the Cuxa Cloister. The small square garden it bordered was deserted and there had been no-one in the last three rooms. An arch of water bubbled from a fountain in the centre of the garden. She stepped down onto the cross-walk, peering at her pamphlet. 'As in most monasteries,' it informed her, 'a source of water occupies the centre of the cross – here, an eight-sided fountain from Saint-Genis-des-Fontaines.'

She stood by the fountain, adjusting her hair, listening to the hum of insects and purling water. The sun was hot. She looked at her watch. Two minutes past eleven.

She heard the man's soft soles scuff the path a moment before he reached her. He was tall and fleshy, with a pastel shirt and a smile that made his eyes look like buttons sewn too tightly into the face of a rag doll. He carried a creased manilla folder and had an accent from somewhere south of Memphis.

'Grace Merrick? I'm Pete.' He opened the folder and removed a wad of papers with Mould's insignia on the first.

'I'm your contact in New York. Mind if I call you Grace?'

'Yes, I do. Get on with it.'

'Whatever you say, Grace.' His smile had not budged. 'Why don't we sit where it's cooler?'

He ambled through the arch into the room with the stone seats around the walls. 'Not many here.'

She sat warily. He sat beside her, so close that they touched, gassing her with his aftershave, invading her personal space.

She shifted along the bench and pointed her finger at the bridge of his nose. 'Stay where you are or you'll regret it.'

'You're a live one.' He held some of the papers out to her as one might feed grass to a cow. As she reached to take them, he pulled them back. 'Uh-uh. Say please.'

She clenched her fists in anger. He dropped the papers beside her. 'Only kidding. Only kidding, Grace.'

He looked down at his own file. 'You have there a breakdown of the assets of Hanford Blair Sinclair as they relate to his animals and wheeled vehicles. The inventory shows two boxer dogs, three horses, and seven cars. Do you believe this? A Rolls. Fancy buying kitsch like that.'

She looked through the papers. 'I'm not interested in your comments.'

'Don't be like that, Grace.' The fixed grin had still not uncreased. 'You're a hard hard woman.'

'You'll find how hard in a minute.'

'Something wrong with the seat?'

The stone seat was agony on her damaged rear and she was squirming. 'Will you get on with it?'

'Sure. Now all we need's how you want it done. Some of the cars are in Europe. So, just to keep it simple, we suggest you concentrate on the South African property.'

'It's Dyson I want. Not Sinclair.'

The man grinned on. 'Guess the faster we get through,

the sooner you can give it your best shot.' He pulled out a monogrammed handkerchief, unbuttoned the front of his shirt and positioned the handkerchief inside under his armpit. 'Hot. Got Niagara right under my arm. Wouldn't want to offend you, Grace. You look like a lady.'

'Will you shut up?'

His eyes almost disappeared. 'Be as quiet as a stunned raccoon. So we kill the dogs? Want 'em strangled with their guts strung on the fence?' He mimed it, hooking a finger in his collar and lolling his tongue out of the side of his mouth. 'We smack the shit out of them? Name it. You got it.'

'Kill the dogs. I hate dogs. I was bitten by a dog as a child.'

'Gum 'em to death? Tooth for a tooth?'

'I'll leave it to you.'

'Okay, Grace baby.' He pulled a pencil stub out of his shirt pocket, licked the point and wrote on his file. 'Now, horses.' He reached inside his shirt and shifted his handkerchief across his chest hair until it was firmly under the other arm.

Grace Merrick went rigid. 'Leave the horses out of this. Horses are God's creatures.'

The man nodded. 'Guess they are. I can tell, Grace, you're a person of definite views. A together lady. Am I right or am I right? Hold the horses, huh? Not even hamstring one leg?'

Her eyes flashed. 'You are not to touch the horses.'

'Message received.' He applied his pencil stub to the paper. 'That leaves a Rolls Silver Spirit and a BMW Z3. Want 'em put in a sandwich with Semtex H? Want 'em ground up and we make the owner eat 'em?'

'Destroy them. I don't care.'

He grinned at his papers and looked up. 'Don't want to give offence, Grace, but I don't see much inspiration here.'

'When's the next draw?'

'After we sort this out, I guess.'

'Then get on with it.' She stood up, her bottom on fire.

He retrieved his handkerchief from his shirt, mopped his brow with it and put it back in his pocket. 'You're a stunning woman, Grace. By the way, what you doing today? Got plans?'

'I'll be in St John's Cathedral, praying you get hit by a truck.'

'You're a live one. I could go for you. I like the way you're wired. Say, you wouldn't give me a blood sample so I could run some tests?'

She walked quickly away toward the sound of voices that were now echoing from the next room.

She heard his mocking voice call after her, 'Be careful. It could get mildew.'

For three days he'd seen it every time he shut his eyes – Rex's blackened mouth screaming in pain to the sky. It was there behind his eyelids, wouldn't go away. He'd cursed Mould with his whole being.

They'd gone to the Tandoori House. It became a wake in honour of Rex. They'd remembered the things he'd done, the practical jokes he'd played. They'd drunk too much, come home, made love. One part of him had gone through the motions. The other part had watched, distrusting her every move.

As he lay half awake beside her soft warmth in the long drift of the night, his mind ran around in its maze, every avenue blocked. He got up once and looked at Mould's rules. They were twisted enough to change things constantly depending on who did what to whom or who won what. He gave it up, went back to bed and, lying there, came to a decision. It wouldn't make things easier, but then nothing would. At least he'd feel less of a puppet.

In the morning, Tess picked up her carry-bag, checked

her face in the hall mirror. 'Are you doing your pre-production for the shoot today?'

'Suppose I'd better get on with it,' he lied.

She frowned. 'I don't know what happened over there but you seem different somehow.'

'How d'you mean?'

'You don't feel like the same person.'

'Not quite as cautious, huh?'

She put a finger to her lip. 'It's like you've been to war or something. When are you over there again?'

'It's not decided yet. The weather's not good right now.'

'Do I get a kiss before I go?'

He dutifully kissed her, wondering what his decision would do to her. Nothing if he had a say in it. He had to get a gun – and fast.

She said, 'Might be back for lunch. I'll see how the appointments go. Just been so flat-chat lately. Byesie.'

He waved at the closing door, stood in the hall as if brain-dead, then trudged down to the studio. The kitten ran in spurts ahead of him, pouncing on flowers, tail straight up, pale anus like the tail-light on a Chev. He'd forgotten the kitten. He went in and looked at the fax tray. There was a request from an old client for ten more dubs, a razz about a multimedia patch panel and, on the bottom, several pages of closely spaced type with diagrams surmounted by a cog logo.

He slumped in his chair and started to read.

Mr Connor,
Here is the information you will need. Your target lives in Constantia, a suburb of Cape Town, along the M41, some 50km drive from the city centre. Follow the directions shown on page 4. A map is provided; also a layout of the house and other preliminary information.

> Cars owned by the family, a Rolls-Royce Spirit and a BMW, are both garaged at the house. Relevant livestock: two bull mastiffs at the house. You will find preliminary information on following pages.
>
> Your first-class return SAA fare to Johannesburg with transfer to Cape Town is booked for the 23rd. You will be staying in the city at the Lord Nelson Hotel, where you will be contacted on arrival and will receive all necessary assistance for the operation. Weapons, poison baits, combustibles or H.E. with detonators will be provided as you require and instruction given. You will note from the following short summary that the house is equipped with elaborate security arrangements and has several permanent staff. This need not concern you as these impediments will be neutralised before you begin. You will notice that your itinerary includes a three-day inclusive visit to Mala Mala, a private game park, as a side excursion after your task is completed, with transfer both ways by private aircraft from Jan Smuts before you connect with your return flight to Sydney.

He almost expected it to end, 'We hope you have a pleasant trip and please do not hesitate to contact us for your future travel requirements.' There was no signature.

Five pages of information followed, including maps of the suburb and the house, details of the Sinclairs' general lives and movements, including the clubs and restaurants they frequented, addresses, phone numbers, details of staff, their movements and more. He'd never been to South Africa and it could have been written in Sanskrit for all it conveyed. Who would have cobbled all this together? Did it involve the woman in the library – Gillian?

The kitten walked across the pages, swishing its tail. He

stroked it roughly, guilty about it. They'd given him the number. What was the time difference? They'd be some hours behind. Too bad. He dumped the animal on the floor. What code? He reached for the directory.

The phone rang three times before a sleepy man's voice answered.

'Sinclair residence.'

'Hanford Sinclair there?'

'Who is calling, please?'

'Tell him it's Connor.'

'One moment please.'

The line went dead, switched to hold. He waited, tapping his foot, wondering what the pause was costing him. He very much wanted Sinclair to be there, needed to talk to someone who understood. He even regretted not getting Dyson's number.

'And who might this be?'

Sinclair's voice. He suddenly felt enormously thankful, no longer alone. 'It's Connor.'

'Christ, man. It's bloody 1am and we're pissed. Just a minute.' The phone put down – perhaps he was shutting the door – then picked up again. 'What's up?'

'Just got a fax from the island. Details of what I'm supposed to do to you.'

'Oh yes? Will my wounds be vibrant? What exactly am I in for?'

'I'm supposed to "take out" your cars and dogs.'

'No horses?'

'Nothing about horses.'

'Thank God. How many cars?'

'Two.'

'And that's it?'

'That's it.'

'Marvellous. Anita'll be delighted.'

'They've even added a sweetener. Booked me into a game park. You credit that?' He was babbling on, craving some connection.

'Which one?'

He looked at the page. 'Mala Mala.'

'Pity you're not a woman.'

'A woman?'

'They choose good-looking rangers to keep the ladies happy. "Be a Mala Mala Ranger/ Lead a life of sex and danger." Mind you, Sabi has better T-shirts.'

'Anyway, I'm ringing you because…'

'You'll enjoy it. Grass is low this time of the year so you'll see the game more easily.'

'I'm not interested in that. I'm…'

'Then go to Bop and see the Lost Kingdom. Or go on Rohan's steam choo choo. He could do with Mould's loot. You hear that, Nick? Bet the twisted bugger's listening to everything we say. Seriously, you'd love it. Edwardian splendour. Double-bed cabins with private lounge and bathroom.'

'Can I get a word in here?'

'Of course you'll need a distaff companion. Take Anita. Might spark her up.'

'Whatever you're on, halve the dose.'

'Sorry, old sock. Bit hyper here. Delayed reaction and all that crud. We're both a tad post-traumatic.'

'Aren't we all.'

'Anita's lachrymose, poor little tyrant. And I'm pretty shell-shocked – not sure from whence cometh my help. Very glad you rang. Better than biting our nails. So when do we suffer the thrill of your attack?'

'That's what I'm on about, if you'll shut up a moment. I'm not doing it.'

'Say again?'

'I'm going to refuse. I'm out. Out of the game. Out. Meaning out.'

'I… *see*!' There was a long and uncharacteristic pause.

'The day I gōt back here, they burnt my partner alive. Burnt him alive. It's murder now. You there?'

'Murder? You sure?'

'Nothing you can prove. They must have set it up ages ago – had it in the works for years – but waited till I got back.'

'Unpleasant.'

'You better believe it.'

'So you're cashing your chips?'

'Right.'

'Mmm.' Another long pause. 'Trouble is, old sock, it won't wash. The bleeding game goes on whatever you decide. What you're doing, according to the game, is refusing to enforce a penalty. Hang on. Hang on, will you.' The phone was put down again. He heard the sound of scuffling before it was picked up. 'Just getting the stupid dirge and the rules. Looked at them lately?'

'Sure. Beyond me. It's a maze.'

'Well, I might have found a flaw. For instance, the penalty after this is rape of wife. But Merrick doesn't *have* a wife. Or Dyson – unless we're expected to bugger his catamite. So I'm not sure Nicolae's thought of absolutely bleeding everything. Might be a chance to do ourselves some good at the expense of Amazing Grace and Adrian. Then twist it the other way. Merrick's a woman and Dyson couldn't get it up. With all that booze, he couldn't even find it! I mean, I'm not fashed about two cars. But if you quit now…'

'Forget it. I'm out.'

'Are you sure? I've just had my lawyers onto the trust Mould set up. The money's there – twenty million, all according to Hoyle.'

'I said I'm out.'

'I'm not trying to twist your arm,' another pause and the sound of rustling paper, 'but see where that leaves you? If you don't come over here and jigger my jalopies then, according to the rules, it's a switch.'

'I cop the next penalty up. I know.'

'Which is... *your* wife raped. And I'm supposed do the honours. Pretty, is she? See, we could avoid that if you stay in the game and we're careful. Then – one needs to be sober for this: bleeding thing's like a minefield – the current penalty... let's see.'

'Mould smashes up my car and kills my cat.'

'No he doesn't. He *doesn't*, old sock. Because that only happens after a switch. But there's been *no* switch yet, so you're in the clear on that.'

'All I know is I'm out of it.'

'Just pointing out the finer details.'

'And if you want to have a go at Tess, you'll have to find her first.'

'You're going to tell her?'

'Have to.'

'Ah. But have you looked at Rule Six? If you talk you score another penalty. You sure you want to go through with this?'

'Sure.'

'Cost you dear, I'm afraid. Hold on now, still thinking, still thinking. Let's steer this our way if we can. I'm so glad you rang. Like a bleeding fresh of breath air. I'm not positive I'll be raping your wife, old son. No offence, of course. I'm sure she's ravishing. But rape isn't my speed. And, as you're refusing to damage me, it would be churlish to rush off waving my prong and know your wife biblically.'

'But if you win, and don't do it, according to the rules...'

'That'd be a switch. I see it. I see it. So... old Nick would have *Anita* raped. Bit of a bummer. Of course, she might enjoy it! Or I could pretend it was her anniversary present.

But still… mmm! You've rather put the cat among the little strutting feathered creatures.'

'You think he's listening?'

'Certain. Or recording it. Hello, Nicolae, you black-hearted bugger.'

'Well, that was it.'

'I'll miss you, Connor. Leaving me to struggle on with Merrick and Dyson. God, they're a dismal pair. You will keep in touch? Tell you what. Come over anyway. I'd be happy to pay for the ticket. I'm thinking of poor Anita. She could do with a lift right now. After all, you've saved me hours of mooning around showrooms and dog-pounds.'

'Thanks, but I'm up shit creek without a paddle.'

'Wouldn't you like four days on a luxury train with my provocative, pocket-sized wife?'

'Yes. Can I hang up now?'

'Offer stands. Stay in touch, will you? Might be important.'

'Okay.'

'Chin up, socklet. Appreciate the call. May fortune speed your passage. Good luck.'

Connor hung up and said to the kitten, 'You're safe, mate.'

He got up, walked through the editing suite and opened the door of the storeroom. He ignored the shelves of tapes and turned to the cabinets that held back files on old jobs. He found his old contact diaries, searched in the second most ancient for the name. Casey. There he was. Casey, a 'well-known Sydney identity', had interesting connections. They'd taped an interview with him years ago on the small property he owned near Dungog. In a country with laws that now prevented everyone but felons bearing arms, Casey seemed the only chance he had.

Connor took the diary back to his desk, dialled the

number, expecting to draw a blank but, to his surprise, Casey answered in his nicotine-damaged drawl. Connor knew not to say much on the phone so mentioned how they'd met, then suggested they might be able to do business. Casey told him to drop by for a beer.

Connor went to the bank, got more cash than he'd ever withdrawn before and walked furtively out with a wad of $100 bills heavy in his pocket.

It was a long drive to Dungog. The small farmhouse looked the same. Connor's impression of the criminal class was that most of them lived simple lives. At the sound of the car, a man wearing overalls and carrying what looked like the armature of a starter motor walked out of a shed beside the house. Casey looked more stooped. He stood without moving, watching from beneath shaggy brows as Connor got out of the car.

Connor smiled.

Casey did not smile. He was a sharp-eyed, seen-it-all, sixty. Most crims, Connor knew, gave it away at forty, and tried to spend the fag-end of their lives without benefit of government custody. But as far as he knew, Casey had never been put inside. 'So what can I do you for?'

'I'm in trouble,' Connor said.

'What kind?'

'Someone's trying to kill my wife.'

'Told the feds?'

'It's not like that.'

'So…'

'I need a gun.'

'And you thought old Case could help out?' He turned and walked back into the shed, saying over his shoulder, 'What sort of gun?'

Connor followed him into the shed. It had an old tractor on one side and a workbench that ran the length of the back.

Half-stripped-down farm implements littered the dirty concrete floor. 'Anything. A second-hand shotgun. Not too dear.'

'Over-and-under. Field? Pump?'

'I don't know.'

'If I have it right, you want to smoke people, not targets?'

'Self-defence.'

Casey put the armature down on the bench. 'How about a nice Browning C3 with Briley tubes and chokes? Or a Perazzi MX8 with spare trigger-springs and firing pins?'

Connor was out of his depth. If the man had asked him about practically anything else at all, he would have been able to cope. About time-reference scanning beams and microwave landing systems, Option and Endorsement Reason codes for insurance claims, Oracle-based stand-alone programs written in GUI, liquid-fill, recyclable hospital-grade polypropylene… But guns? 'I don't know anything about guns. I just want one that'll take someone's head off.'

'Aim for the gut. More chance of a hit.' Casey looked at him rather like a headmaster surveying a new pupil. 'No, we'll forget those, I reckon. Had a nice pump a week ago. Would have been a better bet. How about an auto? Got an old Winchester 1400. Good nick. Plain full choke, gas-operated. Only takes two in the mag, one in the breech, but if you can't do it in three, you can kiss your arse goodbye.'

'Sounds fine.'

Casey nodded. 'Wait here.'

Casey walked out of the side door of the shed. He seemed to be gone a long time. He came back with a long cardboard box, put it on the bench and slid the gun out of the end. He also pulled out a plastic bag that held a couple of aluminium rods, greasy rags and gismos. 'This was worth about seven hundred before they brought in the gun laws. Seeing as my arse is on the line, we'll round it up to a thou. No case with this one. But I'll throw in the cleaning gear and oil.'

Connor picked the weapon up. It was surprisingly heavy with a blued barrel, cross-cut woodwork and a rubber shoulder-pad at the end of the gleaming stock. 'Mechanically all right?'

'Checked over and guaranteed. I'll show you the barrel when I clean the oil out.' The man took the gun from him tenderly, unscrewed something and pulled the barrel free of the gun. He screwed the two aluminium rods together and attached a wad on the end. He worked it through the barrel, handed the barrel to Connor. 'Check that. No pitting at all.'

Connor looked though the barrel at the chromed, mirror-like interior. 'Couple of spots halfway up.'

The man took the barrel back, smiled. 'They're the gas holes. See? Go right through. When you fire, they feed some of the gas into a pressure-relief valve inside here.' He was pointing to the magazine. 'That drives a piston that moves these two rods back. And they rotate and unlock the bolt. Like that.'

Connor didn't see, but nodded. The weapon looked impeccable. As the bold carrier moved back the oiled rails it ran on gleamed.

'I'll take it,' he said.

'Right.' Casey showed him how to assemble it, how to oil the barrel and clean it. 'What about cartridges? Box of twenty-five? Scorpio's all I got. I'll throw them in for the thou.'

'Fine.'

'Know how to use it?'

'No.' He was counting out $100 notes.

'Okay. You'd better come down the back.' He put the weapon back in the box, then lifted a coiled cable with a hand control off the wall. 'I've got a trap set-up down behind the hill. The neighbours use it sometimes. So we'll pretend we're having a spot of fun.'

They walked down the hill behind the house and through a small stand of trees. Beyond the trees was a tree-bounded paddock strewn with multi-coloured plastic cartridge cases and the remains of ochre-coloured targets. Casey told him to stand on a roughly numbered strip of earth, facing a small, battered shed that looked like a shelter for geese. The man patiently showed him how the cartridges were loaded, how to stand with the weight on the front foot. Then he walked to the shed and attached the end of the cable inside it. 'We should have ear-plugs but I forgot the bastards.'

Finally, Connor was allowed to call, 'pull'. Casey pressed the hand control and a ten-centimetre-wide clay 'bird' flew away across the field. He squeezed the trigger and the gun roared for the first time beside his cheek. The target spun away unharmed and shattered on the ground.

'Don't try and aim,' the man said. 'It's not a rifle. If it throws to the side, look ahead of it and let the gun follow your eyes. Hose it – like the gun's a hose. See? Try it again.'

'Pull.'

By the end of the session the barrel was hot and smelt satisfyingly of burnt powder. He'd hit ten targets out of fifty, more by chance than design. There was pleasure in hitting the flying disk on the few times that he fluked it, seeing it powder into nothing instead of falling to break on the ground. But the concentration and the heavy gun made it tiring.

He shook Casey's hand and thanked him for the lesson, put the long box in the boot of his car, shoulder sore, ears still ringing. He now knew the basics of the weapon. If he had to use it, he could.

When he got home he spent the next hour on the floor

of the studio examining the thing, taking it apart, putting it together, like a kid with a set of nesting blocks. Finally he hid it under the back of the editing suite console.

The phone rang.

An accented voice. 'Mr Connor?'

Vo! Christ! He didn't answer.

'Mr Connor, I know you listening.'

He said nothing.

'You refuse to give penalty?'

So they'd heard the call to Sinclair. 'I'm out of the game. Finish.'

'Is no "out of game". Is no way you leave game. Mean you automatically become next loser. Create switch. You understand?'

'Whatever you think it means, I'm out.' He hung up.

It was a matter of survival now.

Chapter Sixteen

Connor parked around the corner from the Bridgeview Hotel on Willoughby Road. It was a regular watering hole for the mob at Channel Nine and Dyson had told him on the phone that it was the only North Shore pub he knew.

Dyson was in the bistro, at a table near the far window. It was 11am and the place almost deserted. Connor ordered a Virgin Mary and took it over to the table.

'Thanks for showing,' Dyson said. He looked dreadful.

Connor sat. 'So what's this about?'

'My job's down the toilet, courtesy Mould.'

'You said that on the phone.'

'I'm looking over the edge and I don't like the view. Got a car. That's it.'

Connor sipped his drink. The tabasco bit the back of his throat, deputising for the astringency of alcohol. 'I'm not a charity.'

Dyson cradled his glass, leaning forward. 'I might look like a scumball. But I'm not asking for a handout. The game's all I got, now. Wanna know what's going down.'

'Didn't they send you something?'

'Got this before I left.' He produced a piece of paper. Connor unfolded it. It was the same as the sheet they'd faxed to him that morning:

> The failure of Mr Connor to impose the first penalty of the second round causes a switch. (See Rule Three.) Accordingly, Mr Connor becomes the next loser and Mr Sinclair the next winner. The penalty is rape of wife.

> The meaning of this is clear and no alteration will be permitted. Should Mr Sinclair fail to enforce the penalty, it will be imposed on his own wife. (See Rule Four.) This will provoke another switch and render Mr Sinclair the loser for the following game.

Connor handed the paper back. 'I've got that. So you know as much as I do.'

Dyson grinned nastily and shook his head. 'Yeah?'

'What're you on about?'

'You and Sinclair. Like you're trying to cover all bases. First, you stage a switch that cuts out the draw. But there's no way you want him pumping your wife. So next move, he gets to refuse, the two of you pull a double switch and I strike out.'

'That's crap. I can't force him to refuse. Anyway, I've told you I'm out of the game. I'm out. Okay?'

'Like hell you are. How the hell can you get out?' Dyson scratched under his arm. 'Told your wife yet?'

Connor frowned. 'Not yet.'

'Because if Sinclair refuses, you don't have to!' Dyson guffawed. 'No, you two have a scam. You're riding the odds while I get sidelined.'

Connor was getting sick of this. 'Look. I'll spell it out for you. One. You're a damn side safer sidelined. Two. If Sinclair refuses, then like that says,' he pointed to the paper, 'Anita gets raped by Mould's little helpers.'

'So what? He won't lose sleep.'

'Three. It'd cause a second switch.'

'Which cuts out the draw again.'

'Forget the bloody draw. It's irrelevant. Look. If there's a second switch, what happens? Think about it. Apparently someone gets slaughtered. It could be Anita. And I'm supposed to do it. Reckon I want that?'

Dyson cackled. 'You wouldn't come at it. And Sinclair knows it.'

'Use your nasty mind, Dyson. If I *don't* go through with it, Mould has *my* wife killed.' Connor sucked down the tomato juice, the ice cold against his teeth.

'He pops your wife?'

'According to their famous Rule Four. So suck on that. So I'm out.'

Dyson looked puzzled. 'U-huh.'

Connor gave him a level look. 'You with it now?'

Dyson screwed up his face. 'Guess I hadn't thought that far. Can of worms, huh?'

'Right. And I don't want any part of it. So I'm glad you're up to speed.' He stood up. 'That it?'

Dyson watched him walk away, a grin spreading on his face. Out or not, whatever way Sinclair jumped, Connor was well and truly suckered. Bing bang boom. He felt a whole lot better. Great to meet someone worse off than yourself.

As Connor drove home, he vowed to speak to Tess that night.

No, damn it. He was fudging.

Impulsively, he swung the car and headed for her office. Perhaps they could talk over lunch.

Her small waiting-room had pastel walls and armchairs covered in muted floral fabric. The colour-coordination was excellent. Most decisions Tess made were excellent. The chairs were empty when he entered, which surprised him: there was usually someone waiting. She didn't have a secretary and the inside door was shut. That meant a client was with her. He could wait.

He flicked through the glossies. On the sideboard was a coffee warmer. He was halfway to the jug, wondering how to broach it with her, when he heard a faint sound through the door.

He froze. A lull. He heard it again.

His wife was grunting – the sound she made in bed when close to coming. And there was another sound too. Gasping. A man gasping.

He put his ear to the door – a sliding door with felt at the edge. It had no catch. He slid it open a little.

He could see her rolltop desk and chair. The treatment table was at the other end of the room. The sounds were definite now. He opened the door wider and peered in.

They were on the floor, both naked, her legs splayed, feet locked around his back. Her head was obscured by his torso but he knew his wife's lush body well enough. The man was muscular and slim, with deeply tanned forearms and strong legs.

He inched the door shut and walked back to the coffee jug. He poured himself a coffee, added the precise amount of milk and sugar, sat down and sipped. The farmer from Moree? Or did she spread herself around? He put the coffee cup carefully on the table and covered his head with his hands.

The faint sound of her laughter from the inside room and the man's answering chuckle. No, he didn't want them to find him here. He stood up quickly and left.

Sinclair stared at his feet, far from him on the stool that matched his club chair. Penelope's lament from *The Return of Ulysses* sobbed from the sound system but the Renaissance sound-heaven did not soothe him.

Anita walked into the study. 'I'm going around to Clifton.' She glanced at the papers on the desk and he tensed. He'd left them exposed beside the yellow folder. She spotted the cogged emblem on the top sheet, lifted it and started to read, eyes widening. 'He's not?'

'Even bribed him with you and Rovos Rail. No deal.'

'Will you please turn that noise down?'

He extended an arm, flicked the volume control.

She was trying to understand the closely spaced type. 'Does this mean... Mould sends around his assassins?'

'No. We're in the clear.' He watched with narrowed eyes as she read on, unable to prevent the inevitable.

'Rape of – *wife*?' She slapped the sheet with the back of her hand. 'This refers to *me*?' She hurled the sheet at him with a stifled sound. It travelled a metre and did swing-curves to the floor.

Sinclair rubbed his finger along his teeth.

She stamped her small foot. 'Hanford?'

He cleared his throat. 'They expect me to rape Connor's wife.'

'And if you don't?' She stormed right up to him.

'Apparently they do it to you.'

'I'm not *in* this game. I've told you to keep me out of it.'

'I'd like to but I haven't much option.'

She turned to the window, her back to him, addressed the wrought-iron bars. 'So who'll it be? Her or me? Well? Are you hesitating, Hanford?'

'If you can point out an acceptable alternative...'

She whirled to face him. 'You mean it's a *question* for you?' Her face was livid. 'How dare you? How *dare* you?' Veins stood out on her neck.

'It's not much of a choice.'

She put one foot against his footstool and side-kicked it out from under his legs. 'I'll divorce you.'

He cleared his throat nervously. 'That won't get you out of it.'

'Not to "get out of it", you horror. To get *away* from you.'

Sinclair frowned. 'You mean you want me to rape Connor's wife?'

'Yes,' she choked. 'If that's what it takes.' She turned petulantly toward the window. 'Above all, I expect you to protect *me*. Can't you even see that?'

'Then I'll do it.' He reached out and got the stool back, grumbling, 'Don't have to talk about divorce.'

'That scares you, doesn't it? Well, count on this. If Mould's gang even touches me, I go.'

He shifted uneasily in the chair. 'Please, dear. You know it's out of my control.'

'That's *your* problem. I've warned you. If you have to rape her, do it. Just keep me *out* of this thing.' Her rage was changing now, to hurt. 'How could you even *consider*... I thought you might have... cared just a little.' She ran from the room like a child, eyes filling with tears.

He stood up from the chair and was across the room in two strides. But he could already hear her steps on the staircase leading to the garage.

He went back to the chair and sat shakily down, assailed by the atmosphere in the room. No love so hot, he thought, but marriage cools it. How much had the last two minutes cost him?

Connor was almost home when the car began overheating. He pulled over, opened the bonnet. One of the belts had gone. He had spares in the boot but he wasn't up to wrestling with them now. He drove to a garage at Cammeray. They couldn't do it straight away so he left the car and went to the post office. He took the Armidale and District phone book from the library of phone books built into the counter. It covered Moree and other towns. There were five Sturtridges, but no Stuthridge. A blank.

He checked his postbox on the way out. An issue of *Hardware International*, a circular about NAB, a promo for a CD effects library, the predictable detritus of his life – a life that was falling apart.

He walked the short way to his home but didn't go into

the house. He went straight around the side to the studio, trying to fight with logic the shock of what he'd seen. The fact of her lover was no surprise. But to see it in the flesh was something else. No point in judging her. No time for that. She was a bitch. But he couldn't just let her be killed. He had to convince her of the danger. And it would be useless confronting her with what he'd seen. The tale about Mould would be hard to believe and he needed her calm and receptive. Recriminations would make things impossible.

He went into the office and looked in the cabinet with his back files. They had to get away. He had outback contacts Mould was unlikely to know. That place in West Queensland. Charleville?

He searched the closely packed job bags. The Water Resources Commission job – a segment on arterial bores. They'd stayed on the property. There'd be details on the call-sheet. A place near Wyandra – a hell of flies, heat, mulga and red dust. The guy would put them up. Failing that, they could stay at the pub. Wooden bar with huge glass ashtrays, ugly red and yellow mats...

The phone rang. Not the office phone – the extension from the house. He must have picked it up a fraction after she did, hadn't even heard her come home.

Her voice, 'Hello?'

A man's voice. 'It's me.'

'Les?'

'You alone?'

'He's not home yet.' She'd assumed that. No car, the house locked.

'I've checked the flights. Should book your ticket now because of the long weekend. Best to start early. Say 6.25am? You'd be there by 7.30. It's a regional service so you'll waste hours if you come later.'

'No, that's fine.'

'So I'll pick you up at the airport.'

Connor was noting the information down.

'How far is it from Narrabri?'

'The airport?'

'No, the farm.'

'Three-quarters of an hour. We'll have a bit of a detour to the Department of Ag. 'cause I've got to drop something off at the lab. Only take a minute. Then, when we get to the farm, you're going straight to bed…'

'And the romantic dinner, don't forget…'

'All organised. And, if you can stand it, I'd like to show you around the farm.'

'I'd rather just see the ceiling of the bedroom.'

'I'd like you to see what I do.'

'You promised me an afternoon in bed.'

'Okay. We'll argue about it in bed. Then we'll be off on our trip next day.'

'Sounds great.'

'Missing you already. Want you.'

'Mmm. Darling.'

'Remember, your tickets'll be at the desk.'

'Okay.'

'Want you.'

'You're making me wet.'

'Love you.'

'Love you, darling.'

'Hello.'

'Hello. Want you inside me.'

'Darling.'

'It's going to be wonderful.'

'I can't even talk to you on the phone without getting hard.'

It dragged on with murmured endearments until they finally hung up.

He put the receiver down slowly, tapped the pencil on the desk. Something strange about the conversation – something that didn't quite ring true. His gut now warned him not to mention her lover – at all.

Tess said to him at dinner, 'You're solemn tonight.'

'Got a lot on my mind.'

'Rex again?'

He helped with the washing up, then followed her into the lounge. She sat on the divan and picked up the TV guide. He perched on the chair opposite, watching her face. On the table to her right was the photograph of them at Lake Eucumbene with their arms around each other. Rex's girlfriend of that year had taken the shot.

Still looking at the guide, she said, 'Okay. Give. What's the problem? You've been mooning all night. You're boring as bat-shit when you're like this.'

He said, 'There's something I've got to tell you but I can't prove it,' he spread his hands, 'in any way. So you're going to have to take it on trust.'

She made a silly face. 'Sounds mysterious.'

'I'm afraid you're not even going to believe it.'

'Try me.'

He told her – the whole thing. About the island, the game, the penalties. Showed her the faxes he'd received, about his injuries, the murder of Rex. He even got the shotgun and put it between them on the floor. That visibly shocked her.

'So,' he finished lamely, 'you're in danger of being raped. What I'm planning is we go bush – somewhere back of Gulargambone – take the gun and wait the whole thing out. You see, Mould'll die soon and then, with luck, it'll be over. We just need to get out of the way till he dies. Now we can't discuss where we'll go here because they've probably got the house wired. Could have put bugs in the walls six months ago.' He stopped. Her face told him the worst. 'You don't believe a bar of it, do you?'

'It's the most tedious load of old rubbish I've ever…'

'Ring Dyson – or Sinclair. They'll confirm it.'

'Anyone can say anything, David. And anyone can send a fax. And the gun only proves you're scared. You'll have to do better than that.'

'Tess, for God's sake, it's true. We've got to get out of here.'

'Do you mind putting that thing where I don't have to look at it?'

He picked up the weapon.

'Out of the house, please. It's not staying in here.'

He took it out to the studio and put it back beneath the console desk. When he returned, he found her in the bedroom. She had the wardrobe door open and was going through her clothes.

'What are you doing?'

'Nothing.' She pulled a skirt out and held it against her, putting one foot forward to check its length.

'You don't seem too concerned.'

'I'm very concerned – about you.'

'I know it sounds mad. But I had to tell you. We can't stay here. Don't you see?'

'No, David. I don't see. She hung the skirt back on the rail and selected another. 'Anyway, I won't be here this weekend. I've got a Chiropractic Convention. It's a five-day seminar. So, as far as you're concerned, I'll be safe.'

'You didn't tell me.'

'Only came up today. There was a cancellation, so I said I'd go.'

He tried to sound casual. 'Where is it?'

'I thought the place was bugged. We don't want Mould to find out, do we?'

'Christ, Tess.' He slammed the wardrobe door shut and she flinched. 'You could get raped, even killed.'

She backed around the other side of the bed as if he might attack her. 'I can talk about something sensible but now you've finally flipped, I don't see the point.'

'What's this "finally" jazz? I'm as sane as you are.'

'I think you're dangerous. I've seen it coming – seen it and tried not to provoke it. Now you definitely need help.'

'Where'd that all come from? It's bullshit.'

'You've been getting more and more withdrawn and now it's reached an acute stage. The Rex thing's tipped you over the edge. You think he's been murdered, you're buying guns. You're paranoid. Can't you *see* it?'

He followed her around the house for another half an hour but her mind was made up. She cleaned her teeth and collected her handbag from the hallstand.

'Now what are you doing?'

'I'm not staying here with you like this.'

She edged by him, 'May I pass?' and opened the front door.

'Where are you going?'

'Somewhere sane.' The door slammed behind her.

He slid down the wall to his haunches and stared at the honey-coloured floorboards they had stripped and varnished together. 'Fuck. Fuck.' He pounded the floor with his fist.

That night he lay awake, his gut flashing red LED lights. Granted, the story was fantastic. But she'd almost determinedly not believed, as if her bias had been established long before.

He didn't expect to sleep but at 5am something woke him. He'd forgotten to switch off the answerphone and the message on the office extension was half through before he got to it. Tess? He pressed the switch, grabbed the handset.

Half awake, he recognised the accent. Anita?

'Hello?' Had she hung up?

'David?'

'Yes. I'm here. Go ahead.'

'David, thank God. I'm so sorry to ring you so early but I'm worried out of my mind. I got your number from Hanford's file. Has he rung you?'

'No.'

'Oh.' She sounded disappointed. 'I've been reading all these things about the game. It says if he doesn't rape your wife, they'll come after *me*. I've told him to keep me out of it or I'll divorce him. I know that doesn't help you.'

'Go on.'

'I know you've been ringing each other. So I thought he might have… told you what he's decided.'

'No, he hasn't. Can't you ask him?'

'He's told me he'll go through with it, but you can never be sure with him. He's such a creep.'

'Know what happens if he refuses?'

'They rape me.'

'Not just that. It causes this "switch" thing. Then I'm supposed to kill you.'

'Kill me? You'd kill me?'

'Course not.'

'God. David?' He could hear her crying. 'I'm sorry to put all this on you and I know you don't think I'm a very nice person but… I've just no-one to talk to. It's a nightmare. What can I *do*? Please help me.'

'You listening?'

The sobbing voice said, 'Yes.'

'Get out of there. Go somewhere no-one can find you. Hide from everyone until Mould dies. What did I say?'

'Hide. From everyone.'

'Right. Get out of the country. Then, a week later, go

somewhere else. Keep moving. Don't stop. And try to cover your tracks. It may not work, but it's worth a go. At least you're not a sitting duck.'

'I could go to…'

'Don't say it. Phones'll be tapped.'

'David?'

'What?'

'Thank you. Thank you so very much. I… I hope you'll be all right.'

'So do I. All the best.'

He put the phone down slowly, worried about her – worried about the woman who wanted her husband to rape his wife.

Mould was tying them in knots.

CHAPTER SEVENTEEN

Sinclair tossed the folder onto the seat of the Rolls. His feet sank into the lambswool rug over the Wilton carpet as he settled behind the wheel. He needed to get out of the house, which reeked of distrust. Anita wouldn't speak to him – had locked herself in her room. He suspected she was packing. He had to get away and think.

He clicked the aluminium door closed, looked along the mirror shine of the bonnet to the winged lady on its prow, then inserted the key in the Italian walnut dashboard and turned it. The 6.75-litre aluminium engine kicked over without a tremor and settled down to 600rpm as the warning lights winked out. It was hard, in this soundproof lounge, to believe that the big V8 was running.

Divorce! The word unnerved him. They had no pre-nuptial agreement.

He put the selector into drive, released the handbrake. The garage began to slide backwards as the blaze of white metal insinuated itself into the sun.

He'd made a fatal move yesterday. Essential to get the next one right. A trip in the beast would clear the head.

The car negotiated the gutter at the end of the drive with every telescopic damper and self-levelling gas spring doing its best to persuade him that the wheels had merely encountered a ripe fig.

He went along Lansdowne and got onto Settler's Way, heading around False Bay toward Strand. A glorious day in the beautiful city he loved – a setting that would soon be the battleground Johannesburg had become. The car's sense of insulation soothed his mood. But he was on the coast road well past Gordon's Bay before his sharp mind could be objective.

Scenario One: If he went through with the rape of Connor's wife, it would hopefully placate Anita but cause a draw. Something he couldn't control. And the next contest implied murder. What were the words? He pulled over and picked up the file, riffling through it.

'Nearest kin destroyed.'

Uncontrollable. And unpleasant if one happened to win – or lose. Uncontrollable was the point. He didn't like that.

He swung the machine back on the bitumen. He loved this stretch. The narrow two-lane road flanked by the steep mountains on the left, grey-red now in this light, and on the right the red rock-rubble and scrub that fell to an azure sea. In the distance, the mist hanging around the base of the headland all the way to Cape Point across the bay. But his anxiety obscured its beauty.

Scenario Two: A refusal would cause Anita to be raped. Then she'd divorce him. Fact. He didn't give a damn if they raped her – but a divorce would be financial suicide. Unless the 'death of kin' contest could…

He needed to check through it all again. But first he needed a pee. No cover here.

The vehicle drifted on, contemptuous of the turns. Its excellent brakes and steering made driving it almost soporific. Hardly a car passed him: the place was left to the cormorants and baboons. He continued past Hanging Rock and pressed on to Kleinmond – as far as he could go without taking the detour around the Bot River. He swung off the road at the south end of the beach, touched the brake and the 28cm discs pulled him up on the red earth above the toilet block, flustering three black-winged seagulls.

The toilet looked unimpressive but the place behind

him, called The Beach House, had a sign reading 'Whistling Whale Restaurant'. Carrying the file, he went down the hall and found the toilet, then strolled into a room at the rear that overlooked a patch of grass. It was a pleasant lounge, sunny now, but the bay was prone to summer gales and the predictable west coast winter storms.

He lowered himself into an armchair in front of a glass-topped coffee table. Apart from a self-absorbed couple, he was the only guest. He ordered a cup of Earl Grey and a piece of carrot cake, then spread the papers from the folder on the table, took a pen from his pocket and held it poised over the bottom of one sheet.

If he refused…

He wrote down 'switch', then, under it, 'Connor winner/self loser = Connor to kill Anita or his own wife killed by Mould'.

He smiled at the scrawl. Unpleasant choice for Connor. He wouldn't be gruntled by that.

The waitress brought the tea and cake. 'There you are, sir.'

'Thank you.'

'I see you've been admiring our teapots.'

He'd been staring sightlessly at the cabinet near the door. It held a collection of decorative teapots. Most looked like anything but teapots. 'Yes. Unusual.'

'Hope you enjoy it.'

He looked back at the paper. But of course Connor wouldn't kill Anita. Being incurably decent, he'd grab his own wife and head for – what did they call it – the outback?

He stirred his tea absently, working through the list of rules again. Then he saw it.

He *saw* it!

In the first game hadn't he…

The waitress stared as the distinguished man in the Summer Lounge bounded to his feet with glee.

Grace Merrick climbed onto the M1 bus and dropped her token in the slot. As usual, there was no seat. She braced herself against the lurching and looked down at her handbag with surprise. An envelope was sticking out of it. She hadn't put it there. An unaddressed envelope with a small cogged emblem in the corner. Her eyes popped and she reached for it. Someone at the bus shelter on the avenue must have… She ripped the end off, eager to get at the message, and read with growing anger.

> Ms Merrick
> You are advised that Mr Sinclair has refused to carry out the required penalty on Mr Connor's wife, thus causing another switch in the game. He thus attracts the same penalty, the rape of his wife. Accordingly the draw is again deferred, with Mr Connor becoming the winner and Mr Sinclair the loser in the next game. This game involves the termination of kin, with Mr Connor required to officiate. A further bulletin will be conveyed to you when more is forthcoming. If you have any further enquiries, you may call the following number between now and noon.

A seven-digit number was added.

She pushed her way off the bus at the next stop and stormed to the nearest pay-phone. A long-faced man in a suit stood almost inside the cowling, peering at his pocket diary for a number. She bulldozed her way past him, jammed in her phone-card and punched the number on the buttons.

'Hello.'
'Merrick.'
'Hello, lovely lady.'
'Why isn't there a draw again? That's twice now.'

'Them's the breaks. One in the dust. One in the zone.'

'I want a draw. You hear?'

'Want to hit a homer, huh?'

'I am *mad*.'

'Want to dish Dyson, right?'

'I will… *kill* him. If you rotten people don't help, I'll fly to Australia myself and…'

'No go, Grace.'

'You can't stop me.'

'Sorry, Grace. You're grounded.'

A hand shoved against her shoulder. She glanced behind her to see two young females wearing heavy boots, chains and tattoos. 'Okay, bitch. Haul ass.'

Tess had come back next morning and had breakfast but said nothing to Connor. A stand-off. The following day he'd kept the conversation strictly domestic, suspecting he'd already said too much. She'd gone to work as usual on the Thursday, then packed that night for her 'conference'. She didn't ask him to drive her to the airport in the morning and he didn't offer. That was the night the fax came saying Sinclair had refused. He took one look at it, then made a phone call to a charter pilot he'd used on shoots.

She went, without saying goodbye, next morning. The taxi beeped at 5.15. The moment she left, he phoned to confirm the flight.

The charter was the only way. If he drove to Narrabri, they'd be gone before he arrived. If he took a commercial flight, his name would go into their computer. He'd also have to declare the gun – because he'd discovered on the Ansett shoot that they X-rayed baggage before loading it in the hold.

He got dressed, broke down the gun, slid the sections into the arms of an old skivvy and packed it in the long grip he used for lugging lighting stands. He emptied the cartridges into a plastic bag and stuffed them in with the gun. Then he got the aluminium case he kept his Kino-Flos lights in, pulled out the lights, the foam, and packed it with things he might need. Essentials. Clothing, maps, a compass, a pocketknife, passport, a few small tools, a first-aid kit. Anything could happen. Best to be prepared. All he knew was that no-one was going to help him. And that he was taking on professionals. People, he imagined, who packed parabolic dish sound-multipliers as routinely as other people packed handkerchiefs and who considered a lightweight carbine with bipod a standard inclusion in a golf bag.

The last thing he did was remove his solicitor's card from his business-card holder and put it in his billfold.

He was ready by seven. The phone rang as he lugged the first case onto the porch.

He heard the overseas pips. 'Mr Connor. You are going for trip?'

They were watching him? His heart pounded.

'Mr Connor?'

'Yes.'

'You receive fax?'

'I read it.'

'You now must kill Anita Sinclair by rule of game. We send detail of method, location, air ticket and full particular within two day.'

'Get lost.'

'Mr Connor, if you refuse, we kill your wife. You understand?'

He said nothing.

'You refuse?'

He thought fast. 'Tell you later.'

'What means later?'

'Later.'

'One moment.' There was a pause on the end of the line as if she were consulting with someone. Then, 'Mr Connor, you have three hour to reply. If you not ring number I give in three hour, we assume answer is refuse. Understand?' She gave him a local number with a 430 prefix – St Leonards. 'You have number?'

'I've written it down.' He hung up. At least he'd bought Tess three hours of safety.

He took the second case out onto the porch, shut the door and stared around. He couldn't see how anyone could be watching him over the high brick wall, unless they had a powerful telescope in one of the blocks of housing units on the hill. He wouldn't put it past them but he couldn't worry about that now. He had to get to the airport by eight.

Anita Sinclair opened the door and clasped her fur about her. Beyond the footbridge over the green slime of the drainage canal was the road – tarred but narrow enough to be a one-way lane. And beyond that was the grass-covered embankment that encased the river which, in that country of polders and dykes, remained the highest thing in the area.

She turned and walked along the lane with its whispering guard of poplars, feeling jet-lagged, thankful for crisp air. Here, less than an hour to Amsterdam and twenty minutes' drive from Schipol, she felt reasonably safe at last. Another day here, then Italy. Meanwhile, it was good to be home.

Her mother wanted groceries from the village. It was a fifteen-minute walk beside rich, sodden fields where placid ducks dabbled in the channels, followed by eager miniatures of themselves.

She heard a car behind her and stepped aside into the gravel as it passed. It continued ahead toward the skeleton sails of the windmill and the ancient leaning church behind the trees. Cars seemed an intrusion in this place where a bicycle or pedestrian was an event. She watched it idly – a small car containing a large, thick-necked man in a cap.

She reached the cobbled streets, walked past the narrow cottages, each with its prim window ornaments and flagstaff holder on the wall, a village so picturesque it attracted tourists in season.

She crossed the old lift-bridge and bought the groceries. She noticed that the car had parked outside the chemist. The man wasn't in sight.

The bridge was up, now, to let a yacht through. She waited for it to lower, watching the bridge-keeper dangle a chipped sabot on a string so that the yachtsman could put coins in as he passed. She gazed along the river at the few moored house-boats and barges, each with its numbered allotment on the bank. Stability. Order. As the drizzle was holding off, and the bag with the groceries wasn't heavy, she decided to walk back on the far side and cross again on the main road bridge.

As she turned into the tree-lined road she heard the car rattle over the bridge behind her. It went past her down the road, past the more expensive homes, picture-postcard places with neat gardens and an air of money precisely applied. The congruity of the place was either stifling or charming, depending on how it was viewed. The man was probably a tourist. She wondered what he made of it.

Beyond the houses, fields stretched all the way to the bridge. No more cars passed either way and no-one else was on the road.

She entered the underpass beneath the main road bridge that lead to the pedestrian walk on one side. It smelt damp and there were graffiti. What did Hanford call it? The folk art of the dispossessed. Against the curved walls the click of her shoes sounded hollow.

As she reached the other end of the tunnel a huge figure

stepped across her path, blocking the way and the light. The cap had been removed. The tree-like legs and piston arms were unmistakable. A shock went through her small body and had the merciful effect of stunning her, weakening her like a rabbit so that she could do no more than wriggle as the chemical-soaked pad was pushed firmly against her face.

When Blore got her to the rented houseboat with the carefully drawn blinds, he undressed her with the anticipation of someone unwrapping a present, as if her tiny, perfect frame was an offering to his fingers and his eyes. She was paler than the child prostitutes from Mae Sai but with the more defined contours of a woman. Not child but ethereal adult, confusing and unusual.

She lay exposed, a thing of shadows, ovals, hollows, of valleys and small peaks, a territory unexplored, so flawless that, for seconds, he just stared. Then he lifted her by the crotch and shoulders, placing her face down on the corner of the bed, spreading her knees on the carpet at each side. He unzipped his pants and applied the lubricant, his field version of foreplay, working it inside her.

Then – he waited.

Waited until she stirred, head one side, staring at the wooden handles of the chest of drawers, as if they were coming into focus.

As she half twisted around, kitten-weak, she saw the colossus behind her.

He grinned. 'Hello, rich bitch.'

She tried to focus on his face. Her hand felt between her legs. 'You... fucked me?'

'Not yet. That's next.'

She was on her knees, taking great gasps of air. 'Why? Why?'

'Spoils of war.'

'No… Hanford. He… refused to?'

Blore nodded. 'What else?'

She subsided back on her haunches, hyperventilating now, her fingers becoming crabbed. 'I… wanted to… hear it… confirmed.'

He laughed. 'So you've heard it. Present arse.'

She staggered up, scrambling away from him across the bed. He grabbed her ankles and yanked her toward him until her bottom was back over the edge. She twisted around, fingers going for his eyes. He slapped her hard across the face, turning her head with the force of the blow. She fell back gasping, then squirmed off the bed again, twisting, struggling until she was half across the floor.

Blore raised one huge fist. 'Shut up or you get this.'

She was on her knees, now, gasping for air, trying to drag herself up by the drawer handles. A drawer slid out. She saw her chance – turned as Blore came at her, trying to thrust the edge at his stiff penis.

He sidestepped, grunting, as the corner drove into his thigh, then brushed it aside with one arm and lifted her bodily off the floor, tossing her back on the bed as if she were as light as a stuffed toy.

She was half up again, eyes huge. He punched her in the stomach to wind her.

As she collapsed, he flipped her over until her bottom was once again across the bed.

He knew his weight would be enough to pin her. He wanted her urgently now.

He spread her vagina with his hands, thrust into her. The novelty was so intense that he came in thirty seconds like a schoolboy, then, spent, withdrew and slumped.

She slid to the floor, gasping as if choking – lay there, in agony from the punch. Blore wiped himself on the hem of the bedspread. Then he stood up slowly and zipped.

He smiled down at her tormented eyes. 'First rule in a battle zone: keep your arse covered.'

She twisted around on the floor, unable to relieve the pain.

He said, 'Hurts, doesn't it?' He turned and left the room.

Chapter Eighteen

Bankstown airport was for general aviation – an expanse of grass and wind surrounded by low buildings and private hangars. Although it looked deceptively dreamy, it handled more air traffic than any other airport in the country. As Connor lugged his cases to the perimeter gate, the pilot strolled out of the office carrying his flight bag and clipboard. 'Hi, David. Been a while.'

'Hi. What've we got?'

The man pointed to one of the shapes beyond the asphalt patch. 'Little Tiger. No sense in a twin for two people.'

Connor followed him over the grass toward the low-wing four-seater. 'How are your isobars and whatnot?'

'Light cloud. No worries. You filming?'

'Pick-up shots.'

Connor knew the routine. He untied the ropes attached to the eyes beneath both wings, then climbed up on the black strip beside the cockpit to help the pilot remove the cover over the canopy. The man threw him the keys. 'You know where it goes.'

He unlocked the small luggage door, pushing the folded cover in. 'I'll do the cases.'

He climbed back on the wing, unlocked and slid the canopy back, then jiggled the cases onto the back seat. He strapped them down, then strapped himself into the right front seat, while the pilot finished peering into the engine and eye-balling fuel levels in the wing tanks. Connor wanted to fast-forward him but knew the ritual was more inflexible than the opening of Parliament.

Finally the man climbed in and Connor mentally chewed his nails while the fellow jacked in headsets, wrote in his log, adjusted frequencies, strapped the sat-nav box to his wheel, positioned his clipboard and maps. He switched on, pumped the primer, pushed in the mixture control, then leaned out and yelled to the wind and the indifferent grass, 'Clear prop!' although there was no-one in sight.

The airframe shuddered as the engine kicked twice and stopped, leaving just the whine of the turn and bank indicator gyro. Connor put on his cans and heard the crackle of the recorded message from the tower about wind speed and conditions.

On the second try, the engine caught. The aircraft settled down to a thrumming as they rocked over tufts of grass, heading for the holding area, stopped for the run-up, got clearance and turned onto runway one-one.

'Looking good.' The pilot shut the canopy, then eased the throttle forward. The prop became a lighter blur as it bit air and thrust them back into their seats. Then they were aloft, banking to the north, the three parallel strips below them growing smaller.

When they were clear of restricted air-space, had established course and height, the pilot went 'bwit' into his mike to get it working. 'What's the shoot about? Cotton?'

'Right.'

'It's a big business. I've been over Colly Farms at Moree. All that irrigation, pumping stations…'

Connor nodded, looking at the ground drifting by 3000 feet below.

'Want to drive?'

'Okay.' He took the wheel. He'd done this before. It wasn't simple.

'Keep your feet off the rudder, nose just below the

horizon.' The pilot lifted his map.

The nose started to rise. He pushed the control column forward a little.

'Watch your direction indicator. You're off course.'

He turned the wheel that controlled the ailerons, slightly dipping the right wing. It felt heavy, rather like driving a truck. He watched his bearing.

'Watch your altimeter. That's the hundreds hand winding up.'

He pushed the column forward. Then they hit bumps. 'You're off course again.'

He flew for thirty minutes. It left his mind no time to brood. A long bank of cloud was nearing. He was sorry when the pilot said, 'I'll take it.'

Narrabri was an uncontrolled airport. They did the circuit and came in at 500. There was wind-shear over the long tarred runway so they touched down on the skew. The wheels hit and vibration tried to shake the cabin apart. Then the nose wheel touched and they taxied toward the small brick terminal with the patch of grass in front.

Connor got out on the wing, carrying the grip. The air was cool.

The pilot handed the square box down to him. 'You going to be long? I've got a ten-hour limit. It's the law.'

'Don't know,' Connor said. 'Just wait. If I have to put you up tonight, I will.'

No hire car companies serviced the terminal. He paced around for twenty minutes until the taxi came and shoved his cases in the boot. 'Department of Ag.'

The driver nodded and they headed through the small town, then over a flat road with nondescript fields on both sides.

'Lovely day for it,' the driver said.

'Pretty good.'

'Been here before?'

'Yup.' He hoped the lie had shortened the trip. Finally they slowed and turned right into a drive with manicured lawns and trees. It was some kind of research centre shared by the CSIRO. To the left of the main office were steel buildings and rows of glasshouses further back. He told the taxi to wait and got out beside two men talking on the driveway. He asked them where the lab was and one pointed to a khaki-coloured building. He hurried up the path and opened the fly-wire outer door.

Most of the inside was a long room with a lab table running down the centre. Female research assistants sat both sides, doing something unpleasant to larvae in segmented plastic trays. The nearest woman slid off her stool and came over. 'Help you?'

He produced his solicitor's card. 'Mason from Mason and Brindle. It's to do with a bequest. We're trying to trace the beneficiary. A Mr Stuthridge?'

'Just take a pew for a mo.' She pointed into an office by the door. 'I'll get someone.'

He sat on the edge of the indicated chair. This was where it could come unstuck. If he couldn't trace them from here, the trip was pointless. Best to look the part – fake unconcern. He leaned back and lifted a folder from the clutter. It showed a chart. '...the green area indicates pyrethroids and endosulphan. The red sector indicates the need to add Bt or ovicide to...' He put the folder down and picked up an issue of *The Australian Cotton Grower*. To someone with no interest in cotton it was all, as Tess would say, boring as batshit.

'Mr Mason?'

He sprang up. An older woman had come into the office, peering at his card through granny glasses. 'What was the man's name?'

'Stuthridge. Lester Stuthridge.'

She moved to the table, peered down at a list and her glasses became momentary mirrors. 'He was in here this morning.'

'Would you know where he works?'

'He's a consultant. They move around. But the samples we did the report on... let's see... winter legumes, chick-peas,' she glanced down again, 'came from Sarridan.'

'Can you tell me where that is?'

'It's up the road – half an hour from here.' He followed her to the front door and she pointed. 'Go out and right. You can't miss it. There's a sign.'

'Thanks a lot. Most helpful.'

He walked back toward the cab, forcing himself not to run.

The driver knew the place and sat the car on 110. Connor glanced at the churning meter. Why was he doing this for someone who'd betrayed him? He felt disgusted with her, but still couldn't abandon her. He'd lived with her for years – and still had to live with himself.

He stared at the paddocks sliding past – black, puggy earth, alluvial, set hard – mostly fallow cottonfields starved for nitrogen. The occasional crop of barley or wheat, some cattle, small silos full of feed. Boring as...

Christ. What were they going to do to her?

The sign.

The cab slowed and took a left, heading along a side-road, trailing dust as it jitterbugged on ruts. They juddered over a stock-gate, sped up a track beside an irrigation channel, the wheels half sliding, then gripping again as they hit patches of loose surface. Deep-ripped black soil stretched into the distance on both sides. Ahead, on a green island in the sea of black, were sheds and administration buildings.

The channel abruptly turned at right angles and ran

away like a river across the field. In the distance the stream was blocked by the concrete wall of a channel gate. He saw the parked pick-up truck first. Then the two figures – standing close together on the metal walkway above the wall, looking down at the water. The man was leaning on the hand-wheel that operated the valve. The woman almost certainly was Tess.

When they reached the first shed Connor told the driver to stop, fed him large-denomination bills, leapt out. As the boot-lid came up he grabbed his cases and slammed the lid. The cab turned and became a cloud of dust. He stood holding his cases, wildly looking around. Straggly bushes, stumps, the rusting curve of a discarded trash rake. The only useable cover was the shed – long and tall with sliding doors. He dumped the lighting box behind it but kept the grip in his hand. Then he peered around the building's steel edge to watch the truck across the field.

The couple were getting into it. Now it was turning, slowly heading back. The man's arm pointed out of the window. She was getting the grand tour.

Then he lost them as the vehicle passed out of sight behind some trees. He jogged along the back of the sheds, heading toward the administration buildings, checking before darting across the gaps. So far, the place seemed deserted. Again, the warning twinge in the gut. At this time of the year there would be few people on the property but he expected to see at least someone.

The last shed was the end of his cover. Beyond was a water tank. Through the gap he saw the pick-up, parked, its covered tray projecting just beyond the building. If only he had a pistol instead of a long, awkward weapon that still had to be assembled and loaded. To get it ready would take a minute and there wasn't a minute. By then, the truck could be gone.

He edged to the front corner of the shed and peered

around. No-one in the cabin. Now what?

A small window around the edge with open louvres. Snatches of conversation. The man talking.

'…my summer cubby-hole…run tests on egg samples here…getting a lot of resistance. Spraying's expensive.…get the reagents, developers in the kit…'

Boring as…

There was no other sound except the wind and the chattering of rosellas. Connor put a foot on the towbar of the truck and slung a leg over the tailgate.

Inside, he lay flat and undid the end of the grip – sliding the gun out, feeling for the plastic bag of cartridges.

He paused as he heard them coming back. The floor pan dipped as they got into the cabin.

Her voice. 'Well, I don't think your job's very romantic.'

'Wait till you see the big machinery. Got a picker in for maintenance.'

'I'd rather go back to bed.'

'I'll just give you a look.'

'Do we have to?'

'It's not far. Then we'll go back to the room and I'll show you a really big machine.'

Her chuckle. 'Men and their toys.'

The truck started and moved off. Connor had the gun clear. It was difficult to fit the barrel with the floor moving and vibrating. On the third try he slid it home and screwed the magazine cap on hard. He thumbed two cartridges into the magazine, dropped another into the open breech, then pressed the catch but held the bolt lever, easing it gently shut. Cartridges were rolling around the tray. He stuffed the strays in the pockets of his shirt, then pushed the safety catch crosswise so the red danger band appeared.

The truck stopped and he slid forward. He lay flat as they got out, waited till he heard the scrape of metal wheels on rails, counted to ten, then peered around the canopy. It was another metal shed, its sliding door pushed slightly open. He climbed out, gun in his left hand, then gripped it at the slope, right forefinger ahead of the trigger guard, and sidled quickly through the gap.

He'd expected to confront them. Instead, he almost walked into the tail-piece of a lathe. The change from glare to gloom blinded him. He hadn't counted on that. The end of the building was a workshop – benches with tall metal racks holding parts. He moved behind a rack while his eyes adjusted to the light.

In the middle of the space was a huge red picking machine. They were climbing its metal ladder to the catwalk beside the cabin. Neither of them had seen him. Their voices echoed in the metal tomb.

'See in here?' the man said, opening the door of the cabin. 'All mod cons. Air conditioning, CD…'

'What's that lever?' His wife's voice.

'Basket control. Raise it, lower it, open, close it, start the conveyor. One-hand operation. Come down and I'll show you the heads.'

As they came down the ladder, a vertical sliver of light widened at the back of the shed. A door. Someone else had come in. Someone careful not to make noise.

They were near the front edge of the machine. It had five raked inlets with vertical drums that obviously turned, studded with long spindles that looked as if they spun as well. Each picking head had a warning sticker on the metal frame above it – a picturegraph showing a figure being dismembered.

She pointed to a sticker. 'That's horrible.'

'First thing visitors say.'

The man released two levers off the end head and lifted the panel off the side. 'This'll show you how it works. See those two big drums?'

A shadow moved from the gloom around the back of the machine. An older man, grim-faced. His cheap rubber-soled riding shoes made no noise on the rungs of the ladder. Next, he was in the cabin and had started the thing up. The roar was like massed Harleys burning off at the lights.

Tess jumped and Stuthridge laughed in a forced way. 'He's only testing it.' He was behind her, arms around her waist.

'Shouldn't we get out of here?'

'Hang on.' He made stirring motions, looking up at the cabin. The roar of the machine changed as the tall picking drums started to rotate, their hundreds of stiletto-like spindles spinning as they moved.

Connor stepped out of cover and shouted – just half a second too late. Stuthridge had dropped to his haunches behind Tess, in one move grabbing both her ankles and butting his head into her rear.

To Connor, it seemed like slow-motion. He saw her fall forward, unable to stop. Her head came up and her hands went out, instinctively, for protection. Connor's shout was lost in her scream as the twirling spikes gripped, bored into her hands and, as they swivelled on the drums, dragged her wrists and arms into the machine. The scream was cut short as her head slammed into the row of triangular spikes. He didn't know that three spindles had speared her upper eyelid, sinus and cheek, or that the spike spinning in her brain, unlike the ice-pick used in a lobotomy, went in horizontally, not up, causing an epileptic seizure. He just saw her stiffen and shake. Then, as the long drum turned, to his horror, he saw the twirling spindles re-emerge as they ripped out the side of her head.

Stuthridge was standing again, giving the man in the cabin the thumbs up.

Before the drum-drive disengaged, Tess Connor's left arm and right arm to the elbow had been shredded into the drums, covering the whirling metal with raw flesh, arterial blood and the ivory of splintered bone.

The man in the cabin was pointing frantically at Connor.

Stuthridge turned to see the inside of a shotgun barrel – before it exploded, point blank, in his face. A face that became a red-black pulp as the back and top of his skull flew off. What was left above his neck collapsed forward against Connor. He stepped back too late to prevent spurts of blood striping his pants.

Connor's next shot shattered the windscreen of the cabin, but the man inside was diving for the catwalk. He didn't bother with the ladder: he leapt. Was in mid-air when Connor 'hosed' him. It was easier than trying to hit trap targets.

The shed resounded once more as the man bellowed, arching backwards. The full-choked load of close-patterned pellets shredded his right kidney. He hit the ground with the finality of a dropped egg, and writhed.

As the Winchester spat its third cartridge, Connor grabbed three more from his pocket, fed one into the breech and pressed the catch. The gate slammed shut as the bolt shot forward, twisting to lock on its lugs. He pressed the others into the magazine, then wiped the spatter of Stuthridge off his face, leaving a pulpy smear on his hand. He couldn't bear to look at what was left of Tess. The body on the concrete in front of him was also practically headless – matted hair, red mince…

The man writhing on the floor was trying to claw his way to cover behind one of the rear wheels of the machine. His face seemed all teeth and gullet and his groans echoed off the walls. A red streak on the concrete recorded the short distance he'd moved.

Connor levelled the barrel at him, wanting to blow him to bits.

But surely the bedlam must have been heard. All he could think of now was escape. He edged back through the gap in the door, prepared to fight his way out.

Two men were watching some distance away on the verandah of the homestead. They seemed interested but more contemplative than concerned. He leapt into the pick-up, shoving the gun against the far door, jammed the truck in gear almost before it started and dragged the wheel around, heading for the drive.

Then he remembered his other case with his passport and personal items. Had to get it. He'd killed a man.

He wrenched the truck around in the dirt, lead-footed it to the furthest shed, skidded to a stop, got out and flung it over the tailgate. He slipped in his haste to get back in the cab, saving himself by clinging to the doorframe, scrambled in and spun the wheels, heading for the drive.

Half an hour later he found a place to stop – a grove of trees by a creekbed near a bridge. He dragged off his spattered clothes, wiped himself down, got a clean shirt and jeans from his bag, changed and combed his hair. Then he unloaded the gun and packed it in the grip. It happened without his participation – as if he were merely observing a different, colder person who took charge in a crisis, got things done.

He drove to the airport but parked the truck further up the road near a hangar that serviced crop-dusters. There were no police at the terminal.

The grass blew peacefully in the sun.

But the lid was now well and truly off. 'Cautious Connor' was irrevocably dead.

He'd killed a man!

But that man had been employed by Mould. That man had killed his wife.

He felt an enormous sadness and emitted a groan, then pushed the thought of it away. He had to get to the aircraft.

When they were on course back to Sydney, the pilot went 'bwit' into the mike and said, 'You shoot what you wanted?'

'Yup.'

Chapter Nineteen

Connor didn't feel the full effect until he'd left the aircraft and was in his car. For an hour he sat in the almost empty carpark, trying to absorb what had happened, work out what it meant. He went through all the stages – rocking and crying, banging on the steering wheel, cursing, rehearsing conversations that had never been with a wife who no longer was. Finally, face streaked, body drained, he got out of the car and walked. Walked to the high mesh fence at the end of the strip and clung to it in despair.

Tess was dead and he'd killed at least one man. For once, Mould had got what he gave. Was it manslaughter or murder? Would the police now trace him, hold him? He didn't know, couldn't plan. He drifted back to the car. On the way home he listened to the news. Nothing.

His house was near a corner. He drove across the intersection, looking at the front. No sign of police. He couldn't stay here for more than a moment but wanted to check the fax. If Mould had…

He parked along the back lane, let himself in through the garage, keyed in the code, opened the studio door. Then froze.

Inside the office there was nothing. Nothing at all. No fax, desk, chairs or cabinets. Just less faded patches on the wall where filing cabinets had stood and where the whiteboard had been screwed. He walked into the control room. Everything was gone. Squares of dust on top of the built-in console table, straggling ends of sub-floor cabling. The monitors, video recorders, speakers – gone. The editing console – even his old effects generator and sound mixer had been unscrewed from their flush fittings and removed.

The mikes were gone from the booth. The storeroom was also empty. They'd taken his lights, camera gear, diopters. The shelves of his tape library – bare. Years of work. Irreplaceable.

The house was the same. Everything had been removed – even the soap and towels from the bathroom. The kitchen cupboards were white strips. Only light fittings and blinds remained. He couldn't even find the cat.

It seemed physically impossible that so much could have been shifted in a day. They'd even turned off power and gas.

The whole of his life – erased. He locked the place and crept out the back. If this was Mould's penalty for telling Tess, why had he gone to such trouble? He could have just blown the house up.

He drove up the peninsula to Avalon, parked in a cul-de-sac, humped his two cases to the highway and waited for the Palm Beach bus. He rode it to the ferry wharf. The ferry was there and he climbed aboard, a tired-looking man with two unusual cases. He sat among the frazzled mums and hyperactive children who were returning to houses across the bay.

He got off at Mackerel Beach. The small West Head settlement was in shadow, the afternoon chill descending the slope. The only access was by sea unless you counted the walk up a fire track to the ridge. Few people came here in winter – only permanents and weekend enthusiasts. He walked along the track behind the beach, in front of the few simple houses, turned into the grass strip by the creek that served the carless place for a road and lugged his cases over the footbridge to the shack.

His friends, the couple who owned the weekender, were in England for two months. Connor and Tess had a standing invitation. He knew where they hid the key, let himself in and opened the windows so the breeze could replace stale air.

He felt weak and knew he should eat. He found a canned steak and kidney dinner in the kitchen, heated it and wolfed it from the pan. Then he sat in the small sunroom, desperately tired, watching the tree-covered slope blur into dusk. It was hard to comprehend. In a day his life had gone – leaving a bitter freedom as raw as a cold wind. He'd bought himself a night's sleep, that was all.

Now it was simple.

Survival.

He switched on the transistor radio. The batteries were weak and he could barely hear the news. Still no report. It was weird.

He didn't put on a light. As night crept down the hill, he spread bedclothes on one of the bunks, lay down and knew nothing more.

The Saab 1200 climbed above Sorrento, negotiating the sharp curves of the Blue Ribbon Road with effortless control, passing the old stone farmhouses and citrus groves until it was over the escarpment and on the Amalfi coast.

Beyond the blur of the low stone wall, Anita Sinclair glimpsed the view that had made Salerno Province her particular love. Deep gorges dropped almost vertically to pellucid green-tinted water that shaded outward into a pristine blue. A sea of glass stretched to reefs that were the Sirens' fabled isles.

Now, as she drove faster, the steering wheel began to vibrate as if the front wheels were unbalanced. She frowned. The garage had sworn they'd tested everything.

Far ahead, on the hillside high above the road, a man in hiking gear lowered his binoculars. A man respected by

Capos for his meticulous attention to detail, a hard-earned reputation he was anxious not to lose. The previous day, in Ravello, he'd attended to the car, removing both right-hand tyres and inserting small charges with transmitters and ingenious sprung gripping-frames. The instructions had been specific, the site meticulously chosen. He felt as confident as one could feel, wedged between two rocks and instructed to operate technology he'd never seen before.

She slowed the car as she neared Positano's terraced gorge. The town's white houses and domed roofs had been the backdrop to their romance – a romance bathed in a liveliness, intensity that rivalled the Mediterranean light. Here they'd met and that night he'd introduced her to his world – taken her down in the lift to San Pietro, the resort built into the cliff, where they'd dined beneath the vine-covered ceiling, exploring each other's minds. Later, they'd explored each other's bodies in the huge bed of the suite below. Then luxuriated in the sunken bath and sipped champagne on their private balcony while the moon made the water pearl-bright.

How life changed. That morning, her lawyers had told her that the settlement would favour her greatly. Now she'd take him for everything she could get. Bitter and determined, she rounded the headland beyond the town. The turbo cut in. Damn the vibration in the wheel.

As the Saab rounded the curve at the maximum possible speed, the man lowered the binoculars and bent forward. He lifted the box off his lap by its rubber-sheathed stub aerial, flicked the safety-cover off the toggle switch. The woman could drive and knew the road – she must be important to rate such an end. He flicked the switch to ARM and held his finger over the button. She was almost to the teeth of the curve. He pressed.

He heard the far-off stutter of two small explosions. The

car, for all its stability, couldn't handle two blown tyres on the same side at that speed and spot. It punched through the retaining wall, flew outward and dived, tilting, nose-down, as if it had all the time in the world.

It slammed into the first outcrop of rock, crumpling progressively as designed, before flipping lazily upside down. The noise delay of the crunch was a full half-second, which seemed odd as it never happened in the movies. As the roof of the cabin was combed back into shreds by the next spine or rock, twin horns began a valedictory blare.

Anita Sinclair never heard it. Her body had been shorn off in the middle and her top half was upside down in the back seat, her head at a strange angle from the trunk, her waist an altar festooned with pale intestine.

The shining scrap barrel-rolled to the water below. The last out-of-sync noise was the splash. The sea parted then closed against the wreck, a symbol of perfect acceptance.

The man on the hill looked at the box in his hand with the veneration of an acolyte contemplating the Blessed Host.

'Mr D.' It was a greeting.

'Harry.'

'Gonna kill 'em tonight, eh?'

'Better believe it.'

As the doorman waved him up the red-carpeted stairs, Dyson felt his pulse quicken.

The casino was doing good business and had a crush of regulars around the bar.

'Hidy, Mr D. Usual?'

He nodded, gulped his complimentary drink and walked to the table with its familiar rectangular markings, his palms beginning to sweat. It wasn't winning or losing that mattered. It was the thrill of the immediate result on this daunting, taunting battlefield of baize. Addictive. Compulsive. To the point of compromising everything: work, life, relationships.

Years of duplicity, cadging, petty theft and eventually full-scale embezzlement. As if to punish himself. For what?

He'd got the poem that morning. He'd asked a professional book searcher to locate it. He didn't hold out much hope but the woman had found it in a second-hand bookshop. An old library book with Romanian poems in English. Perhaps bad news was easy to find. He'd read the third verse. Now he knew there was nothing to lose. So tonight was the end. The last of his money was going into chips.

He settled at the blackjack table, sweating with anticipation. The rectangle in front of him waited to be fed. The key to estimating when high-value cards would appear was visual, not mathematical. But he wasn't a shuffle-tracker. Never been good at that. He tried to remember the BGB strategy. He'd give it his best shot.

The shutter on the card shoe clacked.

Play or stand?

His disadvantage was desperation and the advantage of the house six per cent. Theoretically you could win, but his memory was bad now. He tried to keep track of cards as the dealer slapped them down but the house was using multiple decks.

Concentrate. Stay sharp.

He knew the system. Stand with a hand of twelve or more if the dealer has two to six, with seventeen or more if the dealer has seven to ten or an ace, stand with eighteen or more and double down only when the dealer's card is two to seven, split aces or eights always, split other pairs when the dealer's up-card is two to seven. It worked if your mind could keep track. Yet even with this rigmarole, the house had a one per cent advantage.

Before long he'd dropped $5000 and went home hating

himself, wanting to creep into some hole where nothing could bruise him again.

Connor's head was in a clamp. The light above the operating table blinded him and his scream meant nothing as blood sprayed from the drill boring into his brain.

He jerked awake to find his head jammed against the upright of the bunk and the window framing the glare of a perfect winter day. The sound of the drill became a motor mower slicing through twigs three houses away.

He sat up stiffly, rubbed his neck. His foot touched the cold barrel of the gun. It all came back. Had they found his car? They would have circulated the number by now.

He felt sticky. His teeth were growing fur. He flat-footed it into the kitchen, switched on the radio. Damn. The volume control was down but he hadn't clicked it right off and the batteries had died overnight.

He found a towel and went to the shower. He'd forgotten to switch on the heater. He endured the freezing stream long enough to get clean, dried himself, shivering, and got dressed, dragging on his one heavy jumper. There were cornflakes in the kitchen and long-life milk. He gulped the simulated meal, then tried washing blood off yesterday's clothes. The pants needed soaking and might have to be thrown out. But the shirt came clean, the shirt with the Saks Fifth Avenue label that he'd bought at an extravagant price during a ghost crew job in New York. He put it on a wire coat-hanger and opened the door to hook it on the railing.

Something scuffed the floorboards of the deck. A paper – Saturday's *Sydney Morning Herald*. There were no deliveries here and the shack had been unoccupied for a month. He stared around the she-oaks by the creek, looked into the yards of the cottages on both sides. Just two children with plastic sand-buckets walking along the grass toward the beach. No-one else was in sight.

But someone knew exactly where he was.

He took the paper inside and spread it on the table. The corner of page four had been folded down and the article outlined in red.

TRAGIC DEATH SPARKS LOVER'S SUICIDE

Moree, Friday. A woman was ripped apart bodily today when she moved too close to a cotton harvester and her clothes became caught in the machinery.

A man she was with, believed to have been her lover, later shot himself. The man, a well-known consultant in the area, worked for the farm, which is owned by a New Zealand consortium.

The woman, who was married, had apparently left home. Her husband has moved elsewhere, leaving no forwarding address and police have not yet been able to contact him.

Two witnesses to the accident are receiving counselling. There are believed to be no suspicious circumstances.

The names of the couple have not yet been released.

Next to it was an article in bold type.

FARM WORK RISKIEST

Workers in the agricultural sector are twice as likely to suffer employment-related injury as those employed in other industries, according to the WorkCover Authority.

The Director of the Australian Agricultural Health Unit based at Moree...

He stopped reading, incredulous. A New Zealand consortium? Was the farm Mould's as well? Had Mould put a spin on police and media to play things any way he liked? He knew that, in Australia, it wouldn't be too difficult. Many officials were 'on the take' and the police history of corruption was notorious. Then Sinclair was right. There was no way out of this at all.

Stapled to the bottom of the page were two sheets of paper, both bearing the cogged logo. He tore them off.

Dear Mr Connor

As you see from the paper, despite your insurrection, the game continues. This note will clarify events to date.

1. Your ill-advised disclosures to your wife evoked a penalty (see Rule Six) which you have discovered – the confiscation of your possessions. Because of your actions yesterday, destroying your house would have seemed suspicious. Otherwise it would now be demolished. We will settle for the removal of your possessions, which is consistent with your absence from home. Do not contact the police. A lookalike will do that today. He will confirm that you spent yesterday assisting the removalists, who will vouch for this. The pilot's records now show that he flew alone to Foster. There, he was collected from the airport by a hire boat and taken to town. The boat owner remembers his face. You may see from this brief account how concerned we are for your welfare. If you had been considering a jail term as a way to avoid participation, regard that avenue as closed. You will note from the article above that it is impossible to escape the game.

And so, to the game itself.

2. As you know, if a winner refuses to enforce a penalty after a switch, that penalty is applied to him (see Rule Four). So your refusal to eliminate Mrs Sinclair attracted the same penalty to you – the death of your wife.

3. As a loser can escape only once; a second refusal to enforce a penalty on that loser calls down that

> penalty (see Rule Five) – so your failure to destroy Mr Sinclair's wagons and cattle made it mandatory that he underwent the next loss he attracted, as he initially refused to administer dung to Mr Dyson. Your failure to eliminate his wife made no difference to the outcome. Mr Sinclair has therefore suffered the loss of his wife.

Connor stared through the window at the small rainforest that followed the stream uphill.

Sinclair couldn't escape the game. Had he used it to slot in his own agenda – used Mould to destroy his wife because she'd threatened to divorce him.

Surely the man wasn't that much of a bastard.

He shook the thought off – looked down to read the rest of it.

> We hope you now finally grasp that the game proceeds, whatever you intend. Your own position is currently this:
> As you have sustained two penalties successively – loss of possessions and wife – a further loss cannot immediately follow (see Rule Seven). Thus you will not be part of the next draw. The three other players alone will contend. However, we will need you when the draw is held, for reasons to be explained.

It went on a little longer. It was of course unsigned.

He sat with the papers in his hand, shaking with anger. No way out. He was stuck with this to the end.

He looked at his watch. It was 9.15. He had to get out of the house, walk this off. He left the windows open but locked the door. The shits would get in if they wanted to – were probably watching him now.

He crossed the footbridge and trudged to the beach. The two children were near the water, building castles and moats and a lone man further up was tending two rods stuck in the sand. Moored to the jetty was an impressive-looking half-cabin runabout, its stern buried deep in the water by the tombstone of a Mercury engine. A man lounged across its front-bench seat, as if waiting for someone to return.

Connor walked onto the beach and looked across the water to the peninsula. As the shock of the letter subsided he felt, again, that disturbing sense of freedom. Not the freedom of security or comfort but the feeling that came from their loss – of being totally bereft of involvements – subject to events alone.

He picked up a shell from the sand, studied its rough exterior and smooth inside. He felt like the shell. Empty. Discarded. Adrift.

He walked back in a kind of limbo, feeling the smoothness of the shell with his thumb. His old life had been replaced by the menace of the game. So, as he was obliged to play, he'd play.

But he'd watch for cracks in Mould's armour. 'At least,' he muttered, 'I've scored. Two down and the house saved. Not bad.'

When he got back he placed the shell on the table, picked up the paper again. Incredible. They'd perfumed away a triple murder with convenient misinformation. Even added the bit about farm injuries to lessen the sting.

The deck outside creaked. Startled, he darted to the bedroom for the gun, dropped to his haunches, looked under the bed. Gone. And the cartridge bag as well.

A knock at the door.

He could see nothing around that looked a useful weapon. He padded to the door. 'Who's there?'

A soft voice he knew. 'Come on, Connor. Open it.' Blore

stood there, doing his impression of a wind-break, incongruous in flannel shirt and casual pants. He held out Connor's shirt. 'Dry.'

Connor took it. 'Suppose you think you're a hot-shot, murdering other people's wives.'

'I didn't supervise that personally.'

'Should I clap?' Connor tossed the shirt on the settee as Blore stooped under the lintel, looked around for a chair that might support him and finally lowered himself beside the shirt.

Connor stayed standing, wary. 'You took the gun?'

Blore nodded. 'I don't like large-bore close-assault weapons.'

'I just might have blown your guts out.'

'Yes. You're blooded now, growing up. Like kids do in a war. After you've smelled burning flesh and death... hosed your mate's blood and guts out of a chopper... you're not the same. Shotguns make a mess, don't they?' Connor knew what was coming. Blore the military bore was about to tell him all about shotguns. 'They tried to ban them under the Hague Convention in 1918. Now they have flechette rounds that penetrate mild steel, anti-armour, HE, smoke, illumination...' He smiled. 'Unfortunately for you, that information's academic.'

'You lot are right into it, aren't you?'

'You've taken out two of our men and given us considerable trouble. If it were up to me...' He smiled mirthlessly and drew a finger across the place where his neck should have been. 'But I'm instructed to be your nursemaid.'

'So why are you here, Nursie?'

'Don't push it,' the soft voice said. 'You're visiting Dyson this morning for a special event at 1100.'

'What event?'

'You'll see.' He stood up and cocked a thumb at the door. 'Out.'

Chapter Twenty

It was the boat with the Mercury outboard. It carved a gash in the bay, heading south. They planed over the chop, beached near the Newport pub and transferred to a Range Rover with dark tinted windows. Blore sat beside him in the back, taking up most of the seat, as the other man drove them the long haul to the city. They avoided the tunnel, went across the bridge and took the Eastern Distributor, finally stopping in front of a terrace in Annandale Street. Cables taped to the front step of the house trailed across the tiny front garden, over the wrought-iron fence and along the footpath to a TV outside broadcast van with a satellite dish on the roof.

They got out. Blore pointed to the door. 'Inside.'

'We're on the news, now?' Connor walked down the dingy hall, expecting to see technicians. But there was no crew in the house. He followed the cables to the living room at the back. A camera on a tripod was locked off on two chairs positioned side by side. More cables went to a monitor on a table by the camera. Its screen faced the chairs. Beside the chairs was a C-stand holding a square of poly, with a light shining on it to give fill. The other light came from the glass wall of the room, which looked on a patch of back garden infested with bamboo, and the back of a dilapidated garage.

Now Connor understood. A live hook-up using station equipment. Another example of Mould's influence and wealth?

Blore and his assistant positioned themselves near the hall door, arms folded, like Egyptian temple guards.

Dyson, clad in a soiled dressing-gown, was moaning into a phone. 'You'll get your money ... I know, but ... so it comes down to that, does it? Money? You liked it ... you don't mean this. Zoozie, you know how I feel ... Don't be cruel.'

Connor looked around the room. There had been an attempt, long ago, to make it arty. Two-toned green decor, modish prints of naked men. But the paint was mouldy and dust clung to the picture frames. The chair covers and drapes were tired. In this room of faded dreams, Dyson seemed pathetic.

The embarrassing conversation finished as Dyson swore into the phone, slammed it down, then stood looking out through the glass. He fumbled for a handkerchief and blew his nose hard. Finally, he turned and saw Connor. His hair had flopped over his ear and the cord of his robe, beneath his paunch, was like a strap under a saddlebag. The nails of his bare feet curled over his toes.

'What's this about?' Connor asked.

'Who cares?' Dyson said. He picked up a book from the table and held it out to Connor, who took it. It was a water-damaged hardback with a Sydney City Library Central sticker inside the cover. The title was *Legends and Poems of Romania*.

Dyson sat heavily in one of the two chairs. 'Have a look at your future. Page eighty-five.'

'Give me that.' Blore stepped forward and snatched the book. He found the page, ripped it out and threw the book back on the table.

Connor said to Dyson, 'Got a book on Manners for Mercenaries?'

Blore looked at his watch and switched on the monitor. It hummed and the screen went blue. He said to Connor, 'Sit there.'

Connor took the seat beside Dyson and Blore clipped

lapel-mikes on them both. He positioned them too low so Connor relocated them higher. The screen flashed, became snow. Then they were staring at Vo, seated in front of an out-of-focus curtain. The shock of her non-face on the screen compelled attention like no other image.

'Good morning or evening all. We now begin draw for next game.' She looked at someone out of frame. 'All are assemble?'

The scene switched to Merrick, badly framed, nervously touching her hair. Vo's voice continued under. 'In New York we have Mrs Merrick, and in Australia, Mr Connor and Mr Dyson.'

The red light glowed on the front of the camera as they saw themselves as a two-shot in the monitor.

'In Cape Town, Mr Sinclair.'

Sinclair appeared, clad in a polo shirt. He gave a constricted wave that might have been appropriate for a contestant on a quiz show but was distinctly unpleasant coming from a man who might have arranged the murder of his wife.

The shot was back to Vo, looking out of frame again. 'All can hear?' It was amateur hour on a four-country satellite hook-up. God, Connor thought, estimating the cost of each minute, professional senses outraged. It must have shown on his face because Vo was now looking back, slightly off lens. 'I see that Mr Connor not impress with our production. Not worry, Mr Connor. We are not media company. Just to arrange hard enough. So, we begin. First, Mr Connor will think of number between one and ten. He write down but not say and not show.'

The red light came on as Blore handed him a pad and felt pen. The other man told Dyson to leave his seat and escorted him to the corner of the room. Dyson went passively, all the stuffing knocked out of him.

As Connor took the pen, Blore held his hand between the pad and the camera as if he felt the lens might reveal the scrawl to the others.

Connor glanced over at Dyson. There was no way he could see. He wrote down eight. Blore immediately shut the cover on the pad and removed it.

The red light went out and Vo was back. 'Mr Connor will remember what he write and verify later when number is shown. Next, others will guess number. Nearest guess win. Worse guess lose. Simple. No chance of mistake. Begin with Mr Sinclair.'

Sinclair was on, glancing either side of him as if being prompted by minders unseen. Hands came in with a pad. There was no attempt to frame the action. The shot remained static as Sinclair looked down and apparently wrote something before the pad was taken back.

Vo again. 'Now, Mrs Merrick.'

Merrick looked to the side, gimlet-eyed, grabbed the proffered pad and sat a moment, glazed, before carving something on the page with such force that her shoulder shook as she wrote.

'And Mr Dyson.'

Dyson, now ushered back to the chair, was handed a pad. He looked at Connor. 'Any clues?'

Connor looked away until he saw Vo come back on the screen.

'Now we see result. Please show pad – first Mr Dyson.'

The two-shot came up and Dyson held up his pad but the shot was too wide and the scrawl too small to be seen. Connor went to the camera, zoomed in and adjusted focus until a close-up of the pad showed clearly in the eyepiece.

'Thank you, Mr Connor, for your professional help. Mr Dyson choose number two. Now Mr Sinclair.'

Sinclair appeared holding his pad up. It showed a five.

Merrick was next, thrusting her pad angrily at the lens. The focus was pulled to show a nine.

Vo again. 'Fortunate we have no duplicate number so is clear contest. Mr Connor now show number he choose.'

Blore gave Connor back his pad. The lens was still zoomed in. Connor jiggled the pad into shot.

'Shot of Mr Connor, please.'

Connor got up, readjusted the two-shot, focusing on the now bent-over Dyson. Then he went back and sat in the chair.

'Mr Connor, was eight what you choose?'

'Yes.'

'So no way cheat as Mr Connor not part of contest and no fry fish. Loser – Mr Dyson. Winner – Mrs Merrick.'

Merrick was now on screen, pointing her finger at the camera, her face ugly with triumph. 'Your turn now. Your turn now. I'll kill you.'

They cut back to Vo. 'Game specify penalty as cripple and halt. Mr Sinclair, as last loser, now decide form of penalty.'

Sinclair looked relieved, his glee at escaping clear. He stroked his chin. 'Mmm. Crippled and halt, eh?'

Merrick's voice cut in. 'Amputate his legs.' The vision mixer cut to her belatedly. 'Break his legs.' They faded the sound down as her mute raving continued.

Dyson was rocking forward in his chair, making little moans. His robe had come open, exposing his fat, hairy legs as if fate had displayed them for the sacrifice.

Another shot of Sinclair. 'No, I don't think we amputate his legs. How about some toes?' He grinned up at the lens. 'Say five pinkies from one foot. Best I can do for you, Adrian.'

Vo's face again, considering. 'Five toe on one foot chop off. Accept.'

They cut back to Dyson but he never saw it. Depression had softened his spine into rubber and his head was almost down on his stomach.

Next shot was the soundless outraged Merrick, who looked robbed of her pound of flesh.

Finally to Vo. 'For logistic reason, penalty take place on Tuesday in Sydney, Australia. Not possible Mr Sinclair attend, as require to answer question by South Africa authority. Mr Connor will attend. Broadcast now finish.'

As the screen went blue, Dyson staggered up and poured himself a tumblerful, neat. He drained a third at a gulp, shoved open the glass door to the garden and took the rest of it outside. The keepers of the temple had left the house. They must have told the crew in the OB van to wrap because two technicians came back and started dismantling the gear. Neither showed uneasiness – as if what they had witnessed in the miniature control-room of the van had been a segment on a cooking programme. Perhaps they were plants, or the thing had been monitored elsewhere. Connor left Dyson to his despair and walked to the front door. When he looked along the street, the Range Rover had gone.

Now what?

The next event was two days away. They needed time, after all, to fly the avenging Merrick out.

He stood in the tree-lined street with its listless suburban air. One or two locals were standing near the van, wondering what was going on. A much-powdered elderly resident approached him. 'What's this for?'

'Just an interview.'

'Oh.' She stood, unsatisfied, exuding the smell of age combined with perfume.

He walked up the street to get away, feeling disoriented and hungry, bought two ham and salad sandwiches, then looked for somewhere to eat them. Nowhere. He ate them on the street, hoping to flag down a taxi. If he could get to Wynyard, he could catch a bus to Avalon and his car. Then what? Back to Mackerel Beach? He had nowhere else to go.

He checked for his keys. Shit. He'd left them back at the house – remembered putting them on the table when he'd gone to adjust the camera. He walked back quickly, hoping Dyson hadn't gone out.

The neighbours and the van had gone. Now all the houses looked the same, except for Dyson's, which looked worse. The overgrown garden, flaking paint. He rang.

Five minutes later he was still trying, the dual-tone chime sounding in the hall. Perhaps Dyson was still out the back. He walked around to the lane behind, found the back fence easily enough – corrugated sheets in front of bamboo. No gate. Just the locked garage door – with a car running inside it.

Dyson?

Christ, the bastard was killing himself!

He grabbed for the top of the fence to haul himself up. The thin metal cut into his hands. He winced with pain and looked wildly around for something to stand on.

There was some rubbish further down the lane, including an abandoned space-heater. He ran and lugged the heater beside the fence, stood on it, grabbed the thick bamboo and hauled himself up and over.

Christ! How long had Dyson been in there?

The garage door was closed but unlocked. He yanked it open, expecting choking fumes to pour out, but the air inside was still breathable. A vacuum cleaner hose was stuck into the exhaust pipe and the back window of the car had been closed on the other end. He flicked the hose out of the exhaust and opened the driver's door.

Dyson was slumped against the wheel. Fumes spilled out.

He switched off the ignition, dragged Dyson out of the car and hauled him by the arms though the door until he was lying face up on the grass.

Dyson began to splutter. He couldn't have been in there long.

Connor, feeling relief, turned him on his side. Liquor pumped out of Dyson's mouth. Connor walked away, knowing the man would survive, and retrieved his car keys from the table in the house. On impulse, he went back and threw the vacuum cleaner hose over the fence.

Dyson propped himself on his elbow, looking at him with hatred. 'Fuckwit.'

'I came back for my keys. You got lucky.'

'Lucky? Oh, Jeez,' Dyson sobbed, 'oh, Jeez.'

Blore dashed from the house like the Incredible Hulk late for a train. He must have let himself in. He almost tripped over Dyson in his rush and knelt beside him, panting. His concern made it plain that if a contestant died, he'd be neither popular nor forgiven.

'Some nursemaid,' Connor said.

'I'm getting sick of you, Connor,' Blore replied. 'If the game doesn't take you out, it's my turn.'

Chapter Twenty-one

The building was tired brick with dust-glazed windows, some of them broken where security mesh had been prised back. It was in a Chippendale lane, amid factories and warehouses that shared the garbage of the street with the occasional gentrified terrace. Above the door were the faded words: Stubb and Manxman, Printers. It was a cold Tuesday morning, an ideal time for the severing of toes.

Inside, light filtering from panes in the saw-toothed roof outlined partitions that made the large space confined enough for people. There were signs: Art and Design, Film and Plates. Connor caught a glimpse of inclined boards fitted with the assembly artists' sliding rules and of equipment that colour-separated film.

Beyond the partitioned offices were the presses. Here, everything was new. Aqua-blue paint and glass screens sanctified the latest machinery. There were panels with fancy readouts and rows of buttons ready to light up like a carnival. But there were no lights in the building this morning, no printers, no staff. Only the group of repugnant people Connor already knew.

They had convened in the bindery section, where the stacks of sheets were cut and assembled. Here, among the folding and wrapping machines, was a giant guillotine.

Beside it on the floor were two bricks, a long plank about a foot wide, two G-clamps, rope and a square of thick aluminium sheet. Near one edge of the sheet, slots had been cut and straps fed through, forming a rudimentary sandal with heel-piece.

The Asian nurse from the island was laying out gauze and dressings on the flat top of a folding machine. She wore her white nurse's uniform and the impassive look of a person comfortable with the idea of staunching blood from toes not yet cut off.

Next to her was Vo, wearing an expensive-looking cheong-sam, gold pendant and gold earrings. She looked as if she rarely travelled overseas and was responding to a sense of occasion. The earrings merely enhanced her deformity.

Merrick was there in stone-washed jeans and sweater, looking youthful and impervious to jet-lag. She lifted a plastic apron from her bag, unfolded it and tied it on. It had a flower border and, in the middle, a recipe for pot pourri. She glanced at Connor and hissed, 'This time it's *my* turn.' Then she turned to the nurse, who had just finished her display. 'Can't you let him bleed to death?'

The nurse shook her head quickly, afraid to answer, and looked at Vo for permission before she said, 'He will not bleed to death. No major arteries in extremities.'

Dyson was the last to arrive, frog-marched between Blore and his assistant, eyes terrified, whimpering with fright. The three were followed by another mufti-clad trooper, recording the spectacle on a video camera.

Merrick rushed to Dyson when she saw him and stabbed his paunch with her finger. '*Your* turn, now. *Your* turn. *Your* turn.'

God help him, Connor thought.

While the assistant held Dyson, Blore picked up the metal shoe. He positioned the sheet on the guillotine bed and clamped it securely in place.

Vo said, 'Good morning, Mr Dyson. Are you prepare?'

'Jeez,' Dyson wailed. 'Oh, Jeez.'

Blore laid the plank on the two bricks and as he rose, Dyson tried to break away. He was caught in three steps by

Blore and backed against a machine. Blore pointed to the plank on the floor. 'Lie on that.'

Dyson tried to make a dash for it again. This time Blore held a leg-of-lamb fist in his face. 'Want this? Get on the board.'

'Fuck you,' Dyson said. His last struggle for freedom saw him smashed back against the machine. As the fist jerked in an uppercut, Dyson's chin snapped up and his knees gave. The two men lowered him onto the plank, then trussed him to it, leaving a leg free but removing the shoe and sock. Then they lifted the board onto the bed of the guillotine. One man supported the end at an angle, so that the ad-man's free leg could be bent and his foot strapped securely into the metal shoe.

When Dyson came to, he saw his toes held in position beneath the half-inch thick bevel of the blade. He yelped and tried to pull his foot back, his cries resounding to the roof. The straps held firm, the big buckles on them straining.

He craned back piteously to the man holding the end of the plank as the cameraman recorded every expression. He stared at Connor with the eyes of a Delacroix horse. 'Jeezuz, Connor. *Help* me!'

Connor went up to Vo. 'Do you have to maim him?'

'Stand back or you get hurt. The Major is dying to hurt you bad.'

Blore looked across at Connor and grinned. 'Love you to try it, Connor.'

Although the taunt filled Connor's diaphragm with rage, his head said no heroics. Three against one. But he promised himself one thing. If he ever got the chance, he'd rid the planet of Major Blore – munitions bore and toe-cutter – just to wipe the grin off his face.

Merrick was impatient to proceed. 'What do I do? Press this?'

Blore pointed to the red buttons with their metal guards, far-spaced on the front of the frame. 'You have to reach across him and press both.'

'Two buttons?'

'Together. Safety feature. You have to use both hands.'

She strained forward eagerly but he stopped her with his arm. 'Not till we tell you.' He looked across at the cameraman. 'Ready?'

The man put a thumb up.

Blore looked at Vo.

Connor registered it all – the obscene gathering of people, each convinced that to slice the toes off a pathetic sod was a necessary act. Merrick, wearing her apron, hoping for buckets of blood... He felt sorry he'd left his keys at Dyson's.

Vo said, 'Perform penalty. Now.'

Dyson shrieked, 'No! No!'

Blore's arm dropped. Merrick leapt to the machine and jammed her thumbs on the buttons. The blade descended with a hiss and went *kerchunk* against its cutting face. Dyson's toes seemed incidental, disappearing so cleanly that, apart from his scream, the event seemed an anti-climax.

Merrick augmented the scream with a bellowed '*Yaaaaa!*' lifting her arms high and turning in a kind of jig.

The five toes lay beyond the risen blade. Below the smeared guillotine, a pool of blood was forming on the metal.

Dyson was in torment. They unclamped the metal boot and unbuckled it from the remains of his foot. It had been severed so cleanly that Connor could see the ends of each bone. He felt ill.

They put the plank on the floor and lifted the leg as the nurse applied a tourniquet to the leg, a compress to the mess and did things quickly with surgical tape. The camera stayed focused on Dyson's agony, the better to entertain Mould.

Connor glanced in horror at Merrick. She had plucked Dyson's big toe off the plate and filched some gauze to make a holder for it, as if it were a doll in a miniature crib. She knelt, waving it in Dyson's face. 'This'll teach you to cut your nails. I'm going to *keep* this.' She turned to Vo. 'Let's do his other foot now.'

Vo shook her head. 'Is finish.'

The nurse dug a hypodermic into Dyson. His screams and ranting died to a mumble as the injection blurred his brain. They untied him and took him away, the nurse holding up his leg. The camera followed.

Merrick pulled off her unblooded apron, folded it and put it in her bag.

Vo said, 'End Round Two.' She held out two narrow folders. 'Mrs Merrick, Mr Connor, your ticket. Flight QF363, leaving 10.40 for Auckland Friday morning. You will be met at airport. Round Three is on island. You both free now to go.'

Merrick took her ticket, slid it into her bag and tucked Dyson's toe in beside it with almost jaunty delight.

As Connor left the place the Range Rover was driving off. The nurse was in the back and, presumably, the supine form of Dyson. Blore was walking back to the entrance, with the strictured face of a man who had found the last days arduous indeed. Merrick, however, was jubilant.

'I feel good. Good.' She pirouetted like a school-girl, swinging her handbag wide.

He wanted nothing to do with the ogre but she followed him around the corner to the car, chatting about her flight and the service at her Rocks motel. About Seattle and its bicycle cops. About the salmon in the creeks there made possible by her late husband, a chief sewerage engineer who, each day, had drunk water filtered from his plant. Then she switched to L.A., referring to celebrities she'd seen as if she knew them, studding each sentence with the word 'I' – utterly self-absorbed. As she walked, she swung her hips as if amputations made her erotic.

He remembered that, on the flight back from the island, Sinclair had remarked on her potential in bed. 'She's a monster. All violence, no sex – like American TV.'

He reached the car. There was a parking ticket under the wiper. He shrugged and, for once in his life, threw it away, which felt good.

As he got in, she leaned down to the window to grin at him, exposing a flash of unsettling cleavage as if to affirm that attractive women get their way, and said, 'I'm going to win, you know.' She strode off like a Juno.

Up you, he thought. With luck, the bitch would hit the wall.

Chapter Twenty-two

Halfway across the gulf the Grumman was enveloped by cloud. As the propellers churned into it, the sea below disappeared, leaving the wing and the engine cowlings suspended in grey soup. The tired frame of the old amphibian shuddered in the uneven air, then rose like a lift before sliding off the top of the thermal with a stomach-suspending plunge. Wooden boxes stacked behind the cockpit strained against their webbing. Three rows of seats had been removed to get the small crates in.

Merrick sat across the aisle from Connor, a hard face above a broomstick spine. She had ignored him at the terminal, looking through him like glass, obviously no longer the tourist but the determined winner of $20 million. Behind her was Blore, eyes red with fatigue.

The aircraft lurched and their seats dropped from under them.

'Bloody hell.' Sinclair's voice.

Connor looked back.

The tall man was searching his seat pocket. 'Can't they afford bags?'

There were two other passengers at the rear of the cabin: the nurse, across the aisle from Dyson, reading a Chinese character paper, and her unshaven patient, an appendage of his bandaged leg. His foot was propped in the aisle and seemed to end just in front of the ankle. Connor realised with distaste that they must have cut back the bone to get enough skin-flap to close the wound. A wheelchair, strapped to the rear bulkhead, rattled with each jolt.

The aircraft was tossed back upwards. He heard Sinclair's regurgitating cough and Dyson's 'Jeez'.

The drone of the engines changed as they tilted into a shallow dive. They flattened off in lighter cloud that blew wisps across the wing. Suddenly he saw the sea, no more than 100 feet below.

One of the pilots was pointing, as if uncertain where they were. They held at the low altitude, banking slightly, left, then right.

'They're lost,' Merrick said.

Blore said, 'Pilots are never lost. Just temporarily unsure of their position.'

Smart-arse, Connor thought. He felt trapped and ready to be creamed. But this time there was no way he'd roll over. This time he was after their balls. If they gave him an inch...

'Oh, God,' Sinclair moaned. 'Oh, God.'

The smell of vomit wafted from behind.

They powered along for five minutes, racing above the waves before the flaps wound out and the floats locked down. They skimmed a smaller chop, losing height.

The aircraft settled fast and wallowed, weighted by the heavy boxes. Connor couldn't see anything yet. The co-pilot was winding down the wheels. Then the floats came up again, the engines revved and they powered up on the pebbles of a beach.

Blore unbuckled and went forward. The pilot shut off the power and called back, 'We can't stay here long.'

Blore opened the door. 'You'll have help.'

'Five minutes,' the pilot said. 'That's it.'

Connor stepped onto a beach he'd never seen, no more than a patch of sand surrounded by a slope of rock that rose to undergrowth and bush.

Merrick came out after him, squinting up at the rise. 'What on earth?'

A camouflage-painted wall labelled LEFT-HAND DRIVE was reversing down the rocks, highly geared diesel engine snarling, brake lights winking in metal grids. A trooper stood in the turret, signalling directions to the driver.

Blore yelled up, 'Move it.'

The mobile fort tilted steeply over the last line of boulders and its tracks sank into the sand. It rocked upright again, reversed a little more and stopped, the rear ramp opening down to expose a cavernous inside. Four troopers ducked out.

'Form a chain to the aircraft,' Blore ordered. 'Close order. Move.' The men formed a row, passing the crates out and stacking them on the floor inside the vehicle while the pilots lifted luggage out of the nose.

Sinclair squatted near Connor on the sand, trying not to throw up. 'How'd they get a tank here?'

'It's an APC.'

Sinclair looked blank.

'An armoured personnel carrier.'

Sinclair shrugged, too sick to absorb military details.

The cold seeped into Connor's skin. He was stiff after hours of sitting. And very tense. He stretched and padded around the machine. Jerrycans on the back, spare track links on the front, three whip aerials… the only things missing were the guns. The driver's hatch and turret hatch were open, heavy lids on torsion springs. The tracks had central rubber pads, which explained the spoor he'd seen at the goat track on the headland.

When he walked to the rear again they were lifting Dyson up the ramp. He looked in to make sure they had stowed his aluminium case. One trooper reached up and opened a large square hatch in the roof.

Damp fog was swirling around them now, turning the

late afternoon grey. He glanced back out to sea. The ceiling was almost zero. The pilots were back in their seats, anxious to get off.

'Stand back.' Blore waved at Merrick as the plane's port engine coughed, puffing smoke from the overhead exhaust. As the other radial came in, the rudder swung and the nose swivelled to the ocean, the blast from the slipstream blowing their clothes against their bodies.

They watched it vanish into fog.

Sinclair was still on his knees. 'God. What next?'

'Ask Dyson,' Connor said. 'He's read the last verse.'

Sinclair looked at the personnel carrier with horror and moaned up to the looming Blore, 'Please, I can't get in that. I'm sick enough now.'

Blore looked at him coldly. 'Beats walking.'

The troopers were back in the machine, one standing in the turret, headset on. Connor walked up the ramp and went forward, crouching over the crates, to sit on the padded bench behind the driver. His shoulders felt painfully tight. He knew he might have to fight to survive. He had to stay alert, ready to seize any scrap of advantage. Sinclair staggered in. Blore was last, lumbering up the ramp. The floor at the back of the vehicle was covered with the crates. They'd attempted to lash them to the bench seats on the sides but it didn't look secure.

'Either sit on the boxes or stand up here,' Blore said. He stood on a box to demonstrate and his torso disappeared through the square hatch behind the turret.

The driver put his headset on, turned a lever on his right, then pushed a button on a panel to his left. The engine caught and began to burble like 200 horsepower going nowhere. He revved the engine, pushed another lever forward on his right and the rear ramp came up on its cable. He did something with another lever behind his right shoulder and pulled the first lever back.

That would be the gears, Connor thought, trying to remember the sequence. There were four control levers, two coming up from the floor, two coming down – he supposed they were for steering and braking. And two accelerator pedals, one above the other.

The driver's hatch was open. The man had racked up his seat so that he could drive with his head out, above the crescent of periscope slits. His hands went to the levers, his foot to the top pedal. Connor looked more closely at the panel on the left, trying to read the plates under the switches. The nearest was labelled Bilge Pumps. Did that mean the thing could float?

Blore was leaning down from the hatch. 'Connor, get up here.'

He joined the others where they stood inside the hatch like generals reviewing a parade. Blore pointed to a rail behind the turret. 'Grab that.' He did as he was told, then felt with his other hand below the hatch edge. The armour was five centimetres thick.

The man in the turret spoke into his mike. The engine began to growl again, then snarl as the long box jolted and tipped, its treads clawing at the steep bank of rocks. It climbed without effort, rolling and pitching with sudden sideways jerks as one track or another was retarded. It felt like nothing he'd ever been in.

They clattered over stone, then entered the bush, mowing down ferns and saplings. The tall fibreglass-covered aerials bent under branches, then swung upright again on their base springs. The treads beneath them climbed straight over everything from creekbeds to low cliffs.

The fog was thicker higher up. They could barely see ten metres ahead. The driver changed down and they started crawling up a bracken-covered slope so steep that it seemed they would either slip back or overturn.

Blore was hanging on to a black cable coiled around the base of the turret. Connor decided to try to pump him. He pointed at it and yelled, 'What's that?'

'Jumper leads.'

Good. Ask a military question and the man came in. His motor-mouth might be useful. Any scrap of information might help.

The sheer weight of the vehicle provided the traction it needed. It breasted the slope without faltering, nose in the air, then thumped forward at the top.

Now they were on a gently sloping rise and what looked like a rudimentary track. They changed gears and got up speed, slewing and rattling over the ground, the padded tracks thumping the earth. Sinclair leaned over the side deck. Vomit arced from his mouth and ran along the metal deck.

The fog had become so thick, they switched the drive lights on. The strong beams made it worse. The driver dipped the lights, slowed, then switched to domed lights that pooled just ahead of the driver's bay. Nothing seemed to help. The trooper in the turret called a halt and the diesel burbled in neutral. Speech was possible again.

'Are we on the same island?' Merrick asked, as if each speck in the gulf used armoured personnel carriers for transport. No-one bothered to answer her.

Connor tried again with Blore. 'What's this? Steel plate?'

'Compressed aluminium.'

'And it swims?' That was the money question. He hoped he'd made it sound casual.

'Just.'

'What's "just" mean?'

Blore gave him a patronising glare. 'With the trim vane out and the bilge plugs in and skirts, you can do six knots if you're careful.'

'What're skirts?'

'Curious, aren't you, Connor?' The man was on to him and clammed up.

The trooper was climbing out of the turret.

Blore tapped him back. 'I'll be mother duck.' He bench-pressed himself out of the hatch, squatted on the edge, eased himself over and jumped. Then he walked in front, looking at the ground, occasionally indicating a direction with his arm. He was no more than a couple of metres ahead but still difficult to see. They crawled behind him in low gear.

'Oh God,' Sinclair moaned again.

Connor said, 'Arsehole. I reckon you worked it so your wife got killed.'

'Poor love.'

'...and used me to do it. Deadshit.'

'Completely out of my hands.'

'Like fun. You let Mould waste her.'

'Merely protecting my investments.'

'I knew you were off, but I didn't know you were a scumbag.'

'If we'd stuck together and worked things out – but without you what option did I have?' The tall man hung on weakly as one track went over a rock. They tilted thirty degrees. 'God, how much longer?' He bent back over the side and retched.

Merrick wasn't motion-sick. She stood like a Valkyrie, staring into the mist as if she could hear trumpets proclaiming her advance.

Connor bent to look inside the hull, partly to relieve the tension in his body. He saw a bandaged leg stretched across the crates. He bent a little lower. Dyson was staring at the remains of his foot as if gazing into hell.

He straightened up again, twisted from side to side. His jacket felt damp and fog was creeping in at the neck. He'd prefer wind or rain to this sargasso of mist. The place felt like a purgatory for ghosts.

They crawled ahead until a building materialised out of the grey. The main house.

Blore waved them on. 'You're in the same huts.'

They ground down the hill, guided by the foot-track. To their right, the columns of the pool loomed like a stage set in the mist. They rattled under the branches of the pine grove, the aerials bending and lashing, then stopped. The ramp was lowered and their luggage handed out.

Two troopers took charge of Dyson, unfolding the wheelchair and shoving him in. The third followed with his bag and the nurse walked at the rear.

As the procession faded into fog, Merrick picked up her bags. 'I need a long hot shower, then food. Then beware.' She strode into the whiteness, calling back like a spectre, 'All of you. Beware.'

Sinclair said, 'God, I want to die.' He dragged his designer luggage off and was gone.

Connor, alone now, climbed back up the ramp. The small, square crates – what was in them? No markings. He lifted one, tried to shake it. It was so heavy he had to strain to pick it up. He spotted a toolbox beneath the bench at the side, grabbed a screwdriver that could double as a dagger, shoved it inside his jacket. He could hear someone coming back. He ducked down the ramp, picked up his case and hurried to his hut.

Inside the cabin he half-emptied his case and hung his spare shirt over the mirror. There was a printed card on the bench.

Welcome to Round Three.
Dinner will be served at the house at
7.00pm
Dress informal.

Kind of them not to insist on a tuxedo. He went into the bathroom and hid the screwdriver inside the cistern. Then he went back to the main room, stripped to underpants and pushed the bed to the wall.

He stood in the centre of the space, trying to remember the little self-defence he knew. He tried a roundhouse kick, aiming high. His foot barely rose above waist height. 'Shit.' He was stiff as hell. He tried forward splits, taking it very carefully, but could barely straighten his front knee.

He tried a groin kick, flicking the knee. He couldn't remember the sequence for the blocks. He hadn't practised them enough for them to become automatic.

No good. Useless, in fact, against commando-trained men twice his weight. He showered, changed into jeans and a big sweater. By then it was seven o'clock. He considered taking the screwdriver. No. There would be dinner with Mould, perhaps threats, but almost certainly no contest till the next morning.

The fog hadn't lifted. It dripped from the branches of the pines. It felt damp in the nose, deadened every sound but the distant shell-roar of the sea. From the deck of his cabin the path lights shone yellow, diffused – the first clear, the second a smudge, the third not visible at all.

He'd brought his torch but it only showed the fuzzed cone of its beam. He switched it off and walked toward the lights, the limbo of the island complete.

He arrived at the house at 7.15. There was no-one in the ante-room but several used glasses told him he was late. He walked through the weapons display to a dining room dancing with candles. The other three contestants were seated, waiting.

Sinclair drawled, 'The lady-killer come to judgment?'

Connor came straight back. 'At least I tried to save my wife. I didn't scheme and set her up so someone'd rape her

– then kill her.' He took one of the three remaining seats and shoved his torch on the floor.

Sinclair sneered. 'You sanctimonious bugger – if you hadn't refused to play, if you'd used your stupid nut, both our wives might still be alive.'

'Don't put it on me, shit-face. You killed her. Ever occur to you she was a person?'

'She was more than just a pretty arse. But still prepared to shoot you if you came.'

'Shoot me?'

'Join the twentieth century, Connor. People are animals. Haven't you noticed?'

Merrick said, 'You both thought you were so clever, trying to manipulate the game. And you see? It made things worse. Now you're alone. Serves you right, stupid fools.'

Dyson said, 'Jeez, will you lot can it?' He looked as if he'd been wheeled from some flop-house as a joke – thick stubble, eyes like piss-holes in the snow. Judged on confidence levels, he was off the scale.

Merrick was least shaken. Her triumph over Dyson had renewed her. She was again in her black sheath and had a circlet of lace around her throat. The dim light romanticised her beauty, made the classic face with its belligerent jaw as compelling as any imperative stare from an international perfume campaign.

'We've been here nearly half an hour,' she said. 'Are they going to feed us or not?'

Sinclair, across from Connor, toyed with a silver spoon, a morose man in a modish jacket. 'I doubt I could eat a pea.'

Connor glanced at the head of the table. The chair had no oxygen bottle beside it. Mould was either considerably better or too ill to attend. And the chair beside him was vacant. Who for? Vo?

The nervous tapping of Sinclair's spoon. The small

motors of a camera whirred, announcing their unseen audience. Mould. The room was heavy with fear.

Someone was coming at last. Vo and the woman from the library, Gillian, followed by troopers bearing food and wine. Vo sat at the head of the table, where the travesty of her face was inescapable. The other woman sat quietly beside Connor. He felt the connection with her like a cord.

Gillian placed a folded piece of paper and a pair of half-frame glasses on the table. The man's watch on her slim wrist told him she preferred the practical to the ornamental.

Oysters mornay and wine were served. Then the woman beside him stood.

'Good evening,' she said in her slight continental accent. 'We welcome you back to T55 for the third round of the game. Unfortunately Mr Mould is too ill to join us tonight so he's asked me to make his apologies. He wishes to assure you of his continued interest in events. He's also asked me to read the third and final verse of the poem.' She unfolded the piece of paper, picked up her glasses and looked around. No-one was eating. 'Do please begin.'

No-one touched a fork or moved.

She placed the glasses on her upturned nose, frowned and read:

> Sans teeth,
> Sans ears,
> Too craven to let death heal,
> Gelded,
> Damned,
> Stagger into another dawn.

Sinclair cleared his throat. 'Can we hear that again?'

She read it once more. 'There'll be copies in your cabins tonight.' She sat down.

The oysters were cooling – but no-one moved.

Vo said, 'Now we eat.' She scooped up an oyster with the small fork provided and it vanished into the cavern of her head.

After a long pause they began to tinker with the food. When the hesitant clink of forks was enough to mask his voice, Connor murmured to the woman beside him. 'You still disagree with this?'

The blue eyes looked back at him, startled. Her reply was only just audible. 'Yes. But I can't talk here.' She looked straight back to her plate.

He felt the sense of thankfulness again. Did this mean she might help?

Vo was speaking. 'First contest involve teeth. Loser lose teeth. Winner remove teeth. Clear? You notice game now require you lose body part. Mr Dyson understand already what this mean. And Mr Dyson, as last loser, say how teeth to be remove.'

'More mutilation,' Sinclair bellowed. 'Christ. He wants to watch us get chopped up!' He turned to Vo. 'Can Mould hear this?'

'Mr Mould can see and hear.'

Sinclair looked around for the camera. 'Where's the filthy bugger?' There were two cameras to choose from, one at each corner of the gloom. He stared at one. 'You bloodsucking toad. By God, I'll have you yet.'

Vo laughed, the gaping hole making hilarity horrible. 'I not think so, Mr Sinclair. I think this time he have *you*.'

Sinclair's jaw jerked around to her, his long neck twisting behind it. 'You cold-blooded little…'

Vo continued unabashed. 'Must lose teeth. Mr Dyson, as last loser, will now describe how this be done.'

Dyson looked incapable of descriptions. He'd managed to gulp two oysters but the rest sat like an accusation on his plate and his glass was still full, as if his thirst had vanished with his confidence. He muttered into his collar-grime, 'Gimme a break.'

'So,' Vo continued with the sensitivity of a jack-hammer, 'how we do this, Mr Dyson?'

Dyson rolled his eyes. 'Who knows? Who cares?'

'I care, Mr Dyson. If you not say, then I say.'

Dyson rested his head on his fist, pushing his cheek into a ridge of flesh. 'How many teeth?'

'All teeth. All out.' She pulled out her stopwatch. 'You have five second to say.' The watch clicked.

'Jeez.' Dyson's eyes rolled. 'Can we use a dentist?'

Vo shook her head and clicked the watch. 'Not allow. You not say? I decide.'

'Oh, well done, Dyson,' Sinclair's drawl dripped acid. 'If you want your teeth disposed of thoughtfully, leave it to the Cong – to those wonderful people who brought you Punji sticks. Will you never bloody well learn?'

Vo raised her hand and the trooper who was about to remove Merrick's plate moved to a low cabinet and opened the door. He took something out of it, padded to Vo and put three objects on the table beside her. The first was a rusted cold chisel, its end curved into metal shavings with use. The second was a four-pound hammer, the top of its handle furred with dried cement. The third was a cigar box.

Vo's good eye blinked and the remote-control cameras whirred on their mounts. 'You see,' she said, 'I already prepare.'

'Jeezuz,' said Dyson.

'So what horror's in the box?' Sinclair asked.

Vo upended the box, the top fell open and dominoes clattered on the table. 'We play domino for winner and loser.'

Dyson's expression made it clear that dominoes were as repugnant to him as spin-the-knife. But he was too discouraged now to insist on poker.

The troopers were serving the main course – roast pork with crackling on the side. Another Mould touch? Their last chance to test their teeth?

Gillian, the information oracle, was again served first. Connor had the impression she'd tuned out. She'd been obliged to attend, that was all. What, then, was her status on the island? Where did she fit in? And how sick was Mould? Would he survive to the end of the game? The questions jammed in his throat. Somehow he had to talk to her. How?

The next development was so grotesque that even Merrick's fork paused. Two of the men lugged in a metal frame – made from two-centimetre box-section roughly welded into the shape of a chair. It had a square braced back, a flat piece of steel for a seat and a curved piece near the top with a thick strap attached to both ends. There were straps lower on the frame and two chains hung from the sides, each ending in flat metal hooks. The seat and the curved piece left no doubt about its use. Whoever lost the game would be strapped into the frame and the strap would go around the forehead, making it impossible to move the head forward. Then the two hooks would be placed either side and their chains tightened – to drag the jaw down and hold it open.

As the contraption was set upright near the table, Gillian collected her glasses and rose. 'I refuse to be used for this. It's appalling.' She stalked to the door.

Sinclair leapt up. 'Bravo!' He turned to clap as she went past. The troopers respectfully stepped back to let her out of the room.

Vo jeered after her, 'Now we know where you fit.' She craned up to a camera. 'See? What you think of your favourite now? She shit in your face.'

Mould, Blore and Vo. The planet could manage without the three of them, Connor thought.

The rest of the meal was almost untouched, with even the dessert ignored. The thought of having teeth broken by a chisel obliterated interest in food. Dyson had now fortified himself but the others had drunk little. They each saw themselves strapped to the frame, mouth chained open, helpless, while a chisel was positioned on the gumline and the hammer smashed down. Connor wished he'd brought the screwdriver. If this didn't fall his way he'd need to go for it the moment things looked bad.

Dyson said, 'Jeez, can you believe this?'

Sinclair said, 'I have eyes to wonder but lack tongue to praise.'

Dyson smiled at him nastily. 'Might lack teeth as well in a minute.'

Everything on the table was removed until only the candelabra, the tools and the small pile of dominoes remained. Mess duties finished, the four troopers stood across the entrance to the room – a heavyweight barrier that only a grenade would clear.

Connor was working on an escape plan that involved diving for the hammer, then pulling back the drapes and smashing his chair through the long windows. If he could cripple the first man who reached him and get through before the others could pin him, he could lose them in the fog. His internal shaking had begun.

Vo was arranging the dominoes face down on the bare field of cloth. She must have combined at least two packs as there seemed to be a lot of blocks. She moved them around, mixing them, then said, 'Each person to pick seven.'

The phalanx by the door parted to admit the bulk of Blore. He looked fed up – and angry. He moved to the frame and leaned on top of it, eyes coldly watching the table.

Connor reached forward and dragged the nearest seven

dominoes to him. The others did the same except for Dyson, who couldn't reach. Blore stepped forward and did it for him. Dyson didn't even look up. He seemed no longer concerned what happened.

Merrick set up her small barricade of blocks and glared over them, ready for battle. Sinclair arranged his seven more warily, eyes sidelong, checking no-one could see.

'Chinese proverb,' Vo said. 'Stubborn teeth perish but yielding tongue endure. Good point, yes? So, we begin.' She turned a domino face up and placed it in the centre of the table. It showed a two and a four. She brushed the rest of the blocks toward her.

'You should leave those in the middle,' Sinclair said. 'if we can't go, we need to pick another.'

'No more,' said Vo. 'If can't go, say "pass".'

'That's not the way you play it.'

'Is way I tell you play. I umpire. We start with Mr Dyson, then go clockwise around table.'

'Unfair,' Merrick practically yelled. 'Why him?'

'Must begin with someone.'

'Then begin with me.'

'Objection,' Sinclair snapped. 'Whoever gets out first wins. So it matters where we begin. We should draw lots for it.' He knocked his dominoes face down.

Vo nodded. 'Okay.' She leaned forward like a croupier and slid an extra block in front of them all. 'Begin at person with highest number. Turn over.'

They turned the extra blocks over. Dyson had a double six.

'So,' Vindicated, she retrieved the extra blocks. 'Begin with Mr Dyson.'

Merrick shook her head violently. 'No. No. *No.*' She stood up, glaring at Vo. 'We also have to choose if it's clockwise or anti-clockwise.'

Vo looked at her with one rapidly blinking eye. 'You all very concern.'

'We're concerned,' Merrick spat, 'about losing our *teeth*!'

Vo slid two dominoes in front of her. 'Look now. Is one by my right hand. One by my left. 'Highest win.' She turned them both over. 'The right win. So! We begin with Mr Dyson clockwise. Is what I say first. Begin.'

Merrick sat down, fuming. Sinclair waited until he was sure she wasn't going to slam her fist on the table, then placed his blocks upright again. Disconsolately, Dyson positioned his blocks to face him, then slid one onto the 'two' end of the upturned central block. It now needed a blank or a four. Sinclair selected a block, a double blank, and placed it crosswise on the end.

Connor was next. Four or blank? Luckily, he had a four with a three. His hand shook slightly as he added it to the centre blocks, his stomach burning with acid.

Merrick slapped down a three with a blank, placing it on the blank end. Now it was three both ends. So far, no-one had missed a turn. All eyes swivelled to Dyson.

Vo said, 'Mr Dyson. Your turn.'

Dyson surveyed his six remaining blocks. It couldn't have been a hard decision.

'Bloody hell,' Sinclair blustered after ten seconds. 'Got a three or not?'

Dyson shuffled, scratched his armpit, then sucked his teeth. 'Pass.'

Now the reason for Sinclair's agitation appeared. He also had no three. He looked suddenly drained of blood. 'Can't go.'

Connor had a double three and added it thankfully. Two down. Five left.

Merrick slammed down a three with a five with a small explosion of satisfaction.

Dyson's turn again. They all knew he had no three. But did he have a five?

He scratched his neck with the air of a chess master contemplating the Queen's Gambit. Another ten seconds passed.

Sinclair voice had a shrill edge to it. 'For God's sake. Do you have a five or not? Damn it.'

Dyson scratched the top of his head. He scratched back under his arm, then he furtively picked at his nose. Finally, he said, 'Nope.'

'Bloody hell. Why didn't you say so?' Sinclair slapped down a three with a four.

For three rounds, the cameras panned to each frightened face. Connor missed two moves, Merrick one. The pressure now was extreme. A game of dominoes for a set of teeth, with the inquisitor's rack in the shadows. In the intensely silent room Connor, identified with the next move, found he was touching his teeth. Yet a part of him vowed that he'd smash Blore's skull with the hammer before they could strap him into the frame.

Merrick and Sinclair had two blocks left, he and Dyson three. Then Dyson was obliged to pass again. He ground his fists into his eyes.

It went around again without a miss. The room seemed caught in a time-warp as the candles danced shadows over the blocks. Connor stared over his two remaining dominoes to the hapless Dyson, who had three. Merrick crouched forward, clutching her final block and biting her lip. Sinclair had one block left as well. His eyes were wary now, sly. He'd already saved his teeth and on this last round needed two or four. He frowned at his block and said, 'Pass.'

Connor put down a two, heart pounding, his fingers almost refusing to grip it.

Merrick exploded with triumph and slammed her last block down.

Vo said, 'Mrs Merrick – win. Mr Dyson – lose.'

Sinclair sneered up at a camera. 'Missed me again, you slimy sod.'

As he pushed his remaining block away from him, Connor picked it up and looked. One end was a two.

Sinclair smirked and muttered, 'Gamesmanship, old sock.'

Merrick was on her feet taunting Dyson, eyes narrow with vengeful glee. 'Now how do you feel? *Now* how do you feel?'

She stretched across Connor to grab the hammer. Troopers moved either side of Dyson's chair. The luckless man stared up at them, then at the raving woman brandishing the tool.

Then Dyson did an unexpected thing.

He took his teeth out.

First the pink and yellow crescent of the bottom, which he placed on the table. Then the top set, which he positioned accurately on the first. It was an expensive set, beautifully made, its colour-matching slightly varied, the rows of teeth slightly uneven, to give the impression of acceptable imperfection. 'Like 'em?' he asked. 'Had 'em for years.'

Merrick's face and hands sagged as she became a child robbed of its toy. Sinclair burst into wild laughter. Dyson's chinless grin gave the impression of an old man showing off his party trick.

Merrick, enraged, raised the hammer again as if about to batter Dyson's head in but the two troopers hauled him, chair and all, back out of range. She smashed the hammer down on the teeth. The centre of the heavy table bounced and two sets of candles fell over but the dentures weren't quite destroyed. She scooped up the shattered pieces and fell to her knees on the floor. The hammer rose and fell on the carpet as the sound of her fury filled the room.

Connor and Vo set the candlesticks back. Wax had puddled on the cloth. There was a burn.

Vo glared up at the camera. 'See? What you think of your Gillian now? Not only she shit on you, she not find he have false teeth. Make fool of game.'

Connor subsided back in his chair, feeling too weak to move as Vo fronted Blore, a wisp beside a monolith. She raised her hands. 'What we do?'

Blore shrugged, fed up with it. 'She's smashed his teeth. That was the deal.'

'Is all?'

'What else? Let's get to bed.'

Vo considered his opinion, then shrugged her small shoulders. 'Okay.'

Dyson's collapsed mouth was still grinning. But Merrick was on her feet again, running around the table with the hammer. Blore thrust out a blocking arm, stopping her dead. He grabbed the hammer but she held on to it with both hands and all her considerable strength. 'Let me *go*!'

The huge man twisted the head of the hammer and tore it from her with one hand. It would have taken tremendous power to do it. His other hand slammed her against the table. 'Back off, sick bitch.'

Sinclair was chortling, semi-hysterical.

Blore jerked his thumb at the door. 'It's over. Out.'

Chapter Twenty-three

It was black outside and cold, the fog still blanketing everything. Beyond the light on the front portico, the world seemed to end. Two troopers lifted Dyson's wheelchair down the steps and pushed him into the haze. A third walked beside them, shining a yellow storm light on the ground.

Sinclair said, 'Better follow them.'

Merrick pushed past him, every line of her body telegraphing rage. Connor followed, using his torch to keep her in sight.

Sinclair muttered, 'Can't take much more of this. Bloody Dyson. Can you credit that?'

'Think they're going to kill us?' Connor said.

'It'd be a damned side more cost-effective than shelling out $20 million. Still, I think one of us'll make it.' His voice was unsteady. 'He's going to maim us all first, of course, and I'd say three of us have to die.'

'Great.'

'We should have listened to you, Connor. It would have been better to go down fighting.'

'You've changed your tune.'

'I'm bloody scared, man.' He trudged on. 'I wasn't coming back, you know. Had a rather nifty scheme. Even arranged a dicky passport. Did it all from a mobile phone. But the bleeding buggers knew somehow.'

'You can monitor a mobile on a scanner. You just have to tune in to the frequency.'

Sinclair digested that. 'What happened to you, anyway?

I thought you'd go bush.'

'No point. You can't run. They're too damned good. The only chance of stopping it is here.'

Sinclair pointed to Merrick's back. 'She said you knocked off two of them.'

'One confirmed.'

'Impressive. You're a dark horse.' He stopped walking and put his hand up, then put his finger to his lips until he judged the others were out of earshot. They were alone in the fog. 'I'm ready to listen to you, Connor.'

Connor laughed. 'Bit late.'

'I'm serious. We can't include that mad woman. And Dyson's had it. But if you and I put our heads together, we might come up with something.'

'Am I hearing this? I'm supposed to trust you? After what you did to your wife?'

'Don't be a moral athlete. Time to put away childish things. This is serious.'

'And that wasn't?'

Sinclair used his most persuasive, intimate tone. 'It may be our only hope, old sock. Our bleeding lives are right on the line.'

'Sorry.'

A thin smile. 'You surely don't think you can fight them alone?'

'Whatever I think, I'll keep to myself.'

The tall man blinked in the light of the torch. 'I really don't see why we can't cooperate. Pure self-interest, after all.'

'Because you're a two-timing, tricky, no-good bastard.'

'And you're a stubborn idiot.'

'Maybe.'

They walked on till they came to the path lights near the huts.

Sinclair put a rake-like hand on Connor's shoulder. 'Let

me know if you change your mind.' He trudged off like a stick insect into the void.

Connor diverted to his hut, his gut working overtime. After he'd relieved himself and washed his hands, he decided the screwdriver should stay with him.

He took the top off the cistern.

It was gone.

He put the lid back, cold inside. How the hell did they know? He looked hard at the ceiling. Just the smoked glass of the light fitting. How the…?

Of course. There'd be a pen sized camera with a tiny bug-eye lens projecting down beside the globe. And the translucent glass bowl covering both would be transparent from inside.

He looked down, acting normally, went into the main room. Yes the overhead lights concealed fixed cameras. He was sure of it now. So he could be unobserved in here only on a dark night with the lights off.

Then he heard a gentle tap. Once.

He crossed to the door. The unlatchable door. No-one. He shut it, looking puzzled.

Again, the tap. It seemed to be coming from under the floor. He grabbed his torch, went out, down the steps and under the deck. He shone the beam into the haze. He could hear a slight ticking sound. Immediately, something was thrust into the light. A woman's hand – holding a filing card with words scrawled on it in large black letters:

DON'T TALK

A hand went over his mouth.

He shone the beam up, hand raised to chop. She was almost unrecognisable in a military helmet with some kind of night-vision lens built into the front. The lens projected fifteen centimetres ahead of her face and cables went to a backpack. Only her mouth and chin were visible. The ticking noise was coming from the backpack.

She reached for the torch and turned it back to shine on the card, which she'd turned over. It had words on the other side:

> Don't speak at any time. Go back inside and take your shoes and watch off. Undress. Turn off the light. Wait in bed for a quarter of an hour. Snore a bit. Then dress quietly without the shoes or watch. Very quietly, walk out around the back of the hut, heading for the trees. Remember – no shoes, no watch. Make sure you understand all this. Read it again but don't take the card. Please do exactly as I say and make it look convincing. When you're sure of the sequence, go.

He read it again and nodded.

It was Gillian! Her!

He did it, precisely, knowing there was an extra lens in the light, yawning, getting into bed, turning off the bedhead light. He waited impatiently in the dark, occasionally making snoring sounds.

After perhaps twenty minutes he slipped his clothes back on, opened the door slowly so the catch didn't click, and sidled down the steps.

The fog was still thick. Even the first path light was now just a glow. He felt his way to the back of the cabin and then left the guiding wall, uncertain – feeling the ground with each step, heading for the grove of trees behind the huts. He held his hands out in front of him, expecting to collide with the rough bark of a trunk. Instead, he felt her grab his wrist.

As she led him away he stumbled over the grass, feet

freezing on the wet ground. She seemed to be taking him in among the trees, steering him around things he couldn't see. His eyes were well adjusted to the dark but he couldn't even make out the shape of her arm.

Finally she stopped. 'Okay. We can talk here.'

'Can't they track our heat?'

'They could. But they're not.'

'What's with the watch and the shoes?'

'They bugged your watch at Mackerel Beach with an IC micro-mike. New technology. It's linked with a micro-transmitter in your shoe-heel that relays conversations. The range isn't great but it also acts as a beacon. There are more bugs inside the hut and surveillance bug-eyes in the light fittings. I know you've found the slave camera behind the mirror.'

His hand bumped the contraption on her head. 'What's that? Image intensification?'

'Thermal. Too dark for image goggles. Most thermals can't see through fog but this one's a long-range high-intensity type.'

'Why's it clicking?'

'Refrigeration unit. Skip all that now. We haven't long.'

'So what's this about?'

'I need help.'

'Help?' Incredulous.

'I don't have time to tell you everything. So I'll just explain what concerns you.' A pause.

'Go on.'

'You know I don't agree with the game. I've tried to get it stopped but Nicolae wants revenge. Remember he's terminally ill and this thing's been a ten-year obsession. It's quite mad, of course. It's risking the organisation – distorting all we stand for.'

'*Stand* for? Like mechanised slaughter?'

'Don't make it harder. You don't see it all.'

'There's more?'

She sighed. Another pause. 'Nicolae's a complex man.'

'He's a maniac.'

'I know you're feeling raw. Please try to listen. We don't have long. Nicolae's interested in reducing populations.'

'Not to put too fine a point on it.'

'Because he thinks it'll save wildlife and habitats.'

'So?'

'I'm trying to get into your head that he's serious about conservation. All right – in an amazingly blunt way. But he puts his money where his mouth is. And defending forests from Third World governments eats up huge amounts of money.'

'He told me the tiger bit.'

'The munitions business pays for it all. But not directly any more, because he's invested for years in corporations.'

'Why?'

'Because companies last for generations if they're good. And what we have here can't go on. It'll run down the scale when he dies.'

'So? What are you saying to me?'

'He's set up a trust fund for the areas he's saved. And there's money left over to save more.'

'And that's where you connect with him, right? That's why you're still here. The conservation thing?

'Yes, Mr Connor. That's why. It's something I'm ready to die for. I know you're caught in this terrible game. But it's nothing compared with this. I'm talking about one of the biggest conservation efforts in the world. I know you're interested in conservation. This is something that has to go on.'

'Where do Blore and Vo fit in?'

'They don't. They're military people. Soldiers.'

'You go along with that?'

'Why not? It's a time-honoured profession, with a purpose-built psychology. You have to understand the mindset here.'

'Vo's out to get you.'

'I know.' A long pause. 'I'm no fan of Blore, but I'm sorry for Duyen. She's not so terrible. She's even very sweet. And brave. And she has her crusade.'

'What crusade?'

'Let's just say she… has other uses for the money.'

'Mould knows?'

'Not sure.'

'Why not tell him?'

'It's not easy.'

'How sick is he?'

'Almost dead.'

'And then?'

'When he goes, I'm a threat. You see, they respect what I do, but they can't understand how I think. We connect on the weapons side, that's all.'

'Why a threat?'

'I can't tell you.' A pause.

'Okay. When he dies, what then?'

'The men'll follow Blore, who'll side with Vo. He adores her. And of course they'll see the game through, out of respect for Nicolae. Then,' – a dry laugh – 'I expect they'll kill me.'

'Kill you?'

'And when they do, the conservation programmes will stop. They'll drain off all the money. Finish.'

'And what about us? Do we get killed, too?'

'One player's supposed to survive. The others'll be killed. So I suspect you're safer working with me.'

'Does the winner get the $20 million?'

'Yes. That interest you?'

'No, he can stuff his money. Shit.'

'I'm glad to hear that. Very glad.'

He felt out to her but only touched the heat-seeking lens. 'Wish I had one of those. I could see you.'

'You'd see a green outline with a blur for a face.'

'They killed my wife, you know.'

'I know. And I know what you did with the gun. It proves you can do it.'

Connor breathed out heavily. 'Do what?'

'I've got a plan that needs a second person – someone I can trust completely. You're the only one I can.'

'You trust me?'

A sad chuckle. 'I should be able to by now. I've studied you for ten years. Got a filing cabinet, fifty floppy disks…'

'Thanks for the interest.'

'Can you trust *me*?'

'I have to.'

Her hand found his. 'Shake on it then?'

They shook.

Connor said in a thick voice. 'Thank God for you, woman.'

'It's mutual, Mr Connor.'

'David.'

'David.' It sounded good when she said it. 'And I'm Gillian. Abbreviate it and I'll thump you.'

He held on to her hand.

She said, 'I know you're been under a lot of pressure.' She pressed his hand. 'Come on, I'll get you back.' Her hands moved to his shoulders. 'Let me steer you.'

'So what do I do?'

'Nothing yet. Unless you lose a game. If you do, we'll have to go early. I prefer you with ears and balls. But the longer you can give me, the better. I've got a lot to organise. And you mustn't try to contact me. It can only come from me.

Think you can handle that?'

'Yes.'

'The conservation side's the real issue. Not us – or the game. I'm afraid it'll be a war. We're going to have to kill people who aren't bad in themselves but who want to kill us. Hideous. That's why we're talking now. You understand?' She was almost pleading. 'Please, David. Tell me you understand?' Her hands tightened on his. 'I don't want to make things harder than they are. Please tell me you understand.'

'I'm with you. Two hundred per cent.'

'It won't be easy holding out. If Nicolae dies, I'm next. Then you – if they think you've helped me. You could end up just as dead this way.' She paused. 'Either opt out now and chance it with the game or…'

'And miss getting a shot at them? No way.'

'All we'll have'll be surprise. Fifteen people against two.'

'We'll need hardware.'

'We'll have it.'

'Hope you understand the gear here.'

'I wrote the manuals.' She squeezed his hand again hard, almost desperately. 'Thank you, David. Thank you so much. I knew you wouldn't let me down. I hope one day you'll know what this means to me. Don't talk any more. We're near the hut.'

She led him a few steps further, placed his hand on the wall, and was gone.

Chapter Twenty-four

Sinclair stared at the metal frame and groaned. 'God help us.'

They'd been escorted into a kind of conservatory with a rotunda of sloping glass on one side. It had an ornamental floor of inlaid tile and elaborate cane chairs with floral cushions – a room designed for summer. But beyond the glass was the cotton wool of fog. And in the corner the metal chair.

Connor looked at his watch, remembering not to tell it too much. Not to wear it would have been suspect. All his moves now had to look normal. 'Where are the others?'

'Merrick'll be admiring herself and they're probably making Dyson hop here,' Sinclair said. He slid onto a lounge, spreading his legs like callipers along the smooth floor, then looked at the ceiling and scratched his neck – the overdone movements of a man trying to appear unconcerned but desperately near to the edge. 'So what do we play this morning? Marbles or tiddlywinks?'

'Something like that.'

'Haven't reconsidered, have you, Connor?'

'Forget it.'

The tall man hissed air softly through his teeth. He looked at the lone trooper by the door as if half contemplating a break-out. 'No guns on this island, you notice?'

'Don't bet on it.'

Sinclair hissed some more. 'You know, I'm fond of my ears. You fond of your ears?'

'They're handy,' Connor said.

'See any point in sitting here waiting to have them cut

off?' He was staring around the room. The only exit was the single door. It opened as three more troopers came in and spread out a little around the walls like officials in an execution chamber.

'Got an alternative?'

Sinclair muttered again, 'God help us.'

The door opened once more. A fifth trooper pushed Dyson's chair in and Merrick followed behind. Dyson was in pyjamas, his foot freshly bandaged.

Sinclair, brittle-bright, said, 'Morning.'

Merrick ignored him and strutted to one of the big cane chairs, where she posed on the arm like a fashion model who moonlighted as a vampire.

Dyson wheeled himself erratically further into the room, uncertain how the chair steered. 'Jeez, we gotta go through this again?' His toothless mouth made him almost unintelligible.

'Three sets of ears,' Sinclair chirped. 'Wonder which pair'll go.'

'Shut up, fool,' said Merrick. 'We don't need to listen to your raving.'

'If a toe-cutting, teeth-smashing psychopath thinks I'm a fool…'

'Smash *your* teeth in a minute.'

Dyson half laughed, half sobbed, 'Jeez we're really something.' His finger started pointing. 'He's young. He's rich. She's a looker. And we're all in the same stinkin' can. All of us. No difference. Going to get cut to bits. Like that makes me really…' He couldn't think of a word, just sat there shaking his head.

Merrick said, 'He's smashed. They're giving him booze.'

'Up your rectum, you sick old bitch.' It was hard to understand the words but the gist was clear. She walked menacingly to his chair as he glared up at her with hatred.

'Hit a man in a wheelchair, would you?'

Her arm flew back and then forward to punch him full in the face but he defended himself with one arm. Her other hand came smashing in. He covered his face and cringed. None of the troopers moved to stop her.

'Shit.' Connor stepped in and dragged her back. She twisted, going for his eyes. He instinctively stepped behind her leg and pushed her opposite shoulder – the basic judo trip – and she fell back on the floor. She clasped her hip in pain and whimpered, pushing herself further from him on the tiles, rubbing her bruised side. 'I'll have your ears,' she spat, 'on my shelf, next to that swine's toe.' She hauled herself, wincing, to a chair.

'So Mr Connor's a martial artist!' Blore had entered with Vo. 'Able to trip women. Impressive!'

Around the continent of Blore a rattling traymobile was pushed – the nurse, bringing in her equipment. Medical instruments jiggled on top of it.

'Oh, God,' Sinclair groaned.

Vo walked to the centre of the room. 'Welcome to second contest in Round Three. Removal of ears.'

Sinclair got up. 'Where's Mould? I demand to speak to Mould. I demand to see him *in camera*.' His voice was shrill with nerves.

'He see you in camera.' Vo said.

'Privately, woman. Privately.'

'Mr Mould with doctor. No-one may see. Is very sick.'

'Fuck it, I'm through with this bloody business.' Sinclair stamped around, clenching his fists. 'You can fuck my bloody company. I don't give a fuck. I'm out of it, Mould. Hear me? Through.'

Vo gave her horrible smile. 'Poor Mr Sinclair. He think of this too late. No-one leave game. No-one leave island. Must play game to end. Is compuls…' She turned to Blore.

'Compulsory,' Blore supplied.

Sinclair stared wildly about him. Then, as if Connor's thought of last night had reached him through the air, he grabbed up a small inlaid table and hurled it at the glass. The pane it hit bowed a little and trembled, making the reflections in it dance. But the reinforced wall held and the table smashed to the tile, shearing off a leg.

Yelling, 'Come on, Connor,' Sinclair sprinted for the door. Two troopers grabbed the struggling man, instantly pinning his arms. They marched him back to the others and thrust him into a chair.

Sinclair sat, panting and distraught, staring at Connor, who hadn't moved.

Dyson was grinning maliciously. 'A millionaire. Look at him now.'

'Now we see what you are, Mr Hoity-Toity Smarty-pants,' Merrick said. 'Just a frightened baby.'

Vo clapped her hands. 'Attention all.' She pointed to the inlaid pattern on the floor below her. 'You notice where I stand? Is many circle – like bullseye. And here where my foot is, circle centre.'

Dyson said, 'Coin-tossing. Can't hack this. Can you credit this? Coin-tossing – for our ears?'

'Most clever, Mr Dyson. But not coin. These.' She held up four objects. There were wooden discs about the size of hockey pucks. They'd been cut out of a plank with a hole saw, because there was a drill hole in the middle of each, and the edges had been sanded smooth. 'You all will stand over here, behind this line.' She moved five steps away to the border of the inlaid floor and pointed with her toe. 'You slide disks in from here. Nearest to centre circle win. Furthest lose.' She moved around the room, giving a disk to each of them, then pulled out her stopwatch. 'Allow one minute practice. From… now.'

Dyson said, 'I can't do it in this chair.' He struggled. 'Lift me outa this.'

Blore's two arms came in like cranes. He lifted Dyson's blubber form bodily out of the chair, as simply as a mother removing a baby from a stroller, and deposited him on the floor. Dyson snivelled over his shortened foot until he had it stretched out to the side of him. He started his practice, flicking the disk across the smooth tiles, talking to himself. 'C'mon, Dyson. C'mon.'

Sinclair was already on his knees, frantically trying to get the feel of it.

Merrick squatted near him.

As each disk slid along the floor and stopped near the concentric rings, a trooper kicked it back.

Connor, ice-cold now, was trying to assess the amount of force needed. The disk would slide either too far or too near. It seemed impossible to get it to the centre. Sinclair was way off. His emotional outburst had made him useless.

Merrick was doing quite well. 'About time we had a test of skill.'

Vo was staring at the watch. 'Ten second to go.'

They all tried their last despairing throws. Merrick's landed in the middle. Connor's went two inlaid circles beyond. The disks of the other two were nowhere near.

'Finish.'

They sat up, except Merrick, who remained in her throwing position, practising moving her arm as the disks were kicked back.

'Who wish to go first?'

Merrick put up her left hand, concentrated, intent.

'Mrs Merrick go first in own time.'

Merrick practised the movement of the arm again, then took the disk and slid it back and forth on the floor, not letting it go. Its slight rubbing was the only sound. Then with tiny grunt, she slid it ahead.

It seemed well judged but for some reason went too far, just outside the third ring.

She got up and rushed forward as if to kick it but Blore had his boot on it and a felt-tipped marker in his hand. 'Get her.'

Two troopers dragged her away by the arms.

Blore made a circle around the disk with the marker, then removed it and printed M in the middle.

'Who next?' Vo said.

'I'll go.' Connor knelt low to the floor with his disk. He had to do better than Merrick and wanted to try before he lost the feel.

'Mr Connor next.'

'You'll be worse, Connor. Your aim's off.' It was Sinclair trying to distract him.

Connor said, 'Shut up or I'll do you.'

Sinclair started whistling. Connor tried to ignore the distraction. He wasn't going to shift position. He still had the feel in his arm. He feinted three times with the disk, then let it slide and held his breath.

It stopped inside the third ring on the near side. Relief flooded his body. His ears were safe. Just.

'Oh, oh,' said Merrick.

Blore marked it off. 'Pity.'

'Can beat that,' Dyson gummed.

Vo said, 'Mr Dyson next.'

Dyson did his usual invocation, which involved kissing the disk and murmuring.

Sinclair resumed his whistling.

'Will someone shut the fucker up?' Dyson said.

Vo shrugged. 'Is not against rule.'

'Arsehole,' Dyson said, and threw.

His attempt was surprisingly good. Well inside the

second row. He cackled – his first sign of life since he'd arrived. He gave Merrick a chinless leer. 'Swap you two ears for a toe.'

Blore smiled. As if permitted, the troopers grinned, too.

Merrick, ashen, stared at Dyson caustically enough to turn him to soap. Her eyes slid to Sinclair, who was shaping up behind the line, knees higher than his head. When he crouched he was all limbs.

She struggled and kicked at her captors.

'Mr Sinclair next.'

Merrick began to whistle loudly, off-key, and Dyson joined in, then Connor. But Sinclair seemed immune, as if he'd gathered himself together for the effort. His face was blank, now, with concentration. This was the deciding throw. The disk skittered across the tiles… and landed almost in the centre.

Merrick screamed and fought. Two more troopers hurried to subdue her. Vo was saying something but no-one could hear her in the bedlam. Sinclair stared at his disk in horror, transfixed.

Connor, still on the floor, closed his eyes.

He heard it happening all around him. Merrick being dragged to the frame. Dyson's roars of glee above the noise: 'Cut the slime-bag! Cut her to bits!'

Sinclair's querulous protests: 'I can't cut someone's ears off. It's outrageous.'

Vo said, 'Must cut. Is rule.'

'I'll have to forfeit, then.'

'You not cut and you become next loser. Cause switch. Remember Rule Three. Next loser lose balls. If switch, Mrs Merrick do to you. No jig-a-jig then, Mr Sinclair.' Vo's titter.

Dyson's gummy slur above Merrick's screams. 'You'll love it, kid. Look triffic. Help you swim faster.' The screams became muffled. Connor opened his eyes. Five of the troopers were huddled around the frame and the nurse was primly wheeling the collection of scalpels toward them. The khaki huddle dispersed and he saw Merrick. They'd taped her mouth shut and her arms, legs, waist and shoulders were strapped to the frame. A strap around her forehead and leather chin-piece held her head rigid. Her long hair had been pulled back and taped up, exposing her ears.

'All ready,' Blore said to Vo.

Vo nodded and turned. 'Mr Sinclair?'

Sinclair was shaking his head. 'I... can't, for God's sake. It's hideous.'

'You want to lose balls?'

Sinclair drew his hand across his brow. 'It's... inhuman.'

Blore grinned at him. 'You didn't say that when we took out your little pixie lady. You're happy if others do the dirty work. Now you get to see how it feels up close.'

Vo nodded. 'Major make good point. Is your turn now, Mr Sinclair.'

The nurse took off Merrick's earrings with the nonchalance of a plumber removing a tap washer. She placed them on the tray and pulled on sterilised rubber gloves.

Dyson stared up at Merrick and cackled, 'Want the good news? I'll give you twenty-five cents for your earrings.'

The nurse was swabbing the root of Merrick's ears with disinfectant spirit. She paused and waved her hand over the tray. 'We have several types of scalpel. For this you could use a fifteen, ten or twenty. I think fifteen best. The ears are skin back and front with cartilage in middle. Part of cartilage connect with aural cavity so you need to press hard, behind here.' She pulled one of Merrick's ears forward to show the spot. Merrick's body went rigid. 'You should be able make clean cut right around, close in to head.'

'Give him the knife,' Dyson yelled, like a baseball fan rooting for his team.

Sinclair turned and looked the other way, holding his head with both hands.

Vo said, 'You still not do?'

Sinclair knew he was beaten. He turned and the nurse handed him a scalpel. Merrick's eyes became saucers and the heavy frame shook. Two troopers standing behind it placed their feet on the crosspiece to steady it. Sinclair examined the scalpel with alarm.

Blore was grinning again.

Dyson put his hand up. 'Hey, fella. I'll do the first one – get you started.'

Vo shook her head. 'Not allow.'

Merrick, crimson with terror and dismay, looked close to a stroke.

Sinclair, avoiding her eyes, launched into an apologia. 'I'm very sorry about this situation but I think you see my predicament. If I don't do as they say, you'll be forced to castrate me. Which I know you'd enjoy – and manage without a qualm. But I'd much prefer you without ears to me without balls. I'm afraid I can't offer a better excuse but…'

'Too many word.' Vo was becoming impatient. She was holding her stopwatch. 'Cut off ears.'

Sinclair coughed and turned to the nurse. 'Won't it make rather a mess?'

She said, 'No main arteries in ears. Will bleed much but not serious. Normally would use diathermy machine as cut, but Mr Mould say not to use till later.'

Sinclair made a face, took off his jacket and placed it on a chair. Then he fussed around rolling up his shirt-sleeves.

Vo said, 'You already on purpose take too long. Have ten second to start. Or I say you not do, and cause switch.' She clicked her watch.

Sinclair looked aghast. He boggled at the shiny slide-on

blade in its flat Bard-Parker handle, then peered at Merrick's left ear. She was straining every muscle against the straps, her muffled sounds a pleading scream.

'Five second,' Vo said.

Sinclair looked at Connor. He seemed close to meltdown. 'Dear God,' he squeaked. 'It's bloody rape. But what else can I bloody well do?'

Connor looked away.

'Time up.'

'Shouldn't I have gloves?' he blurted, an obvious attempt at further delay.

The nurse produced a pair. 'Hold out hands.' She pulled them over his reluctant hands while Vo tapped her foot.

Dyson was clutching the arms of his chair and all but bouncing up and down, face florid with revenge. 'Let's see the bitch without ears. Let's see what that does to her looks.' He cackled. 'Won't improve her hearing, either.' He'd wheeled himself as close as he could, was staring into her terrified eyes. 'I'm going to have your ears, bitch-face. Two ears for five toes.'

Vo drew the edge of her hand rapidly across the front of Sinclair's pants. 'Do now or balls go *shiik*.'

Sinclair winced.

Blore shook with silent laughter. The other troopers were enjoying themselves too.

Sinclair stared at his tormenters, then back at Vo, at the dead, ever-open eye and the menacing blinking one. 'Oh, God! Oh, God!'

He pinched the top of Merrick's left ear between his fingers and made a delicate nick at the front. A thin trickle of blood coursed down to her lobe. He looked around at Vo for approval.

Her terrible face told him what hesitation meant.

Rigid, screwing his face up, making hurt-puppy noises,

he began to hack at the ear, dragging it back and outward from her head as fast as the cartilage severed, squeaking with squeamish disgust as he drove the razor-sharp blade in, slicing again and again until the bright tip went deep enough to sever the stiffer part at the back, then ducking to work it around the base with almost feminine revulsion, finally nicking off the last of the lobe with a shudder and a flick.

Merrick's left shoulder was red. Blood poured from the elliptical gash. Sinclair held the severed ear, yelping, like someone with a live mouse by the tail. The nurse held up a metal kidney dish and he dropped the bloodied thing in.

Merrick had fainted, was out to it. Her body sagged in the straps. Thankfully, frantically, Sinclair attacked the other ear. The blade sliced through the skin and paler cartilage. He hacked wildly in his hurry to get it off before she came to, leaving jagged remnants around the hole.

Then he was holding it and looking for the dish. The nurse held it forward again. He dropped the second ear on top of the first, fluttered his bloodied hands and dragged off the gloves. Merrick, earless and unconscious, blood pouring down both sides of her neck, now looked trim as a wounded ferret.

Dyson was yelling, 'Make her eat 'em.' He manoeuvred his wheelchair beside the tray so he could peer into the dish. He poked the severed ears with a finger.

The nurse applied a compress as the troopers loosened the buckles. Sinclair, speckled with sweat and spots of blood, staggered to a chair and hunched deep into it, knees up at his chest but holding his hands far out in front of him as if he'd disowned them. The gleeful Dyson slurred some drunken song with unrepeatable words.

Connor, feeling faint, went toward the door. Two troopers were swiftly there before him. He turned and wandered back.

Dyson had wheeled his chair to Sinclair. He tried to shake one of the limp, extended hands. His masticated voice. 'Great bit of surgery. Loved it.'

Sinclair snatched his hands back and laid them across his stomach.

Dyson withdrew his hand. 'Well, up you, too.' He turned to Connor. 'He's just butchered someone alive and now his sensitive soul's in pain.'

'*You* didn't have to do it,' Sinclair cried.

'Diddums. You've still got your toes, Mr Big Shot. Jeez, she's gonna love *you* tomorrow.'

Connor said, 'I feel sick.'

Dyson's cackle. 'Feel sicker if someone cuts off your crown jewels. Hey!' He called out to Blore, who was talking with Vo. 'Hey! What happens if the bitch loses next time? Mastectomy?'

Vo swivelled to look at him. 'If she lose, she pay penalty.'

'"Gelded", it says. She's a broad.'

'Next game require doctor assist. You want detail?'

'Love it,' Dyson gummed.

Sinclair passed long shaking hands over his flowing hair. 'Will someone shut him *up*.'

Connor said, 'They could knacker *you*, Dyson.'

'Or I might do it to you. Better jerk off tonight. Could be your last.' His glee swung suddenly to alcoholic self-pity. 'Jeez,' he blubbered, 'Jeez. Why didn't you leave me in the car?'

Chapter Twenty-five

It seemed there were to be no more constitutionals on the lawn, no more explorations of the shoreline, no more lounging by the Elysian pool or even fraternising between the contestants. They were escorted back under guard. And the guards remained – stationing themselves outside the huts.

Connor's minder was over six feet of trouble and probably weighed 100kg. He had shoulders an axe handle wide sloping to huge arms. His large gut was firm and quivered when he walked – quivered not with fat but with well-toned heft. The man was almost as big as Blore, but not Polynesian. His face was Slavonic and fixed in a perpetual look of distrust. Above his groper lips bristled a trim moustache. He gave the impression that he quite approved of himself.

After two hours confined in the hut with the monolith outside the door, Connor went out and confronted him. 'I need a walk.'

He trudged down the steps. The fellow followed, staying a pace behind. The fog was dispersing and visibility was now about fifty metres. Above them, a circle like a muslin-covered globe cast light that eight minutes ago had left the sun. He walked up the path to the house, almost to the portico.

A plate-sized hand fell on his shoulder. 'Inside off limits.'

'I'm not going inside.' Connor turned from the entrance and trudged along the building's formidable length, moisture from the crisp grass working into his sneakers.

He passed the french windows of the dining room,

walked to the corner of the building and down the side until he was in front of the tall windows of the library. He paused and stared down at the grove with the huts. Then, just as casually, he turned to look into the room. He could see her desk. The chair was empty. He wondered if she were trying to reach him. How would they communicate now? What if she were watching him? Did she need to contact him? He began walking again and the crunching behind him resumed. He was almost to the back of the house when the voice behind him said, 'Off limits.'

He looked up at the man. 'Just walking around it.'

'Back of the building's now off limits.' The man moved to block him. 'So don't get smart.'

'Okay,' he shrugged. He watched as a white-coated man, perhaps the chef, came out of the building with a metal dish full of peelings and emptied it on a compost mound beside the vegetable patch.

The trooper still stood blocking him so Connor retreated the way he'd come. He walked the length of the building again and around the other end. Here was the tent-like glass projection of the conservatory where ears were summarily removed. The room was empty also. Then he saw the back of a woman, a fair distance up the track that led through the trees. A slim woman with short dark hair. Now he understood.

He said, 'Need to get some air in my lungs,' and began to jog down the hill, heading for the jetty, the big man lumbering behind. He ran along the bay, then up the hill past the pond toward the huts. The man was still behind but puffing hard.

Connor pounded up the steep slope to the house and did the circuit again. This time his shadow was tired of close-order surveillance. Panting like a horse, he stopped at the house and watched.

Connor did one more circuit, feeling winded himself. But when he reached the bay again he dog-legged and darted toward the tangle of vines and vegetation that bordered the forest above the rocks.

He heard a yell from the house. He ignored it and dodged through the undergrowth. The troopers had one disadvantage: they were too huge to be sprinters. He headed up from the shoreline, through patchy grassland with stunted bushes and trees. Bellbirds and tui chimed and there was the screech of kaka from the forest higher up. No pines here but tall timber that seemed indigenous.

He stumbled over ferns, spongy mosses and brittle lichen. Two beautifully plumaged, red-beaked pigeons took fright ahead and beat the air with colour.

He stopped and listened. The cracking of twigs. Someone coming. But not from below.

The trooper would have been easy to hear blundering through the vegetation. No, this was someone smaller, lighter. Then he spotted her head above the sea of ferns. Her finger was in front of her mouth. She pushed fronds away to get to him. She was holding a small instrument with two probes projecting from the end and a readout of winking green lights. She pointed down at his watch. He took it off and gave it to her. She threw it far out over the trees in the direction he had come. 'You lost it.'

He nodded. 'Thought you might find me.'

'It's not finding you. It's getting to you.'

'They've put full-time minders on us, now.' He pointed toward the grass clearing. 'Mine's down there.'

'I know.' She pushed a strand of hair from her temple. Her face looked pale and tense. 'I need your help to lift something.'

'When?'

'Tonight. The safest time is 3am.'

'Sorry. Just lost my watch.'

She slipped hers off and gave it to him. 'Don't let them see it.'

'How do we meet?'

'I'll be at the rear corner of the house on the hut side. Wear something dark. I'll wait half an hour.'

'How do I lose the guard?'

She gestured with impatience. 'I don't know. You'll… just have to.'

'Okay, I'll be there. You still safe?'

'So far.'

'Is Mould still alive?'

'Just.'

A crashing in the undergrowth below.

'Have to go,' she said. Then only shaking fronds showed where she'd stood.

He picked his way back through the vines toward the clearing. He could see the trooper's head as the fellow ploughed through shrubs. As the man got to him, breathing hard, Connor examined a tussock of grass with his toe, pretending to search. 'Lost my watch.'

The man towered beside him, boots sodden and shirt wet with sweat. The moustache twisted above the mouth. 'Smart bastard, huh?' Completely without warning he brought his knee up into Connor's stomach.

The force of it lifted Connor off his feet. Breath exploded out of him and he doubled in agony on the grass.

'Try it again, you get worse,' the man snarled. 'We're sick of you lot. You're no fun no more. You start to give us the shits. You're confined to the hut as of now. You stay there and rot.'

The walk back to the hut was agony. He made it in a doubled-up stumble, crashed through the door and fell full length on the bed. He lay there for almost an hour, hugging his gut. He could hear the creak of the deck outside as the trooper shifted his weight.

The pain slowly subsided but he still felt weak and dazed. He lay, trying to work out what to do, remembering the camera in the light fitting.

The sound outside of a high-geared engine. He slid off the bed to the floor, the pain tearing again at his gut, and struggled on his knees to the window. It was lighter now, the fog gone. Heavy, moisture-laden clouds drifted over and, far higher, in the gaps above them, was cirrus, crystalline with ice.

He got his eyes above the sill and saw the mobile platform pitching down the slope. A trooper was behind the handlebar controls with a white-coated figure beside him. The vehicle stopped inside the grove and the trooper jumped down. The man in white climbed back and opened up containers. Trays were handed down. The hut guards converged on the vehicle and took two trays each.

Lunch.

Except Connor's lunch didn't reach him. The guard hunched on the steps outside and ate first his own lunch, then Connor's, looking back once at the window, mouth full, grinning like a schoolyard bully. If his minder was an indication, discipline on T55 was weakening. Connor watched the man's back as he hogged the food. How did one disable a combat-trained hulk like that? And how did one do it quietly, without raising an alarm? And despite constant camera surveillance? He decided one didn't. There had to be another way.

The only window was at the front, apart from a small louvred window beside the toilet. The walls were thick – lined half-logs. If he had something like a pinch bar, he could lever up the floor. But that would be heard and seen. The ceiling would be easier but then he'd have to prise off screwed-down corrugated iron – unless he could remove the soffits. No. If he tried anything like that, they'd know.

He went to the toilet and looked dubiously at the window. He might get his shoulders through on the diagonal but it'd be an almost impossible squeeze. At least an inch too narrow. Still…

The stippled glass louvres were not puttied, just held in place at the back by the strips of the wooden frame. Two screws on each strip, not puttied, just painted over. So he could feel where they were in the dark. If he'd still had the screwdriver… Then he remembered. He flushed the toilet and went back to the other room.

The trooper was relieved mid-afternoon. By then Connor had unpacked more of his case and put a few things in the drawers and cupboards. Nothing had been taken. Not even the pocketknife he'd stowed in his other sneakers. With the open cupboard door between him and the light fitting, he slipped the knife inside his belt beneath his shirt. The cold metal chilled his skin as he trailed back to the bed.

The knife had been his father's, an ancient navy-issue item with knurled sides and marlin spike along the back. Beneath the loop on the end was a screwdriver blade. With that, the job could be done. Except he'd be working in the dark.

During afternoon trips to the toilet he checked the layout again. He had a beanie he could slip over the light fitting to ensure the camera saw nothing.

The guard brought in his dinner tray and the smell of meat and vegetables filled the cabin. He ate hungrily. There was a card on the tray.

> Mr Mould regrets that his health has not permitted him to join you earlier but hopes to be with you tomorrow for the penultimate game in Round Three.

He didn't dare sleep. When the luminous dial of the watch read 2.30am he rubbed his fingers on the sheet to make them sensitive, dressed silently, leaving his feet bare, and padded through the pitch-black hut to the toilet.

A creak, then a cough. There was still a man outside.

He slipped the beanie over the light fitting and felt for the first screw-head. The knife slipped out of the groove and made a sound. He waited for half a minute, listening, before starting again.

It took twenty minutes to unscrew the strips without noise. He laid them on top of a spread towel where he could find them in the dark, leaving the screws in each hole. Then he slid out the louvres one by one, placing them on the towel, slipped the knife back inside his belt and tried to wriggle through the space.

His shoulders were too wide. Then he worked out that he'd fit if he went through arms first. He attempted it, trying to be quiet. It was worse than trying to play football in a library. He managed to get half out and hung with his torso down the outside wall, thighs twisted against the side of the frame. Stuck. He squirmed and the knife fell out of his belt to the ground.

He touched a pipe on the wall. With the handhold, he was able to work the rest of him through the hole. He fell with a thump that knocked the wind out of him, rolling to take the impact. Listened for steps. Had the man heard? He felt around and finally touched the knife.

He checked the watch. Ten past three. It would take time to approach the side of the house through the trees and he couldn't go directly or he might be spotted by one of the guards.

Away from the glow of the path lights, the night became so black that he had to walk with his hands in front of him and stubbed his toes on roots and stones. He tripped and fell twice. The painful journey took more time than he'd allowed.

When he left the shelter of the trees for the clear ground at the end of the house he could see no lights in the windows. The high square of the building was merely a patch of sky devoid of stars. He approached warily, eyes straining. Three twenty-eight. Was she still there?

A hand on his arm. He almost jumped. 'Shit.'

'Shh.'

'Can't see a thing. Almost killed myself getting here.'

'But you made it,' she whispered. She wasn't wearing the infrared pack but he could barely see her face. 'Stand still.' She felt for his face and started to pat it. 'Blacking you up a bit. How'd you do it?'

'Unscrewed the toilet window.'

'Can you get back without them hearing you?'

'With luck.'

'Thank heaven. If you'd killed anyone, we'd have problems.'

He stood like a small child being prepared by a teacher for the school play. 'Who's awake in there?'

'One person's on duty in the control room.'

'Where's that?'

'Basement.'

'There are the three guards down at the huts. Anyone else?'

'The nurse is in the clinic with Merrick.'

'Poor bloody woman. Christ that was terrible.'

'Don't worry about her. Worry about us. A man's in there with them. Probably the only one awake. They keep the lights on there all night. There are lights in Nicolae's apartment upstairs. Lee's up there with him. Far as I know, the rest are asleep.' She gave his nose a last pat. 'You'll do.'

'What's the plot?'

'We're going into the shelter.'

'What shelter?'

'Behind the house. Underground. Dug into the hill. Come on, I'll lead you. Give me your hand. No more talking till we're in there.'

The back of the building was in darkness except for two windows on the ground floor. She led him a little beyond the pool of light, staying close to the perimeter of the trees. From one of the outbuildings behind the mansion came the throb of a generator that sounded large enough to power a small town. It appeared to be elaborately baffled, like the truck-mounted jobs gaffers used.

Behind the centre of the main building a wide track between the trees led to the rise. They turned and hurried along it, branches crowding overhead. Here, the feeble light of the windows could not reach and they were walking, again, in pitch darkness. Suddenly Gillian stopped and felt ahead toward a small orange glow. A key-pad. Her hand went to it and he heard blips.

The hum of a large electric motor and the rumble of metal wheels on tracks. A reinforced door was sliding open. He saw the vertical line of its moving edge outlined against a glow from behind. The dim light came from a grating set high into a concrete curve. They went in.

A vaulted tunnel, big enough to take a train, with a line of dim lights on one side. On the other side, green 44-gallon drums stacked two deep against the wall. The door was rumbling shut behind them. For a 25-cm-thick door with steel sides it made little noise. He saw the glint of elaborate tandem rollers set deep into double tracks.

She took her fingers off the inside control buttons. 'We can talk now.'

He jerked a thumb at the huge door. 'What's this? They expecting to be nuked?'

'It's a one-bar PF. Got Piller artificial ventilation, gas

filters…'

'U-huh,' he said, no wiser.

They walked along the curving tunnel, dwarfed by its size. She pointed to the drums. 'Spare diesel. And we've underground tanks for fuel and water.'

They passed an open double metal door. Connor stepped into the dimly lit cavern. Switchboard panels, rows of ducting, complex filtering equipment, a maze of pipes on the ceiling. The room was silent, the air stale.

'Air-conditioning plant,' Gillian said. 'All sensitive machinery's shockproof. And we've explosion-proof valves and pre-filters. Protection against radiation, gas, biological attack…'

'Why all this?'

'I suppose you could call it an attractive rental opportunity. Some very wealthy people'll pay anything to save their skins. There's an accommodation area downstairs and we had huge food stores in here once. Now it's mothballed – used for storage. These lights are hot-wired to the outside generator.'

'What did all this cost?'

'Don't ask.'

The tunnel opened out into a space the size of a carpark with auxiliary lights high in the roughly cast roof. A profusion of stores and equipment on the floor. The APC was parked near the centre, flanked by a stripped-down Land Rover with launch mount on the back and a small all-terrain tanker truck that could have used more pressure in the tyres. There was also an elderly LPG-powered forklift with engine parts beside it on the floor.

'The tanker's for diesel. We use the APC for carting heavy stores.'

The rest of the space was stacked with crates and khaki carrier-bags. She led him along an aisle between the stacks.

Connor stared around him. 'Looks like a warehouse.'

'It's got that way over years. Things get sent to us, get left over. They seem to end up here.'

She stopped near the end of the stack and pointed to the bottom. 'Took me ages to find this. Would have to be on the bottom, of course. You'll need these.' She took a pair of rigger's gloves off the forklift seat and handed them to him.

He pulled them on, looking at the battered metal box. Chipped khaki paint and webbing lifting straps, one broken. 'You want that out?'

'Please.'

He climbed the stack and started lifting the top cases sideways. Some were heavy. 'What's in these things?' 'That's a man-pack radio with battery. Be glad you're not in the signal corps.'

He hefted a long sack. 'This?'

'AT4s. Single-shot light anti-armour.'

He heaved away, working down the stack. 'How'd you learn all this stuff?'

'The same way you learned to make films. Working in a specialised job for years.' She was climbing up. 'Can I help?'

'Go for it.' He lifted the end of another long case, his legs each side of it, dragging it along the top of the pile.

She pushed from the other end. 'See why I couldn't do it myself?'

They worked their way down the stack until the long metal box was exposed. He tried to drag it out. 'Weighs a ton.'

She knelt and undid the spring-clips. 'These are the Brownings that mount in the turret.' The lid creaked up and he saw two ugly slabs of steel, one bigger than the other. She pointed. 'That's a fifty-cal heavy machinegun. That's a thirty medium. They mount side by side. That's the barrel for the fifty. Screws in. Forget the tripods.'

Connor squatted, touched the body of the bigger gun. It had a shovel hand-grips on one end and a ventilated sleeve

– a killing machine with no concession to appearance. He got his hands around the two parts and hauled himself up.

The ramp at the back of the APC was closed. Gillian unlatched the door set into it, pushed it wide. 'We can't mount them yet but we have to get them inside.'

He heaved the parts of the gun over the doorframe.

'Careful, or you'll damage the recoil mechanism, bend the sleeve. It's touchy equipment.'

'Bloody heavy.' He shoved it inside.

'The other's lighter. You use the thirty on personnel, the fifty for vehicles.' When the weapons were in the back she said, 'Now we need to get the ammo.'

'So it's going to be a war?'

'It's the only way we'll make it. Without armour and guns we're dead.'

'You don't do things by halves.'

She sighed. 'Please, David, try to remember why we're here. This isn't just about your wife, or Merrick's ears, or Dyson's toes.' It's about us – staying alive. And the…' She looked down and turned away.

'I buy staying alive. But as for carrying on Mould's biodiversity circus – I mean, even with all his dough we can't do much.'

She turned back, close to tears. 'But we can preserve what he's done, don't you see? And do a whole lot more. Look.' She dragged him back to the APC and pointed in the door at the crates on the floor. 'Five-kilo silver bars. Hundreds. And they haven't even bothered to unload them. We're swimming in money here. Money that…' Her eyes were brimming. 'David?'

He pulled her shoulders to him and kissed the camo-creamed forehead, kissed the salty tears. She clung to him, willingly, tightly, her arms around and up his back, pulling him as close against her softness as she could. They held each other for a moment, then let go, startled at what they'd done, surprised at the urgency of their bodies.

He said, 'You're something.'

She smiled through the tears and pressed his hands in hers. 'Help me with the ammo.'

Once the boxes of ammunition were stowed she said, 'I hate to tell you this but we'll have to put that stack back like it was. I don't think anyone'll come in. But if they do, and see something obviously different…'

He whistled. 'Okay.' He started lugging the crates back. It was good to have a workout, good to move. She helped, filling him in on her plan. 'When we go, you'll be in the turret. I'll drive.'

'You can drive that thing?'

'I've done it before. I'm no expert but I'll get there. Next time I'll show you how to use the guns. You'll need to lift them into the mounts. Have to get that shovel-grip off first. I can feed the belts in for you. I'll give you a crash course when they're set up.'

'How does the turret work?'

'It's manual. Traversing wheel. Don't worry about that now.'

'So we clatter out there and chop everyone to bits?'

'If they don't incinerate us first.'

'What with?'

'Lots of things. Like that one you're moving. An M113 protects you against small-arms fire and shrapnel. Beyond that, you're in trouble. Even an M60'll slowly cut through it at under 200 metres.'

'Can't we sabotage this stuff?'

'We'd be here a week.'

Connor lifted a heavy khaki CES bag onto the offending item, then stacked another on top of it.

'Those are Wasp, man-portable anti-armour. One-shot

wonders. Charlie G below that.'

'Come again?'

'Karl Gustaf. Breech-loaded recoilless anti-tank – complete with bore-sighting gear, steel brush and cleaning rods. See what I mean? The stuff's everywhere.'

'So we fight our way out. Where? To the boat?'

'No. We have to cripple the boat.'

'With a machinegun?'

'A fifty-cal round'll chop up the APC, so it'll chop the boat apart.' She pulled the end of what looked like a length of air-conditioning tube out of a pack. It had a sight and firing mechanism on the side. 'You can throw one of those in. Though I don't know how we'll use it unless we're heads up and stopped. Couldn't use it at oyster.'

'Oyster?' He slid one in the back door.

'With the hatch just open a slit.'

'U-huh. Welcome to the army. So the boat's a worry, then?'

'It's armed.'

'Didn't see a gun.'

'Under the front hatch, on a hydraulic lift, there's a Russian thirty mil. If it gets our range, that's it.'

'So we're fighting the navy as well?'

She pulled at his wrist to check the watch. 'Lord! We've been here two hours. You've got to get back.'

'You couldn't lend me a pistol?'

'They'd spot it. The house has metal detectors.'

'So why not fight now? We're here.'

'I've still got things I have to set up. Trust me, David. Please?'

'Okay, commander.'

'Come on, now. We've got to get you back.'

As they hurried down the tunnel he said, 'Never met a female terrorist before.'

'Culture shock?'

'Feels good.'

'But when we go it won't be fun. We'll have a good chance of getting fried. At least we've evened the odds a bit tonight.'

'What happens if I lose tomorrow's game?'

'You won't. I've rigged it.'

'You've what?'

'Thank God you reminded me. Here.' She produced two small sachets from her jeans – plastic foil-wrapped scalpel blades. 'You have to bring them to lunch tomorrow. Hide them between the fingers of your left hand so no-one can see them – and drop them into your plate.'

'I don't get it.'

'Unwrap them first, of course.'

'What're they for?'

'You'll see. Just do it. Please?'

They were at the door. 'No talking now.' She stood on her toes and gave him a peck. 'Good luck.'

He got back through the bathroom window by standing on the pipe. It took minutes of agonising squirming. Then the window had to be silently reassembled in the dark. He covered the worst noise by flushing the toilet. At the end of it his hands were shaking and he was exhausted by tiredness, stress and hunger.

But she'd rigged the next game. That sounded good. He crept to bed and slept in the limbo of the totally fatigued.

Chapter Twenty-six

Connor woke at eleven. On the bench, in watery sunlight, gleamed a tray with breakfast things. He got out of bed, stiff all over, and lifted the plate cover to expose congealed eggs and bacon. Propped against the pyramid-folded napkin was a message telling him to be in the dining room at noon. A shuffle outside. The guard remained.

He wolfed down a piece of dry toast and stumbled to the bathroom, hoping a shower would sooth the stiffness of his body. Next, he got behind the cupboard door, where he knew they couldn't see him, positioned the scalpel blades between his fingers and held his left hand in a natural curve. It wasn't noticeable but he wondered if he'd get away with it.

In the long room the curtains of the windows were caught back to reveal lawn sloping to a sea still greyed by cloud. It was cold outside and he'd worn his leather jacket. He kept it on, afraid that taking it off might dislodge the blades between the fingers. What the hell were they in for now?

For some reason the dining table had been pushed a few feet toward the inner wall. Dyson, seated opposite Sinclair, his face as long as the table, seemed concerned for his safety should Merrick manage to appear.

As Connor sat next to Sinclair, Merrick was marched in – her body flanked by troopers who watched her like hawks. She looked at no-one, tears coursing down her cheeks. Tears had discoloured the bandage that went from under her chin to the crown of her head. She looked up once at Sinclair with eyes full of dreadful hurt. The troopers braced as if convinced that she would leap at him and they would have to pin her, drag her back. Sinclair seemed to think so too, and remained behind the back of his chair. He shook his head and spread his hands as if faced with something impolite. He said, 'I'm frightfully sorry. But I *had* to. What could I *do*?'

Merrick slumped into a chair as if all the fire had left her. She shut her eyes and almost whispered, 'You've ruined me.' Tears streamed from under her lids.

Sinclair emerged from behind his chair, now convinced he wouldn't be attacked. He looked at her a moment longer, then sat with studied slowness. He cleared his throat and said, 'Mould did this, not me.'

She looked up at him once more, her voice still almost a whisper. 'Oh no. Oh no. You did it. Only a coward would do it. Not a man. I can't get to Mould. But by God, I can get to you.' Then, as if intoning a sacred chant, 'You're dead,' she breathed. 'You're *deeeeaaad*.'

Vo entered next, followed, to Connor's huge relief, by Gillian, who looked drained and tense. With everyone seated, the space at the head of the table was still vacant.

'First we eat,' said Vo, and clapped her hands. It was beef stroganoff with mountains of vegetables, accompanied by vintage Grange Hermitage that would have cost $200 a bottle. In that bleak place on that bleak day the meal, their last comfort, was embraced and the full-bodied wine attacked like watered-down chianti. Sinclair quaffed in embarrassed silence. Dyson alternately gulped and mashed his sprouts to compensate for absent teeth. Merrick didn't eat but drank her wine in two long draughts, then raised her glass for more, as if trying to blot out life. Connor managed to hold his fork without dislodging the blades. He was careful not to look at Gillian but still felt their bodies were attached by strings.

Vo said, 'Next we have steam fruit pudding. Draw will be during dessert. Meantime, if you wish for second helping, please not be afraid to say.'

More food? In this dreadful situation it was a comfort of a kind. Connor lifted his plate to a trooper, who took it. He lifted his glass again. Each sip would be worth at least $5. He felt the glow of the alcohol through him. The glass was immediately refilled. Everyone now seemed half awash and Merrick, gulping her third glass, had clearly achieved the desired alcoholic haze. Her streaked face was drying and her chin was up again. Despite her terrible loss, she seemed to be collecting the shreds of her pride and began to pick at the food on her plate as if she'd decided she must stay strong.

Connor's plate came back with another huge helping of stroganoff – far more than he could eat. But he determined to do his best.

Merrick noticed Vo looking at her.

'What are you staring at, horror?'

'So good to see,' Vo said, 'how much you enjoy wine.'

Merrick's tragic eyes stared back. 'Do you feel nothing for me, you gargoyle? How did *you* feel when you lost half your face?'

'Was napalm,' Vo said. She looked down, gave a small shrug. 'Is war.'

'But *you* people did this to me. Out of *spite*.'

'Tough. What about my toes, you banshee bitch?' Dyson snorted.

Merrick, ignoring him, held her glass high, her selective mind oblivious to all but her particular tragedy. 'Thank God for alcohol.' A blighted look. 'Might as well be sloshed the way I am.' She knew her affliction had gained her sympathy, however grudging and reluctant, and felt it her cue to play to the gallery again. Her voice suddenly thundered. 'By God! Be warned. All of you. All of you. I still intend to win.' She turned slowly to face Sinclair, trembling with inner rage, one finger stabbing toward him. 'And I intend to… have… his… *balls*.'

'Ear, ear,' Dyson added, with the courage of the Dutch.

Merrick lunged across, trying to reach him, and was pounced on by the troopers. As her chin hit the table, two glasses and a bottle tipped over.

Dyson almost fell straight backwards in his chair and a slice of zucchini hit the floor. Across the $50 crimson stain he winked at her with calculated insolence.

Merrick bucked again, arms flailing, before she was pinned.

Sinclair examined his nails. 'Must we suffer this?'

Dyson grinned tipsily. 'Untamed passion. She's back, folks, fiercer than ever. New, now, never before, this week only. Gorgeous Gracie. Slightly damaged. Knock-down price. No ears and a message on her arse.'

The ruction was upstaged by the rumble of something large on rubber tyres. Eyes darted to the door as Mould's hospital bed was pushed in. He entered, feet first, complete with drip-stand, ashen form propped up, eyes glazed. The nurse trotted in last, wheeling the oxygen bottle on a handcart.

The troopers positioned the side of the bed toward the table's end so that the man's faraway eyes could survey them. His hooded gaze acknowledged them, touching each like a spectral prod.

'How good,' he finally said, 'to see you in the flesh once more.' The deep voice was far weaker – a hollow wheeze. His sausage finger pointed to the stain. 'Fix that.'

The troopers glanced at each other uncertainly before one trotted from the room.

Sinclair spat, 'You *anus mundi*. You…'

'Torturer!' Merrick screamed. 'Mutilator!'

Dyson crooked his arm, his hand a fist. His other hand hit under his elbow. '*Rompi Coglioni.*'

Mould looked at him with contempt. 'Oh, but I will, Adrian… if I can. And the… reclusive Mr Connor. Which language will you… curse me in? Ancient or modern?'

Connor sensed Gillian's eyes on him. He said nothing.

Mould smiled. 'Well, if you're finished expressing your appreciation, we'll get down to business. As you all see, my health is… assuming precedence over the game. So events have to be… compressed. It's not as I would have… wished it.'

A trooper doubled back into the room, then skidded to a pace of decorum like someone arriving late at a funeral. He padded forward, cleared a space on the table and spread the linen overcloth he'd brought. Another man appeared by the door holding aloft a salver.

Mould gave Vo a meaningful look.

She stood up. 'Next game, balls. Draw now.' She beckoned the man at the door, who lowered the silver tray to the table, revealing the prosaic sight of two small fruit puddings, aflame with brandy, and two bowls holding what looked like brandy sauce and King Island cream. Another trooper placed on the table a small stack of bowls, a cake-server and a knife.

'Pudding,' Vo continued, 'contain some of this.' She held up a scalpel blade. 'And also one of this.' The second exhibit looked like a ball made of miniature pins with the heads embedded in some kind of central mastic and the points sticking out all round. 'None of these item possible to swallow.'

'Compliments to the chef,' said Sinclair.

'Loser get ball. Winner get least blade. Serving begin with last loser and go round table anti-clockwise.'

Merrick was listening intently, trying to absorb the rules.

'Whoa,' Dyson said. 'What if you get two things?'
'Make no different.'
'What if you get nothing, then?'
'Then get least blade and win.'

Connor felt the internal shivering. Now he saw it. Gillian had possibly saved him from winning. But what if his slice had the round thing? Then his balls were still on the block.

'Hold it right there,' Dyson said. 'How do *we* know that *you* don't know where the things are?'

'No-one know.'

'Prove it.'

'All will explain.' She spun a now flameless pudding on the tray. 'Will spin pudding like this, then blindfold person will cut and serve.'

Dyson looked disgusted. 'Dumbest idea yet.'

'Is Mr Mould's idea.'

Sinclair looked at Mould. 'It's imbecilic.'

Mould said nothing, as if speech would cost him too much; as if he were there at all only by a huge effort of determination. Only his squid eyes moved. His body seemed to be already decomposing. The room was charged with the presence of a man who remained alive by will alone.

His eyes slid to Gillian. She glanced up at him and rose. Vo handed her the serving knife and a trooper tied a thick scarf over her eyes. They led her to the table's edge where the puddings were positioned. Vo spun the smaller pudding on its salver, then guided the knife-hand over the centre of the cake. 'Cut now.'

She felt the position of the pudding lightly, then cut it in halves. She turned it and cut again. The quarters were removed and deposited in four bowls. One cut exposed the gleam of a blade and that slice was served to Merrick.

'Ah,' Vo said. 'Mrs Merrick already have blade.'

When every contestant had a bowl, the brandy sauce and

cream were offered around.

Sinclair shook his head, as if he wished nothing to obscure his fate. Troopers positioned themselves behind each chair.

'Why are they watching us?' Dyson said.

'To see if you cheat.'

Gillian's blindfold was removed. She cut two slices from the second cake.

Vo took one. 'Second pudding for, what you say – non-com… non-combatants.'

The two women took their portions back to their seats. Gillian had said nothing since coming in. She looked as if she'd tuned out but he knew it was an act. Women were amazing, seemed able to play any part they wished.

Mould's eyes slid to her. 'Thank you, Gillian.'

She looked up at him.

'For helping us make the contest fair.'

Connor was on his guard. The comment sounded far too pointed. He poked at his pudding with his spoon – mashing the first mouthful to be sure it wouldn't shred his tongue, fighting the numbing of the alcohol, acutely aware of his left hand. If the man behind his chair saw anything…

The normal thing would be to eat. He took his first taste. The pudding was rich, fruity, with the vaguest metallic tinge.

The event was monitored from the bed by Mould's expressionless eyes. There seemed a great distance behind them, as if he were watching from somewhere north of Helsinki.

Merrick, face like thunder, spooned the scalpel blade from her pudding and dropped it on her bread plate.

'One,' she growled. She mashed with her fork, cautiously hunting for more. Her movements were clumsy, her swaddled face dulled by wine.

Sinclair had not touched his portion and was watching the others intently, brow damp with alcohol and stress, as if terrified they might cheat.

Then, amazingly, above the hesitant clink of spoons, came the grating noise of a snore. Dyson was nodding forward, head almost in his plate. Everyone looked at him, astonished.

As if their combined scrutiny had reached him, he suddenly jerked upright again, before his eyes closed and he started to nod once more. Stress, repletion and wine had robbed his sluggish body of attention. The snore resumed. Even *in extremis*, there seemed no way he could stay awake.

Sinclair tapped his spoon, eyes peeled for deceptions. Merrick, delving with hers, disinterred another blade.

'Two,' she announced with a hiss and placed it carefully by the other on her plate.

Connor had also found a blade. He was cautiously probing the slice now, feeling for the ball of pins, hand shaking.

Vo waved a finger at Dyson. 'He not to sleep.'

The trooper behind Dyson's chair shook him. He woke up with a snort. 'Huh?'

The man handed him his spoon.

Dyson's eyes met Vo's. 'How we goin'?'

'Eat,' she said. Then she pointed at Sinclair. 'You.'

'You addressing me?'

'Eat.'

'Shut up, you pathetic creature.' He spooned a corner off his slice, watching the others like a fish-eagle.

Dyson grunted and picked out a blade, 'Like trying to pick fly-shit out of pepper.' Then he found another, grunted and deposited it on his plate. 'Two of the little shits.'

Connor placed his left hand over his bowl, let the blades fall into the cream, then obscured the entry point with his spoon as he took his hand away. No-one seemed to spot it. He pretended to probe beneath the cream, working the blades into the pudding. He didn't seem to have the ball, thank God. Had she arranged that somehow too?

Merrick had ceased her search, as if her two-blade total was final. She seemed strangely abstracted and had not spoken for some time.

'One.' Sinclair had uncovered a blade and placed it on his side plate with relief.

'Three,' from Dyson, who raised a victorious arm aloft. 'Pole position.' He lowered his arm and smiled. 'Looks like more UT infection. Order-of-the-spot forever.'

Connor mashed on until he 'discovered' his first blade and picked it carefully out.

The sun had moved, lengthening the shadows, painting the tablecloth in slanting stripes that made the room seem almost theatrical. From the distant hell of his illness, Mould's dying eyes watched every move.

Connor fished the second blade out. 'Three.' He sat back. 'All I can find.'

Sinclair stared at them, face grey. Everyone now turned to look at him. Slowly, slowly, he pushed his spoon into his pudding, pressing it in from the top. The spoon stopped abruptly, halfway in. He froze. Horrified, he broke off a slice – exposing the spikes of a metal ball.

Merrick's dulled eyes glittered with elation.

Sinclair sprang to his feet. Before the troopers could stop him, he'd used his long reach to split one's lip and kicked another in the shin.

He went down beneath them, on top of his knocked-over chair, his foot landing in Connor's lap, a painful flash of expensive leather, then sliding off as four troopers hoisted him, one to each limb, until he was suspended prone above the floor like a human battering ram. His head came up and he yelled at Mould, 'You fucking bugger. You rigged it.'

Mould painfully shook his head.

Vo called over Sinclair's raving to the men, 'Too much

noise. Take him to gym.'

They carried him out feet first.

Connor glanced at Merrick. Although the remover of her ears would soon be gonad-free, she seemed oddly indifferent, distracted, like someone trying to memorise something.

Mould croaked, 'Who wins?'

The blades were counted, the slices re-probed. Finally Vo said, 'Mrs Merrick win.'

Merrick half smiled, as if her triumph had cost her pain. There was a slight fleck of blood on her lip.

Mould nodded, 'Justice, Grace? Or guile?'

So Mould had noticed too. Even balanced on life's edge, he missed nothing.

Merrick didn't reply.

Vo said, 'Mrs Merrick? Please to open mouth.'

Merrick swallowed and a spasm of shock crossed her face. She coughed and gagged, then opened her mouth. Blood had pooled around her gums. It flecked her teeth from cuts on her tongue and inside her cheeks.

Vo said, 'More wide, please.'

Merrick opened wide. Vo looked daggers at her with her one good eye before prudently inserting not a finger but a teaspoon, to poke round inside the woman's bloodied mouth. She withdrew it and turned to Mould. 'She swallow blade, I think.'

Mould said, 'Get Lee. Tell him what's happened.'

A trooper doubled out of the room.

'You're a brave woman, Grace.' Mould was still expressionless. 'I've never… denied you that. It's a pity such great courage serves no-one but yourself. So you'd rather shred your… insides than miss removing… Hanford's balls?'

'She cheat,' Vo complained.

'But three each is a draw. And it's… really cost her something. No. Let her cut him.'

Merrick sagged against her chair, forehead clammy. Mould said, 'Give her water.'

A trooper filled her glass and handed it to her. She swilled out her bloodied mouth and spat the red water back into the glass.

'What interests me,' Mould said, 'is that there were… eight blades in the pudding but we've… already found nine. And Grace has swallowed at least one.' His eyes slid to his technical officer. 'Do you find that curious, Gillian?'

Vo's head swung around. 'What?'

'We have nine blades,' Mould repeated.

'No. Was eight.'

'I see nine.'

Vo was ticking her finger at the blades.

Gillian shrugged. 'Perhaps they miscounted.'

Connor's whole body stiffened. Christ. Mould was onto them.

Mould's cold eyes didn't blink. 'Perhaps.'

Vo said, 'Is nine. Not understand. You want we play again?'

Mould's faraway gaze moved from Helsinki to Longyearbyen. Connor's heart thudded. The bastard was stringing it out.

Finally he said, 'I… don't think so. The present outcome is… much to my taste. It's time Hanford… slipped up.'

Connor didn't dare look at Gillian, didn't have to, could feel relief surging along the cord between them.

The crisis passed as the doctor entered, carrying a spatula and a plastic packet of cotton balls. He peered into Merrick's mouth, nodded and said, 'Chance of perforation. Right now, need something to catch up point of blade.' He felt her brow. 'Slight shock. Suggest you wet and eat these balls right now.'

She said, 'Is that all?'

'Amazing what can go through gut but scalpel blade not

good. Will need operation. You very silly lady.' He turned to Mould, 'Better to do it on the mainland. If here, then I need certain things.'

Mould thought. 'No. Requisition what you need and prepare to do it here. Meanwhile, she continues with the game. Thank you, doctor, for your help.'

Lee nodded and left.

Vo stood up. 'Now we all go to gymnasium, where Mrs Merrick can have much thrill in slice off Mr Sinclair's balls.'

Chapter Twenty-seven

The gymnasium was the same. The windowless room with its gloomy expanse of shapes and shadows had the same Goyaesque lighting as before. The one lamp was at the far end – above the rack by the mirrored wall where Dyson had been tied and whipped.

But now, on the rack, was the star shape of Sinclair. He hung naked and upside down, like a carcass in an abattoir, suspended from inversion boots hooked over the top rung. His spreadeagled arms were secured to the edges of the frame near the floor and, from the centre of his pale body hung the longest penis Connor had seen. Though half obscured by a dangling scrotum, the appendage was so extended it seemed that the man's forebears must have interbred with goats. His pallid and draining body was a startling contrast to his face, which was flushed with pooling blood. His eyes looked ready to burst from his head.

Dyson, in his wheelchair, gawked at the dangling appendage with its hairy scrotum. 'Jeez, what a tool. It's Donkey Man!'

Merrick had not once glanced at Sinclair's genitals – as if the display were disgusting. She held a fresh glass of water, was dipping cotton balls into it, then eating them. She seemed listless, almost zonked.

The double doors opened back as the end of Mould's bed was pushed through. As the troopers wheeled it down the centre aisle and parked it side on to the scene, the medical contingent rattled after them with the now ominous traymobile. A second rattle, of castors on lino – a man pushing a ringer-mop bucket. He stopped beside the rack, leaned on the mop handle, ready to swab.

'Prepare,' ordered Vo.

The nurse stepped forward and lathered Sinclair's groin with what looked like shaving cream. Sinclair flinched as she took a safety razor from the tray and started to shave his pubic hair.

Then, a curious thing. Sinclair began to talk – not ranting but sweetly conversational. And, above the bulging veins of his forehead, his eyes were now fixed on Mould.

'You know, Nicolae old sock, she was mine after our first lunch – the beautiful Indian continent willing to be explored. We did it that afternoon at my mews apartment in Sussex Gardens, a dull afternoon of Scottish mist. She excused herself to "wash her hands" and came back from the bathroom in the buff. I can see her now – jutting breasts above silken hips, dark hair hanging down the perfect curve of her back, the dimples as she smiled. She sat beside me on the couch as if she were still fully clothed and she said, "You may touch." Just like that.'

Connor was astonished at the deftness of the description. The word-picture was almost lyrical. He saw the strategy. If the bastard could cause enough angst, Mould might be affected – and the medical team diverted. He had little chance of avoiding the gelding but some chance of damaging Mould.

He clearly had Mould's attention. The drooping eyelids had risen slightly. Hatred was enlivening the dying man, pulling him back to life. Dyson, in contrast, was nodding again.

Sinclair kept it going. 'I spent ages stroking her, caressing her, massaging her arms, thighs. I delayed and delayed. Then she couldn't stand it any more and uncovered this thing between my legs. She said, "Goodness me." And I started suckling her breasts, then entered her just a little. I said, "I won't hurt you." She said, "You could try." Ah, that opulent body. Moist, smooth… like diving into dessert.'

It was the longest of long shots but words were the man's only weapon. And he was using them like a master.

'We bonked under your nose for six weeks. Then you took her to Australia. But the feel of her body, that warm bath of sensations, still tempted. So when I went over to Oz for my Bicentenary Issue we got back in touch. She'd leave your barracks in the Kangaroo Valley and travel to Sydney twice a week. Yes, I see you remember.'

Blore said, 'I shut him up?'

Mould shook his head very slightly.

'She'd stay with me at Palm Beach. I had this old wooden speedboat. Perhaps you'd like to hear about her… last moments?'

God, Connor thought. Now it's the Sheherazade ploy. Delaying tactics too. Would Mould be hooked? The nurse had finished her trim. Sinclair's scrotum now hung hairless and defenceless as an embryo.

Mould struggled to speak. 'Do tell me. Then everyone will… approve when she… gelds you.' He whispered something to the doctor. Connor couldn't quite hear – something about not being able to feel his legs?

Sinclair was still expounding. 'We got swamped off Barrenjoey, were left clinging to the seat-covers. When the helicopter found us it was almost dark and we were close to the rocks. Huge columns of spray, breaking against the rocks. Would have broken us too. We were frozen, exhausted by then. The last seat-cover was barely floating and we couldn't cling to it any more. Then we heard the slap of the rotor blades and the harness came down. All I wanted to do was get out of that bloody sea.'

Dyson woke with a start, looked round blearily, frowned.

'I managed to swim to the harness and got my arms through the loop. She was behind me. I fought her off, put my hand on her face and pushed. She couldn't believe what I'd done to her. Can still see the look in her eyes. The downdraft from the chopper was turning the surface of the water into hail and she didn't have any more strength. She looked like a drowned rat as she went under.'

Mould leaned forward in the bed, his swollen fingers trying to form a fist – mouth open, twisted with hate.

'As they started to winch me up, she surfaced. I was dangling half out of the sea. She tried to grab my feet. So I kicked her to shake her loose. Only survival matters, after all. My foot got her under the chin, in the soft part of the gullet. That could have been the end of her. They used the spotlight and did sweeps for half an hour along the breakers near the rocks but couldn't see anything at all. Know what she said about you that afternoon before she died? I'd just fucked her up the arse – she liked that, didn't she? But not from you – and she said, "Nicolae's never learned to screw. I hate his mind and his body, but I'll open my legs for years and suck the bastard off each Saturday night" – you insisted on that, didn't you? – "and pretend he makes me come, as long as I get his loot. The poor dope doesn't see it. He worships me." Then she laughed and said, "If a woman knows how to handle herself, she can make the smartest man as dumb as a nanny goat over a pail."'

Mould strained to sit up further as if in spasm, then fell back. He was panting, his half-closed hand clutching at air.

Even Merrick had seen the point. She began to jeer as well in a shrill, slurred voice. 'And your son, Nicolae. Know how I killed him?'

Mould seemed more concerned with staying alive himself.

'Want me to shut her up?' Blore again.

Mould was thrashing his head sideways. Blore was ready

to take Merrick apart but, good soldier, stood his ground.

'I used a plastic bag. I tied it over his head. Tied it around his neck with a piece of elastic from my sewing bag. I watched his face go blue. And every time he tried to breathe the plastic bag went in and out. In and out – against his face and mouth. In and out – all foggy with his breath. I had to hold his arms down. And he kept… looking at me, his little eyes pleading. He looked so…' She stopped, tears brimming in her eyes. 'He didn't know why, you see?'

Connor gulped, filled with horror. His head was screaming, 'Jesus Christ…'

Mould's fist was still clenched but his body was sliding back, his coughs a rasping wheeze. Lee was at his side, checking his eyes, his pulse. Mould tried to push him away.

Merrick shuddered, looked at the floor, then looked back at Mould defiantly. 'Your son, Nicolae. Your baby.' Her voice became a scream. 'I suffocated him – because of you!'

Mould's seemed to be melting into the pillows, his mouth in the dreadful O sign of near death. 'Clinic!' ordered Lee. 'Now!' He ran for the door and the nurse followed.

The troopers moved suddenly, all together, like toys that had just been switched on. They surrounded the bed and pushed it out, with Vo hurrying in its wake. 'Quick,' she squeaked. '*Quiiick.*'

Blore and four troopers were left.

Merrick stood, chin up, defiant. She knew it was the *coup de grace*. Even Sinclair's upside-down mouth was rigid with satisfaction.

'If I have anything to do with it,' Blore said, 'you vultures'll never leave here alive.'

Merrick, re-animated now, was poking around on the tray.

'Put that down,' Blore spat.

'Why?'

'Mr Mould wants to see it done.'

She gave a deep, dirty laugh. 'He won't see anything any more.'

'You don't know that. Drop it, bitch.'

'I won. I have the right to do it.'

'It needs the doctor here.'

'Who cares if he bleeds to death? You?' She looked down at Sinclair's face with hatred. 'Let him bleed.'

'Nothing happens till Ms Vo gets back. Put it down or I'll break your arm.'

She held the blade defiantly and Connor expected her to make a rush to the frame and start hacking. Sinclair expected it too. His eyes were pure fear.

'Bitch,' Blore said, edging around her. A second trooper was moving in as well. She was outflanked and knew it, but held the scalpel like a weapon, lips red with blood again. She said, 'It's what he wants.'

Blore said to the four remaining troopers, 'Stay and watch them.' He pointed to Merrick. 'And watch that fucking bitch. She doesn't move.' He lumbered to the door.

'You're a tricky dick, Donkey Man,' Dyson turned to Connor. 'Clever arsehole, isn't he?'

Sinclair shut his bulging eyes. Half an hour of inverted crucifixion appeared to have almost blacked him out.

Dyson turned to Merrick. 'Nice one, Grace. You got 'em both. Son and father. Pretty neat.'

Merrick said, 'Don't you dare talk to me, you stinking slime.'

Blore came pounding back. 'Where's Gillian?'

The troopers looked uncertain. 'He wants her. Fan out and find her. Serge, you stay with me.'

Three of them doubled off, leaving Blore and one trooper, the one who'd punched Connor in the stomach.

Merrick pointed at Sinclair's face. 'Don't think you've escaped. You're going to get what you deserve.'

Connor sat on an inclined bench, forcing his dulled mind to think. So Sinclair, the wily shit, and the unstoppable Merrick had done it. Mould was certainly dying and now things would quickly change. But Mould wanted Gillian. Why? Because he suspected her of rigging the game? If Gillian were implicated now... He felt a rush of concern.

He sized up Blore and the Slav. He could out-run both but wouldn't last long unarmed. There was nothing he could do but hope she was all right. Doing nothing would be the hardest thing, she'd told him. He forced himself to sit still.

Sinclair was talking again. 'I'll have a stroke if you leave me like this. For God's sake put me right way up.'

Clever, Connor thought.

'No way,' Blore said.

A trooper looked in at the door.

'Find her?' Blore shouted.

'She's with him now.'

'Come here.'

The man came in.

'Watch them.' Blore hurried out.

Connor stayed leaning against the bench, acting more hungover than he was. Christ. Why did Mould want her? Why? Christ. They could be killing her now!

The troopers watched Merrick with loathing. Her sin had been news to them. If Mould's goons were ever let off the leash, Merrick and Sinclair were dead.

'God,' Sinclair pleaded, 'I'm dying. Let me up. Please let me up.'

They waited for perhaps twenty minutes. Dyson nodded in the wheelchair again. Sinclair still dangled from the bar, eyes shut, mind drowning in blood. Merrick perched on a padded bench, eyes on the instrument tray, dipping the last of her cotton balls in water. Occasionally, through the echoing building, they heard feet running, the slamming of doors. Then nothing but the sound of Dyson's snoring. Connor tried to listen in the spaces. Behind Dyson's snores the island seemed to be holding its breath.

The end of it was unexpected. A single figure walking. The small form of Vo – trailing down the aisle toward them, dwarfed by the big exercise machines with their weights and springs and pads. As she moved into the pool of light Connor noticed her living eye was crying. The other still stared, unblinking, its glass unable to grieve.

'Dead?' Connor asked.

She stared at the floor. A tear trembled on the remains of her chin, pearl-like in the light. Her head came up and, from around her wrist, she took a thick rubber band. It seemed she'd decided on half-measures and looked in at her office on the way.

She stepped forward, gripped Sinclair's scrotum and doubled the band around four times until the skin was stretched white across his balls and he resembled a ringed sheep. Dyson jerked awake as Sinclair pleaded, shaking the frame in terror. He knew his options had run out.

'Cut above band,' Vo said.

Merrick sprang from the bench.

Sinclair's eyes were bursting from his head. 'No. Please. No. Please. Where's the doctor? Where's the nurse?'

'Not deserve,' Vo sniffed.

Merrick moved to the traymobile and lifted the biggest scalpel. The new blade glinted in the light.

Sinclair roared. 'Three million dollars. Three million for each of you. All of you. Everyone in the room. Three million each if you stop this.' He stared at the trooper and Blore and squealed, 'Don't you want to be rich?'

The Slav sneered and Blore said, 'We've all been filthy rich for years. Stiff shit, Long-dong. We'd rather see you defused.'

Merrick walked to the frame, head high, disdainful, not wanting to look at what she had to touch. Finally she peered and the corners of her mouth angled down. She grasped the strangulated scrotum as if it were a beet that needed its top sliced off, and yanked it horizontal. Sinclair bellowed and bowed on the frame. She yanked again for good measure. 'Grace. Twelve million dollars. All for you. Think what you could do. You could…'

She held the scalpel up where he could see it to extract the maximum terror. Her eyes had the fierce glint of triumph. 'This… is… for… my… *ears!*'

Connor shut his eyes as she struck, heard Sinclair's bellow of pain and despair. When he opened them again, Merrick was dancing in time with Sinclair's sobs, dancing in slow circles, holding the severed part high, like the trophy from a bull. The blood from it ran down the inside of her hand and wrist and specked the bandage around her head.

Sinclair's body writhed on the frame, his stomach splashed now with blood that streamed down his chest and dripped into his upturned nose. He was bellowing, sobbing, raving.

Vo turned and walked from the room.

Blore and the Slav freed Sinclair's hands and lifted the hooked ankle-boots off the frame. Sinclair collapsed on the floor. They gripped the raving man by the boot hooks, one to each leg, and dragged him out like a rider caught by the stirrups. The smear behind him awaited the mop, but there was no islander left to use it. The three remaining contestants were alone.

Connor hurried from the room.

Dyson yelled, 'Jeez, don't leave me here with *her!*'

Connor didn't listen. If the bitch sliced him it was too bad. He had to find Gillian.

He looked back once. Behind him, the horrified Dyson

was reversing his wheelchair along the aisle. Merrick was still pirouetting with her trophy. He heard her lilting, little-girl trill.

The laugh was drowned by the yelling of the carpet-burned eunuch as Connor reached the corridor and looked along it. Sinclair was being dragged toward the clinic door but the other end of the passage was clear. He passed several doors, heading the way they had come in. Christ. Where was she?

The library door. He looked in. Empty. He stood in the passage. Where the hell would she be?

The sound of voices behind the next door along. He went to it and listened.

Vo's voice, high-pitched, sobbing. 'Must go on. Mr Mould would have wish.'

Another voice, softer. Gillian's! He couldn't make out the answer. But she was in there. Thank God, she was all right.

He returned to the library, ducked in, leaving the door ajar.

In a minute more, Vo left the room and ran toward the clinic. He pushed the door almost shut as she passed, then opened it as Gillian came out after her. She faltered, her eyes widened.

She edged into the room, leaned against the door.

'Thank God you're okay,' Connor said. 'I thought they might have...'

'You can't stay here.'

'He's dead?'

'Yes.'

'When do we...?'

'Tomorrow. There's one last contest. You're safe one more day. Now listen. Tomorrow they give you guns.'

'Guns?'

'Can't explain now. Soon as the contest starts, take your

shoes off and head for the shelter. I'll be there.'

'Are you going to be safe?'

'Don't know.'

'Should I start trying to knock people off?'

'God, no. They'll kill you. But when you've got the gun you might have to. Try to stay out of sight and double back through the trees on the ridge. Do anything you have to – but get to the shelter. Okay?'

Vo's voice from along the corridor. 'Gilli. Come. Come. Must come now.'

'Wait till it's clear, then get out of here.' She opened the door and was gone.

He spent the afternoon doing a survey of the island. No-one stopped or came after him. He trudged along the path that led to the forest and the headland, all the way to the tunnel through the rock. He turned at the corner of the paddock and walked along the fence-line, still heading away from the house.

The clouds had begun to blow out to sea and he slung his jacket over his shoulder. He felt like an inmate loose from an asylum – an eighteenth-century asylum where watching madness was considered entertainment. The sun remained neutral, warming the just and unjust alike. Birds carolled and, once, a cautious doe flicked its ears at him from behind a bush. It had the softest eyes. He wondered if he'd eaten its mate.

The fence stopped at the top of the rocks just before the sea. He turned the corner around the strainer-post and walked along the ridge above the water. The sea was empty except for a trawler, hull down on the horizon.

He squinted at the small, unhailable domain of normality, wondering what the people on board would think of his earless, toe-less, gelded fellow guests.

The big paddock was studded with salt-tolerant bushes and trees. From a thicket at its third corner the fence-line climbed again toward the ridge. Connor continued along the fence. It was heavier going here in the natural vegetation of the island. Finally he emerged on the grassy patch where Gillian had thrown his watch. That meant he was close to the house and the jetty. He'd traversed almost half the coast.

He left the fence and continued through the bush until he walked out onto the grass slope near the jetty. He looked at the strange cruiser again. The mobile platform was parked near it and three troopers were offloading provisions for the boat. He saw the movement of a head behind the sloping glass of the wheelhouse. He walked on past, scanning the bow. Two hawse-holes but no portholes. Steel hull with small flecks of rust.

A trooper stepped out of the wheelhouse onto the truncated starboard wing and waved him away. 'Out of here. Out.'

Connor walked up the hill to the pond, then turned to look back to sea.

The trawler was now out of sight – the horizon a ragged line beneath sky-castles of cumulus that had drifted far to the east. Long shadows lay across the slope. The sun, half hidden in the treetops on the ridge, blazed its last, most brilliant rays. He was grateful for the afternoon, for the peace and beauty of the walk. Except for its inhabitants, the island was a lovely place. His amateur painter's eye watched the changing play of light. People, the dying sun, the sea. A scene Sorolla would have liked – small figures against the sea's immensity, washed by a greater immensity of light.

The chill had touched the air again. He put on his jacket and headed for the hut.

Later, in the twilight, he saw a group of troopers strolling to the pool. There, like conspirators, they huddled in groups to talk. One or two broke away and wandered down to the bay. They moved as if they were confused. The whole island seemed in disarray.

The civilians were ignored that night. No guards. And no-one brought them food. Connor stepped out later, wondering if they'd be eating at the house. There were no lights in Sinclair's cottage but he spotted Dyson standing outside his hut. He had a crutch, now, under one arm and called across, 'Thanks for leaving me with that bitch. I coulda got diced and boned.'

'You survived.'

'That what you call it? Know when we get fed?'

'Reckon they've forgotten us.'

'Some day, huh?'

'Some day.'

'When're you getting chopped, Connor? About time you got the red arse.'

Connor raised a finger at him. 'Revolve.'

'Ooo,' Dyson minced, 'sounds fun.'

Dinner never came. He went to bed hungry and lay in darkness, listening, his knife open beside him in the bed. The place was as quiet as a blocked-off mine-shaft. Tomorrow's it, he thought. Tomorrow night he could be dead.

Gillian too.

Sleep, he told himself. You have to sleep.

Chapter Twenty-eight

He awoke to the door opening, flooding the room with light. A trooper clumped in and slammed the tray with his breakfast on the bench. 'Be at the pool in forty-five minutes for a briefing.'

He showered, dressed and wolfed the food. Cornflakes, scrambled eggs and toast. No elegant cloth, no plate-cover. The food had just been shoved on the tray. He pulled on his jacket and slipped the marlin-spike knife in a pocket. This was it. Make-or-break day. He felt keyed up but unafraid, looking forward to the chance to hit back.

Sun and wind. He took deep breaths of sea air and walked briskly along the path toward the pool. He soon overtook Dyson, who was managing with one crutch, his bandaged half-foot covered in a sock.

'Jeez,' Dyson said. 'Hurts you under the arm. And I'm so full of steroids my hair's falling in my food.'

Connor passed him without comment, staring at the strange scene by the pool.

Dyson called after him, 'The eunuch's up there. Is *he* going to be out for blood! Gonna have a hit-list longer than his dick.'

As Connor neared the huddle of people he saw a table with a gun on it. Blore stood behind it, with Vo beside him, her hair blowing across her dead eye. In front of the table were four chairs. Sinclair's carpenter's-rule frame occupied one. He cradled a gun across his knees. Except for blood spots on the crotch of his pants, he looked as fit as any man there. But there was murder in his eyes. And they'd given him a gun.

Then he saw guns on the other chairs.

Behind each chair stood troopers with similar guns – hanging by straps, barrel down, from their shoulders. As he came up, Blore pointed to a chair and said, 'Sit.'

Connor lifted the weapon off his seat – a dull-green plastic thing with a stub barrel and a handle on top that doubled as a scope. Its odd, see-through magazine had a square-patterned outside that made it look like a wafer biscuit. It was empty.

Merrick stood near the edge of the pool. Her bandage had been replaced with two gauze pads, taped where her ears had been. As Dyson limped up, she took the chair furthest from Sinclair. Her face was set hard. She was ready to kill.

Dyson said it for them all. 'Looks like serious shit.'

'Today is last game.' Vo brushed hair from where her face had been. 'We continue from respect to Mr Mould. As he would have wish.' Her glass eye still transfixed them but the other looked as if she had been crying.

Dyson lifted his gun and sat down. 'Pay-day.'

'Major will explain how last game work.' Her good eye blinked extra fast and she turned to face the bay. This morning the cameras on the columns were static, one pointing blindly out to sea. The other drooped toward the six-wheeled mobile platform parked in front of the house.

Blore cleared his throat and lifted the weapon. 'Get this wrong, you're dead, so listen up.' He squinted up at the sun, sniffed the air.

Merrick snapped, 'Get on with it, you boring fool.'

Blore looked at Merrick, eyes narrowed. 'Perhaps. But I have a worthwhile life based on discipline, teamwork, comradeship and honour – words a defective like you wouldn't understand.' He glanced at his men. 'We're people who've been trained to fight and die together – with a smile on our lips. Compared with us, you're trash.'

Merrick yelled, 'And you're so damned honourable you cut off women's *ears?*'

Vo turned back to face them. 'Not waste time.' She looked at Blore.

The Major jiggled his demonstration weapon. In his bear paw it looked no bigger than a toy. 'You're now equipped with a Steyr AUG in carbine configuration. Modern design using modern materials. As all of you are right-handed, your weapons have ejector holes on the right, which means you won't get burns or bruises on your faces. Now if you look down the scope…'

Sinclair was already doing it.

'…you'll notice cross-hairs and a small circle. Despite the light weight and short barrel, it's a very accurate weapon. Semi-auto, gas-operated, piston in here, don't worry about it. Foregrip here folds up or down,' he demonstrated, 'for use as a rifle grip or holding by your hip.'

Connor pulled back the bolt and heard the uncompromising sound of an automatic weapon being cocked. Blore did the same. 'Pull the bolt back and release it to chamber your first round. It fires from the closed-bolt position. Put your finger on the trigger. Press halfway.'

Connor tried, felt the first pressure take up.

'First pressure for semi-auto – that's one shot at a time – second pressure for bursts. You're only getting one clip of thirty rounds, so you can't fire many bursts. Questions?'

'What's this thing on top of the bolt?' Connor asked.

'Assist button. Forget that. Worry about this. Safety catch. Push it so you see the red dot if you want the thing to fire.'

There was the clatter of breeches being opened and closed. Merrick drew a bead on Blore.

Blore grinned. 'In case you get ideas, you're limited to a specific area and you'll be shot on sight outside the boundary.

We've got patrols on the fence. You won't see us but we'll see you.'

Dyson said, 'Another test of skill, huh?'

'Final exam,' Blore replied.

'What boundary?' Connor asked.

'The fence around the deer enclosure. Area's roughly square. You'll each be taken to one corner, where you can hole up or hunt. Plenty of good cover.'

Merrick said, 'So?'

Blore looked at her with loathing. 'So what?'

'I presume we're not hunting deer.'

'You'll need all your ammo for each other.'

'We kill each other? That your clever plan?'

'It's Mr Mould's plan. Last one alive wins.'

'And gets the dough-re-me?' Dyson asked.

'And gets the twenty million, yes.'

'Or do you waste him, too?'

Blore looked at Vo.

Vo said, 'Game end strictly as Mr Mould decide. Last one alive get money.'

Dyson looked sceptical. 'No double-cross? What about him?' He pointed at Blore.

Blore shook his head. 'Like she says, it's up to you. And the money's out of our control. If you survive, the trustees pay up. End of story.'

'Except you promised you'd waste us.'

'I'd very much enjoy that, Dyson. But Ms Vo's the referee. And I'm obliged to respect Mr Mould's wishes, even if it gives me acid stomach.'

'Great. Well, it's some shitty contest. I can't even walk,' he pointed to Merrick, 'and she can't hear us coming. So Sinclair and Connor'll clean us up.'

Blore shrugged. 'Then that's how it flops.'

Finally Sinclair spoke, his voice a savage drawl, his face

aflame, knowing everyone there knew what he now was. 'And what if we come after *your* people?'

The troops chuckled and Blore smiled. 'That's fine. We'd like the practice. But if you play it by the rules, you have a one-in-four chance of survival. And if you live, you get the dough. Other way, you're meat.'

Sinclair elbowed Connor and Dyson, then leaned around to Merrick, pointing a long, emphatic finger. 'That revolting bitch is *mine*.'

The troopers chuckled. With the cameras motionless on their columns and their leader cold, they were consoling themselves with barracks bonhomie.

'Any more questions?' Blore waved the gun around, prepared to strip the thing and reassemble it blindfold and one-handed if they asked, then throw in a definitive history of the massacre at Minsk. No-one had any questions. He looked disappointed. 'Good. Keep your gun, become familiar with it, and you'll get full clips when we start.'

Connor said, 'When's that?'

'Soon as you're deployed. The man behind your chair'll take you to your corner now.'

Vo faced them one more time, her good eye blinking, blinking. She cleared her throat and paused, looking very sad and small beside the huge soldier and, for once, a little shy. She said, like a child taught to be polite, 'Wish to say goodbye to three of you which die. Was most interest to meet you.' She gave a little bob, then padded off along the flagging – mission complete.

Dyson muttered, 'Hea-vy shit.'

The other three were led toward the vehicle but Connor's guard pointed downhill. For some reason he'd scored the Slav again. As he walked down the slope, holding the gun, he heard the wheeled platform start up on the rise. He glanced behind him and saw it head off down the track.

'Nice day for it,' the trooper sniggered.

Connor said, 'Butt out.'

They walked off the lawn and started through the bushes, across the clearing and up the next rise to the area with the trees and ferns.

They came to the corner of the fence.

'Inside,' the man ordered.

Connor looked at the close-spaced line wires. He walked away from the brace on the strainer assembly, then squeezed through above the third wire. Just inside the corner of the fence was a metal box with a red indicator light on the lid and a stub aerial fixed to the side.

The Slav pointed to it. 'Your ammo clip's in there. Game starts when they flash the light. Then the box unlocks and you can get your clip. Clear?'

Connor tested the lid of the box, verifying it was locked. The man checked his watch. 'Should have "go" any minute.' He pulled the rifle off his shoulder, took out the magazine and showed Connor how it was replaced. 'Got that?'

Connor nodded.

'Aim for the gut. Biggest target.'

Connor looked at the man's stomach. 'Okay.'

'Remember, step outside the fence and you're target practice for me.' His moustache wiggled in a smirk. 'Hope you try it.' He waved laconically and backed out of sight.

Connor squatted and re-checked the gun. It seemed simple enough to use. He sighted on a tree. The scope worked well in the shaded glade and slightly magnified. He lowered the gun and stared along the line of the fence. Movement, further up behind a bush. He suspected that the rest of the troops had been in position well before they'd been briefed. The danger wasn't Merrick or Sinclair. The real battle was outside the fence. Just thirty rounds in a clip. Not many for what he had in mind.

The solenoid clicked in the box. Adrenalin flooded his body as the light began to flash. He opened the lid, took out the clip, shoved it into the carbine and cocked it. The metallic click sounded out of place among the placid vines and ferns. One in the breech. Time to move.

He walked deep into the thicket where the men on the fence-line couldn't see him. Then he put the gun on a rock and probed the heels of his sneakers with his knife. In the left heel the blade struck something hard. He gouged out the centre and the small round object popped out too. He put it in his pocket. Not time to discard it yet. At least now he could keep his shoes. He picked up the gun, rechecked the safety was off, and moved slowly from the small wetland of thick ferns, walking, he judged, roughly parallel to the fence, hoping he didn't meet any of the contestants on the way. He need to reach the top of the paddock where it met the pine forest on the ridge.

The terrain changed to low bush clumps and gnarled, wind-shaped trees with patches of russet grassland between. He stopped and listened. Just the birds, the sea, the wind. He was glad of his brown leather jacket. It wouldn't be so easily spotted.

The whine of a bullet. Then the crack of the shot. He dropped. God. Where were they? From the order of the sounds, not that close. Troopers sniping from the fence? No, he was away from the fence-line here.

He was crouched behind a thinnish bush, no real cover at all. He waited, eyes darting. Nothing. If they'd seen him, he needed to move. He scuttled sideways, heading for thicker bushes to his left. Waited. Listened. He'd seen no-one. He inched his head around a rock and peered.

Nothing. Just bushes further up. Heart pounding but mind cold, he picked his next move. A clump some way ahead. He counted three and dashed to the next bush.

Nothing. Had the bullet been a stray?

There was more cover from here on. He darted from bush to bush, knowing that movement exposed him, still working his way uphill. When he reached the thick clump on the rise he began to breathe easily again. Here he had to push between bushes so thick they brushed back hard against him, almost impenetrable. Easy to lose direction.

His shoelace snagged on a root. He crouched down among the grey under-bush to re-tie it.

'Bad luck, Connor.'

Sinclair! The shock of the words hammered through him. He froze, gun still on the ground.

Slowly, he turned.

Sinclair, behind him, towered higher than the thicket canopy, the black flashguard of his muzzle pointing at Connor's chest. 'You walked right up to my possie, you silly old sock. But you have to admit it's your turn.'

Chapter Twenty-nine

The sound of the burst was deafening. For a moment Connor thought he was dead. As the blunt gun-barrel dropped, Sinclair's neck and jaw seemed to explode. Pieces flying off to the left, splattering blood and flesh on his shoulder. Face half falling apart as he went down, breath sighing out of the chopped-away gullet. Body yawing into the bushes, crumpling backward, arms jerking. The gun thudding with a tight clatter, butt first onto the ground.

Connor's legs straightened instinctively, propelling him back into the thicket, tumbling him into a shallow depression. As if watching a movie, he saw his hand clutch wildly for his gun.

The shriek of frightened birds like audible silence.

The polished soles of Sinclair's long shoes pointing at ten to two. One shoe wobbled a little, was still, a fragment of red pulp beside the heel, its moist redness incongruous against the earth tones of dried bracken and twigs.

He waited. Waited.

Nothing.

Still he waited, lungs bursting.

A leg appeared. A woman's leg – the smooth bronzed calf of Merrick, framed in the cathedral of the stalks. Then the nose of her barrel came into view, pointing down. It nudged Sinclair, was raised. The leg disappeared, then flew back into sight. She was gasping with effort as she kicked the body with all her force.

'Rot in hell. Rot in… *hell.*'

She finally stopped. He heard her panting. Trust Merrick

to chop the man to bits. She must have fluked a hit with several of the high-velocity bullets and all had angled into bone.

It never occurred to him to shoot her, though he could have done it then. The docked and bandaged ears had saved him. She didn't realise he was there.

He couldn't see her now but knew she was still close. His foot had cramped under him, its agony incidental to the roaring, pulsing silence of the moment.

Then he heard her feet scuff the grass as she moved off down the slope. He waited three minutes more, breathing as lightly as he could, feeling that even to breathe might bring her back.

Then he cautiously retrieved Sinclair's gun, removed the unused clip and shoved it in his belt. He took the bug out of his pocket and threw it into the thicket. Very warily, he stood up.

No sign of her.

Three other people in the field and he'd seen two. Quite enough for one morning. He turned his back on the scene, half expecting a bullet between his shoulders, and started creeping again up toward the track.

Finally he glimpsed the high wires of the fence. He was perhaps six metres from it, well hidden behind rocks. It was clear ground to the wire with the track on the far side, then the wood. The exposed area had to be overlooked by Mould's men. He could die before he got one leg half through the fence. There was no sign of anybody, but they'd be there. Where? How many?

Theoretically he was safe inside the fence. So he could walk over to it and look?

He rejected that. They'd get him before he spotted them.

He felt the roughness of the rock on his face. Pinned down. What now, damn it? Come on, he told himself. Think.

First, there'd only be one trooper near. Or they wouldn't have enough to cover the perimeter. The man would rely on a target delayed by the fence. Enough time to take careful aim and fire.

So where was he? Where? The small dirt lane was clear. He couldn't see anyone among the pines on the slope beyond the track. He looked up at the branches. In a tree? A big man wouldn't climb high. And he'd need a wide view. He remembered the caution to ground-based film crew during an aerial shot – if you can see the chopper, the camera can see you. If the man could spot him, then he could…

He levelled the scope at the lower branches of the trees and began to swing it slowly, using the lens as a focus. Just branches. A bird there. A…

Something paler. He swung the scope back. Then the pale section moved slightly. The side of a face? He waited, trying to be sure. The rim of what could be a black balaclava. He looked up from the eyepiece and sighted along the gun. Nothing visible to the eye. Damn. Now he'd lost it. He looked back through the eyepiece again.

Branches. Damn.

But he knew the spot to look. Methodically, he searched again.

There. A head. The shadow of an ear. He lowered the sight a little. The man's body was hidden. All he could see was the head. And it was too small a target. But enough to show where…

Why hadn't they given them guns with a proper-length rifle barrel?

He practised lowering the scope a little and touching the trigger. Raising it again to the pale spot, lowering it again, like a man taking swings on a golf course.

He felt ready, heart pounding. Hold the breath. Take your time. He centred the small white patch in the circle, then let the weapon sink a fraction. Blore had said the gun was accurate. He hoped like hell it was. He didn't know that the excellent harmonic vibration of the short carbine barrel and the extreme velocity of the weapon made it very accurate indeed.

About… there…

He squeezed.

The carbine bucked once. Little recoil. The crack slapped against the air as the spent cartridge flipped.

The flapping of frightened birds. He flattened himself against the rock. If the man wanted to return fire, he'd see nothing. But next shot, he'd be a sitting duck. The sound of something scrambling in branches, like a possum in a tree. Not a possum. Mould would never have permitted such damaging immigrants to survive here. Something falling through branches?

A thud.

It couldn't be that simple…

He looked around the rock, heart pounding. A man was lying half on the track, under a tree, face down in the gravel, arms ahead of him as if diving, one leg twisted under the other. Connor framed the back of his uniform in the crosshairs and squeezed off a second round. He had an impression of the material on the man's shirt jerking as if the body had absorbed the bullet.

Was it that simple?

He couldn't believe it.

Well, the next bit wouldn't be.

He had to make it through the fence.

He listened. Nothing. No rustling, no sign of movement. He pulled the foregrip down, cradled the carbine at his hip, then dashed forward to the fence, expecting to be riddled.

The wind blew, the trees waved and the sun warmed the field.

Nothing.

Yet.

He dropped to his knee inside the fence, eyes peeled.

Nothing.

Do or die.

He spread the wires and forced himself through, snagging his sneaker on the bottom wire, fell half on the ground, grabbed the gun and sprinted for the trees, feet slipping on the gravel in his panic to get across the track.

As he hit the slope, a burst kicked up dirt ahead of him. He half fell against a tree, feet sliding on the pine needles.

Another burst, this time behind him. Whoever had fired wasn't close – had to be further up the track where it curved, unable to see him on the fence-line. Halfway up the slope he slid and fell face down, gasping, heart pounding through his chest.

He was alive. God. Alive and through. He checked himself for blood. No visible damage.

Frantic not to be ambushed, he struggled up and kept going. Then, drenched by fright and shock, he leaned back against a tree-trunk, panting, gasping, strength draining from his body.

God. He'd killed another man! And been shot at!

The pine forest was featureless – trunks in every direction – with only the slope for navigation. He had to get high, move at right-angles across, head for the plantation behind the house.

A crackling further down behind him. Someone following? He didn't have the energy to run. He stared desperately at the trees. Rough bark but no low branches. Cover.

Where?

Water had gouged out a small gully. It would barely hide him but had to do. He slid into it, grazing his elbow on a stone. Water from the stream trickled down his stomach into his pants but he hardly felt the discomfort. The man was nearing. He fought to stifle his rasping breath.

The sighing of wind in the trees. A small lizard ran onto a rock further up the stream, watched, head up, immobile, the perfectly adapted fugitive, darted off. Pause, then dart, his brain hammered. Pause then dart.

The crunching closer. Steps. Cautious. They all knew more about combat than he did. The only advantage was surprise, she'd said. He picked up a pebble, waiting.

The heavy crunching was very near. He froze every limb tense. They'd stopped.

Where? Where?

He wrist-flicked the pebble further down the gully. It bounced on a rock, plopped into a pool. He heard feet swing around.

Pause then dart.

He surfaced above the lip of the gully. Didn't spot the man immediately. The trooper was further away than he'd expected, uniform blending with the dappled light – huge, motionless, gun cradled, with the barrel aimed at the noise.

The next moment stuttered into Connor's vision like a series of still frames. The man's torso swinging, gun-snout winking with flame, bullets chopping up the lip of the gully, puffs of earth racing toward him along the bank.

A second before the hail reached him, he jammed his finger hard down.

His barrel kicked upward as the air exploded and shook with the roar of two weapons on full automatic.

The man's elbows stabbed into his chest and from his mouth came the elongated sound of someone who'd touched something red-hot or cut off his finger. The rounds had drilled so fast through him, they'd travelled ahead of the shockwave, cauterising as they went. His knees buckled and he toppled back, thudding to the ground like a sack, sliding a little down the slope.

Connor leaned forward and chucked.

When he felt he could move, he scrambled out of the stream and went over to get the man's magazine. It meant looking down at the body, at the face. At the eyes still wide open with surprise, the mouth brimming with blood, which trickled over the lip and down the cheek. The magazine was two-thirds empty. He took it anyway. The man had pouches around his belt but he couldn't bring himself to touch the body. He continued up the slope, feeling almost too weak to walk.

Adrian Dyson knew he couldn't hunt his opponents on a crutch. So, after they left him inside the fence, he found a hide between two rock outcrops and waited.

Grace Merrick knew it, too – knew she'd find Dyson in one of the corners. Which?

She worked along the fence-line nearest the sea until she came to the end of the field. The rock outcrop looked an obvious redoubt. If this were his corner, he'd be there. Just like in the movies. She knew exactly what to do.

She crouched behind a thicket, observing. Nothing happened for a while. Then she heard a cough and a black stick appeared at the cleft between the rocks, wavered once and dropped a little.

A straight stick. The snout of a gun.

Careful not to tread on dead branches, she inched along the fence-line, closing on the corner post, keeping her gun trained on the cleft, the sound of the sea against the cliff beyond the fence masking any small sounds she made.

She was exposed now, but unless he peered around the rock she was out of his line of sight. She reached the sloping brace of the post. She was almost behind the two rock piles.

As she moved the last few feet, Dyson's rear flank came into view. First the end of the varnished yellow crutch with its rubber foot, lying beside him on the ground. Then his good foot, doubled beneath the drooping twin orbs of his bottom. Next, the rounded expanse of his back, broadening to the bulges around the hip-line, almost as wide as the cleft between the rocks. He'd taken his sweater off and turned up his shirt collar as protection against the sun. The bandaged foot was ahead and he was leaning on his other knee. Long strands of his hair hung down the left side of his head like a waterfall modelled from grease.

She smiled with glee. She wanted him to know. To see her before he died. To see the avenging angel.

Oh, this was fun. Glorious fun. First the thrill, the utter euphoria, of executing Sinclair. Now this.

She was going to win!

Like a child playing hide-and-seek, she said, 'Ha!'

Dyson yipped and his blubber shook. He tried to swing around but got only halfway, the gun barrel scoring into the rock, his bad foot unable to be spry. He became jammed, bottom against the rock, shoulders parallel to the cleft.

'Drop the gun,' said Merrick.

'Huh?'

'Drop the gun.' She felt like a goddess.

'Why? We can get 'em.' Below the desperate stare in his eyes he was attempting a conspiratorial smile.

She loathed the way his hair hung down. She loathed his fat jelly-belly. 'Drop the gun.'

'Okay, okay.' He dropped it. 'Have to talk, Grace. Can't win on our own. With your legs and my ears, we can…'

'Remember I told you you were dead?'

'Hang on, Grace. Hang on. I didn't have any choice. You know how it's been. We've all been screwed. I forgive you for my toes. Can't you forgive me? All I did was doodle on your butt. Can't you find it in your woman's heart to…'

'Open your mouth.'

'Huh?'

'Open.' She screamed it.

He did it, gumless, terrified. 'Wayaya go-o to do?'

'You'll see.'

She moved slowly up to him, the barrel of her gun at forty-five degrees, pointing at his belly.

'Ooo. Gaace. Leez. Ooo.'

He went to shut his mouth to plead. The barrel jerked. He opened it again.

'Gaace. Noo. Gaace. Leez. Hnnng.' He whined in terror. 'Hnnng.'

She jammed the flashguard almost into his mouth as his pleading eyes stared up, then knelt down slowly on one knee until the barrel pointed to his palate.

'Gaace. Hnnnnnnng… Leez. Hnnnnnng…'

Blore wasn't around to tell her that a bullet's size does less harm than its velocity. That despite its small entry and exit point it causes trauma inside the body because, as the tissue slows it down, hydrostatic shock does great internal damage. So she didn't understand that a burst into the boxed area of Dyson's skull would cause that box to explode and leave little more than a stump.

As the back of Dyson's head blew off, the sides and front erupted outward and she was showered with pulp from his brain.

'Ahh! Yuk.' Squatting there covered in muck, she reached for his discarded jumper to wipe herself but his leg was jammed on top of it and she couldn't pull it out. Dyson remained wedged upright in the cleft, one side of his face remaining like the rampart of a ruin.

She bolted up, looked at the mess on herself and yelled, 'Now look what you've done!'

A helpless, explosive sneeze from the bushes outside the fence.

'How dare you laugh at us?' she shrieked. 'How... dare... *youuuu*...' whirling, her finger jammed on the trigger, spraying the bushes with the last of her clip. When the reverberations stopped she hurled the gun at the bushes as well. It clattered against the fence wires and hung there by the strap buckle on the butt. She leaned over for Dyson's gun, beside herself with rage – 'Give me that' – fumbling in her crazed attempt to get more shots off into the thicket.

She sprayed another burst at the bushes, bounded to the fence and crawled through it in her fury to reach the man who had considered her act of destiny amusing. The headless witness sat gravely at attention.

A trill of girlish delight, 'We got him.'

She stepped out of the bushes, wiping her face with the man's balaclava, her long hair shining in the sun. 'He won't do that again,' she called to the remains of Dyson.

She'd completely forgotten her ears. She felt invincible – and hungry. After all this hunting she hoped there'd be some lunch.

Chapter Thirty

Connor heard the gunfire. It seemed some distance away. He was sliding down the slope now, feeling like death warmed up, hoping he was just behind the house. Every few seconds he propped his feet against a tree trunk and listened. Two down. Thirteen more. Impossible odds.

When he saw the pale shape of the house between the branches, relief flooded through him. Where was the track to the shelter? He struck sideways along the slope until he came to it. He was almost above the reinforced entrance.

She said she'd be here but he couldn't see her.

Voices. A man and a woman. He dropped behind the concrete cornice above the door to the tunnel, gun forward at the ready.

Now he saw feet, then their bodies progressively revealed in forced perspective beneath the overhanging branches until the heads came into view. Gillian – with the Slav.

'I don't know what you're so concerned about.' Her voice. 'They're not after me.'

'Sorry, Miss G, but the Major told me to stick with you. In case.'

'In case what?'

' "Stick with her," ' he said. That's all. I just follow orders. But it all feels different now Mr Mould's dead. I respected him, Miss G. Looked in at him this morning. Hard to recognise him now. Not a line on his face. All lines – gone.'

'It happens like that after death.'

'Tough way to get a face-lift. All waxy, he was. Like the skin's thick. Like marble. Funny how they go when they're cold. What killed him in the end?'

'A stroke. In the brain stem, Lee said.'

'I see.' The man sniffed hard and the mucous rattled in his nose. He probably wanted to spit, but as she was there he must have swallowed it. 'So what are we doing here, then?'

'Nothing.'

'Need something in the shelter?'

'No.'

'So we're having a bit of a walk, then?'

'No.'

'So why stand around here?'

'I feel like it.'

A pause. The scraping of boots. 'They say you spoke to him before he died.'

'U-huh.'

'Did he give you any idea about... what happens now? The men are a bit concerned. You taking the operation over?'

'No.'

'So who is?'

'Good question.'

She hadn't counted on an escort. She seemed to be stalling for time.

Another burst of fire from the distance.

The man said, 'Sounds like they're getting on with it.'

'I wish they would.'

That was a cue if ever he'd heard one. Connor looked around the slab. The Slav had his back to him, facing away from the shelter. She must have been close by it because he couldn't see her now at all. He levelled the cross-hairs on the camo-patterned shirt and fired a *bruuup* of three. The man staggered forward one step, half turned, gun rising. But his mouth was open, eyes pointing up, the pupils hidden in his head. He hadn't made a sound.

Connor had slid down the embankment almost before

the body hit the ground. He could already hear the door rollers rumbling and the hum of the electric motor.

She ran and grabbed one lifeless arm. 'Got to get him inside.'

She was fit and he was strong but the man's huge body seemed heavier than a dead bullock. Yet even before the door was fully open they'd used all their desperate strength to drag it over the rails and in.

She rushed to the controls to shut the door. The motor momentarily stopped, then hummed again as the monumental slab reversed. 'Thank God you made it. And you got one.'

The dead man's arm was flung across the door rails. As the door base met it, the arm was pushed inside.

'Three counting him.'

'Three? They've only found one. So that makes four.'

'Four?' They were running down the tunnel gasping in dead air.

'Merrick got one. Report came through in the control room.'

'Good.'

'And she… blew Dyson's head off.'

'Shit. Sinclair's too. One-woman hit-squad.'

'Come on.'

They reached the APC, climbed in the rear door and shut it. 'Thirty-cal first,' Gillian said.

He lifted the machinegun.

'Get into the turret. I'll show you how to mount it.'

They worked away, unscrewing the grips, mounting the guns, sliding the locking pins in, positioning the two boxes of ammunition on the stand and feeding the first round from each belt into the breeches. She handed him up the heavy barrel. 'Get out the hatch and screw this into the fifty.'

He did it as she pulled levers on a gun and mumbled to

herself, 'Cock, safety off, working parts forward, cover up, rounds in…'

'Been doing some homework?'

'A lot.' She pushed the feed plate covers shut, fiddled with a knob. 'Safety on…'

He looked down at her as she plugged in wires. 'What's that?'

'Firing control box. This switch gives you left, right or dual. The handle down here's for electronic solenoid firing. The cable runs down the support arm here to the Rotary Box Junction – that's the big green box under the basket. You get lots of breakdowns because the slip-rings corrode and…'

'You've lost me. Worse than Vo.'

'Okay. Left is the thirty. Right is the fifty. Dual gives you both at once. You move this black handle for your elevation and press the red trigger to fire. If you get a jam, it's the RBJ. Then use the triggers on the guns.'

He lowered himself back into the turret. 'So I press this and it fires?'

She fiddled with a knob on the end of the big gun. 'It will when the safety's off. Okay. This is the trigger for the thirty. You press it, like a pistol. This double wing is the trigger for the fifty. It goes down. Press this. That down. Got it?'

'Hope so.'

'Here's your traversing handle. This knob in front here's your elevation pin. Release and you can aim the guns. Try it.'

He did and she re-engaged it. 'See back here? Turret traversing locking pin. Don't pull either till we're in action or you'll flop all over the place when we drive. This turret's pretty well greased so you can traverse by using your body-weight and using your feet against the fire-wall down there. You with it?'

'How does the....'

She took him all through it again. 'When you fire, you have to "walk it" – that means get your aim from the dirt kicked up by the rounds. You can still see the tracers a bit in daylight. They're like an orange flash. Remember. Walk it to the target.'

She handed him a headset. 'Keep this on all the time.' She adjusted the head-band and microphone for him and switched the set to ICS. 'Leave it switched to intercom.' She didn't let him out of the cupola until she felt sure he'd absorbed the whole thing.

He got down off the footplate. 'Crash course, huh?'

'Told you it would be. You set?'

'I'll do my best.'

'I know.' She looked at him in a strange way, placed the back of her fingers lightly on his cheek. 'Now I've got to ignore you and try and remember *my* bit.' She crouched forward to the driver's compartment, settled into the seat and looked around her, then pointed to a space beside her left leg. 'While I'm doing this, get the rifles and shove them in these racks.' She started checking over the controls.

He watched her. 'What are skirts?'

Her reply was abstracted. 'The rubber shrouds over the top of the wheels.'

'So they're on this now?'

She nodded.

'What do they do?'

'Mmm? Funnel water into the tracks.'

'What's a trim vane?'

She turned back. 'What?'

'Trim vane?'

'Where'd you get all this?'

'Blore.'

'It's the panel on the front. Goes forward to make a bow

if you're fording. Otherwise you plough in.'

'So we can cruise?'

She turned back to him. 'In the sea?'

'Why not?'

'Because it's a metal coffin. Eleven tons dead weight. It floats with just a foot of freeboard. And this one's old. I don't trust the seals on the hatches.'

'It's got bilge pumps.'

'They wouldn't hold it long.'

'I checked the sea. It's pretty calm.'

'It's not when you've a foot above the water.'

He frowned and she put a hand on his arm. 'David, forget it. It's okay in sheltered water but not open sea. If you make a mistake, these things turn into a mooring in ten seconds.'

'U-huh.' He sat behind her on the bench, trying to remember all he had to do.

She stood up and checked the driver's hatch cover, then sat back down. 'We go closed down, okay? All hatches shut. Shut your hatch now and the cargo hatch. That's the one behind the turret.'

He got up and did it. The huge springs made the heavy metal manageable. 'What's this round thing on it?'

'Sucks the air in. Now shut up and let me think. You're worse than a kid.' She was mumbling to herself, moving her hands on the knobs and levers.

'How old are you?' he said quietly.

She swung around. 'What?' Intelligent, troubled face, mussed hair, amazed look. She was beautiful.

'How old? And I'll shut up.'

'Forty. Five years smarter than you. Any more questions, Mr Connor?'

He held up his hands. 'Okay, I shut up.'

'Just… get into the turret, put the headset on and… behave.'

He did as he was told.

A crackle. 'Can you read me?'

'Yup.'

'Right. I'm going to start it up and when we get to the door, you'll have to open it. I'll tell you the code to punch in. Then come straight back inside and latch the rear door tight. Understood?'

'Got it. He peered through the crew commander windows, thick glass slits around the base of the turret. 'Your hatch is still open.'

'I'll shut it before we go out.'

He racked down the seat so he could see out the slits. He realised his strength had come back. He felt invigorated, recharged. In this gloomy box with this woman he felt… it was a very good day to die.

They trundled along the tunnel, the rubber pads slapping the concrete, the enclosed box reverberating, the walls sliding past. They stopped with a jerk. The headphones crackled, 'The code is five… one… eight… seven… nine. Go.'

'Travelling.'

He got down from the turret, scrambled across the tethered boxes of silver, swung the heavy door wide and climbed out.

He ran past the burbling machine, muttering the numbers to himself, noticing with a squirm that the bloated form of the Slav was in front of the left-hand track, lying now in a lake of blood. He punched the code in and, the second the door began to move, sprinted back. From the corner of his eye he saw Gillian pulling the driver's hatch shut above her.

He yanked the locking handle on the inside of the door in the ramp and checked that the catch had caught. As he scrambled into the cage of the turret the machine jerked forward. It lifted a little on the left. That would be the Slav. He jammed his headphones on and peered out in time to see that they were trundling down the track behind the house.

As they came out from beneath the trees they slewed hard left and he swayed against the circular turret rim. They stopped.

A crackle. 'On your right.'

He saw a trooper at the rear door of the house. The man looked startled, was about to run back inside. He took off the safeties, grabbed the crank on the traversing handle. Nothing happened. The locking pins. God. By the time he'd released both pins, the man was inside out of sight.

'Too late?' she said, unable to see from her side.

'I was locked up.'

'It's okay. He's the guy from the control room. He'll radio the rest. You'll soon have targets. We'd better head for the boat. Are you unlocked now – both pins?'

'Yup.'

'Turn the turret to face the rear and hold on.'

As he spun the turret around they jerked forward again and the engine tone rose to a snarl. He looked through the glass slits behind him. They were heading straight for a small steel shed near the end of the house. She didn't waste time going around it. The carrier punched the side of it flat, rocked over it as if mounted on springs. Then they were clattering down the grass slope in the sunlight.

She said, 'Guns forward. I'll stop front on. Then go for it.'

'Right.' He spun the turret, braking its travel with his legs. The foot-on-the-engine-bay method worked well. He squinted through the bullet-proof glass. Now he could see the boat.

A man ran into the wheelhouse and did something. The

hatch on the foredeck began to slide back. The thing was automated – controlled from the bridge. He thumbed the selector switch right to fire the fifty, gripped the black handle and lowered the barrels. 'Hold it there. Hold it.'

The vehicle abruptly stopped and almost sent his head through the turret. He jammed the trigger down and the turret vibrated as the huge machinegun gnawed the end off the jetty. He used the traversing wheel this time, walking the fire along the side of the bow, then held position where he imagined the hydraulic gun to be. The big gun's fire rate seemed to be increasing. It was quieter than he expected, muffled by the thick hull. But the plated side of the boat opened up like a tin can hit by a pick.

As he dragged on the juddering handle the dull orange streaks appeared to chop pockmarks right across the deck to the hatch. Then he strafed the wheelhouse as the man inside it dived. All the windows blew out in a shower. Flame licked from the open hatch. The air in the carrier smelt of cordite, sucked in by the fan behind.

'How's that?'

He was answered by hammers on the turret, bullets whining off the sloping sides. He couldn't hear what she was saying but knew they were reversing up the hill. Small-arms fire? He swung the turret, searching for the source.

There, near the columns of the pool on the crest, two troopers with automatic rifles. He switched to the smaller gun, tried to bring it to bear. The rocking stopped as she swung broadside to the slope. The motion swung the turret too. He cranked himself back the other way, pushed the red trigger down.

The smaller gun stuttered. He held it as level as he could, feet braced on the fire wall. The two big men were far up the slope, running for the cover of the pool, but the machinegun didn't mind the distance. The energy of the big, slow rounds threw the first man at the ground as if he'd been hit by a cannonball.

He swung the protesting gun to the other, peppering the general direction. The second before the man could dive into the pool the burst seemed to lift him off the ground. He toppled head first down the slope, mouth visible as a small and open blank. Connor strafed him again and he bucked as if being chopped up from the inside.

Connor, coughing, eyes burning with fumes, yelled into his mike. 'Six. How'd I do with the boat?'

'He's alive and he's put the fire out. But I think you've knocked out the hoist of the gun.'

'Want to hit it again?'

'No time. They'll try anti-armour next. If they get one off, we cook.'

'You mean the tube things?'

'Yes. Watch the trees.'

'Bloody hard to see anything through these slits.'

'It's worse with the periscopes and I'm lower. I can only see left and in front. You have to check the rear and right. You reading me?'

'I'm doing it. I'm doing it.'

'You getting the hang of the turret?'

'Busier than a one-armed paper-hanger with crabs.'

'Don't talk. Watch.'

'Shouldn't we take cover?'

'Not yet. Those two didn't think. With luck, we'll see some others before they remember the stuff in the shelter. Should be safe for a minute. You can aim better if we're stopped.'

'We can't just sit. They're trained troops. They'll pick us off. We'll be cactus.'

'They can do it wherever we are.'

'Move,' he yelled. 'Move! Move!'

The machine lurched forward, tracks rattling, floor plates jumping, as if something had hit it from behind.

'Where? Where?'

'Edge of the pond. Two men and a tube.' He was crouched down in the turret, shouting at her, forgetting she couldn't hear him directly. He saw her hand fly to one of the overhead levers. 'Hold on.'

The box spun on the spot, throwing him against the rubber ejection tube that collected the spent shells from the guns as something whooshed by them like a jet. He clawed himself back onto the seat as the slit windows became searchlights and the inside of the turret flashed yellow, the explosion shattering the air outside.

As he clawed himself back on the seat he got one glimpse of the ridge. The rocket had hit the columns by the pool and the Arcadian scene was now a rolling ball of yellow fire, augmented by sections of toppling marble. A table and two chairs, pure white against the brilliant cloud, hung lazily in the air, turning over, like some motif in a screen-saver program.

'Holy shit.'

They were hurtling down the hill before he had time to crank the turret around. The next eyeful was even more startling – the troopers dead ahead, weapon abandoned, bodies outlined against the pond. One hurled something and dived below the bank while the other ran around the side.

The box shuddered. He heard the whump, felt the concussion, as a grenade exploded below the hull but the tracks must have held because they were careering nose first into the pond, shunting half a tonne of brackish water up the sloping front.

Next, they were pointing to the sky and slewing round, the big diesel screaming in low gear. Now they were changing up and off across the slope like a hare caught in a motorbike tail-pipe.

Connor wrestled the swinging turret back under control. The Panavision slit of the window ahead framed the fat butt of the other man, six or eight metres away, dead ahead, his massive thighs scraping together as he ran. He craned back once, face a mask of terror, changed direction, stumbling down the slope. The carrier lurched, did a right-angle skid and followed.

Each second was a crystal-clear experience. The shovel clamped to the front deck, vibrating, the man's head dead in front of it, nearing…

Gone! Right under the belly.

They slewed again and he saw the bloodied body. The tracks had missed but not the hull. She accelerated, keeping the shape on the ground in line with the right track. A slight bump.

The earphones crackled, 'Eight.'

Connor tried not to think about it. 'Why didn't they use the tube again?'

'They're single-shot disposables.' The racing vehicle slowed to a crawl. 'God. I'm going to be sick.'

'You be sick, you'll be dead.'

'David… oh God.'

'I know,' he said, 'I know. You're doing great. Hang in there.'

'It's…'

He was swinging the turret. 'Land Rover.'

'Where?'

'Went behind a hut. Something on the back of it on a stalk.'

'Don't show you've spotted them. Keep turning the turret.'

'Why?'

'Just do it, damn it.'

'All right, all right.'

'See anything the other side? They'll try two flanks.'

He was already scanning the bushes across the slope. 'Nothing yet.'

She was gunning the engine, speeding away from the huts. 'Keep the turret forward.'

'It's forward.'

'What's happening out the back? Look out the back! Out the *back*!'

He peered through the back slit windows. 'They've edged out. They're stopped.'

'What's on the launch mount? Is it a flat thing with two sections and they're looking through one?'

'Yes. Like a big surveyor's thing. He's got his hands on two handles.'

'How many men?'

'Two. And Vo with them. What is it?'

'Anti-tank missile. Keep the turret straight ahead.'

'Christ. They'll fry us.'

'No. Danger's ahead. Look ahead. *Ahead.*'

'Christ, woman, they're going to cook our arse.'

A shockwave hit the carrier. The turret was bleached by a single flash. When his eyes recovered, Connor looked through the slit behind. The hut was flattened and two pines were on fire, blazing full length, as if soaked in kerosene.

Something bounced on the deck behind him and flew off again into the air – a wheel with a tyre still attached. Now he knew where the vehicle was.

'What the… What…?'

'I fixed it. Rigged it to detonate on the mount. Knew they'd try that one.'

Connor sagged against the turret. 'Thanks for telling me. God!'

'Three of them? You said three of them?'

'Two. And Vo.'

She said, 'Duyen? Oh God.' There was a pause. She was probably crying. Her voice again. 'Makes eleven. God. Keep looking.'

Then he glimpsed crouching men gliding along the rise, obviously on the flat-bed of a truck. They went out of sight beyond. 'Vehicle. Up behind the pool.'

'Can't see it.'

'Get up there. Go. *Go.*'

She spun the carrier on the spot and roared up the slope.

The mobile platform was stopped, broadside on, just above the ridge near the house. The five men around it included a bellowing Blore, unloading and distributing the anti-armour weapons. As they came into sight, everyone with the cylinders scattered.

The two men working at the platform dashed to take cover behind it, shouldering their launchers, training them on the carrier.

'Hold it.'

She skid-stopped. 'Quick. Now.'

He switched to dual and the turret vibrated as both machineguns fired at once. He bit his lip and sprayed left-right-left.

The tyres on the near side exploded first and the vehicle became a cheese-grater, listing toward him, leaking fuel. One man got his shot off as he fell, a flash and black smoke hitting the ground behind his shoulder, kicking up the dirt as the rocket flew into the sun. Then the fuel ignited and the platform was sitting in fire.

Two more. And the other three running. 'Shit, it's like herding cats.' He aimed for the lumbering Blore and pulled the trigger again. Nothing happened.

The men reached the bushes, dived.

Gone.

'How many?'

'Two. Then the guns jammed.'

'It's the RBJ. Use the triggers.'

He pressed the trigger of the small gun. It stuttered, strafing the bushes. Branches shook and chopped leaves flew. He fired again, dragging on the breech, spraying the area in long bursts, then sat back, choking with fumes. Below the cupola, shell casings and belt links danced all over the floor.

'Get away from here,' he coughed. 'Three in the bush with tubes.'

She shifted into a forward gear and snarled the thing toward the track. 'Got Blore yet?'

'No. How many left?'

'I'm thinking. I'm thinking. We said eleven.'

'And two.'

'Thirteen. Less Vo. Twelve. Four left. Those three and the man in the boat.'

'What now?'

'They'll get us if we stay here.'

She took them crashing into the bushes beside the grass slope and he sprayed the ground in front as they went, using the triggers behind the breeches. One gun stopped, then the other.

Then he saw why. The dancing belts had disappeared. 'Out of ammo. We got more?'

'No. Could only find the two boxes. You've gone through 200 rounds. This thing's so old we're lucky anything works at all.'

'Shit. Now what?'

'Trouble.' She swung them violently around.

Grace Merrick knew something unexpected had happened. She'd crossed the paddock again and seen no-one on the way. She'd then seen one trooper running outside the fence, running away toward the house. Not thinking, she left the paddock and walked until she glimpsed the manicured slope. The tank was racing across the grass, and, as she watched, it ran down a trooper, then turned again to mash him flat. It seemed to be civil war.

Then bombs started going off. Even the pines were on fire, right up high in the branches. She retreated back into the bushes, feeling ignored – and concerned that at any moment she might feel the prick of a scalpel blade inside her. The noise from the big gun on the tank made a terrifying sound, a crack so fearsome she froze, unable to move.

Then the awful noise stopped. She tripped and sat abruptly down. She could still hear the tank. It didn't seem to know what it was doing – had churned up half the lawn. They appeared to be attacking it. She wondered where Connor was. Her intense regret was not finding him. She simply had to find him. One more shot and she'd be rich!

One more shot and she'd be repaid for the way people had used her all her life. For the galling, humdrum years that should have been so gay. She was beautiful enough. She should have been a movie star. But she'd never lost her courage, her pride. Except when they'd cut off her ears.

Oh God, her ears!

Her stupid tears were back. Oh please, she mustn't feel like this. She had to be strong – to meet her triumph in this time of all times to be brave.

Think of it! Even under torture, she'd managed to see Mould die. Had lived to geld and kill Sinclair, to blow the wretched Dyson apart – to vanquish them all. One more shot and life would repay… Would repay her for her beauty, her endurance, magnificence…

Oh yes. She was magnificent – had never been more

glorious than now. And cruel life, which cheated one, derided one, would now, finally, be forced to repay.

The tank started firing quite near her. The fearsome noise made her duck. When she sat up again she saw the back of a trooper's tunic. He was three metres in front of her, crouched on one knee, with a tube on his shoulder that appeared to be made from paper and coiled wire. He had his hand around a plastic box on the side of it and his eye to some kind of sight. She could hear the tank clattering down the slope. He was waiting till it came into view.

He was so intent, had no idea she was behind him.

It was perfect.

Perfect.

She brushed her hair back with a self-consciously valiant hand, raised the carbine to her shoulder, and fired a burst across his lower back. He howled, writhed, coughed and kicked in such a satisfying way that she wasn't aware the tank had changed direction - until she heard the snarl of the engine almost upon her and the churning, clattering tracks. She stared, eyes and mouth wide, but couldn't see anything through the bushes until shrubbery near her was forced down.

Her scream was drowned by the noise. A sapling snapped, knocked her back and fell across her like a bar.

Limbs flailing, pinned, face made grotesque by shock, she saw the track now, heading for her chest. It clattered on unstoppably, pressing down on the slim tree until she felt the snapping of her ribs. Last breath gone, unable to even scream, she watched the blur of the dirt-caked metal plates.

Left in the depression of the track was a red mess where her chest had been with the rest of her each side. For seconds, her face contorted. One arm jerked, hand extended to grasp air. Then the horror on the ground became still.

Chapter Thirty-one

'What now?' Connor sat in the useless turret as the machine clattered along the track beside the paddock. 'Where are we going?'

'Getting out of sight. If we can dump this thing without them seeing us, there's a chance we could ambush them when they find it.'

'With rifles? They're not dumb. They know we wouldn't just sit in it. We've done that stunt once. It's their advantage now.'

'Well, if we stay in here, we're dead. They know we've used the belts.'

'Then get off the island. Swim it.'

'Can't. We'll sink. Or the boat'll get us.'

'Not if they can't use it. I got a few down on the waterline and there's a hole in the bow you could dive through. And I've shot up the wheelhouse. We might make it.'

'In the sea? You want to take that risk?'

'I'd rather drown than fry.' He was trying to lock off the turret. The pin went in. 'There's a little beach around here.'

'That's where I'm heading.'

'What about the weight of the silver? I doubt they'll wait around while we unload.'

'These things float with ten men in the back.'

She took them a few hundred metres further, then swung straight into the undergrowth. It was still partly flattened from the day they'd arrived. The machine began to buck and rock, then stopped as she changed into low gear. He opened the turret hatch right back. Fresh air poured in. He took deep breaths.

They tipped crazily down the rock face, navigating gullies and fallen trees. He heard the small crates slide along the floor. He hoped like hell this was going to work.

When they thumped onto the strip of beach she climbed out of the driver's hatch onto the sand.

'What are you doing?'

'Checking the bilge plugs are in. There are four holes in the hull. If the plugs aren't in, we sink.' She crouched down to look under the belly plate.

'They in?'

She stood up again. 'Rusted in. You'll never shift those.' She worked a lever on the front of the carrier. A panel angled forward. 'Trim vane. If a wave gets over this, it'll hit the hull slope and take us under.' And if we're closed down, we'll never get out. You're meant to swim with hatches open.' She climbed back up to her open hatch. 'But if we get some in this hatch we could go down too. Or if the engine bay fills up…' She shrugged, got back inside.

'So we're set?'

'Except for the pre-aquatic check list. You're supposed to put silicon grease around the crew door and…'

'It's got bilge pumps, hasn't it?'

'You sure you want to do this?'

'Take her out and see how she floats. We can always come back if it's no good.'

'Double check that back door's tight.' She closed her hatch. 'And cross your fingers.'

He climbed back up to the turret, looking out the top. The flat panel, now extended on the nose, started to plough into the shore-break, pushing back a heavy wake. Even well out from the shore he could still hear the treads scuffing sand. The box was going down as if on rails, heading under like a slipway cradle. It all felt terribly wrong. The short chop was almost lapping across the deck. Their forward motion stopped.

He climbed back down to her. 'We're almost under.'

'Tell me about it.'

He looked back at the ramp. There were trickles around the seal but he could see no other water coming in. 'Doesn't even look like floating.'

She edged them forward a little more. Suddenly there was slight motion. 'We're off. How does it look?'

He scrambled into the turret, looked back. 'Pretty level.'

'We can't afford to get a wave over the front. If we could lift the head a bit – move those boxes back.' He heard a different noise below. She'd turned the pumps on.

He got down and started hefting the small heavy boxes back to the ramp, piling them up against it to give maximum weight in the rear.

The dark coffin was moving slightly with the sea, but not like any boat. It felt sluggish, like a diving bell, one that might never surface again. The sun from the open turret shone a beam into the hull. She was right. If the thing went down they'd never have time to get out. He slaved away with the boxes. 'How's it coming?'

She was peering through the side periscopes. 'It's looking better now but we're deep.' Water was trickling onto her from the perished seal around her hatch.

When he'd piled most of the boxes in the rear he climbed back into the turret. The hull was slightly higher now at the front but the swell was bigger further from the shore. Water was starting to slop over the vane as they settled into the troughs. Some sloshed into a grid on the right of the deck.

He called to her. She was wet, water trickling down around her with each wave. She turned and pointed to her headphones. He put his headset on.

She said, 'If it gets much worse, we'll be buried at sea.'

'We're shipping some through a grid on top. What's that?'

'Radiator. It's self-draining. But some'll be getting in.'
'Will we stall?'
'No, the engine'll run submerged, long as it can breathe.'

He looked back at the island. They were perhaps 100 metres out, moving very slowly, parallel to the shore.

'How far's the next island?'
'Miles.'
'Think we'd make it?'

'No way. But if we can work around the island we could come back on shore at the jetty and if we could get to the shelter before they…'

'That's no good. We're too slow. They'll spot us going around. They've probably seen us by now.' He looked back toward the shore, squinting along the beach, the rocks. No sign of life. At least deep in the water like this they were a distant and difficult target.

He was about to say, 'Looks quiet over there,' when something moved beyond the upright hatch behind him. He peered around the metal lid to the one quadrant he hadn't checked, the sea behind.

It had rounded the headland without his seeing it – the grey-blue hull of the boat, closing slowly, its bow-wave small, the gaping rent in its side.

He struggled out of the cupola, sliding on the shell casings, and grabbed the long plastic tube with its yellow band and red trigger button. 'Boat!' he yelled. 'The boat. How do you get these end caps off?'

She turned back from her seat. 'Oh God. You…' Then her finger pointed to a small sticker on the side. The label read: Inert.

'Forget it.'
'Huh?'
'It's a sample. A dummy. They're supposed to overpaint the yellow band blue. Hasn't been done. That's why I didn't

spot it.'

'Shit. Can we ram them?'

'At six knots?'

'Get the guns.'

She shook her head. 'We've had it.'

They felt the thrum and the wash of the big craft as it came alongside, heard someone leap onto the rolling top of the carrier and a voice yelling at the open turret. 'Come up hands first or a grenade goes down.'

He said, 'Why are they mucking round?'

'They want the carrier back. And the silver.'

He hung on to the rack behind her. 'Well,' he shrugged. 'Good try.'

She turned and shook his hand. 'Thank you, Mr Connor. I'm sorry.'

'I'm not,' he said. 'My pleasure. Twelve plus Vo. Not bad.'

A clink of metal on the front of the hull. She switched off the pumps, then reached up to the circular waterfall above her. 'I'm going to open this and hope it sinks.' She pushed it open and back. A cascade of water poured in, then subsided. Her legs vanished as she climbed out.

Connor heard, 'Shut that hatch.'

And her voice. 'You bloody shut it.'

Connor put his foot on the driver's seat and followed her up. The next wave practically knocked him back in. As the hull lifted, he scrambled out, drenched. Funny place to die, he thought.

Blore's soft voice, pitched high. 'Shut that hatch or I shoot her.'

He grabbed for it, pushed it down. It didn't want to stay down. The big spring was holding it part up.

'Go back and do it properly.'

He opened it, dropped back inside, pulled the thing shut and clamped it. Water was swilling around his feet. The engine compartment would be filling too, but he could still hear the big diesel running. He thought of the guns again – too late. A trooper had him covered from the turret. As he climbed into the turret stand, a wave bigger than the others rocked the hull. Two of the small cases slid off the top of the pile against the ramp and fell. One broke apart and he glimpsed the dull shine of silver bars.

He put his leg over the turret and stood up, hanging on to the open hatch. The thick wire cable from the derrick was shackled to one of the lifting eyes at the front of the carrier on the radiator side. Blore was shouting from the wing of the shattered wheelhouse. 'More. Or we'll lose the bastard.'

He heard the winch on the boat and the whole vessel rolled a little above him as they tried to lift the front of the APC above the wash of the waves.

Connor took it all in, this last view of the sun, of life. The woman hanging on to the turret beside him, drenched, face drawn, the man with the carbine, legs spread on the sluggishly rolling metal deck behind them, the truck-tyre fenders hung over the side, the trooper operating the winch. The derrick looming over them with the cable coming down. And Blore, leaning over the rail, both hands clamped around a machine pistol, covering them from the deck, face almost black with fury. 'They've turned the fucking pumps off. Get down there and start them.'

The trooper nodded. 'Get out of it.' He shoved Connor back.

'Get back,' Blore ordered.

They moved to the rear of the carrier, clinging to each other to stop falling.

The trooper squeezed his bulk into the turret. He barely fitted. His head disappeared. Then something shifted under their feet. They heard a cry of pain from below.

The back of the carrier came up and the nose dipped well

below the waves.

The boat listed above them suddenly, hauled over by the weight.

Blore yelled back to the man on the winch. 'Ease off! Ease off!' The big boat was listing more. He was so close it seemed they could touch him.

They could feel the metal beneath them settling. The coffin was going down – the man inside, buried under bullion, the water pouring into the grid.

The winch cable went slack, started to pay out as the APC went down like a lift, leaving them helpless in the water.

The boat, released, rolled upward like a barrel above them and Blore's leaning face and gun were replaced by red-leaded hull.

'Swim under the boat,' Gillian yelled.

Connor, choking on seawater, pulled his shoes off, took a deep breath and dived. As he kicked under the rolling hull he saw the keel bubbling toward him like a grader blade. He kicked deeper and it just missed his head, rolling past behind him. Then the hull started to roll back, stabilising. He thrust his hand out, going deeper, lungs bursting, kicking up the other side.

He broke back into the air, sucking in great breaths. He could hear the clatter of the winch, the ratchet off, as the cable rattled through the pulleys – still attached to the enormous weight.

He looked up as Gillian surfaced beside him. There was no-one covering them from the deck. They'd have more on their minds because if the water here were deeper than the cable – and the cable end was attached to the drum of the winch…

The hissing stopped abruptly. He heard the cable twang tight, heard the creak of the overstressed derrick, the yells from the deck.

They watched in amazement as the big hull rolled lazily

away from them, the red dripping out of the waves, until they could see water sluicing down the slope of the keel – until the side of the bridge was pointing to the sky, exposing a sonar pod low on the bow. The craft rolled almost completely over and stayed there, like a red whale.

'It's flipped,' she said.

'It'll sink.'

'No. It's got bulkheads. They always keep them shut.'

'It's got to go down – can't hold up a weight like that. And the hole in the bow's the other side. Holes along the waterline, the deck… Christ, we need a gun.'

She pulled up her sodden jumper, pulled something out of the waistband of her jeans, disappeared beneath the water and shoved something cold inside his belt. He knew what it was. When she surfaced he said, 'I love you.'

'It's cocked and the safety's off. You've got nine shots.'

'Get under the rudder or something where they can't see you.'

'David…'

'What?'

'Be careful.'

He struck out for the hull, hauled himself up onto the exposed starboard propeller guard and pulled the black automatic out of his belt. He wasn't sure he could hit anything with a pistol.

Two men. He'd only seen two. The man by the winch and Blore.

Slowly, carefully, he lifted himself above the crest of the hull.

They must have known what they were in for and got the dinghy cleared in time. It was a smallish aluminium runabout painted black and half full of water. Two oars and an outboard, but obviously no bailer. The thing was awash, floating on its tanks. Blore was crouched in the bow, facing away from him, huge hands joined, scooping water out of the floundering boat but the sea was coming in as fast over the side. The other man was lifting the small outboard over the stern, trying to drop the clamps onto the transom. Connor was high on the hull, the dinghy below him not more than three metres away.

He held the gun in both hands in front of him, aiming along the rudimentary sight and fired four times, two shots at each. The man with the outboard looked momentarily bilious, sagged sideways and flopped out of the boat. He was still somehow attached to the motor, his left wrist caught between its cowling and the handle, because he floated briefly, boots in the air, before going down.

Blore had turned before the last shots came and dived out of the upset dinghy. He clung to the side of it, head poking up, as if the shots had gone wide, the snout of his machine pistol a small black square above the side.

Connor slid back, grazing his foot on the propeller as automatic fire ricocheted off the hull, pinging against the plating and whining into the air.

Blore yelling. 'Bad luck, Connor. You can't beat an Uzi with a belly gun. I'm going to fucking chop you to bits.'

Connor shut up, listening.

The soft voice was raging again. 'Merrick had more balls than you. Got two of ours. But you ran her over with your tracks. And didn't even know. But you won't live to collect. I've got a present here from Duyen. For both of you, you fuckers.'

Connor was onto the bastard. He was trying to lure a response – or target. He was safe for the moment behind the slope of the hull. But Blore wouldn't let it sit that way for long. He crouched in the sun, tasting the salt on his lips. If Blore were unharmed he'd be swimming, could surface anywhere, the gun with him.

Connor's foot hurt like hell. He looked back at the blood

on his instep. Where was Gillian? He couldn't see her. Christ. If Blore got her first…

The hull shuddered and he heard a sucking noise like air sighing out of a vent. A gout of air churned the water a few metres away. The long belly of the boat wouldn't hold the tremendous weight much longer. But he dared not look above the hull and couldn't move further along it.

If he were Blore…

He turned and pointed the pistol directly at the water below him. A calculated guess.

He waited.

Waited.

Just the waves, sloshing against the hull two feet below the big, port screw – green-bronze, three-blade, with a chip in the edge of one…

Blore shot out of the water like a porpoise, hair plastered to the sides of his head, eyes manic, extended cheeks blowing, huge shoulders high and square… the snub-nosed pistol, clasped under his chin, angled accurately up at Connor's gut.

Connor pumped a shot into Blore's streaming scalp… another into his chest… as the snout of the Uzi flamed.

He slammed against the rough surface of the hull as if his head had been torn off.

But he was alive. And Blore was dead. As the huge man slid back into the wave, hands still clasped around the dark square of the gun, blood from the back of his head made a delicate S-curve on the brine. Then, just the hump of his battle-jacket scraping against the hull.

Connor fired three more shots into the camo tunic. Overkill, he thought. He'd never felt calmer in his life.

He pushed the safety catch on the pistol, tucked it neatly in his belt, then felt the side of his head. His hand came away red. He crawled over the rudder post and dived. Water stung and tore at his ear.

He surfaced, swam to the dinghy, looking around for the oars. They'd drifted a fair way but he collected them and swam back with them, paddling one armed and kicking, blood pouring from his head.

Sharks, he wondered? He threw the oars in the dinghy. The waves were sloshing over it. Nothing to bail.

He saw Gillian swimming around the hull. 'We need a bailer.'

'David?'

'What?'

'Where's…?'

'Shot him.'

'And…'

'Shot him. Bailer.'

'God, half your ear's off. And your cheek.'

'Blore. Missed me. Just.'

She opened her mouth, rolled her eyes upward, shut her eyes and sank.

'Hey.' He splashed over as she came up again. 'You'll give me a heart attack.'

She clung to him. 'God. David. God.'

'Bailer,' he said. 'Now. This bloody thing's going down.'

As if to confirm the statement, the hull sighed and settled more by the head.

She swam away to something bobbing near the hull, a plastic flagon half full of juice. He felt and found he still had the knife, cut the bottom off the flagon and scooped enough water out of the dinghy to get them clear of the boat.

They watched the stern rise as the hull slid in, hauled down by the enormous weight – sighing and creaking, the water boiling white around it.

When the sea closed over it, he rowed them back over the spot. There was no longer any sign of Blore.

'Some anchor,' Connor said.

Chapter Thirty-two

She clung to him as if in spasm. 'We've killed… all of them?'

'And Merrick. You ran her over. Blore told me. But she got two of them first.'

'That's…'

'Sixteen. The whole squad.'

They stared at the island as the dinghy pitched in the swell, oars rattling in the rowlocks. Her arms were clasped over her chest. 'I can't stop shaking.'

He took his sodden jumper off, put it around her. 'You're getting the reaction.'

'You're cold too.'

'Won't be soon. It's a long pull. Sit back. We're shipping water.'

'That ear looks terrible.' She retreated to the stern seat but they both still gazed at the island, not believing what they'd done, not believing they were free – expecting a rocket to howl out of the trees.

He settled behind the oars and took a line on the headland, putting his back into the job, feeling the warmth seep back into his body. He looked at the shock in her face. 'It's over now. Over.'

She sat, stunned, staring at the looming waves. Water slopped into the boat as they slid into the troughs. There seemed nothing to say. She started bailing again like a zombie.

Connor rowed for ten minutes until they were safely in the lee of the island and waves no longer sloshed over the transom. Gillian stopped bailing, shoved the plastic bottle under her knee and fumbled in the pocket of her jeans, finally holding up a folded, dripping envelope.

'What's that?'

'A letter. From Nicolae. You need to hear this.'

'Now?' He looked at the blood dripping down his shirt, started rowing again.

'You'd better.'

He raised his eyebrows as she unfolded the envelope and peeled it carefully away from the handwritten paper inside. 'He gave me his safe combination just before he died. This was on top of his papers. A letter to me. To us.'

'To – *us*? He knew about us?'

She stared at him, teeth chattering. 'It's long.' She squinted down. 'Can hardly see it without my glasses.'

'"Gillian. This is for you. It had to wait until now. If you'd known before, you would have lost the chance to prove yourself. You need to be worthy. And if you fail, the others will destroy you."'

'Worthy of what?' Connor looked behind him at the headland. They weren't making much headway but it seemed closer.

'"I'm aware of your intentions. My passion for the planet lives in you. You're a flower among weeds. But the field still had to be ploughed. Connor, of course, has potential. The young man's honest and far stronger than he knows."'

'Huh? Thought the bastard hated me.'

She looked up at him a moment, then went on. '"Your feeling for him? Not unexpected. I'd never seen you so adamant before. I first suspected something when your findings went well beyond my needs."' She paused and shook her head. 'Oh God, this hurts. "As if Connor had become *your* hobby, rather than mine. You were lonely here, I know."' Her voice cracked and she stopped. 'Sorry. I find some of this very…'

'Keep going.'

' "I've admired your independence. And perhaps you had a point. Renegades have the most possibilities." '

'Quite the philosopher. Bastard.'

' "If you succeed in your plan with Connor…" '

'He knew about… How?'

She read on. ' "…you weren't aware of the geo-phone probes. The whole island, including the shelter, has a seismic sensor grid coupled with listening devices. Not line-of-sight perimeter-security types but hard-wired, with probes each twenty metres and audio feedback. Only I had access to the monitor. (Always keep a card or two face down.) So I knew of your scheme and visits to the shelter." '

'He knew the whole…? Was *using* us?'

She nodded. ' "I'm gasping again. This terrible lack of air summons the devil and brings my fear back to haunt me. The ecology trust. Self-funding, self-perpetuating, as arranged. But who can trust trustees? They're scavengers like the rest – with reassuring ways, hard heads, and dead people's money to siphon off every way they can devise." ' She stopped and tried to separate the pages. 'You see the way he thinks? No trust at all. Didn't even trust me. I had to prove I was worthy, as he puts it.' She squinted at the next page. 'Can you stand more of this?'

'Go on.' He looked back at the headland. They weren't far offshore now. He was rowing them around the island to the bay.

' "Blore and Duyen can't understand, so I've never confused them with that aspect. Blore, an efficient ape. Duyen, poor dear, a fanatic. Yes, I know about her scheme to refinance Vietnam with my money. You and Connor are my check on the trustees. If the two of you succeed, you're worthy to replace them." '

'Holy shit. He *wanted* us to wipe them out!'

' "As my step-daughter and surviving child…" '
'You're his *daughter*?'
'Step-daughter. I didn't want to tell you.'
'So Sinclair…?'
'Let my mother drown.'
'And Merrick…'
'Killed my bastard step-brother.'
'And you're…'
'His only heir. I stood between Duyen and her dream. She wanted to wangle the money thing around. See why they needed to kill me?'

She continued with the letter: ' "… surviving child, you'll control everything. There's far more than you suspect. (Read the files and will in this safe.) If you're not killed, you'll be one of the most powerful women in the world. And Connor will have his money – enough to let him paint landscapes all his life. But I think there's more to him than that. His possessions are stored. Details in the file." '

'He was *helping* us?'

She shook her head. 'Oh no. You had to sink or swim with him. He just watched it all go on.'

'What about the scalpel blade thing?'

'Lord, yes. I thought we were really done for then. But for some reason he let me get away with it.'

'Because he wanted to see Sinclair knackered.'

She looked down at the paper again. ' "So if you read this you've captured your island and the weapons division's destroyed. Dispose of the dead at sea. Pay off Lee, the nurse and the cook if they're alive. They're harmless – witnesses if you need them. I've listed certain contacts – people who'll ensure you're not bothered. Suggested bribes are indicated. Always grease the palm. Governments everywhere are corrupt, and legislation pernicious, dumb, irrelevant – so be practical.

' "I wish you and the planet well. Try to safeguard the diversity of her life forms. One day she'll need them again. Good luck both. Be true to my dream." It's signed Nicolae.' Her eyes were brimming.

'You were fond of the bastard?'

'Incredible, isn't it? We all were.' She fumbled with the letter, folding it again, concerned not to tear the wet sheets. 'So you know it all.'

'Holy shit.'

She sniffed hard and frowned. 'See? He's still three steps ahead of us.'

'You're freezing. Put that thing on.'

She tried. 'It's too wet.' She dragged it around her shoulders. 'Sorry the weather's been so bad. It's beautiful here in summer.'

He looked stunned. 'I don't believe this. You've just killed sixteen people, you're the most powerful woman in the world, the sun's out and you're apologising for the *weather*?'

'I suppose I'm saying… I suppose I'm…' She looked over to the island, screwing up her face. 'I suppose you'll… want to go home?'

'We're going home now. And I'm dumping you straight in a hot bath. And when you thaw, we've got some cleaning up. For that bloke in the shelter we'll need a shovel and a squeegee. As for Merrick…'

She covered her face with her hands.

He said, 'Sorry. I know you've lived with them for years.'

They both pictured what they'd done and what they'd now have to face and do. The water was slopping in the boat again, from one end to the other with each wave. She started bailing once more. A long pause. 'David?'

'Yup?'

'I can't do it alone.'

He was rowing hard across the tide now. 'So we'll do it

together, like he says. We'll shovel what's left of them into those bags in the shelter and weight them. Be a few days before they turn into soup. Then we ring for the aircraft, go back to Auckland, hire a yacht, sail it back. A forty-footer should hold them. I can handle a fair-sized yacht solo. With two it's a snap. Sail 100 kilometres east and – shark meat.'

'I know we can cope with that. I'm not talking about all that. It's… I mean… Just here… alone. I'm finding this very hard.' She struggled with the emotion and exhaustion. 'Please… don't leave me alone here. I couldn't stand it. I need you… for a while?'

She stared at the water slopping against her feet. She didn't see how tenderly he looked at her.

'Sorry. Have to go back, put the house on the market, flog the video gear, throw in the easel and…' brightly, 'ship my stuff over here.'

She looked up quickly.

But he was staring at the shoreline, teasing her. 'That's if you think the house's big enough for both of us?'

'You'd do that?'

He looked back at her, slightly smiling. 'Well, it's your empire – but I reckon you've OD'd on the downsizing. You'll need number-crunchers. Negotiators. Not my speed, of course. But I can fix things, do gardening. So if you can use an introverted…'

'…multi-millionaire?'

He scowled. 'I'm not after the money.'

'But you've won it, don't you see? The trustees have to credit your account.'

He looked over his shoulder, could now glimpse the mouth of the breakwater. 'Well I could use a few dollars. 'Cause when we go to hire that boat, I'm shouting you a victory dinner at a place in Parnell. Okay?'

She nodded hard several times, shivering.

He frowned. How to put it to her. 'I'm not trying to intrude on your private life or your island and you've just heard two lies but if you think we… If you think you could…' That was better. 'If you think you could use long-term help, I mean…' He gave up trying, exploded, 'Hell. You've got fifty floppy disks on me and we've just won World War Three and I'm crazy about you and – what are you smiling at?'

'You.'

He jerked at the oars. 'You bloody well *know* I want to help you.'

She managed to control the tremble in her lip, to get the words carefully out. 'Yes, Mr Connor. I think you can help me very much.'

The small boat with its plunking oars rounded the foam-ringed head of the breakwater, then paddled slowly across the harbour's gentle chop. High in the trees, tui chimed bell-clear – as if they knew their piece of the world would survive.